A LONG, LONG DAY

FOR NOVEMBER

by
Moffitt Sinclair Henderson

DORRANCE & COMPANY
Philadelphia

FOREWORD

"We have honored fully the Southern giants who were our Nation's political architects—Jefferson, Madison, Monroe, who helped put the Colonial jig-saw pieces together, and Henry Clay, who strove to keep the pieces joined, and gaunt John Calhoun, who made his compatriots willing to take them apart again.

"But we have not recognized sufficiently the less successful and the later Statesmen—we could do worse than recall them now, and with them the obscure pleaders for the 'little man' in the day of domination by the great landowners. They were in the Southern tradition—the frontier tradition."

—Hodding Carter in
This is the South

PREFACE

Taking my cue from Professor Carter, I have, in this historical novel, brought into focus the life and times of Samuel Price Carson, a Southern statesman who was closely associated with political leaders on the national scene from 1825 to 1838.

For one with political ambition, young Carson had an auspicious background. Nearly a decade before he was born, his father, Colonel John Carson, was elected a member of the 1789 convention held in Fayetteville, North Carolina, to ratify the Federal Constitution, and with three of his sons served at different periods in the North Carolina General Assembly. By birth and marriage the Carsons were closely related to the McDowells of Kings Mountain fame, and some of that drama is incorporated in *A Long, Long Day For November*, which is but an extension of historical documents and newspaper and magazine articles published during the last century and a half.

Although it may claim regional interest only, perhaps it will attract the attention of some of the vast numbers of Carsons and McDowells throughout the nation whose lines go back to the indomitable progenitors of these two families—the transplanted adventurer from Northern Ireland, John Carson, and the venerable and venerated Ephriam McDowell, who as a lad fought bravely in the celebrated siege of Londonderry, and when past sixty, came with his Irish family to these shores on the good ship "George & Ann."

Moffitt Sinclair Henderson

ACKNOWLEDGMENTS

When a writer, through research, undertakes to turn back the pages of history for a period of a century and a half in order to bring to life an individual, a family, a community, it is an impossible task without the helpful ministry of many able assistants in libraries, in colleges and universities, and in research centers and archives. Individually and collectively they have my unfailing gratitude. Many indispensable kith and kin have furnished grist for the Carson family mill. Advice and admonition have been given without stint and without measure. None of these invaluable assistants would expect to be singled out and identified, for the list is long and the space is limited. They would wish me instead to give recognition to those individuals and groups whose copyrighted publications have enabled me to make a more factual and interesting historical novel, and to the following I express my grateful appreciation:

Hawthorne Books, Inc. and Lincoln A Boehm. *The White House Story*

Mrs. Edith Work, Nashville, Tennessee. *American Negro Spirituals*

Mrs. Jane Shaffer Holman, Batesburg, South Carolina. *Carolina Gardens*

William Weber Johnson, Encino, California. *The Birth of Texas*

Paul A. Rossi, Director, Thomas Gilcrease Institution American History & Art. *Indians in Texas in 1830*

J. R. Dolan and Clarkson N. Potter, Inc., Publishers *Yankee Peddlers in Early America*

Prentice Hall, Inc. Rupert Norval Richardson. *TEXAS: The Lone Star State*

Duke University Press and J. Fred Rippy. *Joel Poinsett— Versatile American*

and to:

The Moravian Music Foundation and the Salem College Alumnae Association, Winston-Salem, North Carolina for invaluable information and assistance.

Dr. John B. Shackford, who has allowed me to take advantage of his research on David Crockett.

Norman K. Elliot and Macalester Park Publishing Co., Saint Paul, Minnesota for permission to use direct quotations from Glenn Clark's *The World's Greatest Debates*.

Miss Catharine McDowell, representing the Daughters of the Republic of Texas at the Alamo, for permission to use selections from *The Free State of Bexar*.

The Texian Press, for allowing me to use excerpts from an article, *Samuel Price Carson*, published in 1968 and researched by Mr. and Mrs. Robert L. Jones.

Doctor Richard E. Iobst, Western Carolina University, Cullowhee, North Carolina for his valuable critique and his assistance in helping me to keep history straight.

And to those departed ones whose published works of long ago have made easier and more profitable my challenging adventure in history—Lyman Draper, and his record of the Battle of Kings Mountain; William Fairfax Gray, and his *Diary of the Republic of Texas*; Louis Wiltz Kemp, and his *Signers of the Texas Declaration of Independence*, and to historians Samuel Heiskell of Tennessee and the Reverend Chester Newell, of Texas, I record this appreciation for posterity.

A LONG, LONG DAY FOR NOVEMBER

ONE

As he approached a bend in the road, the young man reined his horse, adjusted his saddlebags and, turning, took a last, long look at the white-porticoed house seen dimly in the distance. He could not distinguish the figures on the upper balcony, but he knew they were there following him as long as he could be seen as he set out on this momentous journey. He recalled the breakfast table conversation, sprightly and light-hearted, in spite of the deep-down emotion at that point well under control.

There were many reasons why he would look with longing at the familiar scenes of his boyhood and young manhood. His family, among the earliest settlers in this mountain region of western North Carolina, had provided him with a solid background of respectability and character. They were a family upon whom had been laid heavily the hand of responsibility. Indeed many of them had already made history—much of it recorded in minute books, ledgers and in local, state and national assemblies. Before he was born, his father, Col. John Carson, had been chosen as a delegate to the Fayetteville Convention of 1789 that was called to ratify the Federal Constitution and was later a member of the House of Commons from 1805 to 1806. Three of young Carson's brothers had served in the State Legislature.

It was a family to be proud of, but more than all else it was a family whose ties were close and strong—how strong would be forcibly demonstrated to him in the now unclouded future.

The young man's father had insisted on having the last word with him as he prepared to mount. "Sam, me boy, there'll be men you'll come to know these days ahead who will be older and wiser than you. Sure and you must learn from them; and there'll be many not so wise who'll be after tellin' ye how to vote, how to dress, how to spend your money and your time. Be wary of them. If ye do as well as ye look, ye'll have nothing to worry about at all—at all." Only rarely did a hint of the Irish brogue creep into his conversation. It was a sign that his

1

emotions were deeply stirred. He slipped a piece of paper into the hand of his son in parting.

"A bit of an Irish blessing it is, and a little bit of blarney for good measure," and once more clasping the hand of his son, he turned away, his greatcoat hugged tightly, his white hair ruffled by the chilling breeze. That picture of his father Samuel Carson would recall many times during the coming weeks.

He did not have to search out the reason for his less-than-light-hearted mood. This was the first time he had left home for a long absence when his mother was not there to give him her blessing and embrace. As this thought came to him he looked toward a knoll in the distance where only a short time ago the loving hands of stalwart men—all sons or stepsons—had borne her to her last resting place. It was for this reason that plans for a gay send-off had been cancelled. The large family had been together so recently for a more serious occasion. He must fight the inclination to dwell on the memory of his mother, because she would have been the first to buoy his spirit for the adventures ahead.

Sam turned his face from home, straightened his shoulders perceptibly, clucked to his impatient mount and was on his way. He had already tarried too long. His hands were numb in his fleece-lined gloves, and his feet were like icy clods in the stirrups.

The early morning sun was beginning to thaw the gravel and mud and to lighten the shadows ahead. He had learned long since how to endure the saddle on journeys that lasted several days. This one would be the longest yet, and as he put his horse to a canter he sat erect, giving evidence of the superb horseman that he was. Then for a few miles he would slouch, his arms hanging heedlessly, his horse choosing her own gait.

There was little activity on the few farms he passed. The harvest season was over these many weeks, and there were few villages on the route he had chosen. Once in a great while he would overtake and pass a rider, usually on a mule, and salutary greetings were exchanged as each pursued his own destination, each busy with his own thoughts.

Young Carson's mind traveled faster than his body, and before the morning was half spent he had already traveled the distance to the Capital—indeed was already there—already answering roll call in the House of Representatives, standing straight and tall and confident.

He was familiar with the procedure. His two years in the State Senate had equipped him in matters of protocol, but instead of the familiar "Mr. Carson of Burke," he would be hearing "the gentleman from North Carolina, Mr. Carson."

He was to find himself during the cold, lonely days of his travels transported a number of times in such fashion to the halls of government. Usually in the quizzical contemplation of his immediate destiny he experienced a pronounced exhilaration, but when he reached the heights of satisfaction a strange, ominous foreboding seemed to engulf him, turning the blue skies into thunderheads, and he would be left with a great longing for assurance. It was as though he could hear the words of an Irish poet in her lament:

> Green rings of rushes came swaying
> Gaunt boughs of Winter made moan
> One saw the glory of life go by
> And one saw Death alone.

"Come now, Sam," he argued with himself, "there are great days ahead for you—days of opportunity and responsibility—yes, and bleak days there may be, for that is Life, and you must go out to meet it and glory in every eternal minute of it." Thus having made his high resolves, thoughts of impending doom were summarily dismissed.

Toward the middle of the morning the sharp outlines of the Linville Mountains could be seen, and after traveling a mile or so he heard the distinct sound of a distant waterfall.

"This is it! I'll stretch my legs and take a look," he thought. Securing his mount, he walked gingerly through the stubble until he came to the edge of a precipice. He dared not look down into the vastness of the chasm below until he could be sure he was well anchored. Finding an overhanging tree securely rooted and clinging to it, he leaned over and looked through perpendicular space one thousand feet where Linville Falls descended into a crashing, rushing torrent.

This was a landmark of sorts. He had never been farther north than the Falls on this route. Ahead was an unexplored region that beckoned to him even in his loneliness, and with this prodding he clipped off the miles with such eagerness that he almost missed a sign indicating that he was approaching the Virginia border. He must take a long look before reaching that milestone. Dismounting, he tied his horse, who had been given a new name for this eventful epoch in her life. The rechristening had caused a deal of merriment. When it had become certain that he had been elected, nieces and nephews bombarded him with questions: "How will you go?" "Where will you stay?" "How long will you be gone?"

To the last question he said, "Oh, I'll be back in time to mend my fences and do a little extra politicking next summer, and to answer your first question last, I am not going by stage because I'll need a horse for transportation and pleasure once I'm there." There was no need to ask which horse he would take. He had always shown a preference for the little "Whirlwind."

"You're goin' to change her name, aren't you, Uncle Sam? Whirlwind is for a racer—not a politican's horse," teased one of the nephews.

"Well, you name her for me, but I warn you, if you don't come up with something I like—a politican's choice—I won't change."

So many names were suggested that his brother Logan, who had joined them, said, "It looks like you can't agree, so why not compromise?"

"That's it! Let's call her 'Missouri Compromise.' That sounds like a politician's horse, all right."

The older ones had heard discussions from time to time on this volatile subject, involving as it did the issue of slavery, and the Carsons, as other Southern planters, were slave holders. Notwithstanding, so great was the admiration of Colonel Carson for Thomas Jefferson that Sam had been schooled in Jeffersonian principles. The "Sage of Monticello" proposed to eradicate slavery by a gradual process. "Nothing is more certainly written," said he, "than that these people shall be free." And again, "I tremble for my country when I reflect that God is just;

4

that his justice cannot sleep forever."

Very few at that time recognized the Missouri contest for what it was—the beginning of the struggle between North and South—a struggle for power, with the humane issue of slavery but incidental.

"Well, let's compromise with the Compromise. We'll give her the full name and call her 'Missy' for short. How's that?"

And so 'Missy' it was, and Sam had not yet grown accustomed to the change.

Some of these reminders came to him as he removed Missy's saddle and his saddlebags to lighten her burden. And then, as if to fix the spot indelibly in his mind, he looked over towering peaks, now bare of foliage except for giant evergreens. Surely nowhere in the Union was there more majestic scenery! How glad he was that his father chose to come to America and to become one of the little band of frontiersmen—Irish immigrants, who for better or for worse were making their imprint on the new world.

He recalled an old Irish folksong he had often heard at home. Throwing his hat in the air, he mounted a log and sang to the hills and the valleys:

> Our Fathers oft were naughty boys,
> Whack fol the diddle lol the dido day.
> Pikes and guns are dangerous toys,
> Whack fol the diddle lol the dido day.
> From Bealnath Buidehe to Peter's Hill
> They made Old England weep her fill,
> But Old Brittania loves us still,
> Whack fol the diddle lol the dido day.

He was surprised at the carrying quality of his voice in this natural amphitheater and sang another verse:

> O Irishmen forget the past,
> Whack fol the diddle lol the dido day.
> And think of the day that is coming fast,
> Whack fol the diddle lol the dido day,
> When we shall all be civilized,
> Neat and clean and well advised,
> O won't Mother England be surprised,
> Whack fol the diddle lol the dido day.

5

One who has written of the highlanders says that so inborn is the poet-craft in the mountain folk that they burst into song on any occasion. "The simple events of their lives, sights seen and unseen—travel, fancied farewells and laments—of these they sing." Was it so strange then that this son of the hill country, who loved music, was stirred into song by thoughts of things seen and unseen, his travels, his laments, the contradictory emotions of exaltation and poignant farewells all pounding in his head and in his heart?

There was no applause to this bit of comic opera, but Missy neighed in approval. Loosing her reins and preparing to mount, he had a second thought as he looked over the towering peaks, declared by some to be the oldest in the world.

"I may not be able to leave my imprint on the Nation's Capital, but I can stamp it indelibly on these hills." Cupping his hands he shouted, "Life!" Back came the answer, "Life;" louder he shouted, "Liberty!" and "Liberty" filled the vastness of the earth above and around him. "Pursuit of happiness," he called loud and clear, and back came the answer, "Happiness." In fine spirit he resumed his journey. Was it a good omen that "Happiness" was all that came back to him at the end of his echo game?

Young Carson was glad that he had planned a stopover in Lexington to visit his mother's relatives, and that he would be there by the weekend. In places where there was no public accommodation, he found the Virginia farm folk hospitable. Indeed they were so glad to get news of the outside world that a stranger was usually welcome, and an arrangement for bed and board could be worked out that was mutually agreeable. At one of these farms he rode into the yard and up to the shed where a young girl was milking. Putting down her pail she called in a voice that could have been heard a mile, "Ma—come out here, Ma. They's a man here wants to see you. Hurry now, Ma. He wants to know can he git supper," she explained as her mother appeared.

The fare was plain but substantial. The table conversation consisted mainly of answers to questions that indicated the chief concerns of a rural family.

wel-
in all
pro-

James
easure
ment.
uld be
neral,

recent
th the
es that
before.
winter
more
his fel-
's visit.

n dur-
op" of
ning of
would
time to
e-deep,
he was
vs were
d glass
vendor,

thirsty,
der his

ew—the
n asked
to the

iss it. I
n town.

cumspect after the meal, Carson repaired to
his surprise an open fire burned cheerily.
early to retire, he reached in his saddlebags
wspapers, and although by this time they
-of-date, he found the news in them ar-

ems that caught his eye was a report of the
ayette to the Hermitage. According to the
d toured the grounds of the Hermitage, and
ouse, some of the friends present implored
how them the arms he had received in the
l yielded with good grace and placed upon
vord and a pair of pistols. The sword had
im by Congress, he said, the sabre by the
ho fought with him at New Orleans, but it
he pistols that the General wished to call
ed them to the French General and asked
.

ember them to be those which I offered to
Washington, in 1786." And the aged
o express his great satisfaction in finding
ds of one so eminently worthy of such an

countenance of Old Hickory was suffused
and his eyes sparkled as in the days of
he same time the pistols and LaFayette's
e said with deep emotion, "Yes, I believe
of them—if not for what I have done, for
my Country."

n to say that General LaFayette was now
deed would set sail on the *Brandywine* on
nswer to the President's farewell address
nvoked an emotional benediction. "God
all who surround you. God bless the
l all of their States, and the Federal
this patriotic farewell of an overflowing
ts last throb when it ceases to beat."
America's guest of honor was coming to
a long while remembering—and there was

so much to remember about his country's exuberance
coming and entertaining and paying homage to the ma
the world to whom America owed so much allegiance,
found a debt of gratitude.

The Marquis had come at the invitation of President
Monroe, at the request of Congress, and every possible n
was taken to insure his comfort, his care and his enjo
Advance notice had been given that "the ceremonies sh
conducted with the least possible fatigue to the veteran C
who is lame, occasioned by breaking his thigh."

Carson also found among the papers he had brought
edition of a New York journal which published, along
story of LaFayette's departure, a digest of published stor
had appeared on his arrival a little more than a year
These he found completely absorbing, and so the long
evening Carson had dreaded had passed pleasantly an
quickly than he thought possible, as he lived again with
low citizens the memorable and exciting days of LaFayett

Night was falling, and whatever activity there had be
ing the day had given place to the desultory "clop, c
riders going home or coming into the Capital for an ev
entertainment. Carson had no illusions about what he
find on entering the city. Disillusioned visitors had from
time made their complaints through the press—mud ank
unsightly and unsanitary streets and alleys. The fact is
prepared for worse than he found, for the evening shadc
kind. Lights in the windows and through fanlights a
doors spoke a friendly welcome. Here and there was a
his leftover wares in a pushcart.

Carson reined in at a watering trough. Poor Missy was
and as she drank Carson signaled to a lad with papers u
arm.

"Morning newspaper here, sir—but the news is still
Gazette and the *Intelligencer*—take your pick." Carsc
for the *Intelligencer*, and asked the boy directions
National Hotel.

"You're almost on it, sir. There it sits—you can't
can leave a paper for you every day if you're staying

It's ten dollars a year, or you can pay by the month."

"Suppose you leave a paper in the morning, and after that we'll see." The transaction completed, he was lifting the reins when the enterprising newsboy accosted him again.

"That's a fine horse, sir. You goin' to keep him here?" On being told that Carson intended to do just that the boy volunteered the information that there was a good stable back of the hotel. This was a fortunate encounter, for Carson was not sure where he could find a stall and rations so late in the evening. It developed that the stable was run in conjunction with the hotel and Missy was entered as a regular boarder.

The lobby was crowded, and a quick glance assured Carson that the gentlemen were only slightly in the majority. He supposed that many of the fair sex were wives of the Congressmen, and unattached as he was, he hoped that there might be some daughters and sisters in the gay company who were waiting for the dining gong. It was good to know that for a time at least he would have all of the necessities and some of the luxuries of life in his home away from home.

His letter of introduction and reservation had preceded him, and the affable clerk lost no time in seeing that he was settled in his new quarters. The rooms were spacious—high ceilings with top-to-toe windows and inside blinds, with the added security of draw draperies. The bellpull hung conveniently near.

The National boasted four floors in addition to the ground floor. Carson's accommodations were on the third level. A large poster bed—plump and inviting with its feather mattress over a cotton tick—was flanked on one side by a commodious desk. Across the room was a drop-leaf table on which was a three-tiered candleabrum. A washstand and chest of drawers with two chairs completed the furnishings. It was a relief to find his room so tastefully appointed. The National was the newest hotel in the city and covered half a city block.

The commodious bed proved to be as comfortable as it was inviting, and so complete was his rest and relaxation that he was not conscious of consciousness until near noon the following day, and even then he probably would not have stirred except for repeated rappings on his door.

It was a white-turbaned chambermaid who came to draw his

9

curtains, pour the water for his ablutions, and ask what he would like for his breakfast. "The dining room is closed, sir, and the only way for you to get breakfast is for me to bring it. What would you like?"

"I'll tell you—what about surprising me? You look like our Binah at home, and she makes breakfast fit for a king."

When the tray arrived there was on it a warm baked apple with cream, flannel cakes, sausage and coffee, plus the *Intelligencer*, thanks to the lad with whom he had bargained the night before. And now he could catch up on Capital comment and news of the world. He had been too tired to read the paper he had bought the night before, and here were two daily papers—a luxury to which he was unaccustomed.

The Capitol was within walking distance of the National, that is, if one needed that kind of constitutional, and Carson concluded that he would use Missy for pleasure and shank's mare for business.

The day was enlivened in the afternoon by a visit from a colleague—the Senator from Halifax, the Honorable John Branch. Theirs was a friendship of several years—indeed both were members of the North Carolina State Senate in 1822.

Branch was sixteen years Carson's senior; in fact, Joseph McDowell Carson, Sam's oldest half-brother, was more nearly the age of the gentleman from Halifax, and the two had developed a warm friendship when both were in the Legislature in Raleigh—Branch, a senator, and Joseph Carson a member of the House of Commons. It was largely because of his attachment to both Carsons that Branch showed a protective interest in the newcomer to the national scene.

The amenities over, Branch took a clipping from his pocket, saying, "You acquitted yourself with unusual decorum—far beyond your years, but not beyond your upbringing."

"What do you mean, sir? I'm very curious."

"This is a comment about the recent campaign in North Carolina that I clipped from a Raleigh paper. There was a very keen interest here in Washington City in this North Carolina campaign, especially among the Southern representatives. Since one or two of your opponents for election in the Congress were former incumbents of the House of Representatives, their con-

10

temporaries here, as I, watched the unfolding of that bit of political drama to its very happy conclusion.

"You have cast your shadow before you, young man. Have you seen this report? If not, let me be the first to apprise you of it. The item originated in Morganton."

Mr. Branch moved his chair to a better light, unfolded the clipping and began to read:

"In the campaign of 1824, James Graham, of Rutherfordton and Dr. R. B. Vance, of Buncombe came out as opposing candidates to the old soldier, Felix Walker, who had been rewarded for his military service with a seat in Congress.

"Mr. Walker was an old man who had been a member of the House of Representatives from 1817 to 1823. He seemed amazed at Carson's aspiring to the position he filled. In his brief speech he announced Vance and Graham as his opponents, and added, 'And I am told there is a boy from Burke who wants to be a candidate.'

"In their speeches, Vance, who was then Congressman, and Graham, made the same excuses for being candidates—each had so many strong solicitations that he was unable to resist the pressure on him and at last, as a matter of duty, had consented to come out for the office.

"Sam Carson was not looked upon as a serious candidate or as being in the way of either, and so all batteries were turned on Walker.

"At first Vance and Graham scarcely noticed Carson in the public discussion. On the other hand, they ridiculed Walker unmercifully, telling the people that when he was in Congress he boarded out of town and walked in.

"When Carson's opportunity came, he was profoundly respectful to the old man. He told the assembled people that he differed from his competitors in the fact that all of *his* friend had urged him *not* to run, but he had persisted because he really wanted to go to Congress. He spoke of Mr. Walker as a patriot who had served his country well in time of war and peace.

"This consideration for the feelings of the old soldier helped to lay the foundation for Carson's political success, for Walker was so captivated by his eloquence and sprightliness that he withdrew in Carson's favor, and became his ardent friend and supporter."

Branch handed the paper to Carson, as he remarked, "The salutary thing about this, Carson, is that your action was not prompted so much by political expediency as by an innate respect for your elders."

"There are some who would take issue with you, Senator Branch—those who put an altogether different construction on my motives; in fact, it's my understanding that my friend and opponent, James Graham, has written to his brother, William, giving an altogether different version of the affair.

"As for Doctor Vance, he will surely find expression for his unusual talents in some other field of honor. He's far too useful to end his political career. North Carolina can ill afford to lose a man of his brilliance and ability. My friends are his friends and they recognize his worth."

"That's very true," agreed Branch, "and if I mistake not, Doctor Vance will step into the political arena again, and so it behooves you, young man, to keep your slate clean and your constituents happy. You will, of course, remember that to some extent you are representing all of North Carolina, but since you have made so many friends in the East this will not be difficult.

"North Carolina does not have a savory reputation outside of the South just now. So many forward-looking, progressive measures have been voted down in the Legislature now on the eve of adjournment—Archibald Murphey's plans for educating our children, the bill for the establishment of a Medical School —both passed by the House of Commons were killed in the Senate, as you know.

"And this particular act of this Legislature directly concerns you and your area. Having been en route to Washington City you probably have not yet received your instructions. In the closing days a joint resolution was passed instructing the North Carolina members of Congress to use their influence to have returned to the State $19,940 dollars which she has paid to the Indians for reservations in the several sales she has made of the Cherokee lands ceded to her by the United States Government, and also to obtain an extinguishment as soon as practicable of all of the Indian titles to the balance of the land in this State. You do not have a choice in this matter, and you will no doubt receive your instructions at an early date."

"I've been interested in this matter for some time, sir, and I shall make a study of it."

"I am sure you will, Carson, and I am just reminded. One

reason for my call is to invite you to a small party—not a caucus, mind you, but a purely social gathering."

"I'm sure you use the term 'purely' advisedly, sir. Where is this gathering to take place, and who will be there?"

"There are some of the old timers at Fuller's Hotel where I am presently staying, and we engaged one of the private rooms used for such purposes. The hotel is at Pennsylvania Avenue and 14th Street. Your hacker will know how to get there, and I shall be on hand to welcome you at six."

After Branch left, and before he dressed for the party, Carson sat at his desk and penned a letter to his father which of course on its arrival at Pleasant Gardens about ten days later would be read aloud to the whole family.

Dear Father and all the rest,

The fortnight just past has been one of the most exciting of my life! Surely the Gods are smiling down on me!

This I have said before, but I feel particularly inclined to repeat now: The good fortune of having you as my mentor, and all the others as my beloved family, are the things for which I daily give thanks.

This is the day before the auspicious date that will mark my first attendance as a member of the House of Representatives—a full report of which will be made to you later.

Now I will begin where I left off in the only other letter I have written since I left home. It was posted at Lexington, where I enjoyed my visit with the Cochranes and the Lewises, who took me to the Academy. I was proud indeed to be introduced as the grandson of one of the Founders. Grandfather Moffett is held in high esteem not only for his brilliant record as a soldier of the Revolution, but as a friend of education.

I could pursue this reporting of my visit to Mother's family *ad infinitum*, but you may be wondering how I am situated.

My commodious and comfortable room is at the National Hotel, which, you can see by the cut on this handsome stationery, has a most prosperous appearance.

So far my time and attention have been given over to a plan of orientation—some of it at the hands of Mr. Branch, and an afternoon visit to the White House with Mr. Calhoun.

In view of the fact that most of the senators and representatives are staying at a dozen or more boarding houses scattered over the City, I feel myself most fortunate to be so highly favored in my living quarters. It is pleasant indeed!

Assure Matilda and Binah that I have plenty of quilts, plenty of hot water, and a good fire when it is needed. I had thought that the new hotel might have gas lights, but that luxury will have to wait—even at the White House and the Capitol.

Since the feminine contingent will be especially fascinated by the President's House and the Capitol where I will be staying most of the time, let me proceed with the best I can offer in the way of descriptions. Take heed, dear ladies, to what I have to say, for I am writing about something hundreds of your kind would give their inheritance to read.

The deepening shadows of a wintry afternoon were upon him. The fire had burned low and was almost out while he regaled his family with a description of the most famous home in the nation, and with sights and sounds of an enchanted city —enchanting to those who had never seen it, and perhaps to some who had, but disenchanting to the majority of visitors who were horrified at the sight of sheep and cattle pasturing in and roaming about the streets, and at the sight and sometimes the stench of refuse that had been thrown into the streets, waiting for a merciful rain to wash it away. But on this last revealing picture Carson did not dwell.

Carson read his letter before folding it, holding it up to the candlelight. He addressed and sealed it with a beeswax imprint of his monogram, and took it to the desk for the earliest dispatch, a letter that would be passed around from family to family and read by a large assortment of his sisters and his brothers, his uncles and his aunts and their neighbors and friends, who would wait impatiently for the next edition.

And then the new legislator began to dress for his first social engagement in the Capital. It turned out to be partly a delegation of politicians from two or three of the Southern states, and they were bent on pleasure—not politics. It gave him an opportunity to meet Tazewell and Stevenson from Virginia, McDuffie from South Carolina and Polk and Houston from Tennessee, and all of the North Carolina delegation who were in the City. The Easterners were in the majority, and Carson wondered if there would be any repercussions or any embarrassing moments because of the recent attempts to balance the power between East and West. Whatever animosity there might have been was held in check, partially because of Carson's youth and his pleasing personality, but largely because he was already favorably known to some of them, and because he was presented as a protégé of one of their own Eastern representatives—the gentleman from Halifax.

These men were realists, and while the East resented more deeply than was on the surface any attempts to infringe on their domain of power in North Carolina, they could be more liberal in their feeling toward the West on the national scene.

Carson immediately sought out one of the group, an old friend—Willie P. Mangum, representing a district in central North Carolina. Young and personable, he was interested in horses and horseracing, as was Carson. But there was little or no time to pursue the subject as the guests mingled pleasantly. Carson was anxious to talk with each one long enough to establish his identity, and in turn to establish theirs in his memory.

True to Mr. Branch's statement, there was little or no discussion of a political nature. It was a convivial gathering, and because it was the Sabbath, before the celebration got out of hand, the gentlemen began to disperse.

December 5 was the day fixed for the meeting of the Nineteenth Congress. At the first session at twelve o'clock, the roll of the House was called by the clerk, Matthew St. Clair Clark, and it appeared that there were present 204 members, beside three delegates from the Territories.

When Carson's name was called he responded much as he had done in fantasy as he and Missy cantered along toward Washington City. He watched carefully when members rose to respond to roll call, and tried to pair names and faces.

On the second ballot, John W. Taylor of New York was chosen Speaker, and as was to be expected he responded with alacrity, setting the tone for their deliberations in these words:

"Gentlemen, when I see around me so many representatives whose virtues and talents adorn our country—whose services at home and abroad, in the cabinet, and in the field, in halls of legislature and judicial tribunals, have largely contributed to our national prosperity—I am penetrated with gratitude for the favorable opinion which has called me to this distinguished station."

15

There was more, but Carson had heard the same kind of platitudes at other times and under similar circumstances, and he was ready, even before the time came, to take the oath of office.

The usual resolutions were adopted containing the Rules of Order set by the last Congress, appointing twelve noon as the stated hour of convening and directing the clerk to furnish newspapers to members.

A message was received from the Senate that they were assembled and ready to proceed with business.

A Committee of the House was appointed to wait upon the President and to inform him that a quorum were met and ready to receive any communication he might have to make. And then the House adjourned.

Carson was fortunate to have secured a seat that promised in some respects to be advantageous—it had a good view of the balcony where the ladies sat. Of the North Carolina delegates in the House he knew Willie P. Mangum, John Bryan, Henry W. Connor and Senator John Holmes of Maine, and others whom he had met casually on last Sabbath evening.

After adjournment he took Missy on a guided tour of the city—guided so far as he was able to find his way along streets that led one round and round in circles. Missy was receptive to a run in the country, and they explored a beautiful rocky region where crystal-clear streams tumbled over boulders and under bridges. So familiar were the sights and sounds that he could close his eyes and imagine he was home again where picturesque Buck Creek Falls tumbled in cascades of foamy splendor.

He felt a tug of nostalgia; here was a place where he could always feel the nearness of home, and he told Missy that they would come often, especially when the warmth of spring was in the air. And for this he was sure Missy was grateful. She had been stallbound of late, and was not a little temperamental and unmanageable.

Very little was accomplished the next day when the House convened at noon. Mr. Trimble from the joint committee to wait on the President reported that Mr. Adams would send a message to each body in writing, and at twenty minutes past twelve the message was brought in by the President's secretary,

Mr. John Adams, Jr., and it was read at the Clerk's table. The reading occupied one hour.

The message of the President was accompanied by reports to the President from the Secretary of War, the Secretary of the Navy and the Postmaster General, with other documents. These were referred to the Committee of the Whole House on the State of the Union and six thousand copies of the message and reports were ordered to be printed. And then the House adjourned, to await on the following day the address of the President of the United States.

After adjournment of the Congress on the seventh, the representatives and members of the Senate who were not in committee gathered in the halls in little cliques to discuss with animation the address of the President.

John Quincy Adams had proposed a radical program for these times. He strongly advocated a system of internal improvements—canals and roads—as an encouragement to commerce, and a National University to insure the country's ability to continue to compete with learned men of other nations. Already the influence of the United States was recognized among the great of all countries. A former President had made certain that no nation, and no individual was to infringe on the lives and liberty of the peoples of the Americas, and other nations had accepted this Monroe Doctrine, not in passive acquiesence, but because the nation, through responsible leadership, had earned the acclaim and respect of international powers.

As the discussion of the President's message continued it was evident that there was dissension, and remarks like these were overheard: *Some states will profit to a greater degree than others when canals are dug and roads built; A university can be a great asset to the state in which it is located; The Government has no right to spend money belonging to all the states for purposes that are local to any one state.*

How narrow and limited was their vision need not be taken into account, because when a vote was taken, the majority went along with the President's recommendations and the measures met with the approval of the nation at large. And although the majority could not see the extent to which these internal improvements would benefit the whole country, the program fostered a movement of expansion that even its heartiest proponents had not foreseen. The canals and roads were destined to open up a flow of commerce and a development in industry and manufacturing that would in time provide an impetus for other and much greater strides of progress.

The election of Adams to the Presidency had been the source of great dissatisfaction to many political leaders. He had been chosen by the House of Representatives when the Electoral College failed to elect a President. The tabulation had been: Andrew Jackson, 99 votes; Adams, 84; William H. Crawford, 41; and Henry Clay, 37. Jackson had received the highest number of popular votes. The Constitution provided a mandate that when no one received a majority of electoral votes, the House of Representatives should select a winner from the three leading candidates. Such was the influence of Henry Clay that he skillfully maneuvered to see that preference was given to one who would most likely carry on his own policies, and that was Adams, who from the beginning did not have the full support of the Senate.

In the aftermath of the election in the House it was Henry Clay who was accused of bargaining, and it was he who received the sustained condemnation of the electorate.

But there were things to reckon with as time went on. At this juncture the role of John Quincy Adams as President had just begun, and something of his courage—his critics would say "gall"—and his stubborn resistance to criticism came to light in his appointment of Henry Clay as Secretary of State. Then indeed the howling began—the howling and the vindictive planning for 1828.

Jackson lost no time in initiating plans to make himself invincible when the time came to elect a seventh President of the United States. He knew where fences needed to be mended; he knew where his proponents had erred in their judgment and in their action. He would not again rely on the role of "Military Chieftain"—the conquering hero of the Battle of New Orleans. He would make his appeal to the common man, who now more than ever was not afraid to raise his voice in the assemblies of men and in the sacrosanct chambers of government. He was convinced that the time was ripe for the hold of aristocratic and autocratic authority to be broken, and for the voice of the people to be heard—heard and heeded, and implemented in the form of legislation that would indeed "promote the general welfare" of the common man.

That Mr. Adams was the recipient of bouquets as well as brickbats was seen in an editorial from the *Intelligencer*:

> There is no part in the President's message in which we are more gratified than that in which he recommends the erection of a monument to the memory of Washington. It has been near his heart, and will contribute to the reputation he has already acquired.
>
> The resolution of 1783 still remains unrepealed on the record of the United States as a solemn pledge, and it is yet unredeemed. The world has long looked with surprise and has spoken with censure of our cold indifference to the memory of one who was the Father of his Country, and the Vindicator of Mankind.
>
> For years his body has lain in the rude sepulchre to which it was at first consigned, and although the spot has been hallowed by the sacred deposits, the native as well as the foreigner heaves a sigh as he gazes on the lonely mound, at the neglect of a Nation who owed him so much, and which had so solemnly pledged its faith to provide a last resting place commensurate with his greatness and the gratitude of the Country.
>
> No moment could be more propitious than the present for the accomplishment of an object rendered so desirable by every consideration of National honor.

Carson was in full accord with this part of the President's address, and indeed with a greater part of it all. It would have been a sobering thought, however, if he had known that full seven years would pass before any move was made to begin work on a suitable memorial to the First President.

Although his fellow countrymen had been derelict in their duty toward President Washington, his memory was annually renewed in the celebration of the Birth Night Ball, which seemed to become more and more spectacular in its observance. This year was no exception. The ball to be held at Carusi's promised to be a gala affair, and Carson made plans to go with some of the bachelor husbands whose wives had not accompanied them to Washington City.

On Tuesday and Wednesday preceding the twenty-second, the weather was the coldest ever experienced in the United

States. At Fort Covington the thermometer dropped to 40° below zero and the mercury froze. And Capitol Hill jokesters were passing the tale of a man walking within sight of the White House who took a bottle of spiritous liquor from his pocket, found it frozen and with amazing *sang froid*, broke the bottle, peeled off the glass and ate the whisky.

On Thursday Carson succumbed to the "cold plague," now prevalent in the District. High fever and chills alternated to produce their debilitating effects, and the misery was aggravated because he was away from home and from his own physician. If he called one of Washington City's doctors, more than likely the treatment would be to bleed the patient, and Carson was in no mood for that.

Perhaps he could have chosen no more propitious time to be absent from the deliberations of Congress. They were now spending most of the time on local bills and executive business, and Carson's illness gave him an opportunity to put on paper his views on "The Mission to Panama," a bill for which was even then bogged down in the Senate. It also gave him the much-needed time to pay his respects to some of his most demanding constituents, to write his family and to read many issues of the *Raleigh Register* that had been laid aside earlier in the press of duties.

One morning when he was feeling particularly miserable, Eloise, the chambermaid who looked after his room, came in and handed him a bottle of brown liquid.

"Mr. Carson, my granny is good at curin' all kinds of sickness. She tol' me to bring you this, and to tell you to take it three times a day. She say this receipt generally cures the worser colds in three days, and it's been known to cure them what is purty near settled into consumption."

"Well, that is very kind of your grandmother, Eloise. What's in the medicine?"

"Oh, she jes takes a spoonful or two of linseed, some stick licorice, a handful or two of raisins, some brown sugar and a tablespoonful of white wine vinegar. She say take it lak she say and maybe sip a little mo' at night when you is coughin' bad."

Carson followed the directions and two days later he was still alive—indeed he felt greatly improved, but the severity of the weather kept him in his hotel room until March had come in like a lion and a week beyond.

And then followed several weeks of legislative routine during which a goodly number of the Representatives were out fighting the cold plague, now in epidemic stage.

When Carson finished his Sabbath meal on April 9th, he kept his usual appointment with Missy, who by this time could find her way to their favorite rendezvous with very little guidance and no urging.

In the weeks following their first jaunt to Rock Creek, Missy had learned that when they reached a certain spot Carson would dismount, bring out a small package and reward her with several lumps of brown sugar candy. As usual that day she slowed her pace and stopped at the exact place, and as usual she was rewarded.

"Missy, old girl, you can almost talk. I should have named you 'Falada.' There is no compromising with you—ever."

The feel of spring was in the air, and although there was not yet enough warmth to coax new growth, it was a welcome change from the severe winter that had exacted its toll of suffering, of sickness and death.

"Yes, spring is in the air, Missy, and you know what spring does to a young man's fancy, do you not?"

Perhaps it was this suggestion that led his thoughts homeward—this time to his second home—Ezeeka, he liked to call it, for that was the name given to Green River by the Red men who discovered it.

Joseph McDowell Carson, his oldest half-brother, had planted his vine and fig tree at this beautiful spot, and it was known far and wide as Green River Plantation. Here Sam Carson was sent when he was eighteen to continue his education under the tutelage of his brother, "with an eye to political advancement," so the story goes.

Many who knew Colonel Carson were aware that he was a man of wealth; they knew also that he was a man of considerable education. For that reason many wondered why, after giving his older children unusual advantages, he was satisfied to let Samuel Price attend one of the old field schools in the neighborhood. The boy had private tutors during his early life,

21

and in addition, his older brothers and sisters, who adored him, gladly took turns in establishing his proficiency in the three R's, and at a very early age he excelled in ciphering and in impromptu speaking.

Strange what tricks memory will play. His thoughts just now were not of his childhood, but of the pretty young girl from Tennessee who had come a-visiting while he was more or less a member of the family at Green River.

Joseph Carson had built his first house of logs on 600 acres of fertile land through which the Green River flowed, and although there were rumors that gold had been found in the general area, he did not buy as a prospector. That a rich vein was found leading back into the hills on his property, and that he had the slave labor to mine it, was just "the luck of the Irish," he told his friends. With this new-found affluence he could better afford a substantial home, and a large, rambling structure was soon ready for occupancy.

His house in readiness and his prospects well-established, Joseph Carson, with a manservant, set out to cross the rugged Smoky Mountains into Tennessee to the house of his first cousin, James Wilson. And when he returned, one of the daughters, the fair Rebecca, came with him as his bride.

On this spring outing Carson was not thinking of Joseph, nor Rebecca, nor of the nieces and nephews who began gradually to fill the house and who brought merriment and heightened activity to the plantation. Rather his thoughts were of the vivacious Catharine who came from Tennessee to visit her sister and to see firsthand the fabulous home where, beginning at midnight, she had been told, one could hear the strains of eerie music—an imponderable mystery that no one had been able to fathom. Why his thoughts traversed the years and the miles that separated him from present realities he could not explain.

Yes, spring was in the air, and the Representative from North Carolina was in the mood to enjoy it.

When Carson entered the lobby of his hotel after returning Missy to her stabler, he saw Thomas Benton standing in the midst of a group of gentlemen. It was easy to see him, for he stood head and shoulders above the bystanders; it was easy to distinguish him because of the cloak of superiority that was his habitual garment.

22

Their eyes met, and Benton pushed his way through the idlers, extended his hand, and clasped Carson's in a vise-like grip. It was a miracle that the smaller man did not cry out in pain, and it was with the utmost power of will that Carson restrained himself from kicking the offender on the shin. He was not sure whether Benton wanted to impress on him his physical superiority or whether his demeanor was calculated to impress his personal superiority. Whatever the motive, this was not the kind of encounter Carson had hoped to have with the Missourian, whom he had heard discussed in family circles.

In the first place, they had much in common. Both were native "Tar Heels," and the wife of Senator Benton was, so he had been told, his first cousin once removed. In any event they had the same great-grandfather, Captain John McDowell of Rockbridge County, Virginia, and it had been his intention to speak of this relationship, but on this he had second thoughts.

Benton suggested that they repair to Carson's room. He found a comfortable chair and at once stated the purpose of his call. "You know, Carson, or maybe you have not heard of the altercation between Mr. Clay and Mr. Randolph, of Virginia, which last week came to a white heat with the usual climax. It seems that Mr. Clay was incensed because of Randolph's speech in the Senate in which Mr. Clay maintains that Randolph's remarks pointedly referred to him personally. Randolph, you know, is constantly offending his compatriots. This much is known to many who heard the debate, but at this point very few know of the aftermath. For that reason I ask your discretion in commenting on the things I am about to relate."

Carson nodded assent.

"Saturday at half-past four the two met on the field of honor, suitable arrangements having been made by their seconds. Mr. Randolph had Colonel Tattnall of Georgia and Major Hamilton of South Carolina as alternates, while General Jessup, of the Army, and Mr. Johnson of Louisiana were Clay's attendants."

Carson listened without comment.

"The parties met on the ground, exchanged salutes and took their stations. The pistol of Mr. Randolph, which was suspended by his side, went off. It was perceived to be an error and was so declared by Mr. Clay. Immediately, however, upon hearing the report of the pistol, Mr. Randolph turned to Colonel Tattnall and said, 'I told you so.' Colonel Tattnall, turning to General Jessup observed, 'Sir, the fault is mine. Mr. Randolph protested against the use of a hair trigger, and it was at my express instance that the trigger was sprung.' The explanation was accepted, another pistol was procured and handed to Mr. R. The parties resumed their stations and an exchange of shots was without effect.

"It was at this point that I came upon the scene, having been apprised of what would take place. As I came in sight I noted that Colonel Tattnall and General Jessup were reloading. I secured the assistance of Mr. Johnson and Major Hamilton in an effort to persuade the antagonists to stop the affair, but without success.

"The parties again took their stations, and the word being given, Mr. Clay raised his pistol and the ball passed through Randolph's clothes, but he reserved his fire, and holding his pistol perpendicularly up, said 'I do not fire on you, Mr. Clay,' and discharged his pistol in the air. He added, 'It was not my intention to fire on you, but the unfortunate incident of my pistol going off instantly changed my determination.' "

"What happened then, sir?" inquired Carson.

"The parties then simultaneously approached each other with both hands extended, Mr. Randolph remarking, 'I give you my hand, sir.' It was cordially received by Mr. Clay and the affair was thus happily and honorably discharged."

Carson's reaction was immediate. "It is always a source of great gratification to me when a duel—an unfortunate hangover from medieval times—ends thus without injury or death. I cannot think of circumstances that would induce me to resort to such evil practice, but if ever circumstances should compel such an act I should count myself fortunate to have you as an intermediary."

Senator Benton smiled sardonically, but hastened to say, "I have not always been so fortunate as to escape such difficulties myself, Carson. You undoubtedly know of my altercation and subsequent duel with General Jackson in 1813?"

"Oh yes, I do know that you came off the victor, or was it your brother Jesse who fired the shot that found its target?"

"I see you *are* familiar with that encounter, Carson. There are some who are so punctillious about the *Code Duello* that they would hardly dignify that episode with the designation 'duel'; indeed, there are those who have described it as a free-for-all," and Benton laughed heartily, brushing aside whatever unpleasant memories he may have had about his own unseemly conduct on that occasion.

"You were too young to know much about affairs of honor at that time. I am surprised that you remember it at all."

"Well you see, sir, General Jackson had been in our home on several occasions, but that was before your encounter with him. When he was studying law in Salisbury he used to come up to race in the valleys and lowlands of the mountains near Pleasant Gardens, our home. My cousins and two of my brothers would sometimes race with him. On one of these visits in our home, my father found that he and Andrew's father were what you might call neighbors in the 'ould Country.' They were from Ulster—Father from Fermanagh County and Mr. Jackson from Antrim—from the little village of Bonneybefore."

"This is indeed interesting, Carson. I had no idea that you had a tie with Jackson—or that your father had. I find it extremely interesting."

"Their friendship is not difficult to explain, Senator. You remember General Jackson never saw his father, and there were many things about his father's homeland that he wanted to know. On this basis their friendship grew, and although Jackson was sixteen years younger than Father, a great bond between them was established. Father used to tell me about him—how when he was fourteen years old he ran away from home to fight in the War of the Revolution; how he loved horses; and how far-sighted he was to study law when he was only eighteen. I was at the age for hero-worship, and he became my hero—my knight in shining armor. My father has never heard of the rumors that emanated from Salisbury to the effect that young Jackson spent much of his time there sowing wild oats. He thinks of him only as a son of a 'son of ould Ireland.' "

The supper hour having arrived, and at Carson's urging, Senator Benton joined him in the Sabbath evening meal, when they again took up the discussion of duelling and the evil effects of uncontrolled emotions. As though drawn to the subject, they brought up a number of examples well known to both.

"You perhaps are familiar with the unfortunate affair that stirred such a controversy in North Carolina about twenty-five years ago, Senator. Of course I was too young to be impressed, but I have heard the story repeated so often I sometimes have thought I was a witness."

"That must have been the instance in which Governor Speight was mortally wounded at the hands of John Stanley."

"Yes, and do you know, sir, Mr. Stanley is now Speaker in the House of Commons, his pardon vouchsafed by Governor Williams after a thorough review of the case. And there's the more recent affair between Louis Henry, who became involved over a trivial incident with Thomas Stanly—not related to Governor Speight's adversary."

"That was fatal to Stanly, I believe. Yes, Carson, I could add to that list, but it would take the rest of the evening. The whole country seems bent on settling affairs of honor and affairs of dishonor in this regretful fashion." Mr. Benton seemed genuinely sincere.

"Let us devoutly hope, sir, that this evil practice will be abolished. There surely must be a better way," said Carson as Senator Benton rose to leave.

"I could wish for you no greater blessing than that you will never find yourself in a position that requires a defense of your honor."

And so saying, the Gentleman from Missouri took his leave, extending as he did an invitation to visit his family in their home. "My wife seldom gets out socially, but she would be delighted to meet so handsome a kinsman."

With a sweep of his arm, Carson bowed low acknowledging the compliment, making less conspicuous his unwillingness to extend his hand.

Carson was left to ponder what manner of man this was. The only reference made to the relationship was a casual one as he was leaving. It might well be that before risking too close an association, Benton actually paid the call to look over this legislative stripling and assess his merits. He mulled over the events of the afternoon and evening, remembered his pledge of secrecy

26

as to the duel and lay down to uneasy dreams. Although he had never been a party to violence, indeed had been spared the witnessing of deeds of cruelty that were commonplace in the area in which he grew to manhood, he was aware that the country was not yet "neat and clean and—civilized," and the thought was disturbing.

The next morning the Capitol corridors were filled with legislators telling and retelling the incident of the duel. The news, it seemed, had leaked out and had been circulated freely during the weekend, and an editorial in the *National Intelligencer* gave wings to the story and gave pause to the conscientious lawmakers.

"We are not a little surprised," the editorial revealed, "at the indiscretion of some of the comments made in our Journals on the language used by different gentlemen in Congress in the heat of debate—the discussion whether A insulted B, or B insulted A, and whether A or B should be challenged to mortal combat, however playfully meant.

"We can hardly conceive how any man could endure existence after being instrumental to a fatal conflict, which, but for his agency, would never have taken place."

Carson tore out the editorial and put it in a convenient pocket for another reading. He wondered if Benton had seen it and if he noted that while many of the colleagues of the two parties involved in the affair of honor were sober-minded and circumspect, other ebullient gentlemen indulged in a deal of back-slapping and ribbing.

Happily the subject was temporarily forgotten in an evening of entertainment. The Ministers of Foreign Nations and their wives, and the Secretaries of the Legations and their families were feted by Congress at the Franklin House. Such a display of beribboned and bemedaled courtiers was becoming more and more commonplace in the City. For Carson it was an interesting experience.

Usually an asset to any group, he mingled gallantly with the ladies. Unattached, he had not yet found feminine companionship that was mutually agreeable, and therefore he was peculiarly fitted to pay court to many. Strikingly handsome, he was sought after by fond mothers whose daughters were delightful dancing partners. When questioned from home about the available beauties who were constantly being entertained or were entertaining, he satisfied the curiosity of the inquirers by reporting succinctly: "Missy still holds first place in my heart."

It was on April 3rd that Carson made his initial speech in Congress. The President had sent a message to the House proposing an appropriation of money to pay the expenses of delegates or deputies to the Congress of American States in Panama. The proposal had long been deliberated, and Carson had outlined his remarks while incapacitated with the cold plague.

The Committee in the House on Foreign Affairs had come up with an elaborate report favoring an appropriation. Carson opposed such an expenditure; first, because the plenipotentiaries who would meet our ministers would not be clothed with authority to make treaties, and the same would be true of our representatives. Further, the making of treaties must be ratified by some authoritative body at home. His speech was long and analytical, purporting to expose the dangers and point out the weaknesses of such an alliance. Although many were in disagreement with him, they were impressed by his logic and his powers of reasoning, and above all with his engaging personality. The House finally refused by a large majority to make any declaration at all on the subject, thus leaving the responsibility to Executive discretion.

For weeks the House had been debating a resolution offered by McDuffie of South Carolina. "Resolved that for the purpose of electing a President and Vice President of the United States, the Constitution be amended in such a manner as will prevent the election from devolving upon Congress."

This resolution reflected the dissatisfaction over the outcome of the last election, which was so skillfully manipulated by Mr. Clay when it was put before the House for a decision. And following on the heels of that resolution was a qualifying one, namely, "That a select committee be appointed with instructions to prepare and report a joint resolution embracing the aforesaid objects." It was clearly the intent of the Congress that never again would the responsibility of electing a President of the United States devolve on the House of Representatives.

Carson, in his spare time, was beginning to think about his

plans immediately following adjournment. He had been away from home half a year—the longest separation from his family he had experienced, and the hills of Carolina were beckoning. On the other hand, a dozen or more members of Congress were planning to accompany Mr. Randolph to New York, or at least to be on hand when he set sail for Liverpool, and he was invited to join them.

Carson had come to know Randolph much better since his encounter with Mr. Clay. He found him quite eccentric, blunt to the point of rudeness at times, but stimulating and witty—a gentleman to the manner born when it suited his mood to convey that impression. Carson was almost persuaded to join the bon voyage party. Besides, he had never been to New York.

Senator Branch had suggested that he plan his trip back to North Carolina over the eastern route that would take him through Halifax County. He very much wanted Carson to visit him and his family at Enfield. That would mean he wouldn't get home until the last of June, leaving but a relatively short while to see his brothers and his sisters, his cousins and his aunts—to say nothing of his nieces and his nephews and most important of all, to mingle with his constituents.

The time would pass quickly. There were only local bills to consider, for which only a bare quorum was necessary. The major bills, except the one just introduced calling for a constitutional amendment, had been disposed of. Only yesterday the long-delayed judiciary bill was rejected and a later resolution to reconsider was rejected also. It was as well for it embraced the kind of legislation that needed consideration and debate.

The pages on the calendar were turned rapidly and on May 22 both Houses met in joint session for the usual preliminaries to adjournment. The Vice President, presiding over the Senate, rose to state that having reached the last business day of the Session, it was his intention to withdraw from the Chair to give the Senate an opportunity to appoint a President pro tempore. Nathaniel Macon, from North Carolina, was selected to receive this honor, and he was conducted to the Chair by Senator Smith, where he delivered a short address expressive of his thanks for the honor conferred upon him, and giving assurance that every exertion in his power would be made to dispatch all business as speedily as possible.

After a round of testimonials and in apparent harmony, the first session of the Nineteenth Congress was adjourned Monday, May 22, 1826.

By the time Congress adjourned Carson had decided to join the party going to New York for Randolph's departure. They had reserved rooms at Washington House, an establishment located near the Academy of Fine Arts. Nearby was City Hall and the Museum—a most convenient location.

Washington Hall was operated on the new European plan with rooms from $3.00 to $5.00 a week. This new English mode of separating the two important concerns of bed and board had its disadvantages as well as its advantages, but it was to become a *modus operandi* for the traveling public as time went on.

A large concourse gathered at the wharf where the packet ship *Alexander* was docked. The sailing of a vessel across the Atlantic was still a novelty and attracted the curious and the sophisticated alike.

Seven years before, the first steamboat had embarked from American shores bound for Liverpool. It was not wholly steam-powered. The *Savannah* had its sails ready for any emergency. Indeed it would be several decades before maritime draftsmen would present specifications for a vessel capable of relying entirely on steam.

The voyage of the *Savannah* in 1819 took twenty-six days, but with ingenious improvements and a demand for faster transportation, the time would be gradually reduced.

The passengers bound for Liverpool, many of whom had been on hand since daybreak, were made aware that these packets never depart on time. Perhaps that was the reason that Mr. Randolph did not arrive with his companions until a full hour after the scheduled departure time. He had made the trip before and had profited by the experiences attendant to a long and tiresome wait for the gangplank to be lifted.

Few were gratified when he did arrive, for leaving his baggage and accoutrements for his companions to look after, with a condescending bow and a wave of his hand, he boarded the packet, his friends from Washington City going with him on board to say last farewells and to drink to his health, to his happiness and to his safe return.

When they took a last look at the departing *Alexander* from wharfside, they noted that the urbane traveler was already the center of a group of ladies and gentlemen, gesticulating, laughing and enjoying the adulation of his fellow travelers. That they were captivated by his charms and he by theirs was evident in the news report of his arrival in England.

"When the packet docked at the English port, Randolph was surrounded by a large concourse whom he greatly amused by his eccentric, instructive and original conversation.

"Dressed in yellow silk neckcloth, mauve coat and blue trousers, he had the appearance of a Grecian sage surrounded by his squires.

"He extolled the virtues of the ministers sent to America from England as well as the interdependent characteristics of the two countries. 'Whatever is beneficial for Liverpool could not be but highly useful to New York.' "

As was their wont, the legislators took occasion to make Randolph's departure a cause célèbre, and the special arrangements for a banquet at Washington Hall provided a congenial atmosphere for the evening of gaiety. The group of lawmakers who started out on this jaunt were augmented in New York by others who were en route to their homes in New England, and who stopped over for the lark. The plain truth was that with the exception of three or four of Randolph's close friends, the entire delegation was bent on pleasure and curiosity.

Those who for one reason or another had had occasion to be rebuked by his temperamental outbursts or stung by his ever-ready barbs were among the least enthusiastic of the revelers. The departure of the irascible Randolph was more an excuse than a valid reason for their presence. Nevertheless they appeared at the banquet in their formal evening regalia.

Counting wives, daughters, staff members and the legislators there were about half a hundred who found their places marked by miniature bouquets of red, white and blue flowers. Mr.

31

Randolph's seat of honor was empty, save for a hastily improvised "John Bull" with England's tri-color emblem festooned on the back. The serviettes were made to resemble packet ships replete with sails.

As was the custom, the drinking of toasts was an important and much-anticipated feature of the revelry. Usually the toasts were in the lighter mood, but not always so. Men in public life were known to clothe in seemingly innocuous words the barbs of malice, envy and suspicion, as well as commendation and approbation. Indeed some took occasion in this manner to launch their political balloons or to snipe their political adversaries at such times of informality and conviviality, and so toasts were heard with more than passing interest and attention.

Nathaniel Macon, close friend of Mr. Randolph, rose and, lifting his glass, proposed a toast:

"To Mr. Randolph, our absent guest of honor: May he find the English belles as charming as ours are beautiful—and the British a match for his barbs."

In deference to the departed member this toast was drunk standing, as was the next:

"To the President of the United States—the Hon. John Quincy Adams:

> "We'll harness our rivers,
> We'll build our canals,
> We'll add to our temples of learning.
> Just where we will get all the money for this
> Indeed is the question that's burning."

"To our First President:

> "Here's to our noble, valiant George,
> Who brought us fame at Valley Forge.
> We'll build his monument lofty and high
> So that his fame may never die."

Carson, remembering the next session of Congress proposed: "A Toast to the Union:

> "We still are united
> Despite all the threats
> To tear us apart and dismember;
> On this glad occasion we're one heart
>   and one mind,
> Our union is safe till December."

Then followed humorous toasts to wives, sweethearts and most important of all people,

"To our Constituents:

> "We're here because of you, dear friends,
> Your confidence we treasure.
> To feel your pulse, we often must
> Put business before pleasure."

TWO

Back in Washington City, last-minute obligations were taken care of, and Sam made arrangements to insure that he would have his room at the National on his return at the opening of the second session of the Nineteenth Congress. He visited the legislative halls, now almost deserted save for a crew of workmen who were engaged in refurbishing the House and Senate chambers.

As he was leaving the Capitol, Carson met his friend, Senator Branch. "Have you decided what route you will take to North Carolina? You haven't forgotten that you have an invitation to visit the Branch family at the first opportunity?" asked the older man.

"I've been reading the enticing announcements of the White Springs in Virginia. It would be a fine opportunity for me to visit this famous place, and I believe the healing springs will be highly beneficial after my bout with the cold plague. In fact I suggested to Warren Davis, Mr. Calhoun's kinsman who has been in the City on business, and who left for South Carolina last evening, that he take advantage of this opportunity to try the baths at the Springs. He promised that if he stopped, he would reserve a place for me. I have just heard from home, and everything seems propitious for me to make this stopover for a few days. Perhaps I should postpone my visit to Enfield until an occasion more suitable presents itself."

"I regret the postponement, but you are following the example of some of our discriminating members. Mr. Clay recommends the Springs heartily, as does Mr. Webster. But tell me about your plans for the remainder of the summer."

"It's my plan to see as many of my constituents as possible. I have thought to go to Asheville, Morganton, Rutherfordton—to follow the circuit—and I hope to get down as far as Salisbury. While it is not in my district, I have some friends there who will not be averse to telling me things that I may need to be told about my stewardship. It's just as you told me in one of our first conversations here, I'd better keep my slate clean and my constituents happy. They may tell me that my slate is too clean —there's nothing on it."

"Oh, I don't know about that, Carson. You have done all right for your district. At least I haven't heard any complaints —not that I have been impatiently listening, you understand."

"Well, sir, as I was leaving home my father gave me, among other things, a little bit of Irish wisdom. It went something like this: 'In politics if thou be wise, and mean thy fortunes be, bear this in mind—be deaf and blind—let *great* folk hear and see.' And so I've deferred to older and wiser heads when broad national issues were debated, and with the exception of a few instances when my own district was involved, I have to all intents and purposes been—not deaf, but dumb and blind."

"The 'great' folk have not always been infallible, as you well know, and I predict that you will soon be numbered among the more knowledgeable of our lawmakers. Besides, you had already cut your political eyeteeth before you came on the national scene. With your astute father's example and that of your three older brothers, to say nothing of your own valuable experience in the North Carolina Legislature, you have been rocked in the cradle of public service. I might go even further and say that you have been reared on the pap of political expediency, nurtured on the bread of Republican principles, supplemented with the milk of human kindness."

They both laughed at this little byplay. "Thank you, Senator. I will accept your picturesque analogy—with certain reservations."

Carson extended his hand, and Branch clasped it warmly as they parted, the older man watching the handsome, boyish figure, reflecting further on the reasons that prompted him to enlist his young life in the service of his country when there were more attractive and perhaps more rewarding areas in which he could have found satisfaction.

The journey to Greenbrier County and the Springs was made without incident. Missy, seeming to sense the direction in which she was headed, needed no spur nor crop to regulate her speed.

Arriving at the Inn, Carson inquired at the desk if Warren Davis had been a recent guest, and was told that he was still a guest, though he proposed to leave for his home in South Carolina shortly after the Fourth of July festivities. And the clerk added, "We would have reserved a room for you if we had been overaccommodated. Our regular guests from the James River will not be here for a fortnight."

There was no dearth of guests, as was apparent when Carson made his appearance. The White Springs, known far and wide for its healing properties, was nonetheless attractive to transients and pleasure-seekers.

Carson did not see Davis until time for tea, when he went out on the veranda, and he hardly saw him then because of the lovely ladies who were vying with each other in animated conversation. Ivory fans and ruffled parasols were much in evidence. A hurried glance convinced Carson that he had made no mistake in planning a stopover here.

Davis was apparently enjoying all of this from afar. He was seated on the balustrade, holding a skein of wool between his outstretched hands, while a motherly-looking companion wound the colorful ball of yarn.

"Oh, Carson," he called, rising but unable to offer his hand. "I'd like you to meet Mrs. Reid, from Lexington. She has been my pleasant chaperone since I came, and she has two lovely daughters who——"

"Mr. Davis has been painting you in glowing colors," interrupted Mrs. Reid, "and I see he has not done justice to his subject."

Carson bowed low in acknowledgment, and the conversation got off to a fine start. Inside they could see the dining room being prepared for the evening meal—supper it was. Southern tavern and innkeepers and those who catered to Southern whims had not been successful in changing the custom of having dinner in the middle of the day.

Through soft lace curtains they could see the flickering light of many candles. Tempting viands were placed on a long buffet by white-coated serving boys, and the delicious aroma wafted through open windows and doors served as an enticing magnet to draw the guests to the dining room.

The first evening, then, passed quickly and pleasantly. The Reid daughters were delightful—really too young for either

36

Davis or Carson, though not too young for dancing partners, and they would have danced until the wee sma' hours but for the fact that Carson pled fatigue from his journey, which was a reason, not a flimsy excuse. And there was the added motive of preparation for the gala celebration of the glorious Fourth of July on the morrow. Because of this significant milestone—the 50th anniversary of the Day of Independence—the day was to be widely, extravagantly and sometimes boistrously observed, not only at this famous resort but in every hamlet and city throughout the land.

At the Old White, prizes were offered for the most appropriately dressed guests in representation of the Fourth. Prizes were offered also for the best collection of toasts to be presented at the banquet which would be climaxed by a grand ball. That evening a committee called to enlist owners of horses in the race that would be a part of the afternoon program. Ribbons would be awarded the winners in addition to other incentives.

Davis entered his two horses, but it took much persuasion for Carson to enter Missy. He knew she was exhausted from her trip, but as soon as the solicitor found that she had participated in many unofficial races when she was in better form, he and the committee were insistent on entering her, and Carson consented provided an experienced rider could be found for her. Ordinarily Carson would have been willing to wager that Missy would be the lead horse. He was not so sure this time, but he entered into the spirit of the occasion and awaited the morrow with no little excitement. He had not participated in a lively race since he left Carolina.

All kinds of games and stunts were in progress when he and Davis and the Reids entered the fair grounds. It was easy to see that elaborate preparations had been made for the celebration. Bunting and flags properly displayed emphasized the patriotic theme. Of course there was a band, and the martial strains could be heard for miles around.

They came by every means of transportation—urchins bareback on mules, riders on saddle horses and ponies, people in gigs and buggies, a number of Conestoga wagons, post chaises and phaetons. One could fairly well estimate the classes represented in the afternoon crowd. They were *all* there—not just the elite

37

and the well-to-do, but the country bumpkin, the lame, the halt and perhaps the blind. In such a conglomeration of humanity it was not surprising to see one or two Yankee peddlers hawking their wares and onlookers being trampled on by eager buyers. These enterprising itinerant merchants always managed to find out when crowds were to assemble, for such an occasion produced results that many miles of traveling could not accomplish.

The patrons from the Old White found seats to their liking where they could watch the horses being put through their paces. There were an even dozen entered, with Davis's two and Carson's Missy accounting for one-fourth the number. Missy's rider, apparently accustomed to spirited animals, seemed to know how to handle her adequately. Davis's entries were really not racers, and he joked about their having qualified at all.

The preliminaries over, they were off amid shouts of encouragement from the sidelines. Carson was sure after the first sixty seconds that Missy could out-perform them all. He even put up a sizeable wager with Mr. Coxe from the Inn, who in the spirit of good sportsmanship was betting on Black Nightmare, one of the horses Davis had entered.

Missy got off to a slow start. She had forgotten her training, but when three or four runners gained on her, she began to show her old form, gradually overtaking the lead horse in the first lap. They kept an even pace for another lap and another, and then she sprinted ahead by a length, and the crowd roared.

And then something happened. She slowed perceptibly. Those nearby watched as she dragged a loose shoe until she lost it, but not before she had inflicted a gash on her right foreleg that put her out of the running. In the excitement Carson did not observe that she limped noticeably, nor could he see that she was bleeding profusely when she was led off the track.

Davis's Nightmare—a name given hurriedly to his most promising entrant for this event only—came in fifth, and the blue ribbon and wild acclaim was given to a local owner whose gelding had outdistanced them all. It was presented by a lanky official dressed as Uncle Sam, striped britches, stovepipe hat and all. There was one other attraction—a showing of trained bears, scheduled especially for the children—and while this was in progress the group from the Inn made their exit. A banquet and ball climaxed the busy, exciting day—a day long to be remembered by old and young alike.

Before dressing for the gala events of the evening, Carson visited the stables, and finding Missy's injury more severe than he had expected, he inquired about professional assistance to prevent unnecessary pain and crippling. The attendant had already administered first aid, and he was experienced. Stage-coaches traveling the North-South route stopped here overnight and it was necessary for them to have expert attention for their animals.

There was little activity around the Inn on the morning following the celebration. Carson, concerned about Missy, visited the stables around noon and found a new hand examining Missy's injury.

"I done tuck it on myself to send for Doc Maynard, sir. Doc, this is Mr. Carson. He's plenty worried about this little horse."

Doc acknowledged the introduction with a grunt and went on with his examination. It was plain to see that the prognosis was not good.

In a few minutes Doc stood up and gave the verdict. "If I'd a been here last night, she wouldn't been so bad. That gash has festered and will take time to heal. I'll fix her up good, but you'd better not take her out for a couple of days—not on any long trip anyway. If you do, you're goin' to have a lame horse for sure."

Carson told Davis the bad news at dinner, and his response was encouraging. "An extra day won't make or break you. Why don't you plan to go back as I do. Better still, plan to go back with me in my gig. That way Missy won't have to carry the extra burden of your weight. If I am not mistaken Pleasant Gardens is in an almost direct line south from here, and if you don't mind traveling some unbeaten paths, I'll have you home in a fortnight. Besides, there are some things I want to discuss with you."

"Mighty kind of you, sir, mighty kind indeed," replied Carson in mock dignity. "And if we are thus importuned by Providence to prolong our stay, I can think of no more pleasant place to while the passing hours—or the days, as the case may be."

Carson led the way to the veranda, where the guests gave every evidence of having recovered from the gala events of the day before. Mrs. Reid and her daughters beckoned them, and soon they were in animated conversation.

"I do declare, gentlemen, the Reid sisters had the most divine dancing partners on the floor last night. We have been asked over and over where we found our handsome escorts. And do you know what I said? I told them that you were distant cousins on the Reid side," and the young girl laughed at her assumed cleverness.

"Which may or may not have a semblance of truth, young lady." Turning to Mrs. Reid inquiringly, Carson said, "Ever since I met you, Mrs. Reid, I have been on the verge of telling you that my father has in his possession a copy of a letter written to a Mr. Andrew Reid of Lexington by Reid's brother-in-law, Samuel McDowell, Jr. It reveals the political tenseness between the Federalists and the anti-Federalists about fifteen years ago."

"Yes, I have heard about that letter. The original is in possession of my husband's family, and on occasion has been read aloud when the family were gathered together. And my husband has another letter he prizes—this one from young Samuel McDowell's father, the Judge who now lives in Mercer County, Kentucky.

"But pray tell me, Mr. Carson, why your father has such an interest in the Reid letter?"

"For two very good and sufficient reasons, Mrs. Reid. Perhaps the most likely is that the father of the ardent Federalist was my Mother's own uncle for whom I am named, Judge Samuel McDowell."

"Is it possible!" exclaimed Mrs. Reid—"and the other reason?"

"The other reason is that Reid was a believer in the program and policies of Jefferson—a Jeffersonian Republican, if you will, and so am I. McDowell, my own blood relative, was a Federalist, but I would not go so far as to impugn his motives."

"Certainly not!" Mrs. Reid spoke vehemently. "His letter to my husband's kinsman is a masterpiece of patriotic sentiment. And besides, the McDowells have always been the first to 'fly to

40

arms' for our country. Not only is the McDowell name synonymous with patriotic fervor, it has now won renown in the field of medical pioneering. Was it not a brother of this Samuel McDowell, Jr. who performed the first abdominal surgery—the young Dr. Ephraim McDowell of Danville, Kentucky?"

"It was indeed, ma'am—my mother's first cousin," answered Carson, "and I have wished that I could meet this eminent man who may find himself in years to come known and respected the world over, even though he has been rejected and well-nigh crucified by some of his contemporaries. I do not know whether he is in active practice or not. He should be, for he is only fifty-five years old, or thereabout. Danville, Kentucky cannot hold a man of such stature and ability—of that I am sure," concluded Carson.

During the conversation the younger Reids fidgeted and finally excused themselves, and when barely within earshot one of them called out, "We hope you will find Mr. Carson is a kissin' cousin, Ma."

"What are these young people coming to!" was the exclamation of the startled Mrs. Reid.

Davis had been absorbed in the conversation but had maintained a discreet silence until he asked about the other letter Mrs. Reid had mentioned—the one written to this same Andrew Reid. "Did that, too, have patriotic overtones?"

"Heavens, no! That letter has caused a deal of amusement. You see, after a successful career as soldier, statesman and patriot, Judge McDowell moved to Danville, Kentucky from Lexington, as you know, Mr. Carson. In the letter to Andrew he wanted to know whether or not the people back in Lexington and vicinity were as religious as they were when he lived among them. He recalled that the Presbyterians would not associate with the wicked, but would meet only for religious purposes or socially among their Presbyterian friends."

"Did the Judge condone this practice?" someone asked.

"No indeed! He advised mixing in assemblies, cultivating friendships and helping to civilize the world, thus improving its manners and removing the sourness and superstition that bigotry inevitably leaves on the mind."

"He should see some of those Presbyterians at Lexington

41

now," laughed Mrs. Reid.

"And he should have seen me with my mother, his niece, at Methodist camp meetings when I was growing up. Many a time I have led the singing, and when there were enough colored folk, as there usually were, to join in, the good old tunes sounded as if they had come straight from the pearly gates. That music brought many a mourner to the bench, as I recall."

Mrs. Reid called to her daughters to join the group, explaining, "Mr. Carson is a singer. He has just been telling us about the camp meetings he attended with his mother."

"Oh, do tell us about it. What were those meetings like?"

"It is not easy for those who have never attended a camp meeting to imagine the excitement and activity that characterizes such an occasion." Carson, recalling a graphic description he had recently read, leaned heavily on it for the telling. "On the appointed day people begin to stream into the grounds much as they did here for the Fourth, only they are laden with provisions—mattresses, tents and arrangements for staying a week.

"The ambitious and the well-to-do are there, for in the region opinion is all-powerful, and they are there to extend their influence or to see that their presence is noted. Aspirants to office are there to electioneer and to gain popularity. Many are there out of curiosity—merely to enjoy the spectacle; children are there, eyes glistening with excitement; middle-aged fathers and mothers are there with the sober look of people whose plans in life are fixed; men and women with hoary hair are there, with such thoughts as their years invite.

"The line of tents are pitched and the camp city springs up in a few hours. The pilgrims mingle, visiting from tent to tent, exchanging apostolic greetings. The candles are lighted, the supper is spread, the moon breaks through a cloud just as an old man ascends the platform, wipes the dust from his spectacles and in a quavering voice gives out the opening hymn—the one to set the tone of the meeting. The words are familiar to most and the tune is one in which every voice may join.

"That is where I'd come in, and it always brought a surge of emotion that is difficult to explain. The aged orator talks of God and Eternity, of judgment to come and always of the

42

heavenly rewards of the redeemed. He speaks of his experiences, his travels, his persecutions, his witnesses and of those he has seen with hope in their hearts in peace and in triumph gathered to their fathers. And when he speaks of the short time remaining to him, his only regret is that he can no more proclaim the mercies of the Redeemer. No wonder as the venerable man of God pauses to wipe the gathering moisture from his eyes, the congregation before him are moved to tears and those who came to scoff remain to pray."

Carson had not meant to stir the emotions of his listeners as he did, and it behooved him to turn the conversation into less emotional channels. He smiled as he remembered some of the incidents of his boyhood, and then continued.

"You know, I have an unusual religious background, almost a paradox, you might say. My mother, devout and proper as she was, enjoyed the excitement of camp meetings, and my father came to these shores to escape the dire fate of becoming an Episcopal clergyman, an ambition of his parents, I have been told."

His listeners laughed and urged him to be more specific.

"Father's story of his flight from 'religious persecution' may not be cut from the whole cloth. It is certain that he was an adventurous lad. He still is—adventurous and very courageous, else he never would have earned a reputation for being an Indian fighter of some renown.

"He did not actually run away from his family, as many have been led to believe. He was not yet twenty when he came over from Ireland with his sister, her husband and their seven children, and he must have had the tacit consent of his parents. If you remember there was a great exodus from Ireland to America at that time. It may be because of the great opportunities afforded my parents and grandparents that I am such a proud and grateful American today.

"I can remember an incident that has been told of him that indicates the kind of courage he had. When he first came over to this country he had a severe illness, and was shown a great deal of kindness by an old couple who were Quakers, and who kept a mill. Afterward, when on a visit to the old people, he was told how a certain bully had been worrying them, abusing them and even cursing them. Father spent the night in the mill, and when the bully appeared the next morning and commenced his railings against the old couple, he was properly and thoroughly thrashed by the young Irishman."

The stories he told evoked great interest among the group, and opened up a flow of conversation that lasted till time for the evening meal. The next morning he persuaded one of the kitchen maids to give him a few lumps of sugar, which he passed on to Missy, allowing her to lick his hand for the last sweet morsel.

It was easy to see that she was better—that she limped only slightly when the stable boy walked her around the paddock. But Doc had left a warning. It would be foolhardy to start on a long journey until she was entirely healed—maybe the day after tomorrow. That would be the eighth, and that would be the last possible day he could in good conscience delay his friend's departure.

They made plans for an early start on the appointed day, and together worked out a preliminary route that would employ some of the shortcuts.

"We can't go all of the way as the crow flies, Carson," Davis suggested.

"Well, how does the crow fly, my friend? I've heard that expression all of my life, and I am no wiser than when I first heard it. I have some serious doubts about the validity of that comparison. Anyway, I'm the passenger *and* the freeloader. I'll defer to you in the route-planning. I'll be making only one request of you, sir. I'd like to go through Salisbury and Morganton on the way home."

Anxious to inquire about road conditions, they joined a group of men on the upper porch. As it turned out they were all familiar with roads and accommodations to the North, but none would hazard a guess about the roads Southward. However, one of them suggested, "I saw one of those Yankee peddlers on the street this morning—possibly one of those who was here on the Fourth. They know more about roads and travel conditions than anyone."

"They should," Carson said, "they fathered much of the system that is now dignified with the term post roads. They know also a very great deal about the backwoods trails, about the thick dust that covers the roads in dry weather and even much more about the miring of wheels and animals in the rainy season."

And then the subject was abruptly changed. Said a gentleman on the right side of Davis, "I am not very familiar with the shades of Southern dialect or Southern accent, if you prefer, but your speech leads me to believe that you are from the deep South."

"Not too deep, sir. I'm from South Carolina, a native of Columbia, the Capital, and I now live in Pendleton, where I practice law. My friend here is a member of the House of Representatives from North Carolina. We are en route to our respective homes, and have tarried to allow time for Mr. Carson's horse to mend. She was injured in the races on the Fourth."

Introductions were acknowledged, and the first speaker continued. "I suppose that cotton and tobacco are your principal commodities," and before waiting for an answer he went on. "I have read much about your plantation life, and of the hardships and injustices dealt the slaves by their imperious masters. Do these reports give a true picture of conditions in your state, Mr. Davis?"

Davis turned in his chair to face the questioner. He seemed to hesitate too long before making a reply.

"Mr. Coxe, I wish it were possible for me to lump together all slave-holding owners and all slave laborers and come up with a composite that would truthfully answer your question. When you speak of the South, sir, one segment of our society will think of magnolias and mint juleps and white-columned mansions, of endless rows of cotton bales and pyramids of tobacco hogheads—of peace and plenty and purity. And that's a damned lie!

"Another will see only man's inhumanity to man—flogging, branding, the cruel slave-market, degradation and human bondage. That too is a lie! Somewhere between these two extremes you will find your answer. To be sure you will find some of both extremes in my state and in other parts of the South. It is the exception that proves the rule, sir.

"Yes, Mr. Coxe, when you paint the South, you must use a

large palette, so that you can employ the use of dark tones—in some cases very dark tones, as well as the delightful pastels—a miscellany of shades, sir, the blending of which gives a beautiful picture, with no particular color dominant."

Carson had thought to enter the conversation to assist Davis in his defense, but he soon saw that his friend was more than an equal for his adversary.

Perhaps fortunately at this juncture the gong for the evening meal sounded, and the group dispersed, some reluctantly, be it said, for in their opinion if there was anything better than a cockfight it was a Yankee and a Southerner engaged in a battle of words.

The meal was strictly sectional, and no one ate with more genuine relish than the Yankee autocrat of the supper table, Mr. Coxe. Crisp, crunchy southern fried chicken, potato salad garnished with radishes, cucumbers and tomatoes, hot biscuits and spoon bread, with an assortment of cakes and syllabub completed the meal. Who could ask for a more substantial manifestation of Southern excellence?

While the guests were feasting, the stage arrived, and the passengers entered the lobby. It was soon noted that conversation of the arrivals reached a high pitch of excitement. Davis excused himself and joined a group clustered around a pile of newspapers just brought in by the driver. Securing one of the papers, Davis beckoned to Carson. "Thomas Jefferson is dead!"

"It cannot be," was the rejoinder. "When did it happen?"

"On July Fourth—four days ago, but wait, there is more. John Adams died the same day. Here is an editorial. Listen." And Davis read in subdued tones.

In another part of our paper will be found an account of the death of Mr. Jefferson and Mr. Adams, ex-Presidents of the United States, Mr. Adams in his ninety-first year, and the former in his eightieth. They both, in conjunction with the venerable Mr. Carroll, who alone survives, drew up and signed the celebrated Declaration of Independence.

These gentlemen both retained their mental faculties to the end.

We regret that our limits prevent publication of some of the memorable letters that came from the pen of each of these gentlemen, who have lived and moved, an honor to their species, and whose memories will be embalmed in the bosom of every genuine patriot for ages to come.

46

"That is but one of many hundred tributes that will be set in print here and in the capitals of the world, Davis. What a staggering coincidence—their deaths on the same day!"

The two men sat talking on the veranda long after most of the guests had retired. They talked of life and death, of pride and ambition, of the seemingly mystical manifestations of Providence, and particularly of the awful responsibilities that rest on the President of the nation as she emerges bearing the imprint of it all.

Next morning they were joined by other guests, and the topic of conversation of the previous evening was taken up where it had been interrupted the evening before. Someone remarked that the President had been scheduled to make the Independence Day address in Washington City.

"Have you read the interesting article that was on the inside pages of the *Intelligencer?*" Davis inquired. "The caption is 'They Were In The End Reconciled Friends,' and it is the kind of reporting that should be made a part of history."

"Do proceed, sir. I dare say we are all curious about the post mortems."

" 'The exigencies of the times, the fulminations of their respective political philosophies—perhaps a lack of communication—had driven a wedge between them. That there was a bond between them became evident while they yet lived.

" 'Over the period of years there was an exchange of letters between them when they were seeking to come to an understanding that would prevent a period of strained relationships. Notwithstanding, there was a period of at least two years when there was no communication between them—written or spoken.

" 'These two encompassed the Birth of a Nation. They had often and forcibly enunciated the principles that should guide the new Nation. But in the end they were reconciled friends. Indeed, Adams' last words were, "Thomas Jefferson survives." And of Adams, Thomas Jefferson said, "There is not upon this earth a more perfectly honest man than Adams." ' "

They sat quietly for a few moments, and then someone remembered that Adams had a keen sense of humor. "It is said that while looking at a portrait of himself with lips parted alongside of one of Washington with his lips firmly closed,

47

Adams was heard to say of himself, 'That fellow never could keep his mouth shut.' "

And another in the group suggested that John Adams, had he been present, would have been pleased with the kind of celebration in which they had participated on the Fourth, because at the time of the signing of the Declaration of Independence he had written to his wife that the day was apt to be celebrated by succeeding generations as a festival, and commemorated as a day of *deliverance* by acts of devotion to Almighty God. He thought it ought to be celebrated with pomp and parade, with shows and games and sports, and with guns, bells, bonfires and illuminations from one end of the continent to another.

"We are a new nation," Mr. Coxe volunteered, and not only should we annually celebrate our birth of freedom, but our history should be carefully preserved for future generations. Let there be an error, an untruth or a misjudgment and half a century later the errors, the half-truths and misrepresentations will be picked up and embellished by numerous historians and pseudo-historians."

"I suppose," said Davis, "that no one has changed the course of history more than historians."

"But isn't it true," Carson interpolated, "that it is impossible to judge an individual or an event until time allows us to put that person and that event in the proper perspective? Customs, traditions and practices change, and what would be considered acceptable practice today might very well be an outrage tomorrow."

So shocking had been the news and so interesting the reactions that no mention had been made of the return trip. Missy was greatly improved, and the afternoon was spent in last-minute preparations.

Davis and Carson decided to go shopping for the homefolk. Carson had bought a few souvenirs in New York, but one of the ladies had told him if he wanted to select a gift that would please the feminine recipients to buy a quantity of nutmeg. "But do provide a small grater to go along with the nuts. Tie a pretty ribbon around each article to make it festive. They'll bless you for it."

When they entered the lobby with their packages they were prevailed upon to join a group in the parlor who were singing currently popular songs. Lyle Reid was at the pianoforte and her sister, Margaretta—the lively one—was trying to bring harmony out of chaos.

"Now listen folks—let's be serious about this and sing," and giving a sidelong glance at Carson, "sing like they do at Methodist camp meetings. Perhaps Mr. Carson will do us the honor of leading our songs."

"Well, miss, you have struck a responsive chord in my breast," and reverting to exaggerated Southern dialect, he continued, "ahs rat at home at a camp meetin', an I loves singin' better than ah loves grits an gravy.

The others fell in with the spirit of the occasion under Carson's clowning and urging, and as the singing grew more spirited, the music-makers were joined by other guests and shyly, one by one, the maids and the kitchen help, whose voices added much to the total enjoyment of the folk songs and Negro spirituals. They warmed up with "I'm going to sing when the Spirit says sing," "Camp Meetin' in the Wilderness" and "Don't Let Nobody Turn You Around," the words of which had a strong appeal for them:

> 'Twas at the River of the Jordan
> Baptism was begun;
> John baptised the multitude
> But he sprinkled nary a one.

> The Baptis', they go by the water
> The Methodis' go by lan'
> But when they git to heaven
> They'll shake each other's han'.

> You may be a good Baptis'
> A good Methodis' as well
> But if you ain't the pure in heart
> Your soul is boun' for Hell.

At the insistance of Lyle and Margaretta, Sam consented to sing one of the popular Irish ballads, and they disbanded after all had joined heartily in the singing of a fanciful Irish round:

Mush, mush, mush too-li-le-aley
Mush, mush, mush too-li-le-o
And I lathered him with my shillaleh
For he stepped on the tail of my coat.

"Why didn't we think of singing before your last day?" Lyle inquired of Carson as they sat on the veranda after the evening meal.

"Yes, the girls enjoyed every minute of your impromptu concert. It was a welcome interlude after all of the serious events of the last several days," Mrs. Reid assured Carson.

"Perhaps it is just as well. An overdose of such carrying-on might have brought an 'overture' from the management. And, as much as I regret it, I must bid you goodnight and good-by. We're leaving at daybreak tomorrow and Davis insists that we get a good night's rest."

It was toward the middle of the morning, after they were sure they were on the right road, that Davis told Carson of his plans to run for a seat in the 20th Congress. Such a back-slapping and commotion ensued that the horses almost got out of hand.

"Let me grasp the hand of 'the gentleman from South Carolina, Mr. Davis!' That's the best news I've heard since I had word of my own election. Do you expect to have much opposition?"

"You never know. I feel that I am pretty well known in my district, having been a state senator."

"Mr. Calhoun's influence should be invaluable," reflected Carson.

"Indeed it will, but I do not expect to trade on that friendship. I want to run my own race, and stand on my own record, brief and nebulous though it is."

"Of course you do, and you will find yourself in excellent company, sir, if I may say it. South Carolina is in the forefront of our Southern states. She has provided the nation with talent, leadership, statesmanship, and in a finer shade of meaning, with statesmen. Excepting Virginia, I believe South Carolina has enriched the nation, intellectually and forensically, more than any Southern state."

50

Carson's evaluation was sincere and spontaneous, and he added, "The name of Davis, I predict, will be added to the other illustrious South Carolinians who have brought honor to our nation."

"Hear, hear!" Davis exclaimed. "We shall see. I may not have an opportunity to leave my imprint in the halls of government. I may not even win the election, but I intend to leave no stone unturned, my friend—no stone unturned."

"If I can overturn any of those stones for you, Davis, you may be sure that I will consider it a high privilege."

They were approaching a toll house, and it appeared that a little settlement had sprung up around it, as often happened; it also appeared that there was excitement of some kind just past the bridge. A group of men, women, children and dogs was clustered around some kind of vehicle.

"That must be a peddler—perhaps one of those who was at the fair grounds on the Fourth—the one who might have given us information about road conditions, as Mr. Cushing suggested."

They were near enough now to see that the vehicle was drawn by one horse—indication that his offerings were of light-weight material. When there were furniture and furnishings—chests, spinning wheels, looms and stoves—the peddler would of necessity drive two horses, and in rare cases more. Drawing nearer they noticed not one peddler, but two, and it was plain to see that the offerings were pots and pans, canes and umbrellas—these suspended from crossbars around the four-cornered frame that had been added to the wagon for purposes of display.

There were hooked rugs, water and milk pails, ribbons and laces, needles and pins and several bolts of bombazine, woolsey and cambric. And for everyone who made a purchase there was an out-of-date newspaper pulled from a stack on the wagon floor.

"Why this, madam, is a December issue of the *Gazette*. Naturally it's full of news *and* it is filled with Christmas receipts and suggestions." And it was pounced upon by the excited ladies as if Christmas were only three weeks instead of three months away. Indeed the old news in these out-of-date papers was new news to many of the bystanders.

Usually there was only one peddler attached to a roving country store as small as this. The peddler's assistant was not peddling wares, but his own highly-specialized service. He was a silhouette cutter. His equipment was meager, consisting only of a pair of sharp scissors and black and white paper—perhaps a pot of glue. When they were traveling he added only his own weight to the caravan, and he paid a small percent of his "take" to the owner.

Business was good. It had been a long time, Carson and Davis surmised, since any of his kind had visited the tiny settlement, and the excitement could not have been more had it been the King of France with forty thousand men. At this juncture the peddler produced a cow horn, on which he blew loud and long, following which he announced: "You good people know me. I've been here before. I am headed south to Fayetteville, South Carolina, and I won't be coming back this way. You'd better get your supplies while you can. I'll be here all afternoon, so step right up and do your picking." The peddler spoke in a New England accent, and his speech showed none of the provincial speech habits that characterized many of those clustered around him.

"Listen to me folks, you haven't seen anything yet. If you'll step right up close, I'll open this chest and this horsehair trunk, and I'll show you do-dads the like of which you've never seen before. Here, young man, give me a hand—help me lift this trunk out where the dear ladies can see and touch the things they've always wanted. There are trinkets here fresh from the old country—things your grandparents never heard of——

"Let alone never seed," volunteered a one-gallus man from the hills.

"Here are some pins from England—rows and rows of them stuck in paper folders for your convenience. We don't sell them by the dozen anymore. Here are steel needles and buckles for your dancing shoes, young ladies. Just look at these elegant combs!" And he stuck in his hair a beautiful tortoise-shell comb banded with mother-of-pearl, put on a gold chain with a handsome locket, raised a ruffled parasol and struck a pose which delighted the customers. The ornamental combs sold well, and so did the ordinary variety, and the fine-tooth combs.

"And here is something for this pretty girl here—a looking glass so she can primp for her young man."

The fine jewelry and silk parasols were eyed enviously, but the price was out of reach for most of the onlookers. Eager to keep his wares moving, he reached into the trunk for other tempting articles. "Here are ribbons and laces, and threads of all colors, and here, good people, is something you need. Take out that oiled paper in your patched-up windows and put in glass panes. These you can see through, and if you can't see through them you need some of my spectacles."

Holding aloft a pair he beckoned, "Look through these and you'll see things you never saw before—I guarantee it." He passed a handful of spectacles through the crowd, allowing each prospective buyer to find his own fit. They were, of course, just different strengths of magnifying lens, fitted with gold rims.

This was the time for him to hold up for feminine delight the bolts of bombazine in gay colors, and velvet and satin. As he watched the women handle the cloth, if they held it at arm's length to see the pattern or weave, he would interrupt. "Now this little lady needs a pair of spectacles. She can't see further than the end of her nose."

Carson and Davis each bought a dress length of bombazine in royal purple to add to the gifts they were taking home. They were interested in the firearms and examined some of the rifles, but did not purchase any. They had their silhouettes cut and that was enough trappings, they thought.

As they walked back to their conveyance, Davis remarked, "South Carolina is plentifully supplied with gunsmiths, and locksmiths, too, of course. Why there's a gunsmith in Charleston who recently advertised in the *Charleston Courier* that he had learned an invaluable secret—he had found out how to crook gun stocks successfully. Not only could he bend the wood for their rifles, but he stated he could crook any gun that was too straight in the breech. And funny thing, no sooner did the ad appear than another Charleston gunsmith named Shirer deposed and said that he could, on short notice, crook any butt of a gun by steam, and would do it at a low price. Charleston alone must have a dozen or more smiths, and there are others over the State. The larger and more prosperous ones have associated with them journeymen adept at making locks, barrels, castings—and others who can cut, polish and finish barrels ready to be stocked."

"Father has always bought his firearms in Charleston when the wagon trains go down for supplies twice a year. He has a rack of guns of every description, and he has insisted that each of his sons learn the correct handling of firearms and that they learn to hit the bull's-eye, and we're pretty good marksmen," said Carson, and he continued, "it is amazing how many things can be bought in Charleston. Of course they have the advantage, as a port city, of having first chance at the shiploads of imports that come in.

"We have a turret clock that came from Charleston, and a grandfather clock, too; in fact, most of our furniture and furnishings have been bought from importers through Charleston agents, and we have some very fine pieces, thanks to my father's good taste and his ability to strike a bargain."

Seated on the wide veranda of the tavern near the toll house, tall drinks in hand, they continued their conversation.

"You know, we didn't inquire of our peripatetic merchant about roads south, Carson. You heard him say he would go as far as Fayetteville, South Carolina, but he meant your state, of course. I doubt if he gets into the mountains west. I figure it will take us two days less to go the direct route south. I'm willing to get off the beaten path if you are."

"Davis, I just don't know. I went up to Washington City by the northwestern route—over roads hacked out of the mountains that are all right for a man on horseback, but it would be rough for a gig and three horses. I wouldn't have any difficulty finding my way back on that route, but I think it's risky for us to try it.

"I'll say this—if we return over the direct route, I can show you in the mountains of North Carolina some of the most breathtaking scenery of your entire life. I doubt if it can be equalled in the nation."

"We'd better save that for another trip, and go back with as little difficulty as possible. Have you forgotten that I may be accompanying you on many excursions of this kind? You see, this drink has been salubrious. Already I feel optimistic about my election, Carson, and honestly it's the first time I have spoken with any certainty about it."

The supper bell was rung at this point, and the travelers sought sustenance and repose against the hardships of their second day on the road.

At the same time the next day they had covered a considerable distance, and two days later were halfway to the North Carolina border. This, because they had so far kept to the post roads, but they were turning west the next day, agreeing between them that they wanted to go through Salisbury and Morganton, in both of which places they had friends who could give them hospitality and bring them up-to-date on events and happenings since they had last read a newspaper.

They had been blessed with good weather, only once having to find shelter in a storm, but there were times when the wayfarers longed for a suitable place to rest and refresh themselves. Hour after hour they had only themselves for companionship. It could have been fatal to their friendship, but there were so many interesting things to talk about, and even more interesting things to see. If they became irritable, they stopped talking, and the first to break the silence paid a wager.

"Carson, since I will be stopping at least overnight with your family, I'd like to know more about them. If the ones I haven't seen are as knowledgeable and as colorful as those I have heard about at the Springs, I'm in for a treat. Tell me about the others."

"You've posed a topic on which I could elaborate for days. If for no other reason than its size and composition, our family is interesting. Let me tell you about my uncles and my cousins and my aunts!

"My father has been twice married, and my mother was his second wife. My father was her second husband, so I have three full brothers and one full sister—Carsons, of course. Then I have four half-brothers and one half-sister—children of my father and his first wife, Rachel, daughter of my step-grandfather. Moreover, I have two half-brothers and one half-sister living who are the progeny of my mother and her first husband, Major Joseph McDowell of Pleasant Gardens.

55

"If you haven't lost count, there are a baker's dozen of us, if you count me in. Eight have homes of their own—not too far away to be a part of our emergency call system. At home now, beside my father are Jonathan Logan, Matilda and John, who is a doctor. They are unmarried.

"The Quaker Meadows McDowells we will see in Morganton are in some instances double first cousins, Colonel Joseph McDowell having married my mother's sister Margaretta Moffitt."

Davis blinked as if he could not believe his ears.

"We will see those who are at the homestead at Quaker Meadows, the older ones having gone these many years."

For a few minutes Carson seemed lost in reflection, and then he burst out laughing. "Begorra, it makes me dizzy to think of all of this vast concourse of relatives—the close, close ones, to say nothing of the second cousins and the in-laws. You see, I have involved only two families—the Carsons and the McDowells, and there are the Wilsons, and the Davidsons, the Prestons and the Chrismans, the Whitsons and the Woodfins, the Kirks and the Millers, the Bowmans and the Paytons, the McClungs, the Irvines and the Reids——"

"Stop right there, Carson! I know about the Reids, and so far as I know the rest may as well be a delinquent tax list. Holy Jerusalem! With those relatives you could get yourself elected President if the family were all of one persuasion."

"Don't worry, they're not!"

"Can you pinpoint the two antecedents who began the begatting of all of those prolific Scotch-Irish?"

"Of those on this side of the Atlantic I would say that Colonel John Carson and the venerable Ephriam McDowell would be an accurate guess. The Carsons are few in number, whereas the descendants of Ephriam—child of the Covenant— are like unto the sands of the sea. The span of his life covered the overthrow of the Stuarts, the rise of the House of Hanover, the establishment of the Empire of Briton in India, the wresting of New York from the Dutch."

"Are you descended from both?"

"Yes, Ephriam begat John, who was killed by the Indians at Balcony Falls. Thus was a brilliant satellite eclipsed, but not

56

before he begat Samuel, James and Sarah, and was assured that his line would go out to the ends of the earth, as it did, for Sarah married Colonel George Moffett of Augusta County, Virginia and they begat eleven children, one of whom was my mother."

"It all adds up to the interesting statistic that your great-great-grandfather was the Patriarch Ephriam, your great-grandfather, Captain John McDowell, who was killed by the Indians, your grandmother was Sarah McDowell Moffitt, and your mother, Mary Moffitt McDowell."

"Your deduction is accurate, my friend, and I will send you to the head of the class—not for your superb memory, but your indefatigable patience. If there's anything more boring than ancestors, I don't know what it is. But you asked for it. Now don't misunderstand me, Davis. I am inordinately proud of my family, but someone far wiser than I has said, 'Birth and ancestry, and that which we ourselves have not achieved we can scarcely call our own,' and that puts me on my mettle, doesn't it?"

Davis turned to look at Carson as if appraising him for the first time. "I think, my friend, that you have made a good start in the right direction."

"I am not satisfied with the start I have made. Some of the more seasoned politicians back home have told me that I would do well to hold my own this year, and later I can experiment in lighting a few fires where heat and light will do the most good."

"If I am there next season, and numbered among the faithful," Davis ventured, "maybe I can scrape up a little kinlin' for your fires, my friend."

"Seriously, Davis, there are so many things that need to be done for my constituents.

"In North Carolina, East and West are unequally yoked together—to the detriment of my section. I want to represent my Western constituents and get some reforms started. Some of these reforms will require constitutional amendments—and that, my friend, is a slow process. The kind of sectional rivalry we have in North Carolina is more than deplorable; inequalities cannot go on forever, nor should they. The West labors under severe handicaps. Conditions now are not the same as those that prevailed when the Provincial Congress met at Halifax and framed the original Constitution of North Carolina.

"Although that instrument proclaimed that 'all power—all political power is vested in and derived from the people only,' that constitution was never submitted to the people for ratification. That's how consistent they were. There are other defects that need to be corrected. Of course these are state matters, and in the final analysis must be adjudicated by the state, but it is my feeling that I can accomplish more for my people by becoming experienced in legislation of a larger scope on a wider horizon."

"That seems to be a reasonable assumption," declared Davis, "especially in view of the fact that you have a much-better-than-average comprehension of the state as a whole, having served for two terms in the North Carolina General Assembly as senator from your district."

"That is logical, Davis. But you know, some of my closest and most trusted friends are in the East, and whatever misconceptions some of them may have had about 'the backward West' have been revised or will be in time. When you consider the calibre of the men who represent the West in the North Carolina Assembly, this is bound to come about. Representation by the land-privileged presupposes that a superior person will hold the reins, but that does not always follow, and I am more and more convinced that that is not the democratic way. As things are now, no man can sit in the senate unless he owns three hundred acres of land in fee, and no man is qualified to vote for a member of the senate in the county of his residence unless he possesses a freehold of fifty acres. Of course the provisions are less restrictive in the matter of representation in the House of Commons.

"But look, my patient listener, methinks I see gray curls of smoke rising in yonder valley. Could it be that we are about to find meat for the eater, mayhap a loaf of bread, a jug of wine?"

Davis shaded his eyes, peering in the distance. "Well, I must say I much prefer a brew of good, strong coffee, and if that is an ordinary, as I think it is, my wish will be *their* command! At least we can find out where we are—where we rightly should be at this juncture. Do you know where we are, Carson?"

"No, I am as lost as the ten tribes of Israel. I have been sojourning with the Philistines—in the beguiling land of politics—and I have completely lost sight of the fact that I had promised to keep you on the right course. I have not kept track of the landmarks, which is of prime significance. My apologies, sir! It is downright uncivil of me to take my duties so lightly."

"Fiddlesticks! At any rate, here we are, and from all outward appearances this is but an ordinary ordinary and not an extraordinary at all."

"Take heart, my friend. These fields abound in ripening grain, there are sheep and cattle in yonder pastures, and if I mistake not there is our host coming to bid us welcome. I'll wager we will dine and sup right heartily."

They did indeed! The innkeeper, helpful in other ways than supplying bed and board, told them that they were not far—perhaps three miles—from Salem, Virginia, not North Carolina, he was quick to point out. "But if you would like to take a shortcut to the Wachovia Settlement, I can map a route for you to go directly south, and possibly reach the Moravian Settlement of Salem by day after tomorrow, depending on the time of your departure."

"Are you sure you can direct us safely with the shortcut?"

"I have made many trips to Old Salem to buy supplies. Besides, my daughter got her education there at the boarding school," and he continued, "the Wachovia Settlement is now almost seventy-five years old, and the church and schools were first in the minds and hearts of these Morvians. A bishop named one of the little settlements 'Salem.' It means 'peace,' and if everyone lived and treated their neighbors like these settlers do, we'd have peace."

"I take it that you settled nearby because you also wanted peace; or perhaps it is because you believe in education, else you would not have sent your daughter to school there," suggested Carson.

"That's about it. We are not Moravians, but we came from Bethlehem, Pennsylvania, same as they did. My wife's folks were from this part of Virginia, and I sold some good land up there—enough to build this little inn. It is not an ordinary in the strict sense of the word, since those of that distinction are supervised and regulated by the government. This is my own establishment, and I am responsible to no outside agency in its management. I thought this way I could keep in touch with the Brethren. You see, although I was not a member of the sect, I could see the advantages of living as they lived. They are industrious, they live their religion, they believe in education and they are skilled craftsmen—at least many of them are. They are not frugal, but they are not wasteful, either; they have fine herb gardens and are famed for their medicinal herbs. They have some peculiar customs that set them apart from others, but they have prospered in a way the outsiders have not."

Davis wanted to know what they would find in the way of craft shops and buildings in the little settlements.

"Well, first of all you will see brick and log houses, well and sturdily built, with nails of their own making. You will see brick walls and walkways of brick, made and moulded from their own soil. You will see brass and iron made into all manner of useful articles by the skill of their craftsmen.

"They make their own guns, their powder, their cooking pots, their candles, their flax hackles, ash hoppers—their tools of every description, and they sing while they work, for they love music. They sing because they are happy, I guess, and they are happy because they are free—free to live as they want to live, and best of all, free to worship God according to the desire of their hearts."

"How large is the largest settlement—how many buildings would you say there are in it?"

"Besides the Tavern, well, let me think. First there is the Home Moravian Church—one of the newer buildings—all the others were built before 1800. Then there's the Sisters' House and the Brothers' House—the girls' boarding school that is now Salem Academy, besides the homes of the settlers."

Carson observed that the Moravians are an asset to any state —like the Quakers. "They serve as balance wheels in our society; they are peace-loving, strong in mind and character.

"I have heard that they are unbending—some would say stubborn in their religious principles and convictions, somewhat like the Quakers."

"Yes," said Davis. "I have heard that Fox, the founder of

Quakerism, was in the habit of attending public worship at the Established Church. When the preacher uttered sentiments of which he disapproved, he would solemnly put on his broad-brimmed hat and leave it on until a strain of doctrine to which he could subscribe was pronounced; then he would take his hat off again. If he had sat long with his hat on, and the unwelcome pronouncements continued, he would rise slowly and silently walk out. Thus it appears that it was for the purpose of habitual protest that Quakers first learned to sit in places of worship with their hats on."

"Davis, that's a good story. In any event, it is to be devoutly hoped that North Carolina and the South will continue to be peopled by such stable and dependable citizens."

Most of this conversation took place at the breakfast table, where the host had joined the two travelers. Shortly after, Carson and Davis set out on the short route described and put in writing, with a crude map drawn by their host. Carson promised to be alert and observe the landmarks, but not at the expense of dispensing with conversation. Indeed they picked up where they had left off when they spotted the inn the evening before.

"Carson, I believe we were talking about North Carolina's handicaps—its unbalanced representation and economy, and the unsavory reputation it has acquired as a 'sleeping giant.' Rip Van Winkle needs to be aroused from his lethargy. How would you go about it?"

"Our transportation system is one of our greatest weaknesses—no navigable rivers in the West, and few in the East. We in the West are several hundred miles to a port. Furthermore we have not improved our roads. They are little better than they were thirty years ago. But Davis, I think our Western section has a rallying point for expansion."

"I hope whatever it is will benefit northern South Carolina— say around the Pendleton area, for example," suggested Davis.

"You know that gold mining on a small scale has been carried on for a number of years. Only last year the first official report of gold mining as a favorable industry was made. And, answering your suggestion, the ones now being worked are in the Southern part of our state, near your South Carolina border.

61

"The prospecting area covers about one thousand square miles, and although my county, Burke, may not be in the profitable area, Rutherford County is. My brother's place, Green River Plantation in that county, has gold on it, though he was not aware of it when he bought the place more than twenty years ago."

"Which one of your 'mixed-up' brothers is he?"

"He is Joseph McDowell—Carson, that is, and he is my older half-brother. He left home in 1800 when I was about two years old. He took a manservant and enough coin of the realm to buy his land and begin his establishment.

"Riding horseback over the hills and valleys he came at length to a river—swift and cold from its turbulent passage through gorges and boulders that obstructed its path, and thence into the cool coves that laced the borders. Its meadows were so rich and green that the redmen called it Ezeeka, meaning green or verdant.

"These lush, green valleys must have spoken to his Irish heart, for here it was that he marked off his boundaries, and 'planted his vine and fig tree.' When he had finished his small cabin of logs, he crossed the Great Smokies into Tennessee where an Irish kinsman lived."

"Don't tell me he married his cousin, like all the others you have told me about."

"He did just that. The lovely Rebecca that he married was one of the daughters of his first cousin—one of the cousins who came over from Ireland with his parents at the same time that Father came. They were Wilsons, and they stayed in North Carolina, then went to Tennessee soon after the territory was opened up for settlers."

"When did he discover gold on the place?"

"It was soon after they returned from their picturesque honeymoon that some of the menservants discovered a rich vein running into a mountain cove."

"A pot of gold at the end of the raindow, eh Carson?"

"Well, in a manner of speaking. Joe didn't go in for mining on a commercial scale then. When there was need for more money, some of the menservants, or 'hands' as they were called, would dig some more of the precious metal."

"What happened to the log cabin?"

"Oh it's still there, but some distance away they built a spacious home—just about sixteen years ago, it was. They gradually added to their family and their entourage, and their plantation has become quite a showplace."

"You know, Carson, Pendleton is not more than a Sabbath day's journey due south of Green River. I hope I can see it some day, and meet these members of your family."

"They would welcome you with open arms, Davis. I know because I lived there two years—from 1818 to 1820—when my brother was tutoring me in both practical and classical education. I also read law under his direction and tutelage. But Davis, this conversation has got out of hand. I intended to pursue the matter of a new enterprize for North Carolina, and I am far afield."

"It has been a pleasant side trip, my friend, and I haven't had enough, but I have a question that may bring us back to our starting point. Do you know personally of any other mines that are in production on a paying basis?"

"Oh yes, the first gold found in North Carolina was at Reid's mine about a hundred miles from Green River. A lucky strike was made there. It was found in masses—one glob of which weighed around twenty-five pounds. It was valued at eight thousand dollars, so Joe told me. It has produced steadily, I understand. Furthermore, I believe there is more to be found in Rutherford County. I'm sure there's more on Joe's property. Some of the men in that area are talking of prospecting on a large scale."

"It might have been more profitable for you, Carson, had you stayed to prospect for gold rather than to gamble your life in the political arena."

"That may very well be, my friend, but I am launched now for better or for worse. I hope I have set my feet on the right path. It's too early in the game to tell. But I am doing more talking than looking. Have we passed any landmarks lately? Let's find ourselves on this elegant map our friend gave us."

The horses were unhitched and allowed to graze and slake their thirst while the two young men studied the map.

"Don't tell me we have already crossed into North Carolina! I fully intended to walk across that invisible line so that I could tell the children back home that I walked from Virginia to North Carolina. But I believe we are once more on hallowed soil, Davis."

By nightfall they were enjoying the comforts of home in the tavern in Salem. It more than sustained its reputation for hospitality and for the scrupulous care of man and beast.

They took time to visit a number of craft shops, and would have been happy to prolong their stay for a time, but their journey had taken longer than they expected, and there would be little time for them to crowd into the remaining weeks of summer all of the duties and pleasures of their respective obligations.

When they inquired of the most direct route to Morganton they were advised by the innkeeper that they could proceed over tolerable roads direct to Morganton without going by Salisbury. Carson had expected to make only a courtesy call on his friend, Charles Fisher, and he could postpone that until later in the summer. As a politician it was incumbent on him to keep the lines of communication open between himself and the influential men in Western North Carolina, but there was more to this obligation. Carson and Fisher were close personal friends, and close personal friends should be garnered and cherished in a special sort of way—at least that was Carson's philosophy, and his many devoted friends bespoke the wisdom of that course.

There was another drawback in changing their route to bypass Salisbury. Davis had welcomed an opportunity to meet Fisher, who had been a staunch supporter of his kinsman, Calhoun, in the last election. He commented on this disappointment while agreeing fully that they must conserve the short time left for their individual purposes.

"Fisher is one of our ablest champions for recognition of the rights of the West," said Carson. "He abhors the domination of the East that has been able to perpetuate its stranglehold on the politics and the economy of the state. He has asserted often and with considerable foresight that North Carolina must have the benefits that will naturally accrue from a strong federal program of internal improvements. He supported Calhoun because he knew that Calhoun favored these improvements."

"Yes, I have heard this and much more about the election of 1824 from my kinsman. But that is all water over the dam, now that he came off second-best. Jackson's majority of the popular vote didn't have a chance with Henry Clay in the driver's seat."

"Do you know, Davis, that during the campaign there were more than one hundred mass meetings in North Carolina where the political ardor of the few generated the political frenzy of the many? It is a fact, and I will be the first to admit that I profited by those held in my district, even though the spotlight was on the Presidential candidate."

"I wish I could have been one of those whoopers-up at some of those mass meetings. We might have secured Calhoun's Presidential prospects, but I keep forgetting—you were a Jackson man, of course."

"Well, you know what I wish? I wish that I had been in the House of Representatives when the election took place—the only time in history when that constitutional sanction had to be employed. It must have been exciting, setting a precedent, as it did, and engendering more heat than light."

"I *was* there, my friend—out of deference to Mr. Calhoun's prospects—and I almost missed the electrifying moment. The galleries of the House had been crowded for several days in anxious expectation. The rules for conducting the election had been agreed on. One of the regulations set down was that the galleries were to be opened subject to the discretion of the Speaker, on whom devolved the responsibility of clearing the halls in case of any disturbance. Do you know who had that responsibility, Carson? Why Henry Clay, of course, and he had wrought wonders in preparation for this event, as subsequent events attested. As I was saying, people had been crowding into the City by every possible means of transportation, and there was literally no room at the inns. People were sleeping in hallways, on benches—anywhere they could stretch out.

"On the opening day of this unusual and significant convocation, General LaFayette was an honored spectator and advisor, along with the venerable judges of the Supreme Court, several ex-members of Congress, and a score of other dignitaries."

"I am sure the beloved General's presence heightened the

excitement of the already excited onlookers and participants," said Carson.

"Yes, but the amenities were observed. You see, the crowded galleries were separated so completely from the body of the House and such perfect silence prevailed that the first idea that a choice had been made was communicated by the report of the tellers. Contrary to all expectations, the election was secured on the first ballot, with the announcement that Mr. Adams had received a majority of the ballots of the electors. The effect was instantaneous. Without waiting for the tellers to conclude their report, the galleries, contrary to orders, responded by clapping their hands. A few audible hisses were heard, as if in reply to the plaudits, but order was restored and the report finished. All shades of emotion were visible on the countenances of the crowd as they left the building—dejection, elation, inexpressible joy and profound sorrow."

"Did you see General Jackson?"

"Only at a distance. He was surrounded by his dejected cohorts, who I am told were vehement in their charges that the Hero of New Orleans was the victim of corrupt bargaining. They then and there agreed to begin campaign plans for 1828."

"It had been a campaign that was likely to leave many scars, Davis, and if he is vulnerable to the sniping of his new kind of enemy, Jackson may not recover from his political wounds. He was attacked for his crude personality, for his lack of education, for anything legitimate or illegitimate that his enemies could scrape together—but he was my man, you know, Davis, and I am betting on him if he runs in 1828. Now tell me about the inauguration. Of course you were there to lend support to Mr. Calhoun."

"Yes, and I had a favored seat, thanks to this nebulous relationship. Almost before daybreak hordes swept down on the City, and the avenues presented a lively and animated scene. Groups of people hastening to the great 'theater of expectation' were to be seen in all directions. Carriages were rolling to and fro, and at intervals the sound of drum and trumpet at a distance gave notice that the military were in motion and repairing to their different parade grounds. The crowd at the door of the Capitol began to accumulate about nine o'clock, and although the ladies were allowed the privileges of their sex in being admitted to seats reserved for them in the lobby of the House of Representatives, they had to reach these seats at no small inconvenience to them and their finery, and the gentlemen who led and guided them in most instances had literally to fight their way to the doors.

"President Adams received the plaudits of the crowds, of course, and among the first to grasp his hand in congratulation was General Jackson. You see he had not received mortal wounds, after all.

"You will be interested in this, too, Carson. Mr. Calhoun was given a glowing tribute as he left the office of the Secretary of War, where he had 'held forth' since his appointment by the previous administration. 'No administration has been so successful,' his mentor said. 'He found the office in confusion, he leaves it in order, attesting his superior organizational ability.' That was of course gratifying to his relatives and his South Carolina friends who were present."

"I wish I might have been present, my friend, to rejoice with you. Did you stay to help him set up his new office?"

"No, I had legal matters pending, and it was impossible. Oh! there's another incident I believe you will find interesting—an incident witnessed by several gentlemen who were watching the proceedings from the top of the Capitol during inauguration ceremonies. No less than four large eagles were seen poising themselves directly over the Capitol for about ten minutes, when one of them, apparently larger than the rest, began to descend, and after making a number of circles around the center of the dome, rose in graceful spirals, and they all wheeled off to the West. There were some who advanced the theory that the large bird was the parent eagle that made her appearance in almost the same place when the last Chief Magistrate was inducted into office—again sent by our Guardian Spirit with her brood from her mountain eyrie to augur continued prosperity to our happy country."

"That is a most fantastic story, Davis, and I want to congratulate you on your ability as a teller of tales. It is a rare gift. Enlarge upon it—perfect it, and it will stand you in good stead in many future instances. And I shall hope to be among the listeners on many of these occasions."

"Thank you, friend. I have always felt that a good politician, or if you please a good statesman, should cultivate the art of storytelling, and for that reason I try to remember the worthwhile incidents so that if I never qualify as an orator, at least I can be an interesting and convincing speaker and conversationalist. Fortunately I have a sense of humor—an asset to any politician."

"Vice-president Calhoun had better look to his laurels, else you will overtake and pass him on his road to Olympus.

"But listen, while you were talking I noted many familiar landmarks. We must be nearing our last overnight stop. Let's get out and stretch our legs. I have thought many times that this has been infinitely more comfortable than riding horseback. The time has seemed short and I've concluded never to make the trip to Washington City alone."

"The sentiment is mutually shared, sir. Now—do we have time to take a catnap? How far are we from Quaker Meadows?"

"I would say about ten miles, and if we could be refreshed when we arrive it would please me."

Davis looked at his watch, and answered by removing his coat, rolling it carefully to make a pillow and dropping to the ground. Carson removed his coat, but did not use it for a pillow. He had always been fastidious about his appearance, and he especially wanted to make a favorable impression on his relatives. He put his head on his arm and both were soon in deep sleep.

Meantime the horses were grazing to the extent their tether would allow, and the first thing Carson noticed on awakening was that Missy was again limping. He had not checked on her very carefully as they proceeded, most of the time being occupied with interesting subjects of conversation. He patted her on the flank, ran his fingers through her mane, and stooping, picked up her right foreleg. Calling Davis to inspect the wound, they agreed that they would have to make it easier for her the rest of the journey.

THREE

Meanwhile at Quaker Meadows there was evidence of unusual activity. Having been apprised by express that they could expect the travelers on the afternoon or evening of the 18th, the Clan McDowell had gathered—at least a goodly number of them—and they were impatiently awaiting the sound of hoofs on the gravel road. The children, tantalized by the delicious aroma wafted from the kitchen quarters, were most impatient of all.

"Please, Aunt Annie, let me saddle Lilliputian and go to meet them," teased a young nephew.

"Let me, let me, let me," clamored the others.

"If they are not here within the hour, Hugh, you may go, but you must let Amzi go with you," and shaking her finger in emphasis, "the rest of you must stay right here."

"Mother, I'll help any way I can," volunteered Eliza, coming down the steps in a new outfit for the occasion.

Anne looked lovingly at her daughter and nodded her appreciation. "Has anyone told you, my dear, that Mr. Davis, like your Uncle Sam, is unattached?"

"Oh Mother! Don't you dare!" was the rejoinder. "Do you want to make me self-conscious?"

Anne smiled, and turning to the children admonished, "Get your playthings now, and here, Jo-ella, put on your clean turban and white apron and keep these small ones from tearing up the place, p-l-e-a-s-e! No you can't go with Hughie! He's a big boy and knows the road. You'd get tired before you got to the covered bridge," and turning to her daughter, "I know how tired they get, Eliza—tired and cross—and I want them to be on their best behavior for your Uncle Sam and his friend."

And so saying pretty Anne McDowell, the mistress of Quaker Meadows, picked up her ruffled skirts and went into the house to put the finishing touches on the decorations.

"Here, Lucinda, if you have finished putting down the pallets for the children, you may start laying the tables."

"Foh how many, Miss Annie?"

Anne started counting on her fingers. "Set twelve places at the long table and ten at the children's table. Master Hugh will sit with the grown-ups, and of course Miss Eliza—and Miss Margaret, too," she added as Margaret joined them.

Anne walked to the window and looked out. "Why, oh why don't the Green River folks come?"

"Oh Mother, don't fret yourself," and Margaret put her arm around her mother and kissed her affectionately. A pretty picture they made, and an exclamation to that effect came from Charles McDowell, Jr. when he saw his wife and two lovely daughters.

"My lady, I think a caravan approaches. Would it be the entire Green River population or just their usual menage?"

They flocked outside to greet their guests, the family of Joseph McDowell Carson. In the interest of sanity, the children with their colored mammies occupied the first two carriages, while Joseph, Rebecca and Catharine, driven by the now aged Jubal, brought up the rear.

The young visitors joined their cousins under the huge oak near the house, and were chattering in what seemed to be unknown tongues as they renewed their kinship, while their elders, almost as excited, sipped cherry shrub on the wide piazza.

Hardly had they settled themselves when shouts from the yard proclaimed: "They're here, they're here," and Hugh, whose pony had outdistanced the others, galloped into the yard. It was several minutes before the others came into sight, followed by Amzi leading Missy, who already had become his special charge.

And then pandemonium! Such noisy commotion ensued that the geese and other barnyard fowl joined in the noisy spontaneous welcome, and it was as difficult to keep from trampling them underfoot as it was to keep the children in tow, their usual restraints having been overlooked in the general rejoicing. Surely there was not as much confusion when the redcoats swarmed all over the place in an earlier period, and in this demonstration of uninhibited family devotion Davis, for the first time, understood Carson's deep feeling for his uncles and his cousins and his aunts, to say nothing of his nieces and his

70

nephews—all of whom he seemed able to encompass in the wide-open arms of his affection.

It was still quite light when they sat down to the evening meal. The host, on whose right Davis was seated, rose and, lifting his wine glass, proposed a toast to the guests of honor.

"We greet our guests, reminding them with Milton's permission, it was 'Bacchus that first from purple grapes crushed the sweet poison of misused wine; whoever tasted lost his upright shape, and downward fell into a groveling swine.' "

"Charles, how could you! What will Mr. Davis think?" But in spite of herself Anne joined with the others in the laughter that followed.

Sustained conversation was impossible, but when the table was cleared for dessert, Davis observed to the host, "On our way from the Springs, Sam and I stopped overnight at Old Salem, where we were told that the same Bishop Spangenburg, who had much to do with the founding of the Moravian settlement of Wachovia, came first to this fertile valley—and proclaimed it the richest he had seen in North Carolina. I understand that he was responsible for the name 'Quaker Meadows.' "

"That is the legend, Mr. Davis. At any rate the name preceded us. Regardless of its origin, the name has been given historical significance because of the dramatic incidents enacted here during the harrowing days of the War for Independence. That huge tree you see outside, for instance. As long as it stands it will be a landmark of peculiar significance in this area. Yes," Charles continued, "we hope it will be here to shelter the children of our great-grandchildren, and their children, and others yet to follow, but more importantly, that they will never forget it also sheltered the group of patriots and soldiers as they planned the campaign strategy for the Battle of Kings Mountain—the battle that was the turning point in the War for Independence. It is well named—the Council Oak."

"This would seem an appropriate time for me to soak up enough of the firsthand facts of this strategic battle to pass on to my own descendents, if any, a heritage of reality and not of tradition. They can add their own accounts of the glorious victories achieved in South Carolina if they choose," Davis said.

"There are no glorious military victories, Mr. Davis. Does the number of slain make slaughter glorious?" inquired Sam's brother.

"Don't let Joseph Carson's quips discomfit you, Mr. Davis. He is as much a patriot as the rest of us, and I, Charles McDowell, intend to keep alive the stories of the bravery and heroism associated with this most unusual conflict. So much of it centers right here on this spot, Quaker Meadows—the home of my father, Charles and my uncle, Joseph McDowell—patriots and commanding officers of distinction."

"Let me say right here, Charles, even though I was named for one of an earlier generation, I am honored to bear the name 'Joseph McDowell.' I say this humbly and without equivocation," said the senior Carson.

"Your explanation and implied apology are accepted, Joe." And Charles rose, leading the way from the dining room.

So that their smoking might not offend the ladies, the men, except Sam, moved their chairs under the towering oak that dominated the landscape.

"This, I take it, is the Council Oak," commented Davis, "and this tree, the valiant over-the-mountain men who clustered 'round it, the courageous and farsighted officers who drafted their campaign strategy under it, spectacular military achievement and the beginning of the end of the War for Independence—these are synonymous, are they not?"

"They are indeed!" assented Charles McDowell Jr., "and though I had no part in it, being of a very tender age, this whole place speaks so eloquently of patriotism, of courage and of achievement that I am indeed fortunate to have had it bequeathed to me. I can never forget that it was a grant in trust, and that my obligation is to pass untarnished the peerless heritage that is the McDowells', so that one hundred years—even one hundred and fifty years hence—these significant events will have become a part of the heritage of everyone who bears this noble name."

"Do you know what the year will be one hundred and fifty years from now, Uncle Charles?" asked Hugh. "It will be 1976—two hundred years from the date of the Declaration of Independence and of the beginning of the War to secure our freedom."

Hugh paused as if trying to comprehend the span of years. "That's a long, long time. I spec' nobody will be thinking about Quaker Meadows then."

"Which leads me to remind you, Hugh, and all of the next generation, that this heritage is placed in your hands to keep alive, and pass to each succeeding generation the love of freedom and liberty so dearly bought, not by your ancestors alone, but by all valiant American patriots."

"Then, if I am to pass it on, I need to know more about it. Oh! I'd like that, Uncle Charles. I can just see them now—all dressed up in their fine soldier suits—those brave over-the-mountain men as you call them. What color were their uniforms?"

"Wait a minute, son, the dress of the soldiers who secured this important victory is of least consideration. What you should know and be able to relate to posterity is not just the spectacular events of that glorious day—that glorious hour—but all of the interlocking events that preceded it—the individual heroes, many of them spies who risked quick reprisal and death in the event of capture. These—many of them—were country folk inexperienced in war, unrehearsed in their roles as pretenders, who mingled with the enemy, fearful of being betrayed by some of their neighbors on the other side—neighbors who might recognize them and impede their mission.

"No, son, this engagement was not a full-dress affair, but it was unique in the annals of war. These brave men were not commanded to do their part—they were not ordered by any one authority to participate in the bloody struggle. The ties of discipline were slight—the commanders elected their own chief without regard to rank or seniority. In fact, the one who was entitled to lead the entire command was my father, who was given no share in this engagement, but was sent off bearing a mission to General Gates. Their method of completing the formation of the company was unique. Four days before the actual conflict at Kings Mountain, Colonel Cleveland commanded the troops to form a circle that he might impart to them important news. Colonel Sevier assisted in forming the circle, and very shortly they were joined by Campbell, Shelby, Colonel Winston and Uncle Joe McDowell. Colonel Cleveland

73

addressed them. 'Now, my brave fellows, I have come to tell you the news. The enemy is at hand, and we must up and at 'em. Now is the time for each of you to do his country a priceless service, such as will lead your children to exult in the fact that their fathers were the conquerors of Ferguson. When the pinch comes, I will be with you, but if any of you shrink from sharing in the battle and the glory, you can now have the opportunity of backing out and leaving, and you shall have a few minutes to consider the matter.'

"Colonel Cleveland paused, and almost immediately Uncle Joe, with a winning smile on his countenance, asked, 'What kind of story will you who back out have to relate when you get home, leaving your braver comrades to fight the battle and gain the victory?'

"Shelby then stepped up, saying, 'You have all been advised of the offer; you who desire to accept it will, when the word is given, march three paces to the rear.'

"Not a man accepted the unpatriotic privilege, and a murmur of applause rose from the men, who rejoiced that there were no slinks or cowards among them. Colonel Shelby stepped into the circle, giving them the high praise they were due, and continued with their instructions, climaxing his persuasive message with these words: 'Your officers will not shrink from danger; they will be constantly with you, and the moment the enemy give way, be on the alert and strictly obey orders.' "

"It will be great fun to tell about it, Uncle Charles. I know the younger ones will learn fast if we let them 'play soldier.' Have you told me all I need to know?"

"Far from it, Hugh, my boy. I have spared you the details of the horror of that war—of the atrocities, of the blood and gore, of young men advancing gallantly with a rallying song on their lips only to be thrust through with well-placed bayonets."

"Please spare us, Charles," pleaded Rebecca. "Hugh is too young to feel the bitter anguish of an antagonist, who, jerking the rifle from the hands of a dead soldier, found on turning him over that it was his own brother. Can't we spare these young ones the terrible realities of war until they reach an age when they can better accept man's inhumanity to man? There is a brighter side we can remember."

"What brighter side, my dear?"

74

"I'm thinking of the evenings around the campfires when a certain harmony was achieved in song. I have been told that before the actual battle, there were instances when the opposing sides were bivouacked so close that if they were not in sight, they were in sound of each other. That happened at least once here at Quaker Meadows."

"Yes," replied Charles, "Uncle Joe demonstrated a rare kind of harmony when the enemy encamped here after their defeat. He rode among them, and noting that they were drenched in the cold, November rain, he invited them to take the rails from his fences and build fires. I would say that almost amounted to 'heaping coals of fire on their heads.'

"But speaking of harmony in song, Rebecca, and the brighter side of the picture of war, Uncle Joe often told about the campfires at night and the songs that broke the stillness of the autumn air—songs sung back and forth from loyalist to patriot and from patriot to loyalist. He remembered having heard the story of one John MacRae, Gaelic poet, who in due time after landing on our shores found himself with Pat Ferguson, and the mission he enjoyed most was a mission of song—a song of enticement and pleading directed to the rebel Scotsmen, of whom there were many in the patriot encampment; a song sung in Gaelic that pointed to the dire consequences that would befall them if they did not all surrender. 'There'll be hangings and wounds and wholesale confiscation, for no argument or law can save rebels alive.' "

Meantime, Sam and his half-sister had been bridging the span of months since they had seen each other.

"Anne, you are taking up where Mother left off in continuing the custom of family gatherings. She loved nothing better than to bring us all together for feasting and frivolity."

Anne's eyes were tear-filled. "Sam, we miss her so. Your father has been superb in helping us all to accept the loneliness of her absence. I'm afraid you will find Pleasant Gardens a far different place than when you left it. But that precious Binah—my own colored mammy—believes firmly 'dat de Good Lawd expecs her to hold the family together.' You remember she took over completely before Mother relinquished her fragile hold on household management."

"Then I suppose your father, had he known the circumstances, would have forgiven Mother for taking Binah into our home when their separation had made poor Binah sick unto death," suggested Sam.

"Oh, I'm sure of it. Father was a very humane person, and the provision in his will to allow Mother to keep Binah and the others until she married again was done more or less because of custom, and not in a spirit of vindictiveness. You must remember that your father and my father were not only brothers-in-law but very close friends.

"I'm glad we had the same mother. She was so proud of you—a State Senator at twenty-four years! I'm proud of you, too, my dear!"

Remembering her duties as hostess, Anne rose and with Sam's arm around her, they joined the lively group under the famous tree.

"Uncle Sam," Margaret called as he came near. "I hope you have kept a diary of all of the interesting things you have been doing in Washington City. How I would like to read it!"

"Nothing of sufficient import has happened to beguile me into such an undertaking, my dear Margaret. But you have given me a splendid idea." Then turning to his sister-in-law he said, "Rebecca, as much as I have always admired and respected you, you are now entitled to all of the superlatives in my vocabulary. Until I made the trip on horseback from Pleasant Gardens to Washington City, I did not know how to appreciate your remarkable feat. How you ever survived the arduous journey on horseback from East Tennessee through the Smokies to Green River is beyond my understanding. Though I traveled farther, your route was more primitive and difficult. It is nothing short of amazing! Pioneer women usually travel with some of the necessities and a few of the comforts of travel. All you had was the comfort of your husband's arms."

Rebecca smiled at her husband. "I found that to be entirely sufficient, Sam, though I doubt if I'd ever make that trip on horseback again. Women are not built for such endurance tests.

"And speaking of diaries, Margaret, I wish I had kept one, because I doubt if there are many—perhaps not any ladies who could boast of honeymooning in such fashion through the wild vastness of the formidable Smokies."

"Did you see any Indians, Aunt Rebecca?" It was Hugh who was eager to explore such a possibility.

"As a matter of fact we did, Hugh," answered Joseph Carson for his wife. "You know we were very near—actually sometimes in the Cherokee territory, and we came upon a band of hunters bent on replenishing their supply of venison."

"Please tell us about them," and Hugh moved closer so as not to miss a word.

"There were a dozen of them and only four of us. At first we expected they would give us trouble, but old Jubal, who drove us here today, and who went with me from Green River to Brentwood, Tennessee to claim my bride, had had some experience acting as an interpreter. He did not know the Cherokee language, but he did know the language of the Catawbas. While all Indian talk is not alike, there are certain similarities, and they understood enough to invite him to share their campfire and the meal they were preparing.

"It was not until by signs and symbols Jubal conveyed the idea that he was acting as a guide for a newly married man and his wife that they wiped the scowls from their faces and made the circle wide enough to include all of us in the celebration of a hastily contrived tribal rite—perhaps akin to their marriage rite. It was curious and impressive and we left giving thanks for Jubal and his incantations."

"Did you see any more Indians on your journey, Mrs. Carson?"

"No, but the Indians played an important part in the story I am going to tell you now, and since it is familiar to some of you, I shall address myself to Mr. Davis."

Sam dropped to the ground beside Catharine, and Davis hitched his chair nearer the storyteller.

"My mother, Ruth, was born into a family of Davidsons who were early settlers, coming to North Carolina from Ulster, Ireland, by way of Pennsylvania. It was about forty-five years ago when Grandfather Davidson crossed the Swannanoa with his wife and six-week-old daughter and her nurse. He built a cabin on Christian Creek near what was then an Indian Trace running through the Swannanoa Gap.

"It was the custom in those days for a settler to turn his

77

horse out to graze at night, a small bell tied around the neck of the animal so it could be easily located next day. One morning after the horse had been out all night, Grandfather went in search of it, following as he thought the sound of the bell up the mountainside. As he reached the crest he was attacked and killed by Indians who had lured him into their trap by using the horse's bell. Grandmother heard the shots, and knowing that Grandfather was not armed, understood what it meant. Taking baby Ruth, my mother, she and the Negro nurse escaped by different routes through the mountains to Davidson's Fort—a stockade sixteen miles away. Friends and relatives organized a searching party for the marauders, and they did apprehend and kill some of them, but most of them escaped. They found Grandfather's body and buried him at the foot of a tree where he was slain, and they cut his initials, S.L.D., on the tree for identification.

"It was only a little distance out of our way on that trip and my mother secured my husband's promise that he would take me to see his burial place. At once I had a new feeling for a grandfather I never saw and knew only in stories my mother told me."

"I would think that you would hate the Indians. Do you?" inquired Hugh.

"I fear them but I do not hate them. They have been shamefully treated in many instances. The truth is my grandfather had gone farther into their territory than the white man was supposed to go, and he actually built his cabin on Indian land. That was when the urge of many pioneers was to push farther and farther into unoccupied territory; and in many cases treaties were conveniently ignored."

"Aunt Rebecca, your story was so real. I have an eerie feeling that there are Indians lurking behind these trees waiting to ambush us. Really I do! I have cold chills all over."

"Nonsense, Margaret, but I believe other stories can wait for the morning. This night air may cause all of us to have chills if we stay longer. And we *have* heard too many terrifying stories tonight, my child."

"My lady, you have just forestalled the telling of a tale which I know will interest Mr. Davis, and any others who have not heard it—the story of how my father and Sam's father out-witted the gallant Patrick Ferguson just before the Battle of Kings Mountain."

"Oh please, I want to hear it," pleaded one of the younger ones.

"We'll get to that in the morning, so be on time for breakfast. Now get on with you, children, and get your night clothes on."

There was a great race to see who would reach the porch first, and then shepherded by Jo-ella and Lucinda, they scrambled off to bed, excited over the prospect of sleeping on the floor. In the parlor the older ones made themselves comfortable until a later bedtime. They did not want to miss any of the moments of being together. There was much to talk about, but the conversation was kept in light vein—no problems—no politics—no polemics.

"Sis Anne, you couldn't have planned a more perfect surprise than having so many of the Clan here to welcome us. And to have Catharine here is the greatest surprise of all," and putting his arm around Rebecca's sister, Sam kissed her ever so lightly on the forehead.

Davis, sitting on the other side of Catharine on the cut-velvet sofa, agreed enthusiastically. Turning to Joseph Carson he asked, "Do others who come into the family circle as strangers find it confusing to unravel the relationships of members of the Clan, as I do?"

It was Sam who answered. "Many of them do not try, my friend, and since I left you hopelessly confused when I tried to prepare you in advance for my uncles and my cousins and my aunts, to say nothing of my nieces and my nephews, perhaps it is just as well that you spare yourself the ordeal of solving this genealogical puzzle."

Joseph Carson agreed with his brother, and pointed out, "To add to the complexities of this Clan, there were all shades of loyalties at a time when loyalties were crucial, many times embarrassing and often tragic. For instance, my wife's Grandfather Wilson, who was my uncle and Sam's uncle by marriage, was a Tory, as were others around the area. All of the McDowells, so far as I know, were patriots and rebels—the fathers and the grandfathers, and Lieutenant Allaire, one of Ferguson's officers,

79

said that in this community, the young ladies were the most violent rebels of all."

"Now that you have admitted that you are a family of divided loyalties, I am very curious on this point. What was Sam's father, Mrs. Carson?"

"I am glad you asked that question, Mr. Davis. Colonel Carson was a patriot in the guise of a Tory. Is that an accurate description, Joe?" she asked her husband.

"I would say that is putting the kernel in a nutshell," responded Joe, while all laughed at the unexpected witticism.

"Don't forget we promised the younger ones they would hear in the morning about the Carson-Ferguson incident. Shouldn't we save the telling of that tale, especially since I know instances where a number of women outwitted Ferguson, and I'll tell you the ones I know best," Rebecca suggested.

"It was while the British were camped at the Davidson home, two miles west of Colonel Carson's, that one of the soldiers was tempted to kill a chicken and have a savory meal. Being discovered by Mrs. Davidson, she reported the theft to the Colonel. The British commander had the culprit punished and gave Mrs. Davidson a dollar to compensate for her loss."

"That must have been a rare sample of Patrick Ferguson's justice," remarked Charles, Jr. It was plain to see that the son of General Charles McDowell gave no quarter as far as the English officer was concerned. He knew firsthand of his father's long and courageous fight for American freedom, and remembered some of the heartbreaking episodes of Colonel McDowell's life immediately before and after the Battle of Kings Mountain.

Thinking to steer the conversation into a less emotional area, Anne said, "I remember Father telling us a story about an encounter that a Mrs. Lytle had with Colonel Ferguson when he and his men were engaged in foraging expeditions near Father's home and the Carson House."

Rebecca broke into the conversation at this point. "Ferguson and his men knew that a certain Thomas Wilson, a redheaded Irishman and loyal to the Crown, lived on Buck Creek near the home of his brother-in-law, Colonel Carson. He knew that Wilson could and would supply his army with corn and beef and other necessities, and he made it convenient to tarry in these parts where there seemed to be more friends than he had expected to encounter."

"Rebecca, why don't you tell Mr. Davis that the redheaded Irishman was your Grandfather Wilson?" Joe Carson suggested.

"I was coming to that. I was going to suggest that now he has been introduced to both my Grandfather Davidson—a patriot—and my Grandfather Wilson—a Tory. But I have very rudely interrupted Anne's story of the Captain's Lady. Let's hear it, Anne."

"It seems that Mrs. Lytle was young enough for adventure and vain enough to think she might distract the enemy. Hearing that Colonel Ferguson was in the neighborhood, she put on her best and newest gown and her handsome beaver hat. She took pains to look her best, and at length the Colonel, at the head of his squadron, rode up to the house inquiring for Captain Lytle.

"Mrs. Lytle came to the door in full costume, and dropping a polite curtsey, invited him to alight and come in. It must have been a shock to the Colonel to see so handsome a woman dressed in finery that might have come from the finest city emporium. Ferguson thanked her, but pointed out that his business required haste; he was coming to pay a visit, and now that the rebellion had been quelled, to offer a pardon to Captain Lytle and others who had taken up arms against the King.

" 'My husband is not at home,' Mrs. Lytle said.

" 'Madam, do you know where your husband is?'

" 'To be quite frank with you, Colonel, I do not. I only know that he is out with others whom you are pleased to call "rebels." '

" 'Well, Madam, I have discharged my duty. I was anxious to save Captain Lytle because I have learned that he is both brave and honorable. But if he persists in rebellion, his blood will be on his own head.'

"But Mrs. Lytle was not to be intimidated. She knew the war was not over and that the British officer was seeking information by trickery. Drawing herself up to her full and commanding height, she said, 'Colonel Ferguson, hear me, I don't know how this war will end. It is quite possible that my husband will fall in battle. All I know positively is that he will never prove a traitor to his country.'

81

"To which Colonel Ferguson replied, 'Mrs. Lytle, I admire you as the handsomest woman I have seen in North Carolina. I even halfway admire your zeal in a lost cause, but take my word for it—the rebellion has had its day. Give my regards to Captain Lytle,' and bowing he led his troops away.

"A straggler in the rear rode back, accosted Mrs. Lytle, took off his old battered hat and, replacing it with her precious beaver, he made her a sweeping bow as he said, 'Mrs. Lytle, I cannot leave so handsome a woman without something to remember her by.'

"As he rode off wearing the beaver at a jaunty angle, he heard her shout, 'You'll bite the dust for this, you villian!' "

The saga of Mrs. Lytle was enjoyed by all of the listeners, who were agreed that without these human interest stories, the bloody tales of war would be well nigh unbearable.

"Yes, the women—God bless them—performed nobly and often heroically those bitter days," said Charles, Jr. "My mother and my grandmother among them. All of us here, with the exception of Mr. Davis, know that my grandmother was born Margaret O'Neill in the Emerald Isle, and that Grandfather brought her to these shores equipped with a ready Irish wit, and a goodly supply of the sterner stuff of which true pioneers are made. She was at her best when faced with a ruthless antagonist. That was Margaret O'Neill McDowell, and wherever she is tonight, I salute her!

"You know, Mr. Davis, that the enemy in considerable numbers were encamped on these grounds on two separate occasions—just before the Battle of Kings Mountain and after defeat. The first time was when Father and Uncle Joe with their men, and Shelby with his band, had retired before Ferguson's pursuers and were camping in the Watauga settlements, where they waited to be joined by Colonel Campbell and Colonel Sevier before renewing their attacks on the redcoats. My widowed grandmother was hostess here at Quaker Meadows when the enemy paid their first visit. They were under command of Lieutenant Allaire, of whom we have just spoken. He and his subordinate officers made themselves comfortable in the house here, while the soldiers were scattered over the grounds wherever they could stretch a blanket. Without being reprimanded by their superiors for their conduct, they brazenly ransacked the place for spoils and coldly appropriated the best clothes of my father and Uncle Joe. They taunted Grandmother with tales of what they would do when they found her two rebel sons. Colonel Charles, my father, would be killed outright, but as for Uncle Joe, they would first compel him by way of humiliation to plead on his knees for his life, and then they would slay him without mercy."

"And what did Margaret O'Neill McDowell say to that?" inquired Davis.

"She talked back to them. Looking straight in their eyes in her most effective Irish style, she reminded them that in the whirligigs of life they might sooner or later have to do a little begging themselves."

"And they did didn't they, Uncle Charles?" queried Hugh.

"Indeed they did, son. In the short space of a month they were back as crestfallen prisoners of war. The shoe was on the other foot. Lasting only an hour and five minutes, with upward of eight hundred men locked in mortal combat, the Battle of Kings Mountain was over. It was one of those glorious military victories you were talking about, Joe Carson."

"Without any shadow of doubt, it was an early turning point in the War for Independence, as history now confirms. And from the standpoint of military strategy, it was one of the most unusual battles ever fought on our soil. I wish," continued Joe Carson, "that all Americans could have firmly implanted in their mind's eye the spectacle of this engagement; brother fighting against brother, neighbor against neighbor, according to their loyalties and their convictions. Then indeed would they remember how dearly bought was our independence and with what suffering and sacrifice was vouchsafed our freedom from the yoke of tyranny."

"As interesting as this subject is, there are two of us who need a few hours sleep before starting on our trip to Pleasant Gardens tomorrow," suggested Sam.

It had already been determined that the Green River Carsons would stay another day, and at the suggestion of Charles, Missy would be left in Amzi's care until she could safely travel.

"By the way, Charles, I am in need of some respectable

clothes. I think I'll stop over in Morganton long enough to have Silas McDowell take my measurements. I suppose he is still in the tailoring business?" questioned Sam.

"As a matter of fact we are without a tailor in these parts. Your kinsman has moved to Asheville. It seems that some years ago he bought some land west of Asheville, and that he has become as much enamored of plants and herbs as of the tailoring profession."

"I'll look him up and pay my respects the first time I am up that way. Perhaps I can persuade him to leave his herbarium long enough to outfit me. I'd like to talk with him again, for he is a man of many interests and attainments."

Meanwhile, in another part of the room Davis was exploring a different topic.

"Mr. Carson, your brother has told me in glowing terms about your Green River Plantation, and about your gold-mining interests there and in the area. Pendleton, my home, you know, is not so far away. Is it unthinkable that we might find it profitable to do some prospecting ourselves?"

"Very likely there has been a deal of digging done in northern South Carolina, and there will be more if there is ever a genuine gold rush, and if the natives succumb to gold fever. I have been talking with Father and brother Charles and with Charles McDowell in an effort to have them buy up some of the property that may become valuable. As it is now, much of the gold here is 'branch gold.' Vein mining is more profitable, but more expensive, of course. I was fortunate to have a rich vein on my property, but we do no commercial mining at Green River."

"Sam thinks that this new industry will go a long way to compensate the Western part of the state in its struggle for economic survival," Davis observed.

"Well, it has started a chain reaction in the Western counties. I hear that on Sunday afternoons after church service whole congregations, armed with pick and shovel, cradle and rocker, head for the nearest streams, and that their favorite hymn is 'When The Gold Is Found Out Yonder I'll Be There.' "

To speed them on their way, the travelers had requested an early breakfast, and had offered to serve themselves so as not to disturb the household.

"We will have no slipping away at daybreak, Sam. I'll see that the breakfast is served promptly at seven. We must have one more happy meal together. The children would be hard to live with if they couldn't help us speed the parting guests."

And a happy meal it was, with much planning about a gathering at Pleasant Gardens in September, and promises to tell some of the untold tales that would delight the children. But they would not forego the anticipated story of the outwitting of Ferguson, and Joe Carson was elected to tell the tale of his father's brash encounter with the British commander.

"It was your father, Charles, who really instigated this maneuver, and it was while Ferguson was still in the community whose inhabitants seemed to be more friendly to England than he had dared expect. The Pleasant Gardens area was a lush, fertile valley. It still is, we know. When it appeared that Ferguson was determined to feed his army by appropriating and slaughtering the cattle of all of the rebels in the territory, Colonel McDowell called a council of the leading men. He was careful to exclude the known Tories, and the meeting was held in secrecy. Explaining the necessity to take drastic steps to save the cattle from Ferguson's grasp, Colonel McDowell suggested that some of those present agree to take protection under the King by registering their intention with Cornwallis, then quartered in Charlotte.

"Hunting John McDowell, Anne's grandfather, and incidentally, my grandfather too, was asked if he would agree to the ruse, but he refused. He felt that the end did not justify the means. 'I'll drive my cattle into the mountain coves, and the British be damned!' he said.

"Seeing that there were no volunteers, a selection was made of two or three who were convinced that saving their herds in such a manner was no more reprehensible than the wholesale slaughter of their herds by Ferguson. They agreed to become Tories temporarily in a good cause. Colonel Carson, my father, was one, and as I remember, William and Ben Davidson were the others."

"Was Colonel Carson a redcoat or a turncoat and was that disgraceful?" asked Hugh.

"He was neither. There was no disposition on the part of anyone to regard this act as anything but expedient. You must

85

remember, Hugh, that Colonel Carson was only twenty-four years old, and had been in the United States only six years when he was asked to perform this patriotic service. To this day I have never heard anyone cast suspicion on his motives or condemn his action, have you Sam?"

"No, I have never heard anyone reflect on his patriotism, but this doesn't mean that he has escaped censure. We would be the last to hear. It doesn't disturb me because I know his allegiance to his adopted country is certain."

"Was that the way he outwitted Ferguson?" asked Margaret.

"The incident we had in mind happened later. The word was put out that Colonel Carson was loyal to the Crown, and Ferguson sought him out; in fact, he spent a night in our home. Actually he and his army were billeted on the farm of a Tory neighbor when he persuaded Father to go on a cattle-hunting foray with him. At this point the wary Ferguson had begun to suspect that Colonel Carson and his friend were deceiving him and saving more cattle than properly belonged to them, and resolving not to be foiled by such backwoods diplomacy, he fitted out a party from camp to go in search of beeves being smuggled out of harm's way.

"Father accompanied the foraging expedition, and soon a large herd was found grazing near the farm of one David Greenlee, but Father was closemouthed about the ownership until the Tory party had slaughtered over a hundred head of fine cattle. Then he quietly observed that he expected they were the property of Joseph Brown and perhaps of Dement and Johnston, who even then were soldiers in Fergusons's camp. When Ferguson realized that he had been outwitted by a backwoods diplomat, his anger and chagrin were hard to conceal."

"We have been speaking in such glowing terms of these kinsmen of ours who were heroes in the War for Independence. Since in most cases they are of another generation, we hope, Mr. Davis, you will forgive our show of pride in their accomplishments," said Charles.

"This has been a revelation to me—an opportunity to hear firsthand a most exciting slice of history—some of which I knew, of course, but which is now more personal and meaningful. Someday the history of these deeds will be published,

86

and in the publication there may be errors and omissions that will be detrimental to the true picture."

"There *has* been one omission in these reminiscences, Mr. Davis."

"I think I know what you mean, Charles," Anne suggested. "It is about my father, Joseph McDowell of Pleasant Gardens, a cousin of my husband, and of the two McDowells who have figured in the story. I am glad you thought of it, Charles, for I am a little prejudiced in behalf of this other member of the Clan."

"Indeed the picture would not be complete otherwise," volunteered Sam, "and it seems to me an opportune time to give each of the Joseph McDowells his due. Already there is discussion and argument among the knowledgeable people of Burke County as to which Joseph McDowell was the real hero of Kings Mountain."

"I would rather not belabor that point, my dear brother. There were many heroes, and as someone has just said, the heroes were not all officers—far from it. I would be inclined to memorialize every patriot soldier who took part in this memorable affair. In my own mind I have not drawn distinctions of bravery. Besides, we do not have time for more revelations of history—these young ones are getting restless and our two travelers should be on their way."

"Your modesty is becoming, Anne. Nevertheless I will make it brief, and I especially want the young ones—even the very young ones—to hear these stories of bravery and patriotism firsthand. It is far more impressive than reading about it when they are older.

"But to get on with the story. Anne's father, Joseph McDowell of Pleasant Gardens, was little more than a boy when the Revolution broke out, but he went into service with the patriot army, and soon rose to the position of Captain in the Burke regiment commanded by his cousins—Charles, as Colonel, and Joseph, as Major. You have already heard of their distinguished service. Joseph McDowell of Pleasant Gardens, Anne's father, was with the patriot army in every skirmish or battle in which they were engaged, serving from the beginning to the close of the War for Independence. In the Rutherford

Campaign he killed an Indian in single combat. Educated as a physician, his distinction as a statesman was not less than that which he attained as a soldier.

"He served in the North Carolina House of Commons from 1787 to 1792. He was a member of the 1788 Convention at Hillsborough, and some of the present-day historians say that his able and intelligent speech against the adoption of the Federal Constitution had much to do with delaying ratification."

"On what grounds?" one of the younger ones inquired.

"On the grounds that the Federal Constitution did not guarantee the rights of the states; that it did not provide trial by jury, and there were other objections. You see, the people of North Carolina leaned strongly toward individualism and democratic principles, and their fear of a strong central government led them to reject the Federal Constitution at this convention by a vote of 185 to 84. They suggested a number of amendments, some of which were later incorporated into the Constitution as the first ten amendments."

"Did any other state object?" inquired Hugh.

"Yes, Rhode Island and North Carolina were the only states that failed to adopt the Constitution in the spring of 1789, but at the Fayetteville Convention in November of that year, Sam's father, Colonel John Carson, with others voted to ratify, but we came under 'the Federal roof' too late to vote for the first President of the United States."

"Necessity compels me to interrupt this instructive session," announced Sam. "We must be on our way, or we will not be able to reach home until dawn."

When dark overtook them, they were so near Pleasant Gardens that they concluded to drive on, even if the hour was late. Nighttime traveling in these parts was extremely rare, occasioned only by emergencies or perhaps by a noisy celebrant who had indulged himself too freely away from home, and who was happily returning to the hinterlands, depending entirely on his horse to see him home.

By midnight they were nearing their destination. Farms and houses were not so widely separated, and now and again a lighted window seemed to speak a welcome and to stir an emotion—half joy and half nostalgia—one of those un-accountable reflexes that travelers in the night feel at such times and cannot explain.

Carson spoke of this to his companion. "There's something about a lighted window at night that compels attention. You drive along in the darkness, and there it is—a beacon to lift one's spirits. I almost never associate this circumstance with ugliness or depravity. Always behind a lighted window is a happy little family, sharing their experiences and their joys—content with their lot in life."

"When you know damned well they may be staging a free-for-all, or that the man of the house is sprawled on the floor in a drunken stupor and the poor wife and mother, distraught with all of the complexities of *her* lot in life, is nursing sick children, keeping them quiet so as not to waken the brute on the floor."

"Old wet-blanket Davis! Why couldn't you let me have my dreams and the euphoria that goes with them?"

"Because I am realistic. You know, Carson, I feel that I have come to know you quite well these past few weeks, and the more I know you, the better I like you—except . . . "

"Except what?"

"Except that you are almost without exception prompted by your heart and not your head, and this can hurt you more than anyone."

Later, as they rounded a bend in the road, they could see silhouetted against the star-bright sky the towering peaks of the Blue Ridge Mountains, and as they approached a white home with columned porch in a valley framed by the mountains and hills of home, Carson said to Davis, "This is where Anne McDowell was born—the home of her father, Joseph, about whom you heard at breakfast this morning."

"Who is living in the home place now?"

"It was inherited by James, my half-brother. I am glad that it has not passed out of the family."

Less than a mile further, Carson exclaimed, "The journey is ended, my friend, and I shall forever be in your debt for your very great forbearance and your favors of many kinds. Pleasant Gardens welcomes you! It is my hope that you will stay several days with us and be refreshed when you reach Pendleton."

"We will not get much sleep tonight, so I won't take the road until day after tomorrow. Is that the house I see over on the left?"

"It is indeed, and I could gather it in my embrace. It's good to get home again. You have no idea how deeply and sincerely I mean that! Now, if we can manage to get to our rooms without waking the family, it will be a miracle. This way to the stables, Davis," and Carson took the reins to direct him.

Just then a candle light flickered in one of the cabins, and a hoary head appeared through the opening of a door.

"Who goes dar?" the old man called, peering into the darkness.

"Well, if it ain't my Sam boy! Becky, it's Mr. Sam come home! Lordy, iz I glad to see you. Done clean giv you out, you wuz so long comin'."

"Sh-h-h, let's not wake the whole kit and kaboodle. My friend, Mr. Davis, and I will put up the horses."

"Not so long ez I'm able to get about, you won't. Now jist you leave 'em to me an' you go and git some sleep. 'Pears to me it's nigh on to mornin'!"

"It is, and you need your rest, too, so don't ask me where Missy is. I'll tell you tomorrow."

"You mean our little Whirlwind, Mr. Sam?"

"Yes, Eben, I mean Whirlwind."

FOUR

They entered the house from the back porch through a wide hall that ran lengthwise of the house—open at both ends, without benefit of doors. The front hall opened onto a porch of ample width and length, above which was an identical porch, both supported by large square columns. To be sure that they did not intrude on any of the sleeping family, Sam led the way up one flight of stairs and then another to an unfinished third floor, where beds were always in readiness, dormitory style, to take care of the overflow when the Carsons gathered for special occasions. Dog-tired, they lost no time in seeking the rest they both so sorely needed. Although neither required it to lull them to sleep, the little rivulets of Buck Creek, flowing almost under their window, had a kind of hypnotic effect that attracted and sustained repose.

They were awakened near noon the following day by Eli, Sam's special charge, who brought coffee and a message from Binah that dinner would be served at one. Sam slipped down ahead of his guest so as to dispense with the noisy welcome he always received on returning home.

After he left, Davis looked about him, examining the wide boards used on the ceilings under the roof, and the wider ones used for flooring. He noticed especially the solid construction of the house—huge beams put together with wooden pegs, the floating beams under the roof denoting the type of construction of the period. He was interrupted in his examination of the unusual architectural features by the bell announcing dinner, and he joined the family in the downstairs hall. The venerable gentleman who met him at the foot of the stairs extended his hand in greeting. "Welcome, Mr. Davis, a very hearty welcome."

"And you, sir, are Sam's father. I do not know when I have anticipated meeting anyone as much."

"We are greatly indebted to you for rescuing Sam from the misfortune of Missy's accident, and for seeing him safely home." Turning, he introduced his daughter, Mathilda, his son,

Doctor John, and his youngest son, Logan. George, the only other brother still at home, was helping his brother Charles with the harvesting. "We will not wait for Samuel. He will have to jolly up everyone on the place before he comes in. Binah will keep his food hot. So you had to sleep under the eaves last night. I hope it was not oppressive for you."

"It was very comfortable, and lying in bed this morning I had an opportunity to note the sturdy construction of the house—the walnut timber, the hand-planing and finishing."

"It is solid as the Rock of Gibraltar, Mr. Davis. It can weather many storms—it already has demonstrated its soundness from roof to cellar."

"Father built a log cabin when he first came to this section around 1770. It, too, was well built, and is still standing," commented Logan.

Sam stuck his head in the door. "May I come in? You'll excuse me, Father. I had some catching up to do. Looks like everything is cantering right along. Don't see how you got along so well without me all these months. I'll bet Binah and Tillie missed me, now didn't you Tillie, girl?"

Of course Tillie had missed him—more this time than ever before. There had been the added hurt of her mother's absence, too.

"Yes, I did miss you, Sam, and if you had sent an express telling us the time of your arrival we would have given you and Mr. Davis a right royal reception."

"You know, Tillie, I wish you had been with Mr. Davis and me at the White Springs. You would have loved it! There was a Mrs. Reid and her two daughters who were spending a few weeks at the Old White, and I believe the girls were just about your age."

"That would have been wonderful—a truly wonderful treat for me. I need to know more young people who are not cousins."

"But they were cousins! How near we did not figure out exactly, but I believe they were great-nieces of Andrew Reid, Father. You remember, you have a copy of his patriotic declaration here somewhere. Maybe you can find it for Mr. Davis to read, since he has heard so much about it, and the letter from

Judge Samuel McDowell to Andrew Reid."

"Now there's a stalwart for you! Judge Samuel McDowell, a fearless man of iron nerve—a civil servant who was as selfless as he was magnificent under fire! He was a mighty influence in affairs of state in Kentucky when the infant commonwealth was suffering the birth pangs of separation from the mother state of Virginia. Yes, Samuel McDowell of Mercer County, Kentucky was an ardent Federalist—a man of great influence and even greater convictions."

"Yes, Father, we know, and that sort of puts him in a suspicious category as far as I am concerned."

Doctor John spoke up for the first time. "The Federalists performed a unique service for America in the critical days of our first steps as an infant republic. Here we were—thirteen little biddies anxious to leave the nest and try our wings—to leave the protection of the mother hen. These little fledglings might very well have gone off in thirteen different directions, but for the fact that the Federalists kept them together till they were sufficiently mature to strike out on their own."

Logan took issue with his brother. "That illustration is an oversimplification, but it can serve as a starter."

It was not difficult for the Carson men to find a "starter" for stimulating conversation, and reminiscences of the early days of territorial expansion as it affected North Carolina continued as they lingered over their coffee, interrupted at length by William, one of the Carson sons, whose home was in walking distance up the way.

"Keep your seats, all of you, and go on with what you were saying, Father. I had word of the Prodigal's return, and I came to help kill the yearling." Grasping Sam's hand warmly, he then acknowledged his introduction to Davis, pulled up a chair and accepted the cup of coffee that Tillie brought. "Don't let me intrude in the conversation. If Father is telling something he likes to remember, and I warrant he is, then by all means let's proceed."

"For some reason—I don't remember how—we got into a discussion of North Carolina's tardy entrance into the Union."

"Mighty serious subject you're discussing—serious and not very timely. Why don't we talk about something exciting these

93

city fellows can tell us—like the girl that Sam has been going around with in Federal City," said William.

"I'd like to hear about that duel—you know, the one between Henry Clay and John Randolph. I don't see any sense in hatching up something about Sam and a girl. If he had found one, he'd have waked all of us up to tell it, now wouldn't you, Sam?" inquired Logan.

Sam smiled. "Senator Benton did give me a first-hand report of the duel, Logan. He was there as an interested friend, and he claims he tried to persuade them to desist. Probably because of the harmless outcome, a great many people joked about it. Someone down in Orange County wrote my friend, Willie Mangum, that he was sorry to see Mr. Clay and Mr. Randolph had been pretending to shoot at each other, and he added, 'I fear it will cause some of our headstrong boys to think they ought to do the same, and be foolish enough to take good aim.' "

Whereupon Davis commented, "It's too bad that duelling is accepted as a custom of the times—a most unfortunate thing if there are fatalities, but a sort of sporting event otherwise, according to its proponents."

"Since this is an off-year for elections, we will not likely have the serious altercations that often provoke gentlemen to use their swords and pistols indiscriminately," commented William. "And speaking of elections, Sam, I hear that you may have some opposition the next time around."

"I'm glad of that. It's always more challenging to have to contend for the prize than to have it laid on your doorstep. Besides, it's a healthy thing to have men of high calibre anxious to serve their country and willing to compete for the honor," commented Sam. "But we have been so busy talking about our own affairs, I have not told you that my friend Davis here has his hat in the ring for a seat in the House of Representatives. He is going home tomorrow to read the political barometer in his district."

"If we could leave electioneering in the hands of our supporters, as they did in the early days of the Republic, it would not require so much energy and effort," said Davis, addressing

94

his remarks to Colonel Carson.

"Yes, it takes flowery speeches, reckless promises and a lot of spiritous liquor to enhance the prospects of some candidates. It would be interesting to see what would happen if a campaign were waged without recourse to these alternatives. I'm not suggesting that you try it, Mr. Davis. I am confident that you will do well without such questionable aids. And speaking of electioneering, I saw Abner Burgin some days since, and he says that David Crockett would like to extend his political boundaries from the grassroots of Tennessee to the national scene. Like you, Mr. Davis, he may become a candidate for Congress next year."

At the mention of David Crockett's political ambitions, Sam interrupted. "He's not in Swannanoa now, is he?"

"They expect David and his family this fall, according to Abner's report," answered Colonel Carson, as he noted the incredulous expression on Sam's face.

"Davis, it may be that I will soon have two friends fighting with me in the mighty effort to establish justice and insure domestic tranquility, although I can think of no two more unlike in personality and manner of life. This is amazing! Tell us more, Father."

"There's not much more to tell, except Abner did say that Crockett had had a bad accident when he swapped his coonskin cap for that of a commodore."

"You're talking in riddles, Father, and that idea is so farfetched I can't follow you. Now please start from the beginning and tell it slowly so your uncomprehending son can get it straight. First of all, does he really intend to run for Congress?"

"According to Abner, he does. So far I have found the Burgins to be reliable, and I have no reason to doubt Abner."

Noting Mr. Davis's quizzical expression, Logan prodded his brother Sam. "Maybe Mr. Davis doesn't know who it is who has these Congressional aspirations. Do you know who we are talking about, Mr. Davis?"

"I am not sure you are talking about the same backwoodsman I am thinking about. If you are, he is the last person I would think of as an aspiring candidate for Congress, or in the

95

role of commodore, for that matter. Your mention of a coon-skin cap, though, has a familiar ring."

"Go on, Mr. Davis."

"This man I know only by tales some of our South Carolina game hunters have brought back from Tennessee. He is famous in his own territory, but I have never laid eyes on him, have any of you?"

"Oh yes, Mr. Davis," the elder Carson answered. "I think perhaps he had roots in North Carolina before he married a neighbor up the way."

Davis interrupted. "Hold on there a minute, I just remembered. I have had occasion to represent some former North Carolinians in their claims for settlement of land warrants in East Tennessee. They frequently mention a Mr. Crockett, who, as a member of the Tennessee legislature had used his influence to crack down on holders of those warrants by fixing an expiration date on the instruments, jeopardizing their holdings and causing them much concern. Could these two people be one and the same?"

"They could be and they are, my friend," said Sam. "I've known Crockett in his role as backswoodsman, Nimrod and legislator, but as a commodore—never! Let's hear it like Abner told it to you, Father."

"Well, you have laughed at the idea of Commodore Crockett. He is fully entitled to the title of Lieutenant Colonel Crockett of the Tennessee militia. It seems that David Crockett is a man of many parts, for in addition to the categories named in which he has made himself known, another will have to be added, and that is as a manufacturer and shipping tycoon."

"Manufacturer and shipper of what?" Logan inquired.

"Of barrel staves, Son. Abner says that last fall David decided it was time he ventured into some sort of business beside politicking and bear hunting. He went twenty-five miles west to Obian Lake and with the help of hired hands, he started his enterprise. One venture called for another. In order to get the staves to New Orleans where there was a market for them, he had to have boats, so he put some of the hands to work building boats. He had no sooner begun this work in earnest when the insistent call of the wild caught up with him, and leaving the manufacturing to the hired hands, he went off to indulge in his favorite sport. He bagged bear, deer and buffalo, then returned to his barrel-stave project.

"By the middle of January he had about 30,000 staves and two boats almost ready for navigation. He picked his crew for both boats and started confidently down the Obian River, thence to the Mississippi.

"Because he could subdue nature, and had held communion with her visible forms, Crockett was not only sure he could navigate in calm waters, but could successfully ride the rapids and harness the seas."

"Now Father, I know Abner did not adorn the tale like that, but as Crockett is wont to say 'Go ahead.' "

"Don't interrupt me, Son. I'm just indulging in a bit of imaginative prose. But if you insist I will stick to Abner's tale. Abner, by the way, Mr. Davis, is Crockett's brother-in-law. But to proceed. Once they got to the Mississippi all Hell broke loose. Inexperienced landlubbers that they were, they were at the mercy of the elements. They could neither navigate nor make a landing. Night came upon them in their futile attempts. People at the landing places along the way would run out with lanterns and shout directions that they were powerless to follow. They did manage to lash the two boats together for a measure of protection and security. David finally gave up and went below deck. Shortly thereafter there was a great commotion overhead, and the next instant there was a crashing blow and an inrush of water.

"The craft had struck submerged trees and debris that were not visible in the darkness. The foredeck of Crockett's craft nosed under the companion craft, and the aft section was standing perpendicularly out of the water at a precipitous angle. His only means of escape was through a hole in the side of the boat too small to accommodate his body. With much pulling and tugging on the part of his deck hands, and with his clothes literally torn from his body, he was finally extricated. Crockett had been in tight spots before, and but for the discomfort of spending a night in the chilly dampness without clothing, he was not too put upon."

"I wish I could have heard Crockett spin that yarn himself," commented Sam. "He has an uncommon gift in that direction, but it would have lacked the 'imaginative prose' with which you embellished it, Father. Besides, I don't think you imagined that prose. If I am not mistaken, it came from the pen of the New England poet, Bryant. At any rate, it has a familiar ring."

"Imaginary or purloined, I say David will cut quite a figure in Congress with the dignified and sartorially correct New Englanders," Doctor John observed.

"That he will, John, but there are other colorful figures making legislative history in the Capital—Sam Houston, for instance, though I believe his term of office expires next year, and there are rumors in the cloak rooms that he intends to run for governor of Tennessee."

"Well, if you ask my opinion, I think Crockett will be a miscast actor on the national stage—if he gets elected. I like him better in his role of backwoodsman," observed Logan.

Davis had heard the storytelling and comments with the keenest interest. "The more I hear about the prospects for the next Congress, the more anxious I am to participate in its deliberations. I gather that you have known Crockett as a sometimes neighbor, Sam. He is older than you, is he not?"

"I would judge about twelve or thirteen years older. He certainly doesn't look older, and of course in many respects, he is not as old. It could well be that his very naiveté will make him more friends than enemies. We shall see! I confess I am more than a little interested in the prospect of his candidacy."

The next day on his way to Pendleton, Davis began seriously thinking about his own campaign plans. His talks with Carson had provided him with intimate glimpses of some of his would-be associates in Congress. It would be tremendously helpful to have this advantage, and now, more than ever, he was determined to win. He congratulated himself on the prospect of being a practical politician and a States' Rights advocate at a time when the transition from autocratic to representative government was in prospect, and when government of the people, by the people, and for the people was referred to in terms of possible accomplishment rather than the mouthings of irresponsible politicians, or as empty words on a printed page.

Unfortunately, what Davis was not aware of at this juncture

was that being a States' Rights activist *in* the Palmetto State was not the same thing as being a States' Rights advocate *from* a Southern state in the national Congress, particularly when that state is South Carolina. If there were one revelation more than another that made a lasting impression on him during his visit, it was that the people of Western North Carolina were far from being the uncouth barbarians they were sometimes represented to be, and that Eastern North Carolina and, indeed, South Carolina did not have a monopoly on culture, wisdom and abilities.

During the month of August Carson did little but relax and enjoy his family. He did a little paper work in anticipation of his visits to his constituents in September and October. In his district there were seven counties, the more populous being Burke and Buncombe. "I believe I will go westward first," he told his father one evening when they were discussing his plans. "When we were at Quaker Meadows, Charles told me that Silas McDowell had moved his tailoring shop to Asheville. I want him to measure me for a new suit. If I see him soon enough he may be able to get it to me before my return. I'd rather not risk the mails, as unpredictable as Uncle Sam's carriers are in bad weather. From Buncombe I can go to Macon County and back by Rutherfordton. Now that the Green River folk have given up plans to visit us, I will spend a few days there with Joe and Rebecca."

"I'm sure if Catharine had not gone back to Brentwood you would have made a longer stay," his father ventured with a sly smile. "I haven't seen Catharine since she grew up. Is she as pretty as Rebecca?" asked the Colonel.

"In a different sort of way she is, Father. I'm sorry the plans did not work out for their visit here. Her mother's illness changed everything."

"Do you think Almyra will undertake the trip to Brentwood, or is her aunt's illness that serious?" Almyra, the wife of William Carson, was a first cousin of Rebecca, Catharine, and of Margaret, who had married Charles, another of the seven brothers. Three Wilson daughters had married three Carson brothers—first cousins to begin with.

"I have heard nothing of Almyra's plans. Catharine is the one who should be with her mother now. She has fewer responsibilities."

The quiet summer evenings had been memorable ones for father and son, who shared their experiences of the past winter months. Sam suspected that his father had been much lonelier than he would admit this first winter without his devoted helpmate. He talked about the "ould country," describing his home on Loch Erne with as much enthusiasm as if it were being revealed for the first time. "I'll never forget, my boy, how upset was your Aunt Katie when that redheaded Irishman, her husband, decided to come to America. They lived in the village of Enniskillin—the island town just a few miles from our home, it was. They usually came visiting on Sunday, but when Kate came bringing the bairns on a weekday, sure and it was a sign that something unexpected was brewing.

"I well remember one of the last of those visits, the one before we set sail, though at the time it happened the thought of coming to America had never tantalized me. Katie came one afternoon crying, and broke the news that Tom Wilson—the man she had vowed to love and cherish through a lifetime of ups and downs—was secretly making plans to go to America. Oh, of course he offered her a choice! She could stay and wait for him to come back in five years, or she could go with him so he could be comforted and cared for in that strange new wilderness of America. She cried her fill, then, as I knew she would, straightened up and confided to Mother that there was really no choice. Tom knew she wouldn't let him go without her. It was then I began thinking of making the journey with them. Mind you, they hadn't asked me to come along, but the more I thought about it, the more enticing I found the prospect.

"I haunted the docks, inspecting the boats and talking with every seafaring man who would listen and answer my questions. I read everything I could lay hands on about the New World and its beckoning invitation to fame and fortune. Finally I screwed up my courage to talk with Katie. To my joyful surprise she had been thinking these very same thoughts. I could help with the seven children and I would be family to her in a very special

100

way. She would get Tom's consent, and I should get transportation and a nest egg to carry me over rough times. But first of all I must get the consent of my parents. The last was not easy. My parents had great plans for me. You'll wonder when I tell you that they wanted me to become an Episcopal clergyman. But with Katie's pleadings added to mine, they finally gave in three weeks before sailing time."

"So that's how it came about! An Episcopal rector! Why you might have been a bishop by now had you stayed in Ireland! But now that you've picked up the threads of your early years, tell me about Enniskillen and Loch Erne, Father." Sam realized that in recent months his father had spent more and more time reliving the early years of his life, and he wanted to share in the reminiscences.

"To tell you about Loch Erne and Enniskillen, I must tell you of the charm of Fermanagh County—all of it. Sure and its the loveliest corner in all of Ireland, where primroses grow in profusion—wild primroses sprinkling the roadsides and the hills with their splashes of color. Loch Erne is dotted with islands, many in their native state, with forests and woodland abounding in plants and animals But how can you put the beauty of it and the wonder of it into words? Have you ever wondered why I settled here in Western North Carolina? It was because here I was able to recapture some of the beauty of my native land. Within five miles of Enniskillen there were thirty lakes and rivers—a fisherman's paradise. But I was no fisherman. We need some lakes and more rivers to make a true comparison, but Ireland cannot boast mountain ranges like we have around us. We have beauty enough and wonder enough to fill one man's life, and I have been satisfied!"

"It makes me very happy to hear you say that, Father, and hearing your high praise of the beauty that is ours in this choice spot, I am moved to say I hope that those who possess this land through the years will have an awareness and an appreciation of its beauty that will inspire them, even as you have been inspired. I hope this scenic grandeur will never be desecrated by the hand of man.

"But let's go back to Ireland for a few minutes more. Tell me, were you like your father, James Carson, or like your mother, Rebecca Hazzard, and do you spell 'Hazzard' with an 's' or with a 'z'?"

"It is spelled both ways in the ould country, my son, and here it doesn't matter. My mother used to say I was like my Uncle Jason, her brother. A fine man he was! I think your brother, Jason, is like him."

And so, with intimate sessions like this, with visits to and from the many relatives, with fence-mending plans made and carried out, the colorful autumn season was soon over, and Samuel Price Carson was on his way to the nation's Capital.

The opening of the second session of the Nineteenth Congress took place on December third, according to the proscription of the Constitution. Vice President Calhoun, who had but recently returned from South Carolina, took the Chair of the Senate, and both Houses reported that they were completely organized. On Thursday, December fifth, the message of the President of the United States was delivered and copies were placed on every desk, as was the usual custom.

The next day Carson prepared to walk the six blocks from his room to the Capitol. The sun was shining but shed no warmth on this December day. Indeed, the weather had been so severe that there was notably less activity on the streets and in and around the government buildings. Wrapped securely in a great-coat, a woolen scarf wound tightly around his throat and loosely up to his nose, Carson strode along Pennsylvania Avenue, facing the wind. Now and again a sharp, cutting pain interrupted his breathing. He stopped at an apothecary shop to feel the warmth of the pot-bellied stove around which were clustered a few of the drifters who always seemed to claim the first fruits of another's industry.

Carson reached the legislative chambers a few minutes before nine o'clock. On entering the House, he was shocked into questioning unreality by the scene that met his eyes. Usually dignified and sedate, the members were pushing and crowding around the Southern windows of the room, and the distracted clerk was gavelling the table in an endeavor to bring the body to order. Spreading his muffler on top of his desk, Carson stood on it to find a more commanding view—an act which at any other time would have brought an official tongue-lashing, indeed would have been an unheard of breach of dignity and protocol. That the commotion was caused by a great conflagration was readily seen—the flames and billowing smoke in full view over the heads of the spectators.

Finally, one of the observers walked to the desk and conferred with the clerk, who again tried to gavel the assembly to order, shouting, "Our neighboring city of Alexandria is burning! You are needed now to assist them. Get to your seats and quit you like men!" The assembly seated and tractable, the clerk continued, "It will be impossible for us to proceed with cold deliberation when a scene so calamitous is before our eyes."

Mr. Miner, obeying the promptings of his humane disposition, superceded all other considerations and immediately got to the practical aspects of the situation by offering a resolution to appropriate a sum of money for the relief of the stricken sufferers. The afflicting view, the burning town, and the extreme severity of the weather appealed so powerfully to the feelings of the House that no objection was voiced on the first reading, but so great was the excitement, rendered more insistent by the clanging of bells from the Capital firefighters as they raced past the building, that the second reading was dispensed with and the lawmakers did not proceed on the order of their departure, but emptied the Hall in record time. Carson boarded a tram car that had interrupted its regular route and was hauling the populace to the scene of the disaster, and on arrival he began immediately to assist the bucket brigade in its attempt to halt destruction.

That night, after thawing out in front of an open fire in the lobby of the hotel, and at the insistence of various and sundry guests, he indulged in not one, but two or three strong hot toddies, then, returning to his room, he penned a round-robin letter to his family:

> We have had no mail from the South since the New Year came in—the propitious year of 1827! It is reported that rivers have been closed to transportation—so much ice that boats cannot ply, and mails coming in by any route have been delayed.
>
> In this letter I had planned to regale you with a description of

Christmas in the nation's Capital and to give you a report on the annual Eighth of January celebration. As to the latter, suffice it to say that Judge Hugh Lawson White of Tennessee lauded Andrew Jackson and the now famous Battle of New Orleans, whose anniversary was the occasion for the event.

The urgent news now relates to a devastating happening of today, and the other events will have to be slighted, for you must know that much of Alexandria, the beautiful sister city of Washington, is in ashes, destruction having been caused by a fire that broke out in the early morning as most of the legislators were assembling for the day's activities.

It was easily observed from the Halls of the Houses, and cold as the weather was—the thermometer at fifteen degrees—our townsmen turned out with alacrity, and almost literally flew to the assistance of their neighbors.

The engine from Capitol Hill, with its hose, was underway a few minutes after the alarm was given. About three hundred persons from the Navy Yard, headed by Captain Booth, were underway almost as soon, but having further to go did not arrive quite as early at the scene. The engine from the Post Office Department got under way almost immediately.

As soon as the fire was ascertained to be serious, an express arrived from the Mayor of Alexandria to our Mayor, soliciting aid, whereupon the engine from the second ward and that from the first were notified and lost no time in plunging ahead.

Nor were our Georgetown neighbors behind hand. With great spirit they went down in numbers by carriages, on horseback and on foot. All the Marines in the station were taken down by Captain Howle. The whole number of persons who went down from the City to the River could not have been less than a thousand—a distance of more than seven miles from most points.

There was cause for rejoicing and exultation, for with all of this assistance, the fire was brought under control and a vast amount rescued from the jaws of destruction.

When I arrived, our friends in Alexandria, exhausted by fatigue and anxiety, appeared to be in shock, and without the hose and the supplies we sent would never have been able to spare their own or their neighbor's property.

The conflagration was awful and the destruction of property was great, as would be supposed with a fire raging for five hours. The river supplied the water and although the water, thrown in streams, descended in the form of ice and sleet, mantling the firemen in icy garments, only one engine was put out of service.

And now, at a quarter past ten, I am feeling a great fatigue from my exertions and from the near-frozen extremities I sustained, and so I will send my felicitations and sign myself,

Yr humbl & ob'dt servant

On the following morning when the House convened, Mr. Powell moved that all the orders of the day be postponed in order to deal with the bill for the relief of the citizens of Alexandria. The motion prevailed and the House went into a Committee of the Whole. A letter was read from the citizens of Alexandria, giving a statement of the loss sustained and the amount that would be needed to relieve the distress. The number of dwellings destroyed was sixty or more, and the sum needed for immediate relief for food and clothing was $20,000. It developed that many of the members had been firsthand witnesses of the destruction and many, like Carson, had participated in the effort to contain the conflagration.

A proponent of the bill explained that the amount stipulated was not to make up for any losses sustained, but to relieve personal distress and suffering, while another was anxious for it to appear that the appropriation would be made because the distressed city lay in the District of Columbia, and the bill should be worded in such a manner as to emphasize this point in order to forestall any future involvements by emergency situations occurring outside the jurisdiction of the House. There was no doubt that the House under the Constitution had the power to enact such legislation; moreover, they were in duty bound to pass the bill, not for relief of a city in the District, but because the city was a part of the District.

Some of the members opposed the bill, and after one had given his "justifiable" reasons for opposition, Congressman Newton called for a reading of the act appropriating $50,000 for the purpose of sending provisions to the people of Caracas, in Venezuela, South America when they suffered the effects of an earthquake and consequent famine. The Act of 1812 was accordingly read. Nonetheless, another long speech of opposition was recorded. After the members had listened to the tedious, drawn-out pronouncements, both pro and con, they began to grow restless. It was evident that those who opposed the bill had forgotten that they and they alone had been given the responsibility for the protection of life and property of all of the people of the District, and that their relief was as much a sacred obligation as that of a father for any or all of his minor offspring.

On the heels of a skillful argument in behalf of the bill, Carson rose to try to bolster the effort. "When last night I returned from the smoking ruins of Alexandria and lay down upon my bed, I could not but reflect on the situation of many of my fellow beings who had, the night before, slept in security and last night had not where to lay their heads; who had that very morning risen in comfortable, even in affluent circumstances, and last night found themselves without a dollar in the world. I saw beautiful edifices tumbling into ruins. I saw delicate females, as well-bred and well-dressed as are to be found anywhere, throwing themselves in the ranks and handing water in the bucket line till their hands were stiffened with ice and their limbs with the cold, and who refused to retire though repeatedly urged to do so.

"After witnessing a scene of destruction like this I am unable to refuse my assent to such a bill as is before this House. In such circumstances could the House refuse the sufferers such a sum as $20,000—a sum scarce sufficient to purchase beds for all who are without any?" Carson was an attractive and forceful speaker—now as on other occasions. That he would, by a combination of circumstances, have occasion to defend himself on this humane issue would never have occurred to him, nor indeed that the aftermath of this day would have repercussions that would affect his whole life.

There were other speeches for and against the passage of the bill, but the cause of compassion won by a wide margin.

It was very late when the business of the day came to an end. The sittings of the House were becoming more and more demanding. Instead of convening at noon, as was the usual custom, the sessions were begun at nine, and during the early part of February they were often in session nine or ten hours consecutively. For that reason, the plans for a gala celebration and holiday on February 22 was a pleasing prospect.

The Birthnight Ball was always a notable occasion. Remembering his indisposition of a year ago, Carson determined to be on hand this year, and he hoped that he could find an agreeable young lady to share the festive Ball with him. The difficulty had been that he had had little time to cultivate feminine com-

106

panionship. Surrounded as he was at home with the beauty and congeniality of ladies, even if most of them were his nieces and his sisters, his cousins and his aunts, he felt bereft indeed in his staid surroundings, and he made a solemn pact to remedy the situation.

Carson was delighted on reaching his room to find that at last the mails had come through and that there was a sufficient accumulation to keep him pleasantly occupied. There was a letter and a package of shortbread and cookies from Mathilda "baked by Binah—and with them she sends you her love." He had no way of knowing how long the package had been in transit, but the contents had not suffered from the delay. He poured a glass of wine and settled down to enjoy his repast while he read the letters piled on his desk. He put aside those from constituents until he saw one in the bold handwriting of his father, and he lost no time in breaking the seal.

My Son,

I am sorry to convey to you in my first letter since your departure the distressing news of the death of your aunt, Katy Wilson. It was inevitable from the inception of her illness, and there should be fewer regrets when one considers her full and satisfying life. Almyra and William, Charles and Margaret made the trip together, and Joseph and Rebecca went to Brentwood direct from Green River. They are returned now to their respective homes in time for Christmas.

You will be pleased to know that Missy is once more in her own stall. Charles McDowell and Anne came up for a visit with James at McDowell House and brought her along. Old Eben was almost tearful with joy when he curried her yesterday. He says, and I confirm, that there is hardly a scar that you can see, though he "expecs" her racing days are over.

My activities are about as usual. I served on the Grand Jury shortly after you left, but I did not go with the wagon train to Charleston.

Mathilda says to tell you that we will have syllabub for Christmas, for which she will grate fresh nutmeg—thanks to your thoughtfulness. She and Binah are baking today, and whatever it is smells tempting.

Present my respects to Mr. Mangum, Mr. Branch and any other of my acquaintances.

Your occasionally venerable Father

Pleasant Gardens
December 20, 1826

107

As he sorted further into the stack of mail he found a letter postmarked Brentwood, Tennessee. He thought he recognized Catharine's delicate handwriting, and he was surprised at the impatience he felt in opening the letter. As he read, his face showed a variety of emotions. Catharine wrote of the difficult adjustments that followed her mother's death, and of the responsibilities of homemaking that had necessarily fallen to her. She remembered so pleasantly the short time they had together at Quaker Meadows, and already had begun to anticipate her return to Green River next summer. She hoped he would not be too busy with affairs of state to write to her occasionally, for she was beginning to realize that all the young men she knew suffered by comparison with her sister's brother-in-law.

There was an expression of pleased amusement on his face, and as he tucked the missive away in a secret compartment of his desk he found himself whistling a gay refrain. Toward the bottom of the stack was a letter from Davis, his friend and traveling companion of the summer.

Dear Carson,

It is with considerable embarrassment that I begin this, my first letter to you since our most pleasurable summer experience, and since I was shown such favorable hospitality at Pleasant Gardens.

That my time was well spent in campaigning for a seat in the Twentieth Congress, you have no doubt been apprised through the papers. Although I did win handily, I had left no stone unturned to insure my victory, as I promised you last summer. And now "to the Victor belongs the spoils."

It is my plan to drive my spirited team in the same conveyance used on our trip from the Springs, and I shall allow myself ample time for all of the caprices of the weather. I shall hope to be settled in my quarters at Fuller's Hotel by the nineteenth or twentieth of February.

In the event of my arriving on schedule, I would like very much to have you reserve a place for me at the Birthnight Ball, and incidentally, if you expect to escort a young lady, do see if she has a friend or twin sister who will consent to accompany on this grand occasion,

Your humb'l & obd't servant W.R.D.

Pendleton, S. C.
January 16, 1827

P.S. Has Commodore Crockett made his debut in Congress, or has his election come off yet? I have had no time for anything but South Carolina politics, and am sadly uninformed about developments elsewhere.

Sam chuckled at the remembrance of Crockett's dilemma with the barrel staves, and made a mental note to tell Davis at the first opportunity about the status of the would-be congressman. Carson anticipated with no little pleasure the companionship of his South Carolina friend, and he was not reluctant to admit that he anticipated with the greatest satisfaction the advent of a States' Rights champion at a time when whispers of disunity and sectional disagreement were audible without the aid of an ear trumpet. Abolition, anti-slavery, insurrection, compromise—all were inflammatory subjects—not just straws in the wind but thunderheads that threatened to dislocate and tear asunder the moorings of the Ship of State.

Even last year Carson had heard rumors that Southerners were beginning to unite for self-protection, and the terms "State Interposition" and "Nullification" weighed heavily in their councils and in their caucuses.

As a newcomer, he tended to ignore or pass over lightly these sinister implications in which the South was presumed to play a stellar role. That was last year. This year he found himself an unwilling member and an occasional participant in groups where one or two reckless individuals seemed bent on fanning the flames of prejudice, suspicion and sectional malcontent. A man of uncommon resolves and of unquestioned integrity, Carson had no intention of evading or avoiding issues, but he was equally determined that he would not "go off half-cocked"—that he would be sure of the ground on which he stood before making commitments and pronouncements. He felt easy with Davis; together they could discuss these issues dispassionately.

It was the opinion of many Southern statesmen and politicians that if there were one man whose counsel was reliable, one who had the "inside track" and the insights provided thereby, it was Davis's kinsman, the Vice President, John C. Calhoun. It was unthinkable that Davis would become a puppet for his kinsman's manipulation—even if Calhoun should

109

entertain such ideas, which he never did. By the same token it was unthinkable that Davis would not have the ear of the most influential man in the South. The prospect was at once awesome and intriguing. In any event, Carson welcomed the idea of becoming better advised without the opprobrium of collaborating with strange bedfellows.

It was not until he was ready to snuff out the candles in his room that the thought of the Birthnight Ball and his friend's request came to him. Carson consulted the time and, finding he had an hour to spare before midnight, brought out his writing material and re-read Catharine's letter. So much time had elapsed since she penned it that by the time his letter would reach her it would not appear that he had hurried his reply.

He told her briefly of his activities since he saw her last, expressed his condolences and passed on to lighter and brighter happenings. He knew that she would be interested in anything pertaining to Davis, and he wrote,

> I am expecting Warren Davis momentarily. He will take the oath of office as the representative of the Pendleton District in South Carolina on March fourth. This ceremony will not be as important or as exciting as will be the swearing-in in March of next year, when, if my sanguine wishes are fulfilled, one Andrew Jackson, of the Hermitage, will be elevated to the Presidency.
>
> There will be gaiety aplenty this year, however. Perhaps it is because of the serious and weighty problems attendant in the daily lives of the lawmakers that they seem to welcome with unusual expectation the social outlets, of which there are not a few.
>
> Beginning with the private parties when the men of Congress assemble in December, Christmas and the New Year are celebrated with enthusiasm, as they are elsewhere. Then on January eighth is the annual celebration of the Battle of New Orleans, when Andrew Jackson and his cohorts are toasted and acclaimed with enthusiasm.
>
> The birthday celebration of our first President seems to become more spectacular each year, often beginning in the morning hours with parades and military display and the booming of cannon, and ending with the colorful Birthnight Ball and a magnificent display of fireworks.
>
> If my man is elected, perhaps you can come to Washington for some of the festivities of the inauguration. This is a pleasant prospect, but I shall delight in seeing you at Green River in the meantime.

On Saturday, March 12, the last session of the Congress came to an end. For Carson it had been all too brief. To be sure, there had been the long, drawn-out hacking away at attempts to transact in an orderly manner the important business of State, but being interspersed with occasions of social enjoyment in the celebration of special events, the time had passed quickly.

There was no doubt that the tempo of his social life had been stepped up because he had Davis to share the occasions with him. Together they made favorable impressions upon the Washington hostesses, and jointly and separately caught the attention of the lawmakers in both Houses, particularly of the Southern delegation.

They had planned to return home by separate routes, but the two were meeting on Tuesday the twelfth for a farewell session.

At the appointed time, Davis rapped on the door, and Carson noted as he entered the room a look of amusement on his face.

"What's so funny, my friend?"

"Have you read today's *Intelligencer?*" Davis queried.

"No, I read Duff Greene's sheet. Why?"

"Would you like to behold a mirror image of the Nineteenth Congress as reflected in the editorial office of the *Intelligencer?*" Making himself comfortable in a chair drawn up for him, Davis unfolded the paper and began to read:

> The representatives of a mighty empire are now returning to their respective homes to render an account of their performance of the great trusts which have been confided to them. How they shall accomplish this last duty is an inquiry of the most serious import.
>
> Are there many who can look back with unmingled satisfaction on the history of their official labors? The period of cold reflection has arrived.
>
> Are there not some who stand rebuked for a crafty and insidious purpose in the gratification of personal animosities and the promotion of party interests? Are there not others who, commencing with purer intentions, have gradually yielded to the irritation of their feelings and have ventured into and persisted at length in practices which they would otherwise have condemned as unbecoming equally to their honor as men and their duty as public servants?
>
> And how many more are there who, disgusted either with the low intrigues, or the corrupt practices and unmanly dissension, have recurred in their seats in shameful silence with scarcely an effort to arrest the degeneracy and restore the dignity of the National Councils.
>
> It will be happy indeed if the task of self-examination be accompanied with neither of these results to some who are now on their way to their homes.

111

The floor of Congress has been literally converted into an arena for contending partisans, whence the public have been excluded, or into which they have been only occasionally admitted that they might witness the worthless and the unprofitable games and sports!

Such is the mortifying reflection of those who, removed from the excitement of party feelings which have too much swayed the discussions of the Nineteenth Congress, are now scrutinizing the few insufficient and important enactments which they have passed, and the postponement of measures that most vitally affect the interests of the Union at large.

It is therefore most devoutly to be wished that the labors and results of future years will speedily erase the reproach which is thus left upon the annals of our Legislature.

"And that is the bitter end," said Davis, folding the paper and glancing at Carson for his further reaction.

"You will have to admit, Davis, that there has been no world-shaking legislation accomplished in this session, but there has been plenty of steam under the lid clamped down by the conservatives, and plenty of opportunity for a boiling over of the political cauldron. There was no explosion on the slavery question and no insuperable wedge driven between the Northern and the Southern factions, for which we can thank your kinsman, the Vice President and presiding officer of the Senate—and to those like-minded in the House."

"Yes, these and other issues of great moment will most certainly come up for the attention of the best minds in Congress, and I predict we will not be kept waiting long."

"What other issues do you have in mind, Davis?"

"The tariff—that issue of abomination!—surely will demand enactments that undoubtedly will provoke controversial debate."

"Yes, I believe *The Intelligencer* has made a point well worth considering, but I am wondering how our constituents will take that critical analysis. Of course our state papers will give it prime space, but you know, Davis, we are on the eve of departure and will be going our separate ways. I may not see you through the summer, for I will be campaigning, you know. Aren't you glad that item is not on your agenda this year?"

"I am indeed, and since I will have some time on my hands,

sir, I will do you the honor of offering my valuable services in any way that I can further the successful outcome of your campaign. Do you know for a certainty who your adversaries will be?"

Carson appeared not to have heard the question. He walked to his desk and took a letter from a leather folder. "Since you have asked specifically, I am going to share with you, confidentially, a bit of intelligence that is a little premature for public consumption.

"You have heard me speak of Silas McDowell, kinsman of the Quaker Meadows McDowells. This letter is from him. He begins

Since your re-election comes in August, it is not too soon to apprise you of developments in your District.

Recently, Doctor Vance, your predecessor, and one of your antagonists in the last election, notified some of his most abiding friends to meet him at Asheville on a certain day for consultation and advice on whether he should run against you for a seat in the Twentieth Congress. To a man they all advised him to take the field—all but one man, and that was myself. My reasons for trying to dissuade him from the contest were in his own best interests.

I pointed out that you are decidedly popular, as well as a fast-rising young man, and that all of the measures you have advocated so far have had the approval of your constituents. I further stated that he—Vance—would have nothing on which to ground an argument against you.

In my last assertion, I was flatly contradicted; and it was reiterated by the entire company that Doctor Vance had ample grounds for making a damaging charge against you, to wit: In the matter of giving $25,000 to the citizens of Alexandria after the city burned.

I gave my opinion that such a charge would not damage you at all, and that our friend, Vance, had better keep out of the contest.

It was plainly evident that I had excited the indignation of all present except Vance, and among them were men for whom I have the highest regard—one of them an uncle to the lady I intend to marry.

One of the number stated it as his opinion that Vance could drive you from the District because you are a coward and would rather quit the field than fight.

It was then that I rose to take my leave, stating "Gentlemen, I know Carson, and let me tell you, you mistake the man."

This is where things now stand, except I should add that I am now looked upon as an enemy in camp by all except Doctor Vance.

113

He knew I was speaking the truth.

You will soon be coming back into the District and can assess matters at that time.

Carson replaced the letter in his wallet. "So that is the answer to your specific question, Davis. It appears that there are threatening clouds on my political horizon."

"Do you remember that you said in a conversation at Pleasant Gardens last summer that you would welcome honorable competition?"

"I did, and I still do, but I would rather it be almost anyone other than Vance."

"There are two things I would like to have unraveled, Carson. I want to know more about Doctor Vance, and more about charges of cowardice that have been made against you, if you are agreeable."

"Certainly, my friend. As to Doctor Vance, his father, Colonel David Vance lived in Burke County during the Revolution, and some years subsequently moved to the new county of Buncombe. Colonel Vance was a Presbyterian in doctrine and a Christian gentleman in practice, and he held an unsullied record as a patriot during the War for Independence. He had a large family of daughters and three sons, one of whom studied medicine and opened an office in Asheville, but did not long pursue his profession, preferring the political arena. He is my opponent, or is likely to be.

"He had a childhood disease that left him a cripple physically, but he is a mental giant, or so I have heard him described. It was at my insistence and with my considerable help that he was elected to the position of responsibility which I now hold. When he first appeared in Congress his unprepossessing appearance mitigated against him, but not for long. The strong and influential men in the House soon discovered that an Aesop's mind could not long be hid under an Aesop's form, and at the close of his term, he had the respect of every distinguished man in the House.

"That, my friend, is a brief sketch of my adversary, who like myself, has never been married."

"Already he has my respect, Carson, and I've never seen him. Now—when did you play so much the coward that Doctor Vance concludes that you would rather run than fight?"

"This is the kind of thing I prefer not to remember, Davis, but it has come up and I must make an explanation. I prefer that the person involved remain nameless, and I shall have to rely on you to make whatever judgment you wish in the matter. A member of a very prominent North Carolina family, who was a lawyer and for a brief period took a high rank at the bar, became the victim of strong drink and made a wreck of his former self. He challenged me to a duel over an inconsequential matter, and because his condition played a large part in his display of temper, I refused to meet him on the field of honor—the field of dishonor, I should say, for that is what it would have been. Now, let's quit this unpleasant subject and repair to Carusi's for our repast and our reluctant farewells."

Davis was less inclined than Carson to let the weight of the world settle on his shoulders. He was always the one who could find humor in a situation if there was any to be found. During the meal he thought of a clipping he had cut from one of the papers that might offset the sting of the harsh editorial on the caliber and performance of the legislators that they had read together a few hours earlier. At a lull in the conversation he produced it.

"*The Intelligencer* is not the only organ concerned about the dull performance of the lawmakers this session. For example, I have here a clipping from *The Connecticut Mirror*. 'Let any man look at the papers or out of the window and see for himself if anything is happening in this part of the world which can fairly be designated as news. The Congress of the United States, the Legislature of New York, that of Massachusetts and a half-dozen other solemn and dignified bodies are now in session, and we have gleaned from the resolves, the speeches and resolutions all we could, with the hope that our selection may be instructive and worth reading, but such hope is futile.

" 'A noise is heard in the streets, but no stagecoach is run away, and nobody is run over, no necks broken, no damage done; it is but an avalanche of snow from the roof of a building

115

that hits no passerby. The horn blows, and the mails come in, and down we go to the post office, to get an armful of papers with no news in them.' "

Both men laughed at the caricature of the current crop of lawmakers, and both conceded there might be a grain of truth in the accusations.

Several weeks later, after a brief period of relaxation had restored his aplomb, Carson and his father and brothers began their perennial discussion of politics, the subject uppermost in the minds of many this election year.

The sons knew instinctively that Colonel Carson was bent on revealing his thoughts about his favorite candidate, and they did not have long to wait. "I notice that one of our Eastern representatives favors the incumbent, Mr. Adams. He believes him to be an enlightened statesman who is honestly disposed to promote the best interests of our country."

"I hope that does not represent the sentiment of the majority in Eastern North Carolina," interposed Logan.

"Let me finish, Son. On the other hand, the Philadelphia papers are crowded, literally overwhelmed, with sentiment that points to Jackson. This editorial says, 'If our sheet were as large as the mainsail of our Men O' War, we should scarcely find room for all of the toasts at a recent public dinner in his honor.' "

"And on the other hand, Father," Sam commented, "Clay is doing all in his power to counteract this groundswell for Jackson. He has on more than one occasion inveighed against the trend to make Jackson in the image of the formidable hero of the Battle of New Orleans. While he refers to his own obligation of gratitude to Jackson, the soldier, he warns against the evils of allowing public gratitude to manifest itself in political appointments and promotions."

Colonel John looked over his glasses at his son. "Mr. Clay's oratory will appeal to some elements of our society, but not to the bulwark of the nation—the common man. Our people are shrewd and intelligent—yes, and they are suspicious of public men who are active in their own cause. There's no doubt the national political pot is boiling, but here and now we need to tend our own fires, eh, Sam?"

"Yes, Father. I do not relish the thought of my own campaign, which I intend to begin immediately. And contrary to my expectations, I will have to defend my record in Congress. I believe I can satisfy the majority of my constituents on any debatable point. How many of you are going to the first rally in Asheville next week?" he inquired.

Three of the brothers and Colonel John indicated their intention to be there when Carson and Vance would meet for the first time in public debate.

As they entered the courthouse, Silas McDowell stepped forward and greeted them. They talked briefly and proceeded to their seats. When he mounted the platform, Sam was dignified and decorous. As was the custom, he shook hands with his adversary, and they drew lots to determine the first speaker. It fell to Carson to launch the campaign, and he reviewed the legislation he had supported in the last session.

Vance followed in a brief reply, observing that he took no exception to his opponent's voting record except for one instance. "I note that my competitor was careful not to mention that he voted away $25,000 of the people's money to the City of Alexandria."

Carson replied, explaining that the City of Alexandria had suffered severe destruction by fire and thousands of its citizens were homeless. "I did what each one of you would have done. I voted for their relief $25,000, and if my competitor had been in my place, he would have done as I did, and the reason I make that statement is I know he has a heart." Carson took his seat amid loud demonstrations of applause. This confused Vance, and his friends looked grieved and crestfallen, albeit he rallied quickly with the retort, "Yes, Gentlemen, Mr. Carson was correct in saying he was impelled to vote away $25,000 of your money, but if you can admire, as some of you seem to, a prompter who sends a man's benevolent hand into some other man's pocket than his own, all I can say is—I can't."

Carson's face was flushed, and it was evident that he was making an effort to control himself when he rose to reply. His words were slow and measured. "Gentlemen, I am glad that some of you know me and can say whether or not I would likely put my hand into another man's pocket save my own. My former friend, Doctor Vance, has told you by implication that I

117

would. I must confess that I am deeply mortified that such an accusation comes from him, and until he retracts the charge, we can be friends no longer, tho since boyhood I have looked upon him as one of my truest friends.

"I have not the slightest word to say against any vote he cast when he represented you in Congress. All I have to say about him is this: he is lacking in justice to me, and in his charge against my Alexandria vote there is bold-faced inconsistency."

"Inconsistency in what?" demanded Vance.

"In finding fault with my vote of $25,000 to the sufferers in Alexandria when you, as a representative, voted $250,000 to General LaFayette, besides many townships of land."

This brought the doctor promptly to his feet, and pointing derisively at Carson, and with a sneer, he said, "That demagogue who objects to my vote in favor of the LaFayette appropriation, I don't envy him his feelings, and I don't see how any gentleman can."

Carson replied, "Doctor Vance, if you were not such a diminutive dwarf I would bring you to account for your vile utterance."

"You are a coward and fear to do it," returned Vance.

The battle of words ended here, and the meeting was adjourned, a disappointment to a few who expected the heat of debate to start a conflagration. Very little was said on the way back to Pleasant Gardens—the Carsons realizing that the injured member of the family was stunned at the charges leveled against him.

Vance and his cohorts met before they left the building to plan their strategy. The consensus was that Carson was indeed a coward, and the suggestion was made that Vance insult Carson so damagingly that, as a man of honor, he would be forced to leave the District.

"But how?" inquired Vance. "The avenues of legitimate insults are few in this case."

Someone suggested that he attack the character of Carson's father. One of the old-timers remembered having heard a floating rumor that might serve the purpose. They agreed to proceed on that flimsy premise, but to guard well the secret of their strategy.

118

Silas McDowell had been excluded from the clandestine meeting but the winds of chicanery blew near enough for him to have an idea what was going on. The candidates were to meet for the second and last time in the courthouse at Morganton, and McDowell accepted Vance's invitation to accompany him to the contest, and exerted all of his powers to dissuade Vance from making an attack on Colonel Carson, plainly asserting that if he did, Vance's life would be at stake. McDowell insisted that young Carson was anything else but a coward, but Vance laughed at the reference to Carson's bravery.

Nor was Vance's competitor without friends and relatives who would have proffered advice, but Sam allowed it to be known that he wished to finish what had been started in his own way. He did not need to go out of his way to invite them to be on hand as silent supporters when the two adversaries met in Morganton. They were there, as were Vance's supporters, in impressive numbers. Only those who came early were able to crowd into the courtroom. Again it fell to Carson's lot to speak first. He carefully avoided any reference to Vance, though he spoke for nearly two hours and held the rapt attention of the crowd.

Vance followed in a short address, pungent, venomous, and substantially in these words: "Gentlemen, our Bible tells us that because the fathers have eaten sour grapes, the sons' teeth have been set on edge. This is a Bible doctrine, and I am not here to say whether it is right or wrong. I can only say that my father never ate sour grapes, and my competitor's father did. In the time of the Revolution, my father stood up to fight, while my competitor's father skulked and took British protection."

All of Carson's brothers were in the room, and without hesitation they rushed toward the platform as though they would attack the speaker, when prominent citizens restrained them, and the excitement died down.

As they were leaving the courthouse, Silas McDowell stopped for a word with Colonel John. They talked earnestly in subdued tones, and while they were thus engaged, Abner Burgin came up to Sam, who was standing with his brothers on the lawn.

"Samuel, you had bad dealings today. I can't see what possessed Vance to lose his bearings like he did. Why, you were the one most responsible for his winning his seat in Congress before."

"It won't be long now, Mr. Burgin, and we must just hope that the best man wins. How are your folks, sir?"

"As usual, Samuel. We are looking for the Crocketts next month—as soon as the Tennessee elections are over."

"I have been so much on the run in my own campaign, I have not had time to read up on the campaigns elsewhere. Does David write very much about his prospects?"

"David doesn't write, but my wife hears from her sister pretty regular. Elizabeth says that David thinks the campaign is just another bear hunt, and as long as he has Betsy and nobody gets in his way he can stand a fair to middlin' chance to bring down one—maybe both of his competitors. He figures he can cripple them some—if he can't put them out of commission."

The boys laughed and Doctor John asked, "Who are his competitors?"

"Well, let me see, David carries on so much foolishness I'm not sure that Elizabeth knows, but from what I gather they are General William Arnold—a right smart educated man, and the one who is now their representative, Colonel Adam Alexander. Don't see how David has much chance against them, now do you, Samuel?"

"That's a contingency I'd rather not bet on, Mr. Burgin, but I'll tell you that I will be disappointed if he is not elected. Now be sure to let me know how things come out. You'll likely get the word before it gets to the papers."

"I'll make sure you get the word, Samuel, and I'll bring David to see you as soon as he gets here."

Silas McDowell and Vance were lodged at the same boarding house, and after returning from the Morganton courthouse where Vance made his insulting charge about Colonel Carson's conduct at the time of the War of Independence, McDowell spoke in the most serious manner to Vance. "Doctor, you have this day sounded the knell over your grave or Carson's—perhaps both." To which Vance replied, "You are mistaken. There is no fight in Carson. I wish he would fight and kill me. Do you know why? My life has no future prospect. All before me is deep, dark gloom. My way to Congress is being closed forever, and I

120

shudder to think of being thrown back on my former resources. I have no wish to kill Carson, nor to injure him. This you must believe, McDowell."

The next morning at breakfast at the Carson home, last-minute voting plans were discussed. It was agreed that by this time the only votes that would be switched were those that would be bartered to the highest bidder, and Carson wanted no part of that. He was sure that Doctor Vance would not be a party to such irregularity, but neither was sure of what their henchmen might do—in a pinch.

All in the Carson home were thankful when election day dawned fair but sultry. It was reported that the crowds that milled around the courthouses at Asheville, Rutherfordton, and Morganton, presented the usual election day appearance. In the early morning they were sober, orderly and well-behaved, but as the heat of the day intensified, so did the unkempt appearance of the motley, perspiring crew, and they were less restrained in their behavior. Toward sunset the fighting and swearing tapered off, and the stragglers left the polls. It took three days to assemble and count the ballots and declare the election, which was done at Morganton.

The news of Carson's victory—three to one—over Vance was brought to Pleasant Gardens by one of the McDowell cousins. Ordinarily an occasion for rejoicing and celebrating, the victory had a hollow ring. After grasping his son's hand in hurried congratulation, Colonel Carson rode from the house in the direction of Asheville. He had some days since penned a fiery letter to Vance—ill-natured and abusive, according to those who later read it. He was determined to personally start it on its way. When he returned he reported his mission to his already-suspicious family, most, but not all of whom approved his action. "Sam has won, Father. We ought to let it go at that," suggested William.

Colonel Carson stood in the midst of his family. His voice trembled and he was visibly shaken as he replied as calmly as the circumstances allowed, "This is my decision, William, and I have not acted without due consideration. I have been thinking it over since that nefarious rascal condemned me at Morganton. An unfounded accusation of disloyalty to one's country at any time is reprehensible, but being charged with being a traitor in time of war is damnable, and I will never tolerate it!" They had not realized until now how deep were the wounds Vance had inflicted on their father.

The note had been sent by an express from Old Fort, and by express the reply was received: "Colonel Carson, I will have no altercation with a man of your age, and if I have aggrieved you, you certainly have some of your chivalrous sons that will protect you from insult." The note was dated September 6, 1827.

When Colonel Carson was deliberating on the manner in which he would call Doctor Vance to account, he fully recognized the possibility of a fateful outcome. In his note he had given Vance an opportunity to reply with a retraction of his charges. Now that he had refused the opportunity there seemed only one course open to any man of honor, and this he announced to his sons. "I intend to proceed personally with a challenge to Doctor Vance," the old man declared, but the sons overruled him instantly and emphatically.

They were in the midst of this serious contemplation when Captain Alney Burgin was announced. He was welcomed as a friend of the family, and as a close associate of Sam Carson. They had served from the same district in the State Legislature of 1824—he as a member of the House of Commons and Carson as Senator. "I have come to offer my services in whatever capacity I am needed, my friends. It would seem that the Doctor is bent on forcing a challenge."

Colonel John spoke, expressing appreciation for the offer of assistance. "We may very well need it. The boys and I have been weighing this matter seriously, and the decision is that Sam will challenge Vance, and if he falls, each one of the brothers in turn, beginning with Joseph, will challenge, and if they all fall in defense of their honor, then I will make a last attempt to wipe out the insult. They will have it no other way."

"The marksmanship of the Carson men is well known," replied Burgin, "but Sam, you are out of practice—why you haven't even been bird hunting in years, have you?"

Carson's face was drawn. He looked as if he had not slept for weeks. "That's right, I have had other pursuits demanding my time and attention, Alney. But we have discussed that contingency—not only for my sake but for the Doctor's as well. I doubt if he can hit the bull's eye, either."

"So I have suggested, and the others agree," said Joseph, "that if the challenge is accepted all parties concerned have a period of three weeks to make essential preparation—a time that seems very short in view of the possible consequences."

For a time the men sat in silence. It was as though the awful finality of events had just struck home. Sam broke the silence. "Realizing that there was no time to lose, I have sent an express to my friend, Warren Davis, a man thoroughly conversant with the *code duello*. I have asked him to come to Pleasant Gardens and refresh me somewhat on some of the techniques and to otherwise oversee my training. And I should like to have you as my second, Alney."

It was almost as if a charge of gunpowder had exploded in Alney's face, but he had made his offer of assistance in good faith, and could do nothing less than meet his friend's request.

"Could we ask another mission of you? I have made a rough draft of the challenge. I will copy it at once. Will you deliver it to Vance, ascertaining before presenting it if I am the 'chivalrous son' he alluded to in his note to Father; if so, hand him the challenge."

August 12th 1788

Sir

When a mans feelings & charector are injured he ought to seek a speedy redress: you Rec: a few lines from me yesterday & undoubtedly you understand me my charector you have injured: and further you have Insulted me in the presence of a court and a large audiance I therefore call upon you as a gentleman to give me satisfaction for the same: and I further call upon you to give me an answer immediately without Equivocation. And I hope you can do it without dinner untill the business done: for it is consistant with the charector of a gentleman when he Injures a man to make a speedy reparation: therefore I hope you will not fail in meeting me this day from yr oft &c.

Andw Jackson.

Coll. Avery

PS This Evening after court. adjourned.

FIVE

It was on the afternoon of the thirteenth that General Burgin confronted Vance with the question, "Which one of Colonel Carson's sons did you allude to in your letter to him?"

Doctor Vance did not hesitate. "Sam knows well enough that I meant him." And so the challenge was delivered and accepted. "And you may tell Sam that my second will be Franklin Patton and my surgeon Dr. George Phillips."

As he rode back to Pleasant Gardens with Vance's acceptance and with the sobering thought that he had let himself become involved in what undoubtedly would mean tragedy for one or the other party, Alney Burgin had time to think on the deplorable concept of honor that was held dearer than a life. It was true that duelling was widespread through the South, and the North had not escaped. It was more or less a gentleman's game, resorted to largely by professional men and politicians. The quarrels of lesser lights were satisfied with the good old "fist and skull" method, seldom fatal to either party, and requiring no rules and no paraphernalia.

Burgin knew Carson's kindness and gentleness of nature had enabled him to be willing to endure the taunts of his accusers; that Vance and his cohorts had every reason to charge that "there was no fight in him" when he refused to challenge Vance immediately upon being called a coward. Men of high rank and high position seemed insensitive to the twisted sense of honor that demanded redress by such means. It was none other than Andrew Jackson who wrote to his one-time friend and associate, a native of Burke County, "When a man's feelings and character are injured, he ought to seek a speedy redress . . . My character you have injured, and further you insulted me in the presence of a court and a large audience. I therefore call upon you to give me satisfaction for same, and I hope you can do without dinner until the business is done."

Jackson's antagonist was a Presbyterian, whose forebears were Puritans, and he was opposed to duelling on principle. But he so far yielded to the imperious custom of the times as to accept the challenge and repair to the field of honor, where he allowed Jackson to shoot at him but did not return the fire. Their altercation began during the progress of a lawsuit in Jonesboro when the two men were on opposing sides. Jackson's anger flared at some point in the proceedings, and sitting down he wrote the challenge on a page of his law book and, tearing it out, handed it immediately to his associate. Now, having satisfied Jackson that he was not afraid to die, Waightstill Avery, Attorney General of North Carolina, walked up to the younger man and delivered a lecture much as a father would counsel his son. In spite of this, Jackson's quick temper would again place him in a similar situation.

Vance's acceptance of the challenge was expected. After delivering it to Carson in person, Burgin stayed at the Carson home long enough to hear final instructions. Joseph, the oldest son, reminded them that every precaution had been and would be taken to conduct the affair within the legal confines of North Carolina law. "Since it is illegal to permit a duel to be fought on North Carolina soil, the challenge stipulated the procedure which will insure absolute legality. It will be fought on neutral ground, and the determination is that it will be fought at the Saluda Gap on the South Carolina turnpike."

During the interchange of statements Sam Carson sat, impassive. Those who knew him best noted that he had been perceptibly ashen in contrast to his usually florid complexion, but no word escaped his lips to indicate that he was frightened or apprehensive.

During the ten days he had been at Pleasant Gardens, Warren Davis had discussed with the Carson men the provisions of the *code duello*, especially the provision that prohibited members of the family from witnessing a duel, although it was customary for either principal to invite friends. "The seconds," he said, "are charged with the responsibility of making every attempt at reconciliation, but you have satisfied me that every reasonable effort has already been made. Another stipulation is that the seconds are required to load the pistols in the presence of each other."

One or two preliminary rehearsals with the brothers substituting for the other principals satisfied Davis that there would be no bungling of the pseudo-military precision of the procedure, and it was on the last practice that Captain Alney Burgin was on hand to take his position as second to Carson. After they had finished, Burgin called Carson to one side. "You know, Samuel, that I do not want a hitch in this affair, and I think you are making a mistake not to have Congressman Davis as your second. He is skilled in the *code duello*, and he is as anxious as I that you have every advantage."

"Let's think about it until tomorrow, Alney," suggested Sam.

The three weeks' armistice had extended itself through October and into November. At breakfast on the morning before the duel, the Carson family appeared to show no outward emotional strain. Instead they seemed bent on showing their guest every consideration of hospitality. They did not mention the impending event, but entered into a lively discussion about the political shenanigans of one David Crockett, then visiting at the home of his brother-in-law, Abner Burgin, just twenty miles away.

"You know, Mr. Davis, we speculated last summer on David's chances of being elected to the House of Representatives when Abner told us that David might throw his coonskin cap into the ring."

"I remember quite well, Logan."

"And now the talk is that he will represent more voters than almost any other congressman because they are enlarging his District. It stumps me how he got himself elected."

"Well, that election, my son, will probably go down in history as a tall-tale victory."

"You see, Mr. Davis," continued Colonel Carson, "Abner tells us that one of David's opponents, like the opponents of Jackson, attacked him unmercifully on grounds of incompetence, illiteracy and indecency. For every attack that was made David manufactured a more dastardly charge about his competitor. He put on such a show that the crowds clamored for more, and he received such an ovation that this early opponent withdrew from the race, saying that he would under no circumstances represent people who would applaud such a liar."

"It would seem that he resorted to his native wit and his uncanny knowledge of human nature, and wherever he spoke he so captivated his backwoods audiences that his popularity was manifested at the polls. And now," laughed Colonel John, "David is no longer Commodore Crockett, but Congressman Crockett of the Ninth Tennessee District."

Colonel John continued, "As soon as the election was over and his victory assured, Crockett started with his family to the home of his wife in Swannanoa, but on the way, according to Abner, he took down with a 'billes fevere' and has been prone on his back for weeks. He is almost recovered and ready to 'stand up to the rack,' as he puts it, and Abner has sent word that he and David will be with Sam on the fateful tomorrow."

Doctor John interrupted to say that Sam had considered asking David to act as his second, but because Crockett had introduced a legislative bill to outlaw duelling in Tennessee, it would not be fitting for him to participate, "although if he is recovered he will probably be on hand tomorrow."

"I shall be pleased indeed to meet this man who shows signs of becoming a legend in these parts," said Davis.

There was no tearful farewell when the horses and conveyances were brought to the door after breakfast; only old Eben, holding Colonel John's mount, was seen to bring out his bandana for surreptitious use. The others—Eli, Becky, Binah and a dozen or more like them were near enough to give silent encouragement and support to their beloved "Mister Sam." At the suggestion of his kinsman, Davis had come to Pleasant Gardens in Calhoun's carriage, bearing the Vice President's expression of esteem and concern, and in it they started out on their fateful journey.

As they left the grounds and came into the public road, Davis turned his horses left toward Asheville, and Colonel John, with a brave salute, turned right. He had not indicated to his family what his errand was; they suspected he would be busy about something—anything that would take away the anguish of his heart, an emotion that up to this point had been skillfully concealed.

For a long interval Sam did not speak. He knew that his friend sensed his need for reflection, and he thought how fortunate he was that these difficult hours could be shared with someone who understood him and who could almost read his thoughts. It was not until they turned south toward Greenville that Sam broke the silence. "Davis, I have been thinking that it was a lucky day for me when Missy's ill fortune started us on a chain of circumstances that have brought about this Damon and Pythias relationship. You have always sensed my moods—I am sure that you do now, as we go together to this ill-starred event." Carson did not wait for comment, but continued, "I have been thinking I would like for you to act as my second. Alney will be so greatly relieved. I am sure you have sensed that only his loyalty and his offer of help have enabled him to go this far."

There was something in Carson's pleading expression that stirred the heart of his friend. Davis agreed, and Carson's relief was undisguised.

The fateful day dawned cold and crisp and fair. They had four or five miles to drive from their overnight stop. When they reached the scene there were fewer than two dozen on hand, and that was the first thing to be thankful for.

As Carson stepped from the conveyance he noted that Doctor Phillips and Doctor Shufflin were already preparing bandages and sorting supplies. He hoped there would be no delay, lest he become unnerved. He avoided looking directly at Robert Vance, who stood about fifty feet away, surrounded by his friends. Instead he turned to Alney Burgin to release him from acting as his second.

As Captain Burgin and Vance's second were marking off the paces and positions for each principal, Carson spoke to Davis. "You know I can hit the Doctor where I choose, but I do not wish to inflict a fatal wound. I can graze him, and that is what I prefer."

Davis wheeled around in astonishment. Looking Carson straight in the eye he said, "Unless you shoot to kill Vance, I will have no part in this affair. If he receives only a superficial wound, Vance will demand another chance to kill you. He does not intend to spare you—of that I am certain."

In the end reason prevailed and Sam said, "Let's get it over, Davis."

Doctor Vance's second came up and with Davis began the exchange and examination of the duelling pistols. While thus engaged, two men on horseback, riding furiously reined in when they reached the scene. Securing their mounts, they approached Carson and the three were seen in close conversation for a short while. Abner Burgin and David Crockett had made good their promise to be present in support of their friend.

"Samuel, I have been rasslin' all of the varmints in tarnashun, and I made sure my time had come. I never knew I could have such an enemy as this 'billes fevere.' I musta' bin lef for a purpose, an maybe it was to help you today. Mighty late showin' my colors, but here I am! What kin I do?"

"Not a thing, David, unless you take the word back to Pleasant Gardens. You can do it faster than anyone I know. It won't be good news no matter what happens, but they will be mighty anxious to hear."

"I'll sure do it, Samuel. You can bet your last continental I'll ride like Jehu—and Samuel, the news I take back will be good news for them. Understand?"

A shrill whistle interrupted the talk and the principals took their stations. Only briefly did Carson look directly into Vance's eyes—without evidence of malice, he hoped, for he felt none.

Suddenly Doctor Vance held up his hand for a reprieve, and a hush fell over the spectators. Had he suffered last-minute qualms? It was a tense moment for all concerned. Reaching in his pocket, he took his watch and handing it to Franklin Patton, Vance requested, "Give this to my friend, David Swain— if the worst happens." Franklin noticed that Doctor Vance's hand trembled ever so slightly as he placed the watch in his hand. Vance and Swain had been classmates at the Newton Academy in Asheville, and were fast friends.

The principals again took their positions, back to back. Davis gave the instructions. At the signal the combatants were to reverse their positions, walk ten paces and at the command, "Fire—one—two—three," should proceed, using the rising or the falling pistols, as each had chosen.

Carson chose the falling and Vance the rising position. Neither showed outward sign of agitation or trepidation, as they waited in an agony of suspense for the word of command. At the signal word, Carson fired, the bullet striking Vance, and he slumped forward.

The color drained from Carson's face as he rushed toward Vance, saying, "The Doctor is hit." Whereupon Davis seized Carson by the shoulders, turning him around just as Vance's surgeon and second caught the victim and lowered him to the ground, but not before Vance gave Carson a look of incredible kindness.

"He has lost consciousness," said Doctor Phillips, "but he may revive."

In a few minutes, Vance regained consciousness, and at Carson's request, Captain Alney Burgin was at his side. "Doctor," he reported, "Carson tried to speak to you just as you fainted, but was led away."

The doctor spoke haltingly, and in apparent great pain. "Oh, I'm so sorry . . . they did not let me . . . speak to Sam. Poor Sam . . . I do not have . . . the first unkind feeling . . . for him."

Captain Burgin observed, "Well, Doctor, you have fallen on the field of honor."

"Yes, Alney . . . just where . . . I have . . . wished to die." Then he lapsed into semi-consciousness, as his second and surgeon lifted him from the ground and removed him to a nearby residence on the road to Asheville, where he died the following day. His last words, whispered faintly, were, "Out, out brief candle."

It had been a long day at Carson House—a long, long day for November. About two o'clock Colonel John came in and went immediately to his room without speaking, except to say, "Call me when there's any news."

On a clear day in winter, when the trees are bereft of foliage, one could see from the upstairs porch an approaching vehicle at least a mile away, and in the late afternoon the family took turns watching for a courier. At length old Binah shouted, "Come on folks—they's a' comin, leastways I see a rider comin'—comin' mighty fas. Oh Jesus, Jesus, let it be po' Mister Sam!" And in the same breath, "He's sho' layin it on to that horse, whoever he is."

131

David Crockett turned into the grounds at high speed, waving his hat in the air and shouting, "The victory is ours! The victory is ours!"

Without a thought of decorum, the Carson family, their friends and relatives, emptied the house in a split second. They surrounded the breathless courier, and would not allow him to dismount until the day's events had been recited.

Just before retiring, and after they had seen Crockett off on a fresh horse, the visibly relieved Carsons discussed the events of the day. Colonel John tried not to appear jubilant as he reported bits of the private conversation he had had with David as he took his leave. "Mr. Davis thought it best to go back to Pendleton direct from Saluda on the turnpike, and Sam is to spend the night with Alney or Abner, Crockett could not remember which one. With all he has gone through this day, it is too much to expect that Sam can return to Pleasant Gardens tonight. That's why I sent Missy with Crockett."

"What else did David say?" questioned Logan.

"He hopes that he and Sam can go on to Washington City together. His original plan had been to go back home first, but his bout with the 'billes fevere', had shortened his time and his patience, and he plans to send the family back to Tennessee under John Wesley's 'protectin' keer.' "

"I suppose John Wesley is big enough and man enough to look after his mother and the children. I haven't seen him lately," observed William.

"He's past twenty, and 'he's a strappin' feller and feared of nothin', so David says. Elizabeth will fare all right," Colonel John replied. They were all agreed that it would be a fine thing to have David accompany Sam to "the City." He would be the very medicine Sam would need.

And so it came about that as the lengthening shadows deepened into darkness on a cold and biting evening in early December, 1827, two weary travelers dismounted at the National Hotel, signed the guest register, and were shown to their rooms. The journey had been long and arduous for Carson, who was unable to put from his mind the events of that black day when he faced his friend on the "field of honor." For David, who made frequent attempts to enliven the journey and to distract his friend, every mile they took brought him nearer and nearer to the fulfillment of his cherished desire to become a part of the Federal government, and he was in fine fettle.

Both Carson and Crockett answered roll call on the opening day of the first meeting of the Twentieth Congress, and Carson was pleased that the election of a Speaker elevated Andrew Stevenson, of Virginia, to this honorable position. Among the new faces was that of the successor to the late Doctor Young— Mr. Chilton, of Kentucky, who was to become an active protagonist in debate and procedure, and with whom Crockett was to become intimately associated.

Meantime, back in North Carolina, conventions were being called for the promotion of one or the other of the Presidential candidates, as indeed similar meetings were convened in other states. These national conventions were, in the strictest sense of the word, regional or state conventions, called to promote a national ticket, and as usual there was much speculation on the outcome—with vote-swapping, voluble haranguing and side-betting to enliven the proceedings. Generally speaking, the women saw "their men" off to the county seat or other designated polling places without a thought of their personal participation in anything so degrading as "politics." They were interested in the outcome only as it affected the whims and personal fortunes of "their men."

Press reports seemed to indicate that John Quincy Adams, the incumbent, would be the favorite of the majority of the voters, and this was disturbing to Carson, whose allegiance to the gentleman from the Hermitage was so well established that his close friends jestingly referred to him as "Young Hickory." They were discussing this one evening when he and Davis and Crockett were in the home of Senator John Branch. "If the convention held in Raleigh two weeks ago is any indication of the sentiment of the majority of the voters in the South, then our candidate from the Hermitage will have rough sledding," Sam predicted. "As you know, the delegates lost no time in framing an electoral ticket for Adams, whose qualities of states-manship, they proclaimed, far surpass the military achievements of Jackson as qualifications for the high office of President of the United States. I suppose, Davis, no South Carolina journal

133

would be caught red-handed in such seditious outpourings as filled the columns of my state papers reporting this convention."

"With one or two exceptions, South Carolina conventions will support Jackson, certainly the Pendleton district will."

"And there's no use to ask you, Mr. Crockett, where Tennessee stands," Branch observed.

"All I kin say is the Adamses had better pack their belongins' and start headin' for home."

On or about January 4, Sam settled himself for a long past-due letter home.

Dear Family,

Last Tuesday, the first day of the year, was exceedingly propitious for the enjoyment of the promenade and the exchange of the compliments of the season.

As usual, the President's house was thrown open for the visits and salutations of his friends and fellow citizens. Davis had asked me to accompany him to the annual New Year festivities, but having so recently on the floor of the House expressed my disapprobation of the manner in which the President has handled certain fiscal affairs (and in my enthusiasm having been reprimanded by the Chair), I declined the invitation of my friend and of the President.

Davis reported to me as we were dining that evening that Vice President Calhoun was there, as were most of the senators and representatives, the heads of departments, etc., etc. There was also a respectable showing of the average citizen—gentlemen with their families or their ladies—all enjoying the hospitality of the White House, the while being enlivened by the Marine Band.

Since you, Father, have access to *The Intelligencer* and the state papers, I will not be repetitious, and will write only briefly of the issues that are being debated.

Before us now is the perennial tariff question, which almost certainly will not be resolved this session; indeed President Adams in his State of the Union pronouncements, omitted any reference to tariffs and imports, for which he has been roundly criticized.

Nor will the matter of retrenchment, introduced last month by the newcomer from Kentucky, Mr. Chilton. As is customary, everyone wants to cut the salary of the "other fellow" and prune expenditures outside his own baliwick. This is a subject on which I may yet take the floor to air my convictions.

The other matter on which debate is begun is my own bill for a satisfactory adjustment of Cherokee lands—a matter, you will recall, on which I was instructed to act by the Legislature of North Carolina.

The ladies will be interested in Crockett's reception in the Congress and elsewhere. Already he has demonstrated that he is not the uncouth, unlearned backwoodsman that many believed him to be. He has a certain naive charm that throws his opponents offguard, but with it he is "as stubborn as a Kentucky mule." He knows what he wants for his District, and he says he "will spit on his hands an' plow a straight row till he gits it." He is not overcome or awed by the dress and manners of "the top layer," as he calls them. He has associated with fine folk before.

It is too early to make a prediction for the finish, but he is holding his own in the first heat—"standing up to the rack," as he says he fully intends to do—the rack in this instance being the machine back home and any who may oppose his measures here and who try to prevent him from "layin' it on the line" for his cherished constituents.

Mr. Webster arrived only the day before yesterday. He came by land, having been detained because of sickness. He reported that the roads were in terrible condition, in some instances so bad that they were obliged to procure a team of oxen and drag the stage out of the mud. The foregoing with reference to Mr. Webster is corridor gossip. So far I know the gentleman from Massachusetts only by sight, but I respect his ability, and up to this point his fair-mindedness, and I shall hope to know him better as time goes on.

My great annoyance is that I do not have time to read the accumulation of state papers, and my great concern is the apparent enthusiasm in North Carolina for the Administration. What can be done to turn the tide in favor of *our* candidate?

It would please me very much if you, Father, or John or William or Logan would keep me advised about North Carolina and the Presidential prospects. From my limited reading of the North Carolina news, there are more active Federalists in North Carolina than I imagined—either that or the "antis" are holding their fire.

I did not write at length about our journey to the Capital City. As you have probably anticipated, it was a godsend to have Crockett with me.

We really suffered with the cold. "Horseback riding in winter is fer tougher hides than yours, Samuel," was David's pronouncement on the second day out. I was concerned lest he have a backset and would have to be laid up at some farmhouse on the way.

The boys will be interested in this: one afternoon when we were almost frozen, David suggested that we "strike a blaze and thaw out." We piled some brush together and he took out his flint and steel. It was then I brought out my new Congress matches that I had been hoarding, drew one through a fold of sandpaper, and *voila*, I had a light! Crockett was amazed and delighted at this demonstration. He had heard of the brimstone match, but this 1827 model—a tip of potash and sulphur at the end of a splinter stick—was new and fantastic. If he had had his way I would have exhausted my supply then and there.

We stayed to enjoy the fire for a while, and I encouraged David to tell me about his election, and he gave me this account.

Being at one of the Hustings and hearing one of his opponents speak, it seems he asked how to get the attention of the crowd. One of them told him to mount a stump and cry, "A bear to be skinned!"

David took his friendly enemy seriously and mounted the stump, but I will let him take it from there.

"And so I got up on the stump and cried in a loud voice, 'A b'ar to be skint!' An' when the crowd gathered aroun' I seen my chanct and I said, 'Feller citizens, friends, brothers an' sisters. On the first Tuesday of next month you will be called on to perform one of the most important duties that belongs to free white folks. On that day you will be called on to elect your members of the Senate an' your members of Congress. And feelin' that in times of political commotion like this it becomes you to be well reprisinted, I feel no hesitation in offerin' myself as your candidate to reprisint such an onerable, high-minded and magnanimous free white set.

" 'Friends, feller citizens, brothers and sisters. Carroll's a statesman, Jackson's a hero and Crockett's a mule's cousin. They accuse me of adultery; it is a lie. I never ran away with no man's wife who wasn't willing. They accuse me of gambling; that is a lie, for I always planks down the cash. They accuse me of being a drunkard, and that's a d—d eternal lie, for it is well known that whisky can't make me drunk.' "

It was evident that David enjoyed the tale as he told it, but whether or not there was a word of truth in it, you must be the judge. It provided a refreshing interlude, anyway.

Space permitting, I would send my deep affection to each of my sisters and my brothers, my cousins and my aunts by name, and to all the retinue—Binah, Becky, Eben, Eli and the rest, but I must be content just to sign myself

Y'r hum'bl & obd't servant
S.P.C.

P.S. I am convinced that there is no political chicanery so base as that which seeks to destroy the character and reputation of another in order to advance the prospects of the candidate it promotes, especially when the abused is a lady. Of course you know I refer to Mrs. Jackson and the diabolical rumors started last year, and even now growing in intensity.

Washington, D.C.
January, 1828

The letter-writing had consumed all of Carson's spare time

during three consecutive evenings. Now finished, he folded, addressed and mailed it the following day—a letter received with much rejoicing and intense relief by his family.

From time to time during the remainder of the session, Carson heard from his father and brothers, reporting on General Jackson's prospects in Western North Carolina and over the state. Carson's half-brother, Doctor John, was the one most interested in the issues at stake, or it may have seemed so because he wrote more often and was more vehement in his stand on these issues.

On May 6, the House again considered Carson's bill to reimburse the State of North Carolina in the amount of $22,000—the amount expended by her in extinguishing the title to certain Indian lands in the Cherokee reservations within the state—the same land that was granted to them in fee simple by treaties with the United States in 1817 and 1819. When Carson rose to address the Assembly he reminded them that the bill in question had been introduced in January, had been voted on affirmatively by the Senate and negatively by the House, and now in amended form was being presented to the House for reconsideration.

"In the earlier argument," Carson reminded them, "the most prominent objection voiced by Mr. Clark of Kentucky was that, 'If we pass this claim, it will be a precedent by which other states can come in, and with equal justice demand similar remuneration from the Government.' No state in the Union has such claims upon the government as North Carolina, except Georgia. Our claims are founded on these reasons: during our Revolutionary struggle, the Cherokees seized that opportunity to wage war on the frontier settlements of North Carolina. That state, at her own expense, subdued them. Sometime in '77 or '78 a treaty was held by commissioners representing the sovereign state of North Carolina with that tribe of Indians on the Holston River. One of the commissioners was that able gentleman, Weightstill Avery, among whose papers the original treaty may no doubt be found. It was held in effect until 1785, when the government enacted a measure called the Hopewell Treaty by which North Carolina extinguished the Indian title to all of the lands within her limits, but permitted the Indians to hold as hunting grounds certain portions of the country

137

described in the treaty. North Carolina assumed control of these lands and sold to her citizens considerable quantities of the same."

Those in the Assembly possessing legal minds and legal talents could well recognize here the maze of complications and controversy that could and did arise from these loosely-defined arrangements.

Carson went on to show the further steps by which North Carolina had been discriminated against by the then Confederated Government. "What did the government do? Why, sir, in the year 1785 she extends her paternal care over the Indians, takes them from the guardianship and control of North Carolina, and expressly prohibits them from holding treaties with any power on earth save herself. What is more, the government retrocedes to the Indians the very lands which they previously ceded to North Carolina. Not content, Mr. Speaker, with giving away our lands, she was graciously pleased in Article V of the Treaty of Hopewell to empower the Indians to cut our throats or otherwise treat our citizens who dare cross within their borders or to disturb their rights in any way.

"I repeat, Mr. Speaker, no state in the Union has been treated in the same unjust manner by the government, nor has any state in the Union acted with more loyalty or dealt with more liberality toward the government. North Carolina, sir, ceded to the general government not lands to which she had no title, but to which she had a *bona fide*, undoubted and unquestioned right—and that cession includes not only what is now the state of Tennessee, but its entire Western limits as bounded by the Pacific Ocean. It is clearly manifest, Mr. Speaker, that the great object which North Carolina had in view in parting with her Western lands was the extinguishment of the public debt contracted in our Revolutionary struggle, and I refer you in this regard to the Preamble of the Act of Cession.

"And here I might pause, Mr. Speaker, to pay a just compliment to my state for her liberality, her magnanimity and loyalty to this government. Although this act of hers—this cession of her Western lands to the government—must remain as a monument to her credit, while this Union exists or the name of Tennessee is remembered, I would to God, sir, that this monument to her had never been erected, and that this act had never appeared on our statute books. Then could North Carolina have reared her head among the proudest of her sister states. Then, sir, would her influence and her weight have been felt, and instead of having assigned her to the humble position as a follower, she would have proudly led the van."

There was no doubt that had North Carolina held title to her Western lands, which she could rightfully claim, she would have held a commanding place in the affairs of the nation. That Carson lost no opportunity to enhance the prospects of General Jackson for the Presidency was manifest in his closing remarks. "Let it be understood by my friends from Tennessee that I wish no injury to that state. Far from it. While I regret that the parent state has parted with the dominion and soil of that desirable region, yet North Carolina does and will always feel a just pride in the recognition of the State of Tennessee as her daughter, and at the same time, sir, we must be permitted all of the gratification and pleasure which a parent can derive from seeing her offspring the belle of the Union. And permit me to hope, sir, that the Old State will be pardoned for the part she must act, and the pride she must feel in seeing the favorite son of a favorite daughter elevated to the first office in the gift of the Nation."

Despite the length and complications of Carson's presentation, he had been accorded respectful attention, but with the injection of this partisan allusion to Jackson, there was noticeable unrest and whispered comment among the lawmakers, which was quickly subdued by the Speaker's gavel. Nevertheless the skillfully-presented claims of this native son were rewarded when the vote was tabulated showing a clear majority in favor of a reimbursement to the state of North Carolina.

During the month of May there were many warm days conducive to outside interests and enjoyment, but Carson had little time for such pursuits. His committee assignments kept him busy, and in the spare time he had he worked on the Circular Letter that he intended to mail to his Western North Carolina constituents. It was addressed, "To the Freemen of the Twelfth Congressional District of North Carolina," and concerned his stands on major political controversies of the period. Carson first took the opportunity to express his dismay over rising expenditures during the Adams administration. He followed with a bitter attack upon the Tariff Bill which he, like the other Southern Congressmen, had opposed vigorously, but to no avail: in his opinion the Tariff Bill that favored Eastern industrialists would have a calamitous effect upon the South. Only the anticipated election of Andrew Jackson to the Presidency could mitigate this severe blow to the Southern economy. Other matters discussed in the Circular Letter included appropriations for the Chesapeake and Ohio Canal, which Carson opposed as being too costly. He concluded with a long quote by Henry Clay, whose impassioned, clever oratory advised voters to resist military government by withdrawing their support from the military hero, Andrew Jackson. Carson fully believed that Clay's only weapons were words, words and more words. By his skillfull use of them he sought to detract from Jackson's irreproachable reputation as a hero who had served and now was celebrated by the American people.

The letter was mailed on May 20, and on May 27 the first session of the Twentieth Congress terminated at an early hour, the two Houses having met in concert at six o'clock in the morning and adjourned after a session of two hours—long enough to receive the final notice of the signatures of bills by the President. Little other business was attempted—a meager quorum being present. Most of the members were on the road to their homes by ten o'clock.

It was not until the first days of July that Carson began to get a reaction to his Circular Letter. Some of the communications came direct to his home in Pleasant Gardens and others were forwarded from Washington. He gave careful attention to each one and noted with surprise that whereas the majority were indifferent to his analysis of the relative expenditures of the Monroe and Adams administrations, some of the more knowledgable ones took him to task for his displeasure at the increase of eight and a half million dollars for Adams's incumbency.

"Is it not a sign of growth and progress that more money was expended for legitimate causes in the last three years? If, on January first of this year, there was an estimated balance of $6,269,585.29 in the Treasury, then we are far from dissolute," observed Doctor John when these matters were discussed around the family table.

While approving of his strategy in procuring favorable acceptance of his bill on Indian Affairs, many of his constituents and members of his family objected to his vote on the appropriation for the Chesapeake and Ohio Canal.

"You show a consummate lack of faith in your Government by suggesting that this appropriation would provide an opening wedge for similar indiscriminate appropriations," was the gist of such reactions.

"Do you want to strengthen the opinion outside our boundaries that North Carolina is one of our most backward states by voting against internal improvements that will benefit most of the states and ultimately will help North Carolina?" asked his brother. "Why we're doing enough right here to give us a black eye nationally."

"What do you mean, John?"

"Are you so ill-informed that you need ask that question, Sam? Just see what they've done down at Raleigh to hold back the tides of progress! They voted down a resolution requesting that a survey be made by a corps of United States engineers of a proposed route for a railroad from Newbern through Raleigh and the central part of the State. And 'dang it! They're always complaining that North Carolina is being overlooked by the Federal Government. Then they turn around and refuse to ask aid calculated so essentially to benefit the whole state."

"Now I think——" Sam began.

"Just don't interrupt me! Do you know what these obstructionists have done to Archibald Murphy, the best informed man in North Carolina today? They have shattered his dream for a system of public education that would meet the needs of our boys—and even our girls—especially for these 'youngsters' in the Western section. Only the rich can provide an education in the home, and the very rich in this whole Western area can be counted on four hands. You know it, Sam!"

"If I may be permitted to speak, let me say that Archibald Murphy's dream may be shattered for the time being, but he has provided a frame on which to build an adequate system of education for rich and poor alike. That frame may prove useful for the future. And furthermore, since you have such strong feelings, I would think that you would run for the Legislature—do some missionary work where it will do the most good. Since you are unattached, you have more time than many others."

Provisions in the proposed program were for white children only, and girl children were to have the advantage of a primary education only. In some plantation homes limited attention was paid to the children of the slaves and their educational needs, but for the most part, they were neglected.

The subject was pursued at some length in the discussion that morning, and to illustrate the lack of prejudice on the part of the more enlightened, Carson told the tale of John Chavis—friend, counsellor and advisor to Carson's friend, Willie P. Mangum, who last year had ended his term of office as congressman from the Raleigh District, and was again taking up the role of superior court judge. It seems that Chavis, a full-blooded, freeborn Negro, had had the advantage of a superior education for that day, having been tutored under Doctor Witherspoon at Princeton, and had attended the Academy at Lexington; that he had taught many of North Carolina's most prominent citizens—the sons of Chief Justice Leonard Henderson, Archibald and John L. Henderson, and Charles Manly, Priestly Mangum and others. Although Chavis taught in many of these homes, he also had a schoool in Wake County. Carson pointed out that Chavis was a minister, licensed to preach in both North Carolina and Virginia.

"What kind of minister?" inquired Colonel John.

"A Presbyterian minister," his son replied, "and you know that Presbyterians set high standards for their men of the cloth." And he continued, "Mangum has shown me a number of letters from Chavis—all written in fatherly style—advising, criticizing and reproving, but often commending 'my son,' as he addressed Mangum and other of his youthful protégés. He was devoted to Mrs. Mangum, Willie's mother, and he was often a guest in their home."

Before the family conclave was over Sam had been strongly advised to "ride the circuit" and talk with his constituents and get a true picture of their satisfactions and dissatisfactions with his vote on the issues they had discussed, and this he did, returning just in time to make preparations for his journey to the Capital. It was when he stopped over in Lexington en route to Washington City the last week of November that he heard the good news of Jackson's election, and he verily believed that this significant event would usher in a new era in these United States, as well as to enhance his own political fortunes and interests.

Aided and encouraged by the weather and by a facilitated means of travel, the members of Congress began to converge on Federal City about the first of December. The opening session of the Twenty-first Congress convened on the seventh, and Carson noted at roll call that there was only one vacancy in the North Carolina House delegation and one in the Senate.

In the opening remarks someone ventured to compare the present Congress with the First Congress held in New York. In the Senate on the opening day of that first session, eight members only were in attendance and it was twenty-nine days before a quorum was got together, while in the House on the first day of that early Congress, only thirteen members attended and it was nineteen days before there was anyone present from New York, New Jersey, Delaware, Maryland and Georgia, and it was twenty-nine days before a quorum could be formed. Now, from the widened bounds of this extended Republic, from regions then unexplored by the white man, and from every region then under foreign sway, there assembled on the first day of the session, December 7, 1828, nine-tenths of the whole number of 264 senators, representatives and delegates, nearly half of whom traveled hither from a distance greater than that traveled by any member of the First Congress, with a few exceptions.

During the closing days of the year, the House had agreed to reconsider Carson's motion to inquire into the expediency of establishing a mint in the gold-mining region of North Carolina. Speaking to the resolution, Carson stated that since his bill was introduced, opposition to it had been brought forward by his colleague, Mr. Connor, "and it may be that he is withholding his support because of his kind feelings toward me, wishing rather to cover than to expose the defects of the bill." Carson fully intended after inquiry into Connor's objections, to pursue the matter further. How else could he serve the best interests of his constituency?

"It may be that some of my colleagues do not know that of the nine million dollars in gold coined at the mint in Philadelphia until this date, all of it was from North Carolina, and that even now we are becoming known as the 'The Golden State.' I do not speak boastfully of these matters. I call attention to them so that you may put into proper focus my intent in introducing this bill. And to make further clarification, let me point out that these are natural—not man-made resources, and it has ever been incumbent upon man to make use of the God-given resources at his hand, just as he should make use of his God-given talents in the best interests of his fellow beings.

"It is my firm belief that the establishment of a mint in the area of the gold mines, just as the securing of the Ohio Canal, will benefit the local area first, and ultimately will be of inestimable value to all of the United States."

No further action was taken at this sitting of the House, but Davis, who probably knew more about the facts presented and the integrity of the proponent than anyone, congratulated Carson on his effort and encouraged him to try again.

When David Crockett told Carson as he was about to enter the National Forum that he intended to plow a straight row until legislation favorable to his constituents was passed, the "straight row" Crockett alluded to was his determination to let nothing stand in the way of the protection of the squatters who had settled on bits and pieces of vacant land in West Tennessee, and who had built homes and begun to improve the land. Their rights were being threatened by the Vacant Land Bill which proposed that all vacant Federal land in Tennessee be relinquished by the government and sold at public auction, the proceeds to be used for education—in Tennessee, of course.

As Crockett viewed this seemingly provident issue, there were many cockleburs in it, and the ones most painfully irritated were the poor pioneers who had cleared the wilderness and claimed their rights as squatters. To this end he introduced a bill early in 1828 to prevent the encroachment of federal and state authorities on those settlers.

On April twenty-fourth of that year, Senator James Knox Polk rose to lay claim for the state of Tennessee on the vacant lands in her boundaries. The issues arising out of this seemingly meritorious action were to bring Carson and Crockett face to face in conflicts of interest, and were to severely test their friendship. As far back as April, 1806 the Congress had authorized Tennessee to proceed to locate and grant all North Carolina land warrants. And this order had not been revoked.

Carson recognized Crockett's humane intentions and weighed in the balance as against the state's practical consideration of reaping financial rewards at the expense of those with undoubted claims on the very land it would confiscate, he was inclined to side with his friend and throw the weight of his influence in favor of the hardy pioneers, who could barely eke subsistence from the poor lands and who most certainly did not have the money to repurchase what they had always thought was their own property.

Whether from expediency or unwillingness at that juncture to alienate himself from the Tennessee delegation, David had gone along with Polk until the bill was tabled in the closing days of the session, but on January 5, 1829, he proposed an amendment that indicated he had had a change of heart. From this time forth he intended to pursue legislation that would benefit the inarticulate poor in his district—regardless of party machinery, which he called "a stranglin' machine." To this end he changed his tactics. On January 5, 1829 he proposed an amendment that would give the land directly to those who occupied it, and State revenue could go hang as far as he was concerned.

Enlarging on the import of this amendment, David made one of the most powerful speeches of his career. Few could doubt his sincerity and his honesty of purpose. When the question was put on Crockett's amendment, the ensuing discussion was favorable, and noting this trend, Senator Polk attempted to salvage his amendment by lambasting Crockett for abandoning the whole Tennessee delegation and for defying the instructions of the Legislature.

At this juncture time ran out and the matter rested until January twelfth, when a member of the Tennessee delegation moved the postponement of the amendment. It was at this point that Carson rose to face his friend in opposition to the bill under consideration. He stated that if the vote had been taken on the fifth, following Crockett's able and persuasive presentation, he would have favored the amendment, but that subsequent reflection had convinced him that the passage of this measure would be a direct injury to the very persons it was intended to benefit, and that it would most certainly mitigate against the best interests of North Carolina, now holding land warrants for some of the precise tracts that his honorable friend would give to the squatters in his District.

Carson argued in this wise at great length, going into North Carolina's claims on Tennessee lands, as provided by the Act of Cession of the Confederated Government, claiming that because these were legitimate claims he would propose a further amendment—the same as Crockett's amendment, but containing the provision "that enough of these lands be reserved to satisfy yet outstanding North Carolina warrant claims."

Crockett drew laughter from the legislators when he replied that North Carolina land warrants were of a multiplying nature —they bred like rabbits—"and as far as my friend Carson's proposed amendment is concerned, I object to it! There is an abundance of good land in Tennessee—let North Carolina warrants be settled out of good land, not out of the little homesteads of the poor!"

For the time being Crockett's plea for justice and mercy for his belabored constituents met with sympathetic response, and he was later to state in his Circular Letter, "I was utterly astonished at one thing. It was while gentlemen from other states were aiding me in my humane attempt that my own friends were bending all of their powers against me. The measure met with no serious opposition with *one* exception." Though Crockett made no identification of the person who was "the one exception," he was in all probability referring to Carson.

146

But Carson's was not the only voice raised in protest. Barringer and Connor, both of North Carolina, repulsed Crockett's idle charge in terms of just indignation, and David later remarked that Mr. Connor was more terrible in a fight than any panther he had met.

Crockett's star in the legislative canopy had been in slow ascendency until this point, when it reached its greatest brilliance. Hereafter the trend would be reversed. Commenting on his many unsuccessful efforts to secure passage of his measure, a contemporary remarked that "the bill was talked to death." It was a slow death, characterized by fits and starts, though continually shepherded by the redoubtable Crockett, who seemed to thrive on discouragement.

Toward the latter part of January word reached Washington that the President-elect had left Tennessee and was expected to arrive in the City about the fifth of February. "The death of his amiable lady," the announcement stated, "has occasioned his early movements. He is accompanied by Mr. Andrew Donelson, his private secretary, and Mr. Andrew Jackson, his adopted son, and others."

Someone writing in the *Baltimore Gazette* noted, "I have just walked through the apartments at the National Hotel for the accommodation of General Jackson. They are in all respects comfortable and well-furnished. He will have a parlor and chamber adjoining the hall and fronting on Pennsylvania Avenue along North Sixth Street. The parlor opens onto the uncovered terrace and the West Portico, where he may be saluted from the avenue by any number of people who may throng to gaze at their favorite." Carson was reading this news bit just before retiring after a rather difficult day with Crockett and the Tennessee land matters. He had been thinking again about the events of the day and speculating on the rift that had developed between his friend and himself, and he was not sure at this point whether he would be able eventually to placate David, who seemed deadly serious in his remarks.

The news about Jackson's temporary quarters at the National served to distract him. He remembered that just prior to his arrival on the national scene in the fall of 1825, Jackson was then a senator and that he and Senator John Eaton had rooms

147

at the Franklin House. Carson read on. "The National Hotel is a stupendous establishment. Besides the apartments of General Jackson, the judges are lodged there."

The news report continued, "Invitations were issued to the General from numerous towns and cities along the way from Tennessee to Washington City—committees seeking to entertain the President-elect and his party at various public dinners and receptions. He declined them all, reminding the issuers that the death of his beloved lady prompted him to refuse all social engagements."

On March 4, 1829, John C. Calhoun, Vice President-elect of the United States, took the chair and the Senate was called to order. The oath of office was administered by Mr. Smith of Maryland. At half-past eleven, Andrew Jackson, the President-elect entered, attended by the marshall of the District and the members of the Committee of the Arrangements, and he took his seat immediately in front of the secretary's desk. The chief justice of the United States Supreme Court and the associate justices entered soon after and occupied seats on the right of the President-elect.

A large number of ladies was present and occupied seats in the Eastern gallery, the Western gallery being reserved for members of the House of Representatives. At twelve o'clock the Senate was adjourned and a procession was formed to the Eastern Portico of the Capitol, where in the presence of an immense congregation of spectators filling the porticoes, the steps and the enclosures, the President delivered his address and having delivered it, the oath of office was administered by Chief Justice Marshall. Salutes were fired by two companies of artillery, which were repeated by forts and detachments of artillery on the plains. When the President retired the procession was formed. His horse had been in waiting on the Capitol grounds, and mounting, he led the procession to the President's Mansion, where he received the salutation of a vast number of persons who came to congratulate him.

The National Intelligencer reported, "The day was serene and mild and in every way favorable to the wishes of those who had come from a distance to witness the ceremony of Inauguration. We believe we do not fall short of the estimate that ten thousand persons were present." On March 6 it reported editorially, "The great concourse of strangers in the city has already subsided, and the steady rain yesterday kept indoors most of those who remained. What particularly gratifies us and does credit to the American people is that amidst the excitement and bustle of the occasion, the whole day and night of the Inauguration passed without the slightest interruption of the public peace and order. At the mansion of the President, the sovereign people were a little uproarious, but it was in anything but a malicious spirit."

Again Carson and Davis met at Carusi's on the week before adjournment for a farewell celebration. There was much to talk about, a great many things to laugh about, and a few regrets and disappointments as they discussed chiefly the events of the past ten days. They had both attended the reception at the White House following the Inauguration, and had stayed long enough to witness the destructive tendencies of the convivial celebrants. "*The Intelligencer* should be given a medal for the understatement of the decade in its restrained reporting of this unrestrained carnival," laughed Davis. "I doubt, my friend, if you saw all that I saw of the melée—you were giving so much time and attention to the President's pretty niece! I lost you about that time, and never saw you again. You probably stayed to help snuff out the candles."

Carson made no direct reply to speculations raised, but commented, "I was proud of our President through it all, proud of his dignity and bearing and his gallant consideration of the ladies, whose unrestrained enthusiasm must have made him miserable. His outward manifestations belied the deep-down emotional strain—his loneliness without his beloved Rachel."

"You are no doubt pleased with him for honoring two of your native sons in his Cabinet appointments—Branch as Secretary of the Navy, and Eaton as Secretary of War."

"I had lost sight of the fact that Eaton is a native of North Carolina; he has so long been identified with Tennessee. And since you have reminded me, both of these new Cabinet members are from the same County—Halifax. Of course you know I am delighted with the appointment of Senator Branch. I know Eaton only casually."

The two friends reviewed the highlights of the year, deplored

149

the lack of significant legislation, and discussed their plans for the summer.

Davis noted that Carson was less jubilant than usual, and he was canny enough to guess the reason. Of late there had been a rash of journalistic criticism of the evil practice of duelling, and other states had followed North Carolina's example of outlawing this method that displaced argumentative persuasion. As if he had been able to read Davis's mind, Carson remarked, "Did you see the statement attributed to Dean Swift that 'none but madmen and fools fight duels, and the sooner the world is rid of such the better?' "

"Yes, my friend, I did, and I also read the comment that followed. Perhaps you did not pursue your reading. The commentator related the story of a Doctor Akenside, a celebrated poet, who challenged to mortal combat a member of the Bar, whose name I don't remember. But they did not get as far as the field of honor, for one would not consent to fight in the morning, and the other was equally determined not to do so in the evening. One wished to fall in a blaze of glory mingled with the brilliant rays of the morning sun, and the other, with an equal display of poetic feeling, thought that the shades of evening more congenial to the horrors of dissolution. The upshot was 'no shot.' "

Davis was not sure that his turning of the subject in this wise was beneficial. He was sure that his friend often felt a desperate need to clear his mind so as not to allow the building up of tensions and recriminations because of the unhappy affair of the past year.

They were distracted at this moment by a party of *bon vivants* at a table adjoining them. From time to time they had ordered and had drunk an immense quantity of wine, and they were now being presented with the bill. The amount must have been enormous, for one of the company, not so far gone as the others, stammered out, "It is impossible that so many bottles could have been drunk by only seven persons." Whereupon the waiter replied, "True, sir, but your honor forgets the gentleman under the table."

On Tuesday, March 17, the Senate adjourned *sine die* and the Vice President left the following day for his home in South

Carolina. Davis and Carson were at their respective homes within a fortnight.

Some weeks after he reached home, Carson received a marked copy of the *Halifax Minerva* which commented, "The people of the State view with peculiar pride and full appreciation the services of Messrs. John Branch and S. P. Carson and others whose indefatigable exertions were mainly instrumental in procuring the Cherokee lands and other appropriations which the government has of late years made for the benefit of the State, and those gentlemen are now enjoying the enviable reward for their faithful public labors."

It was election year again, and because of the growing concern of some of his more knowledgeable constituents about the tarriff, Carson spent more between-season time than heretofore in public speaking and private conference. This was his first campaign since the duel that cost the life of his friend, and even though it was not an issue, Carson dreaded the thought that it might be injected into the campaign. It never was, and he thanked God for that. If he read the signs correctly, there was sure to be more and more protest about the protective tariff. Carson was confident that Calhoun would provide adequate leadership in this regard, and he was reassured by the willingness of his constituents to trust the leadership of Calhoun. He did not reckon on the voices of dissension that would ultimately be heard in other parts of the state, but other issues were being debated over North Carolina. At Hillsborough, a meeting of the "Friends of Internal Improvements" was held in the court-house, with Dr. John Webb as the featured speaker.

But the issue that was of primary concern to Carson, as indeed it was to all of Western North Carolina, was the booming gold industry. There was no longer any doubt about the validity of the claims for this expanding venture. Indeed, the clamor for a branch of the United States Mint to be located within the area had reached the point of demand rather than request. Carson's efforts to this end would be bolstered by such timely reporting as appeared in the *Raleigh Register* of May 5: "Few persons not residing in the immediate vicinity of the gold mines have any adequate conception of the operations which are carried on in procuring the precious metal. In this section of the state, the people talk of the gold mines, but they have little knowledge of the vast sums which they annually yield—that already there are several companies from the North and from the South engaged in the business, nor are they aware that monied men from over a quarter of our Union are purchasing up land for which they pay extravagant prices. One Northern speculator, who has just returned from a visit to the mines in South America states that those of our own state greatly exceed them in richness."

It was shortly after his election had been secured that Carson set out to visit the mining areas, gathering statistics and information that would bolster the prosecution of his requests for the establishment of a branch mint. He went to Rutherfordton to talk with the Bechtlers, German immigrants who had bought property in the area and had begun prospecting. He found they had planned to establish their own mint if they were favoured with good results, and if the government were too slow to move in this direction.

While in Rutherfordton, Carson took occasion to visit James Graham, local barrister, his opponent in the 1824 race for Congress, and his contemporary in the North Carolina Legislature of 1822-24. Though neither was aware of it at this time, Graham was destined to fill the role in Congress now held by Carson.

"Well, if it isn't my old friend, Sam Patch," exclaimed Graham as Carson accosted him. "What tricks are you up to now, my fine friend?"

Carson could not feign ignorance of the sobriquet, "Sam Patch." For weeks the press of the United States and Canada had been filled with reports of his acrobatic performances—his high jumps and daring leaps. He had, with elaborate fanfare, jumped over the Falls of Genessee at Rochester, New York, and indeed a crowd of many thousands watched, breathless, as he made the leap at Niagara Falls. Of him the *New York Courier* said, "Sam Patch is neither fool nor madman, but is possessed of great coolness and judgment and performs exploits no created human being has ever attempted before." Carson was sure that the sobriquet was applied to him mischievously, perhaps because his name and middle initial were the same as that of the showman's. Even if it were a malicious jest, Carson had no intention of dignifying it with comment, and he soon began

152

Andrew Jackson on Sam Patch, a magnificent white horse presented to him by the citizens of Pennsylvania

to discuss with Graham his plans for securing favorable consideration of his resolution already introduced in Congress to establish a branch mint in the gold mining section—probably in or near Rutherfordton.

This subject was a most agreeable one for Graham. He offered his assistance in whatever capacity he could further the prosecution of this timely consideration, and they discussed the subject at great length.

As he prepared to mount on departure, Carson called out, "I suppose you know that our new President has a beautiful white charger that he has named Sam Patch."

"Tell me more," shouted Graham, but Carson was off in a cloud of dust.

It did not take long to ride the distance to the Green River Plantation, and it was no surprise to Carson that Catharine was among the number who gave him an enthusiastic welcome, albeit he noticed a restraint in her enthusiasm that had been absent on other occasions when he visited his brother's family. Should he interpret it as a new pattern of behavior, or read into it an effort to subdue her real feelings toward him; or, could it be that she had heard some of the idle talk that seemed to be going the rounds during elections last August that he had found his heart's desire in the Capital City?

He scarcely had time to speculate on the reasons for her changed attitude, for he had hardly finished his greetings and embraces when a smiling Negro boy advanced. "Let me take yo' saddlebags, Mr. Sam—de dinner bell done rung, and I specs yo-all is hongry."

"Thank you, Peter. You have grown up since I lived here, and I almost didn't know you," Sam said, and turning to Rebecca added, "Am I to stay in the big house or the bachelor's house?"

"In the big house this time, Sam. We know your visit will be short, and we want you close by, especially since Joseph is in Raleigh. The Legislature is in session, you know."

"Your wishes, dear Rebecca, are my command, but I can't help remembering some of the gay and unconventional evenings spent under the Bachelor's roof."

Built to accomodate an indefinite number of men and boys when there was an influx of summer visitors, or when the hunting season was at its height, the bachelor's house was of hand-hewn chestnut logs, with chinking that every now and again reflected sparkling flecks of gold. An open aperture called a dog-trot separated two ample rooms. Stone chimneys covered with ivy filled most of the width of the gabled ends.

The dining room of Green River Mansion looked out on the front piazza but was easily accessible to the outdoor kitchen— itself a room of large proportions, with huge open fireplace equipped for every culinary achievement. There were bakers, broilers, toasters, and waffle and wafer irons. Gleaming copper pots and skillets were rubbed to mirror perfection, and the cavernous fireplace accommodated crane, spit and trammel for the preparation of venison, wild turkey, brook trout, quail and pheasant.

Today the specialty of the house was home-cured ham, hot biscuit, wild rice and spiced apples, with golden brown yams and gravy for those with lustier appetites. As they lingered over their coffee, Sam gave a glowing account of progress in the nearby mining region. "This bit of news has just come to light, and it opens up a wide field of speculation—not monetary speculation, but the kind born of curiosity," he said. "Recently, prospectors for gold in upper Burke County came upon a crucible deep down below the surface of the earth. The crucible bore evidence of having been much used. They wondered if it could be that the Aborigines were aware of the formations of gold in this area, and that the crucible was used in fluxing the precious metal. It was a logical deduction, because close by they found a sandstone slab containing indentations or excavations of various sizes. It probably had been used for molding orna- ments to decorate the ears and the noses of Indians who were here centuries ago, and the crucible would have been used to melt the gold."

The children were wide-eyed at the mention of Indians who wore ear and nose decorations. "Do you suppose they wore war paint and feathers a long, long time ago?" And before Sam could answer one of the little boys began to beg for an Indian story.

"I am not as well versed in ancient Indian lore as I am on present day Indians, but I can tell you a tale that happened not too many weeks ago, and mind you it is a true story! You'll have to let me look in my bags for something I will need for my story."

Sam excused himself and came back with a portion cut from *The Halifax Minerva*, Senator Branch's home town paper. Seating himself, he explained to the children, "You know all Indian tribes have Indian names. The Cherokees and the Catawbas are the ones nearest us, but down in Alabama there is a tribe known as Creeks. They are the largest and the strongest of any of the tribes in the South, except the Cherokees. They had been living peacefully with the white men until a few moons ago when they went on a rampage and killed two of the white men. Then trouble began, and a delegation went to Washington to see the President and to ask for his help in keeping the peace.

"The President was disturbed, and he talked with some of his advisors about the best way to keep down an uprising. They decided it would be best to remove the Creeks from Alabama and send them West to live in the country that had been set apart for the Cherokees and other tribes. But the President was troubled and he talked again with his advisors about the best way to deal gently with the Creeks. He did not want bloodshed and bitterness and he did not want to send troops to make them go, so he decided to write them a letter, and this is what he said:

Dear Brothers and Sisters:

By permission of the Great Spirit above and the voice of the people, I have been made President of the United States, and now speak to you as your Father and your Friend, and I request you to listen.

Your warriors have known me long. You know I love my white children and my red children and that I always speak with a straight and not a forked tongue; that I have always told you the truth.

Your bad men have made my heart sicken and bleed by the murder of one of my white children. Our peaceful Mother Earth has been stained with the blood of the white man, and they call for the punishment of the murderers, whose surrender is now demanded by the solemn obligation of the treaty which your chiefs and warriors in council have agreed to. To prevent the spilling of more blood you will have to surrender these murderers and return the property they have taken.

156

Friends and brothers, listen: where you now are you and my white children are too near each other to live in harmony and peace. Your game is destroyed and many of your people will not work and till the earth.

Beyond the great Father of Waters, where part of your nation has gone, your Father has provided a country large enough for all of you. There your white brothers will not trouble you; they will have no claim to this land, and you can live upon it, you and all your children, as the grass grows or the water runs, in peace and plenty. It will be yours forever.

For the improvements in the country where you now live, and for all of the stock which you can't take with you, your Father will pay a fair price.

In my talk to you in the Creek Nation many years ago, I told you of this new country where you might be preserved as a great Nation, and where your white brothers would not disturb you. Where you live now your white brothers have always claimed, but the land beyond the Mississippi belongs to the President, and he will give it to you forever.

Listen, my children: I have sent my agent and your friend to consult with you on the subject of removing you to the land West of the Mississippi in order that my white children and my red children may live in peace, and that the land may not be stained with blood again. I have instructed Colonel Crowell to speak the truth to you and to assure you that your Father, the President, will deal fairly with you. Should any of you desire to come under the laws of Alabama and remain where you are, land will be laid off for them and their families.

My children, listen: My white children in Alabama have extended their laws over your country; if you move across the Mississippi, you will be subject to your own laws and the care of your Father, the President. You will be treated with kindness and the lands will be yours forever.

Friends and brothers, listen: This is straight and good talk. It is for your Nation's good, and your Father requests you to hear his counsel."

As he folded the paper, Carson said, "It is signed by the President and it will be preserved in our history forever."

"Did the Indians leave their homes and go beyond the Mississippi to live?"

"Some of them already have gone, Ruth Margaret. Nine hundred passed through Pike County, Alabama and joined fifteen hundred from another place, and they are on their way West. Others will follow, but some of the old and the sick—and maybe some of the young ones will stay where they are."

"Do you ever talk with the Indians' father, the President?" asked one of the younger ones.

"Oh yes, I see him often. He sometimes asks me to speak for him on the floor of the Congress. I am glad to do it when I have the same thoughts about measures that come before us as he does. He knows that I will not compromise my thinking and feeling about issues, but most of the time I believe in the things that he wants to do for our country."

"Does he get a vacation like you do, Uncle Sam?"

"Well, he is at the Hermitage now, and he told me before he left that he was having wood cut from the land there to make a walking stick for your Grandfather Carson. The President likes to remember that his father and your grandfather came from the upper part of Ireland, 'where the grass is always green and where the little people go dancing in the moonlight on the shores.' "

"Please, please tell us about the little people," they clamored.

"Oh no, not now. It's off to bed with you, but if you calm down and take your naps, you can hear about the little people tonight." And so saying, Rebecca led the way from the dining room, happy in the realization that apparently Sam had not once thought of the fact that exactly two years ago at this same hour he had been surrounded by his family at Pleasant Gardens awaiting the answer of Doctor Vance to his challenge. She was glad that the tragic episode had apparently left no scars. He had been devoting himself so assiduously to his responsibilities and labors as a representative, which of itself was the best therapy. She had never seen him look handsomer and in better spirit. Perhaps there *was* something to the rumors that had been floating at election time—rumors about his affair of the heart."

Reluctantly she admitted disappointment that Catharine had not been her usual witty, vivacious self. It was apparent that she was more deeply infatuated with Sam than anyone had realized. It was a well-established fact that the Wilson girls had found the Carson men prime targets for matrimony—three of them had already taken the Carson name, producing well-nigh a score of double first cousins. Perhaps it was just as well that Catharine conclude this much-frowned-upon biological complication.

Left to themselves, the two in question found conversation difficult at first. Sam did not wish to be put on the defensive about his attentions to the President's niece, especially since the affair was not going so well. He fully intended to press his suit with more ardor on his return to the Capital City, and there could be no harm in avoiding the issue in the meantime. Deftly he turned the conversation away from himself and his pursuits, plying Catharine with questions about herself, her interests and her plans for the rest of the winter.

Suddenly there was a great commotion in the backyard, with much screaming and excited talking. Catharine and Sam rushed out to one of the Negro cabins in time to see Peter carrying a small boy inside. "He bin bit by a copperhaid," one of the little girls explained.

"Not this time of the year," Sam ventured. "Maybe it was a bee sting. Had he been near the stands?"

"It were a copperhaid," said an old Negro, "kaze I seed it and tried to kill it, but it got away. Guess it was winterin' up under dem bricks de little feller pulled from under de corn crib."

Sam went in to have a look, and there was no doubt about it. Already the child's arm had doubled in size and he was screaming with fright and pain. Someone handed Sam a vial of whisky. "Open de woun' an suck out de pizen, den pour some of dis whisky on de place en mek him drink a swaller or two."

Sam did as he was ordered—with some assistance. They had to hold the boy to get the spirits in him, for they did not take time to dilute it. Just then an old woman came in with two raw chicken breasts, and when he was about to protest, she looked at Sam menacingly. "Git outen my way, man. Lem'me lay dese on him. De pizen will go outen him to de chicken bres'."

The little room was crowded with the distressed and the curious. Sam took Catharine by the hand and led her outside, where they met Rebecca, who had just been told of the accident.

"Rebecca, that child must have a doctor. I will ride into Rutherfordton and bring one out." Sam paid no attention to the protests, saddled Missy and was off in a matter of minutes. Dark overtook him before he reached the home of the physician, whose office adjoined the residence.

"You laughed at the chicken breast remedy, Mr. Carson, and you may laugh at my remedy, too," said the doctor, and going to a cabinet he brought out a large quantity of dried roots. "This is the root of the yellow poplar, sometimes called the American Tulip Tree. Make a strong decoction and divide it in half. Wash the swollen arm with part of it, then give the patient a half pint of the brew every half hour. It will greatly speed recovery if you have some of the women make poultices of the bark, which I will give you, boiling it to make a soft substance. By morning the boy should be almost recovered, but you will have to continue the treatments the rest of the night."

Sam did not reach the plantation till late bedtime, and it was Catharine who carried out the doctor's orders and who stayed with the patient until daybreak, when he dropped off into fitful sleep. The swelling had subsided and his fever was almost gone. As she went into the outdoor kitchen to get an early breakfast, Sam was already there in readiness for his long day's journey. Suddenly, and to his surprise, he was overwhelmed with a tenderness he had never felt for her before. He took her in his arms, kissing her and holding her in his embrace. "Catharine, if the boy lives, he will have you to thank for his life. You were wonderful, and I love you very much."

As he rode away, the red and gold rays of a November sunrise suffused the skies and proclaimed the advent of another beautiful day—another beautiful day for November.

SIX

It was almost the last day of December when Senator Foote, of Connecticut, introduced a resolution that would limit for a certain period the sale of public lands to those that had already been offered for sale. The purpose of the resolution was to slow up the sale of Western lands and to retard somewhat the growth of Western immigration. On the surface it seemed a reasonable proposal, but it brought sharp response from those representatives who could read into it sectional advantages or disadvantages, depending on their own self-interests and self-concerns, and those of their constituents. Almost the first to rise to his feet in protest was the senator from Missouri, Thomas Hart Benton. He assailed New England, proclaiming in stentorian voice that the states of the East were bent on crippling the Western development by interfering with its settlement.

While the sectional cauldron was boiling, the old year slipped into the new—the propitious year of our Lord, 1830.

One of the first to take advantage of the sectional controversy was Senator Robert Y. Hayne, the gifted orator from South Carolina, who, having obtained recognition from the Chair, walked to the front of the room and faced the assembly. Davis, sitting to Carson's right in the balcony, caught Carson's eye as if to say, "Now for better or for worse the issue of States' Rights, South Carolina style, will be injected into the question."

Carson thought Davis's conclusion, if he read him correctly, might be premature, but as Hayne, in his opening words, caught the attention of his listeners, he began to reassess this opinion. "—That the centralizing power of a central government has proved inimical to the best interests of the people in the handling of public lands. Do you not remember that the payment of a penny or a peppercorn was the stipulated price which our forefathers along the whole Atlantic seaboard paid for their lands? Was not the policy then founded on the universal belief that the conquest of a new colony—the driving out of the savage beast and the still more savage native, cutting down and subduing the forests, and the conversion of a wilderness into cultivated soil—was that not considered sufficient payment for the land?

"Contrast that, if you will, with the present policy in the United States in the West: Lands which had been for fifty or a hundred years open to every settler without charge beyond the expense of a survey were, the moment they fell into the hands of the Government, held up for sale to the highest bidder, with the limitation that they could never be resold below a certain minimum price, thus making it the cardinal point of our policy *not* to settle the country, but to fill our coffers by coining our land into gold. Under a drain like that, when a system is constantly operating on the wealth of a whole community, it may be said to be afflicted with a curse more grievous than the barrenness of the soil or the inclemency of the weather."

There was no shuffling of feet—no rasping coughs in the assembly, and every word of Senator Hayne was clearly audible as he continued. "The present condition of the Southern states has served to impress more deeply on my mind the grievous oppression of a system by which the worth of a country is drained off to be expended elsewhere. In that region, Mr. Speaker—the region of the South—it is our misfortune to stand in this relation to the Federal Government. The fruits of our labor are drawn from us to enrich other and more favored sections, while with one of the best climates and the richest products in the world, furnishing with one-third of the population two-thirds of the whole of the exports of a country—we exhibit the extraordinary—the painful spectacle of a country enriched by the bounty of God, but blasted by the cruel policy of man!"

"Hear! hear!" resounded the approbation of many Southern representatives, but as they spontaneously rose to their feet, the Chair gavelled for order with the admonition, "Let the gentleman from South Carolina proceed."

Senator Hayne smiled. "Mr. Speaker, I see I do not stand alone in this conclusion, and it is one I have long entertained. Stripped of high-sounding oratory, and put in its simplest terms, these issues of which I have spoken can be resolved into the question: shall the states or the central government rule?"

This was not the first time that the controversial issue of States' Rights had injected itself into a national forum, nor would it be the last. Between the years 1787 and the present, any issue of States' Rights or the issues growing out of it made all men contemporary. A man discussing the question of States' Rights in the Spring of 1788 would talk in the same terms and with almost as much emotion as a man discussing the same issues for the next half-century. There were more—and more— and more skillfully-devised pronouncements—thought-provoking questions. Through it all the lawmakers sat immobile, intent on every word.

As Hayne concluded this first in a series of the greatest debates ever heard in the New World, he admitted that he had not formed a fixed policy, "and I must reserve for further light and more mature reflection the formation of a final judgment. Of this I am convinced—the public debt must be paid. These Western lands have been solemnly pledged to the public creditors. In short, our whole policy in relation to public lands may be summed up in the declaration that they ought now to be kept and administered chiefly with a view to the creation within reasonable periods of great and flourishing communities to be formed into free and independent states, with the control of all of the lands within their respective limits."

"Free and independent states," Carson repeated almost audibly. "This is the opening volley, and now the battle is on."

Senator Daniel Webster, of Massachusetts, who had been arguing a case before the Supreme Court, came into the Senate chambers in time to hear all of Senator Hayne's speech. It was a foregone conclusion that he would reply in opposition to the South Carolinian, and when the lawmakers and a host of visitors assembled the next day, their tongues were wagging at both ends, so excited were they over the prospect of hearing a rebuttal in the language of an orator who had already won renown in the forum.

Reputedly one of the best-dressed men in Congress, Webster's courtly appearance on this day added to the dramatic effect of the setting. A contemporary commented, "No one understands better than Mr. Webster the philosophy of dress, and what a powerful auxiliary to speech and manner it can be." On the occasion of this debate with Mr. Hayne, he appeared in a blue coat and a buff vest—the revolutionary colors of blue and buff—and a white cravat. Mr. Webster walked in slow dignity to the dais, and turning, paused long enough to provide dramatic suspence, and then addressing the Chair and the assembled group, he began skillfully handling his opponent in this wise:

"The claims to the Western lands held by all the Eastern states were relinquished to the United States in the ordinance of 1787. From the very origin of the government, sir, these Western lands and the just protection of those who settled on them have been the leading objects of our policy and have led to expenditures of both blood and treasure. Those colonists in passing the Alleghenies did not pass beyond the care of their own government. Wherever they went, the public arm was still outstretched over them. I deny, Mr. Speaker, I deny altogether that there has been anything harsh or severe in the policy of the government towards those in the New West. The government has been no stepmother to the new states. On the contrary it has uniformly pursued toward those states a liberal and enlightened system.

"It was not until 1794, the time of General Wayne's victory, that it could be said we had conquered the savages. It was not until this period that the government could have considered itself as having established an entire ability to protect those who should undertake the conquest of the wilderness.

"And here, sir, let us pause and survey the scene as it existed thirty-five years ago at the epoch of 1794. Let us look back and behold it! Over all that is now Ohio there then stretched one vast wilderness, unbroken except for two small spots of civilized culture—one at Marietta and one at Cincinnati. At these little openings, hardly a pinpoint on the map, the arm of the frontiersman had leveled the forest and let in the sun. These little patches of earth were all that had been rendered verdant by the hand of man. In an extent of hundreds and thousands of square miles, no other surface of smiling green attested the pressure of civilization. The hunters' path crossed mighty rivers flowing in solitary grandeur whose sources lay in remote and

164

unknown regions of the wilderness. It was fresh, untouched, unbounded, magnificent wilderness!

"And, sir, what is it now? Is it a reality or a dream that in so short a period as thirty-five years there has sprung up on the same surface an independent state with a million people—an amount of population greater than all the cantons of Switzerland; equal to one-third of all of the people of the United States when they accomplished their Independence? This new member of the Republic has already left far behind her a majority of the old states. She now is beside Virginia and Pennsylvania and in point of numbers will shortly admit no equal but New York herself!"

Mr. Webster used an effective weapon in pointing out the rapid development of wasteland into a thriving commonwealth, long since weaned from its mother's breast and now contributing to the strength of the nation. He drew a delicate comparison of the terms "union" and "consolidation," and quoted from a letter that accompanied the Constitution when it was submitted for ratification of the country, which indicated the intent of the framers of that sacred document: "In all our deliberations, we kept steadily in our view that which appears to us to be the greatest interest of every true American—the consolidation of our Union."

Skillfully, Webster introduced the subject of the tariff, denied that New England was its author, and charged that the tariff of 1824 was literally forced upon New England.

Newspaper criticism of the inept caliber of this lawmaking body notwithstanding, the settlement and sale of public lands was to proceed, leading inevitably to the next stage when these new lands, formed into territories, should become applicants for admission into the Union; and whether they should enter as free or slave states, as had already been adjudicated in the case of Missouri, would depend upon whether or not the South or the North should control Congress.

That forces were already at work that would threaten the solidarity envisioned by the Founding Fathers most informed representatives and the literate public were fully aware, but Carson did not foresee his personal fortunes affected by the intermittent squalls that brought temporary chaos to the Ship of State. So impressed was he with the talents and abilities manifest in the speeches of the two contenders that he sometimes lost sight of the issues. Having himself been recognized as an effective orator, he was guilty in this instance of weighing words rather than issues.

How was he to know that he was privileged to be among veritable giants of intellect, whose luster would increase with the passing of the years! And how was he to know that this and subsequent encounters between Webster and Hayne would provide the most brilliant illustration of the highest type of debating skills which could be found in the history of oratory—ancient or modern! Such determination must await the passing of time and the evaluation of enlightened citizens.

It was soon recognized that the issues involved in this debate—those that had separated and would continue to separate North and South since the founding of the nation—States' Rights, slavery and westward immigration—were being drawn out into the open and subjected to the sharpest criticism and the most logical minds in the Senate.

Carson was so moved by these experiences that he wanted to share the highly-charged, exhilarating atmosphere with those at home who would appreciate most the height and depth of emotions and oratory displayed. He intended to go to his room and put on paper for the benefit of friends and family the thoughts that were racing through his head.

Was it treason that he could not put out of his mind the appearance, the sincerity, the powerful emotion of Webster when he concluded his peroration? Liberty *and* Union, Now and Forever, One and Inseparable!

He should have been remembering Hayne's words—his dynamic statements—his persuasive arguments as he presented the cause of the South.

Before he knew what had happened he found himself in a cluster of Webster's friends and well-wishers. Too late to extricate himself he went forward, hand extended in sincere and unaffected warmth for one with whom he only recently had disagreed as violently as his temperate disposition would allow.

Mr. Webster grasped the outstretched hand proffered him. "Carson, I always liked you. I knew you to be an honest man."

As he made his way out of the group he was accosted by one whose accent betrayed his deep South lineage, one who was slightly inebriated and who apparently mistook Carson for one of Webster's New England friends.

"I say, sir. I see you have already started consolidating, but it won't do you any good, sir. The South knows that as Peter she is being robbed to pay Paul. At least South Carolina knows it. Might may be on your side, sir, but right is on ours, and we shall win. Mark my words, sir—we shall win!"

As was usual in the opening days of the session Carson found himself behind in his schedule. There never seemed time to write to his family. After he had hand-written his speeches—a laborious task at best—attended committee meetings, placated or encouraged individually the constituents who took time to write to him, he had little time for personal correspondence. He had not written to the Green River family since his return. He was not yet ready to begin a correspondence with Catharine, but he needed to report to his brother and to the Burke and Rutherford mine owners.

His bill to establish a mint in the North Carolina mining section had been sent to committee and had found favorable consideration—at least a beginning toward the desired end. They were favorable toward establishing an assayer's office in the district in the event the proposition for the mint was not approved. Thus the gold could be assayed and a standard value affixed; it could be made into ingots which would answer the purpose of a circulating medium, while it would tend to keep the gold at home. As at present there were hazards of inconvenience and risk in transporting the gold to Philadelphia, from which place it found its way into other markets.

A number of new mines had been discovered in the area and improvements were continually being made in the mining process. His brother and the company he had formed were using machinery to pulverize the rock and collect the gold, and in his last letter Joe had reported a substantial increase in the daily output with these improved methods.

Invitations had been issued for the annual Birthnight Ball—an occasion which, in addition to honoring the Father of His Country, offered an opportunity to relax from the daily harrassments and to unite in the enjoyment of an occasion when patriotism and pleasure go hand in hand. This year the managers had planned something especially handsome. The stage and pit of the Washington Theater were to be thrown into one area for the dances, the banquet room to be above, and the announcement had been made that "all the conveniences for the ladies and the gentlemen will be amply provided for by arranging the Green Room independently of the amusement of the dance, for which a first-rate orchestra has been engaged. Both vocal and instrumental music will be featured, and in addition a distinguished artist and his assistants from New York assure us that decorations and scenery will be employed to give every assurance of a splendid spectacle."

Carson had thought to make this occasion the opportunity to climax his attentions on a certain fair lady and to be rejected or rewarded according to her wishes and desires. His fond hopes were shattered when he read her polite refusal to accompany him. Halfway expecting that sooner or later his attentions would be rebuffed, he had steeled himself for a development that came sooner than he had thought. Mary Eastin had other plans. Casually, as if nothing had happened, he made plans to attend the gala affair with Davis, who seldom attended any public functions except as a bachelor. Their friendship had continued to grow, a source of great satisfaction to both of them.

When, a fortnight later, Davis dropped by to discuss with Carson some of the debatable points in pending legislation, he noticed a volume of Shakespeare open on the night table. Picking it up with care, so as not to lose the place, he asked jestingly, "Do you intend to have the Bard of Avon bolster you in your arguments against the proposed road from Buffalo to New Orleans? Let's see what we have here."

His eyes fell on a line from *Macbeth* that had been heavily underscored—"Out, out brief candle," and he immediately recognized the words as having been the last uttered by Doctor Vance on whom Carson had inflicted mortal wounds three years since. Already concerned about the physical health of his friend, Davis wondered if there was cause for alarm about his emotional condition. While considering some way to deal with his blundering intrusion in an interlude so personal, he read on:

> Life's but a walking shadow,
> A poor player that struts
> And frets his hour upon the stage
> And is heard no more.
> It is a tale told by an idiot
> Full of sound and fury—signifying nothing.

"All right, Davis. I see you are making deductions of your own, having come on this bit of incriminating evidence. Yes, I'll admit I am guilty of harking back to that black day in my life. How do you expect me to ignore the railings of the press? The papers are filled with comments on the deplorable practice of duelling. That recent affair in Kentucky produced eight or nine long columns, with the minutest details reported—most of it purporting to show that the close friendship of the two antagonists was evident throughout—indeed until the fatal shot was fired."

"Which shows there is indeed something wrong with the system, my friend. Who would applaud such an event?"

"The editor certainly did not. He pointed to Sallust, who said wisely that men have quarrels, differences, feuds, *only* with enemies—friends seek to excel one another in great actions, in the arts and sciences, not in single combat for personal quarrels. You know, Davis, Vance was my friend. *I* was the one who suggested to him a career in politics—*I* was the one who encouraged him to launch his career and sustained him while he pursued it!"

"Carson, my friend, duelling is and will continue to be not only tolerated but encouraged by that which is stronger than all law—public opinion. Nevertheless it is a crime—it is an ir-religious practice. North Carolina has put her seal of disapproval on this immoral and evil showmanship. Would to God—and I say this fervently, for I see what a toll it is taking in your life—would to God that Congress would blot out this evil by an act of legislative mercy. But such an act must be induced by mass dissatisfaction with this medieval practice that has no place in the nineteenth century!"

The emotions of both were at such high pitch that Davis was in no mood to discuss affairs of State, but he knew that Carson's thoughts should be directed to other channels, and he asked gently, "Have you forgotten that we came together tonight to review an improvident act that may be foisted on our country if we do not exercise our best persuasions tomorrow to prevent it?"

Carson took from his desk a meticulously hand-written argument—too long and involved and tending too much to a display of the erudite vocabulary of the orator—at least that was Davis's appraisal after reading it hastily, but the two discussed it at length.

When on the morrow Carson gave his reasons for opposing the construction of a road—"a miserable, paltry, earthen road" to connect the two widely separated points in New York and Louisiana, he compared the ease, convenience and dispatch afforded by steam power on connecting, navigable rivers, citing the speed of uninterrupted steamboat passage from Memphis to New Orleans, and giving in detail the report of the postmaster general containing unquestioned proof that so far as mail service is concerned that steam navigation is superior and will undoubtedly supercede earthen roads for such purposes. Davis was close at hand while Carson was presenting his case, and at least once interrupted him to bolster and strengthen his point.

In his closing remarks, the young legislator from North Carolina took occasion to eulogize the President. "Mr. Speaker, I supported General Jackson in the last election because I believed him to be honest and meritorious, and I shall continue to support his administration, sir, because I *know* him to be so. He will realize the expectations of his friends throughout the nation if his friends here by their misguided policies do not prevent him."

In spite of his physical indisposition and the discouragement of unrequited love, Carson was present at almost every session of the House throughout the entire long, drawn-out delibera-

170

tions of the Congress. He was active in debate on the important measures, with the exception of the dialogue on the impeachment of a district court judge that consumed much of the time of that body for weeks.

A number of events transpired in the spring of 1830 to enliven the otherwise drab proceedings. There was the Jefferson birthday celebration of April 13—the beginning of an event that would be celebrated throughout the years—a rallying call for statesmen and politicians and friends of good government and Republican principles, the two not always synonomous.

Internal improvements were a major concern of state and national legislative bodies. When a state or territory could not raise sufficient revenue to provide improved highways, bridges and canals, the assistance of the government was sought to underwrite the project by subscribing the amount of the deficit, especially when the improved roads, canals and bridges provided a link in the chain of major highways and waterways.

Jackson's first Presidential veto was given to just such a bill. Local to the state of Kentucky, the proponents sought to minimize the local aspects and to emphasize its national importance. So thorough had been the investigation preceding this request that the company engaged to construct the road hired a man during one month to record the number of persons, wagons, horses and cattle which passed over the road at a given point, and the average for one day derived from this record showed that 351 persons, thirty-three carriages and fifty-one wagons had been serviced.

Mr. Polk opposed the bill on the grounds that it was unjust, unfair and unconstitutional. Mr. Carson objected to the system that would make the government a stockholder in public companies incorporated by a state. Mr. Crockett did not make a speech upon the controversial subject. Indeed, he was convinced in his own mind that if they were to speak for five days on it not a single vote would be changed. Everyone, he thought, had already made up his mind on the subject. But Crockett's surmise was incorrect. The bill passed the House on April 29 and the Senate on May 15. Jackson summarily vetoed it.

Writing to a constituent who had made inquiry about it, Carson noted, "The bill owes all its celebrity to the veto of the

171

President, which blow destroyed it." It is true there were angry cries and great excitement when the announcement was made, and the demands for a vote to overthrow the veto, but the bill failed of passage by a scant majority.

Carson in his letter to one of his constituents gives an interesting sidelight on the political picture of that time.

I called to see Mr. Van Buren, and among other subjects we held a conversation relative to the Maysville Road Bill, which had just been sent to the President for his sanction. The conversation we had is substantially as follows: I remarked that I hoped the President would veto the bill, whereupon Mr. Van Buren exclaimed, "That is impossible!" "How is it impossible?" I asked.

"Because the the principle (of government subscriptions to stock issues) has in some way or other been sanctioned by every administration since the commencement of the Government."

I answered that the principle had indeed been sanctioned by his predecessors, but that formed an obligation on General Jackson to veto the bill if he believed it to be unconstitutional.

Mr. Van Buren thought that the many precedents for such sanction constituted an obligation on General Jackson, "and besides, the veto would lose us the state of Kentucky and Ohio and probably Indiana and Pennsylvania.

I then rose from my seat and with some warmth said, "Is it possible, Mr. Van Buren, that you place popular considerations in the scale as against high and lofty principles?" He then remarked something about the heat of my feelings and the rashness of my judgment, etc. I left him with the decided feeling that he was against the veto.

Some few evenings after the veto message, I happened to be at the President's mansion, and found Mr. Van Buren in conversation with Colonel James Polk. Van Buren remarked that he thought the veto would be one of the most popular acts of the Administration, to which Colonel Polk assented.

I then said to Mr. Van Buren that I was gratified to see his change of heart.

"What change of heart?" he asked.

"Why, sir, when I had conversation with you some days since, you then expressed it as your opinion that the veto would lose the General several states."

"I was only trying to find out your opinion, Carson." To this I replied that our efforts were mutual, for I had visited him on that occasion for the same purpose.

Referring to Carson's letter to his constituents the *Western*

Carolinian, reflecting the sentiment of many friends of the congressman, commented, "In another column of our paper will be found a letter from the Hon. Samuel P. Carson to Thomas Gilmer. We call attention to this letter because it establishes most completely the duplicity of Mr. Van Buren. Those who know the character of Mr. Carson will not for a moment question the truth of this assertion. If there is one high-minded, honorable and chivalric gentleman in the United States, that man is Mr. Carson, and not to believe his assertions would be tantamount to saying that no one is to be believed."

Extravagant praise, that, but to one in a state of dejection because of physical and emotional handicaps it was as balm in Gilead. There was a mountain of correspondence to claim his attention, but Carson felt it incumbent on himself to be in attendance at all sessions when matters were debated that affected his District or the good of the nation and the sessions lasted far into the night hours.

Returning to his room after an especially trying day, Carson picked up a letter addressed in feminine handwriting. It was Catharine's reply to the short note he had written her many weeks before. She was still in Brentwood. Her father was beginning to need and claim much of her attention in his declining years. Indeed, her gaity and banter seemed forced and stilted. He suspected that she had found out from many available sources that whereas during the past months he had been a constant visitor at the White House, he no longer called there socially.

The next letter he turned to was from his friend, Charles Fisher of Salisbury, who urged that he follow up the very commendable move he had initiated to establish a branch mint in the gold mining section of North Carolina. He reminded Carson that the resolution he had introduced in the House on this subject was couched in words that did not require prompt action. "It takes a long while for the Congress to 'inquire into the expediency' of *anything.* Meanwhile we are suffering severe handicap in taking our gold on the long haul to Philadelphia."

Carson took up his quill and addressed his friend:

> The committee meets on Tuesday next, and we shall come to a conclusion whether or not we will make a report this session or wait

and see the developments of the present year before we move further.

I perfectly agree with you on the importance of the subject. Indeed, I am deeply impressed—so much so that I fear I shall not be able to do justice to the matter or to match the expectations of my friends.

And as to other matters of import, General Jackson *will* run again! We shall have a 'blowout' for him on Tuesday, the thirteenth instant in celebration of Jefferson's birthday.

I think the fate of the Buffalo-New Orleans Road Bill doubtful. I was much provoked with the committee on account of them selecting the Western route. It was the result of a combination—if not corrupt, at least fraught with too much injustice to be borne patiently. I did not let them escape. My speech is published today in the *Telegraph*.

Your friend & obdt. servant,
Samuel P. Carson

April 9th, 1930

Although ostensibly to honor the illustrious Jefferson, the birthday celebration held at the Indian Queen Hotel was an occasion to honor the seventh President of the United States. According to newspaper announcements, "No occasion has ever taken place in this country at which there was a greater assemblage of public men distinguished for respectability and talent. An immense concourse from all parts of the nation joined with the utmost cordiality in celebrating the birthday of him whom they loved while living and whom they honored equally in death, whose political principles they adopted as their standard and will follow as their surest guide. What time more propitious than at the commencement of the administration of his steadfast friend, disciple and follower is held this first celebration of Mr. Jefferson's anniversary. We hope it will be repeated annually in all time to come by all who are really and in truth of his political faith."

Twenty-four toasts had been scheduled and there were many volunteer pronouncements befitting the occasion, and in the intervening pauses a number of eloquent speeches were delivered. It was on this occasion that President Jackson, rising for the first toast of the evening, proposed, "Our Federal Union—it *must* be preserved." He was followed by Vice President Calhoun, who said, "To the Union—next to our liberties

174

most dear; may we all remember that it can only be preserved by respecting the rights of the states, and distributing equally the benefits and burdens of the Union."

Here then was the emergence of conflicting ideologies or conflicting interpretations of the powers delegated to the states by the Constitution. Here were two gladiators in the Forum, testing in a convivial assembly the reaction of their respective philosophies, with Calhoun intimating that there is no provision in the Constitution to authorize the general government, through any of its departments, to control the action of a state within the sphere of its reserved powers, and that the Constitution is a contract between individual sovereign states and not a consolidation uniting them all into one great state.

It was to be expected that those who followed the Vice President would touch on the matter of sovereignty, but neither Van Buren, Stevenson nor Branch, who spoke almost immediately, touched on the matter. Senator Eaton's toast skirted the issue: "The people will regard with warmest affection those who shall be found to act from principle." It remained for Carson to illuminate the subject. His toast was, "To the sovereignty of the people—the fundamental principle of democracy—the ultimate tribunal in the last resort to decide all political contests."

Carson was followed by Major Andrews and Mr. Speight, from North Carolina, who produced raised eyebrows when he said, "The division of surplus revenue: It will be a series of eternal scrambling among the members to see who can get the most money wasted in their states, and they will always get most who are the meanest."

By this time Carson had decided he must spend a few weeks in the health-giving baths of the White Springs, and because he did not have time to write a full Circular Letter to his constituents, he wrote a brief summation of his legislative efforts and sent it for publication to the *Carolina Watchman*, published in Salisbury, and other Western North Carolina papers.

To the Freemen of the Twelfth Congressional District of North Carolina: It has always afforded me pleasure to communicate with my constituents the result of the deliberations of the national legislature, and to state the condition of our country.

175

At the close of this long session I have been worn out with fatigue, and in such feeble health as requires my immediate departure from this place for the purpose of seeking to restore my health.

I do not expect to be at home until August. My intention is to visit the different counties in my District and also to attend Superior Court, where I hope to see you individually and render an account of the manner in which I have discharged my duties.

In closing Carson paid a glowing tribute to Jackson for his firmness and moral courage in opposing corruption.

The brilliancy of General Jackson's military career sinks into insignificance when compared with his resisting influences which have borne many men into office backed by the delusive hope of obtaining millions from the public treasury, when they know full well that no money can be taken from the Treasury until it has first been placed there, having been taken from the pockets of the people.

He praised the message of Jackson in which he gave his reasons for vetoing the Maysville Road bill.

"This courageous act, taken in connection with his determined resistance to a rash of appropriation bills rushed through the House on Sunday morning last, is destined to place his name on the brightest page in American history. He must stand the center picture on the American canvas, between the Immortal Father of His Country and the no less memorable sage of Monticello."

The full text of the President's veto message was carried in the same issue as was Carson's letter, as well as the statement that "on Monday, May 31 was terminated the first session of the Twenty-first Congress."

On June fifteenth the *Watchman* reported that "two of our congressmen passed through Tuesday on their way from Washington," and noted, "We are sorry to learn that the Hon. S. P. Carson is confined in Washington because of serious illness."

Carson's illness was more serious than he had allowed his family to know, and his rehabilitation was of longer duration than he had expected. He did not reach Pleasant Gardens until late August.

So as not to undo what had been accomplished for his health, he did not begin the tour of his district until October. Having been warned by eminent doctors he consulted that he was a prime target for respiratory diseases—pneumonia, pleurisy, and even the dread white plague, tuberculosis, he determined to see only as many of the key people in his District as his energies would permit, thus sparing himself the ordeal and debilitating effects of arduous travel.

He intended to return to Washington by way of Raleigh and Halifax. There were matters of prime importance to be decided by the 1830 Legislature now in session at Raleigh, the most pressing of which, in Carson's opinion, was the election of a United States senator to replace the venerable Nathaniel Macon, recently resigned after forty years of public service. The name of Willie P. Mangum, his friend and former congressional colleague had been advanced as the likely candidate to defeat Governor John Owen for the senatorial position. Aside from personal feelings of friendship for Mangum, Carson, with other of Mangum's friends, believed him to be the superior in talents and legal capacity of the Governor, and he had been advised that the vote would be close.

This would be a timely opportunity to confer with Charles Fisher, now speaker of the House of Commons, on possible measures to secure action in the Congress in the matter of expediting the establishment of a mint. There needs must be some private sessions with his friends. But first he must bolster his persuasions with the latest records of mining operations and affidavits of the mine owners and operators, and to do this he must spend time in the area of the most extensive operations. Naturally that would place him in favorable position to spend at least one night at Green River, a prospect he entertained with mixed emotions. That Catharine would be there was more than a remote possibility, and he could hardly endure the remorse he felt at having avoided facing up to the dilemma in which he had placed her.

Now that there was no longer any uncertainty about his amorous pursuits at the White House, and now that the rehabilitation of his health had been accompanied by an equally beneficial rehabilitation of heart and spirit, he welcomed the opportunity to make peace with Catharine, whose vision of

177

loveliness had been a part of his confused delirium when his illness was most critical.

On his arrival at Green River, he was given a noisy ovation by an array of the children of the Plantation, both black and white, who were attended by a middle-aged nanny, and by Peter, his young friend, who explained, "They's all in the back settin' room. They's workin' lak they didn't have no longer dan sundown to finish. I specs you'll have to sleep in the bachelor's house. We'se got cumpny."

Carson could hear them before he could see them—chattering, laughing, sometimes shrieking. As he stepped into the open door he thought he had never seen a more appealingly distracting sight. They did not note his appearance and he was loath to make it known. He did not want to break the enchantment.

Seated on the floor with her back to him was Catharine. Standing beside her and being properly fitted for the length of her gown was Rachel Rebecca, sixteen, the oldest daughter of the household, while her mother and two of the women seamstresses were fitting, measuring and cutting yards of material in both gay and subdued colors.

"Stand still, Ruth Margaret," her mother admonished. "We'll never get your wardrobe finished if you keep fidgeting. And you, Mathilda, thread these needles for me while you wait for your time to be fitted."

Mathilda looked up and on seeing her uncle shrieked with delight. "Why Tilda, baby, what are you doing here?" Sam questioned. The answers came in a chorus of excited voices. "We're going to boarding school, and these are our dresses—just see how pretty they are!"

Mathilda seemed to be the most excited of all—or the most talkative. "Ruth Margaret and I have dresses just alike. We'll be twins, won't we, Aunt Rebecca?" Both near the age of thirteen, they fanced themselves too old to be called "baby" by anyone—except perhaps Uncle Sam.

Catharine made a move to get to her feet and Sam, taking both of her hands in his, lifted her from the floor, meeting her eyes in an effort to convey a meaningful message, but to no avail.

"What a pleasant surprise!" she managed with a forced smile, as she turned aside to allow Rebecca to greet her brother-in-law.

"Sam, how thin you are! You *have* been ill. I had hoped the reports were exaggerated. Did you know Charles is here? He brought Mathilda over so that her wardrobe can be made like her cousins'. He will be going back to Brindletown tomorrow, and the two of you can have a 'caucus' in the Bachelor's House tonight. Suppose you find him and have Peter help you get set up for the night while we make progress for another half an hour or so. We'll join you in the dining room for our evening meal."

"Please, Mother, let me show Uncle Sam my wardrobe—what is finished, I mean."

"Let them parade for me in their finery, Rebecca. I'll promise not to interrupt for long." Snatching up the dresses that were ready, they went into the drawing room to change, calling back, "You come too, Aunt Catharine," but Catharine had disappeared.

"You haven't told me where you are going," Sam called after them, and the excited answer came back, "We're going to the Academy—you know, the Academy at Salem!"

"How splendid! How perfectly splendid! Whose grand idea was it?" Sam exclaimed.

Before replying Rebecca suggested that the two women take their sewing and go to the drawing room to help the girls dress. Pulling Sam into a chair near her, she said in lowered tones, "Sam, we have been quite concerned about Catharine since last spring. She has had too much responsibility with Father and the housekeeping, but there's something other than that that has disturbed her." Rebecca looked inquiringly at her husband's brother, but hastened to say, "We'll have to make a long story short, for they will be coming back any minute. Joe and I decided to enroll Catharine at Salem, thinking a complete change would be beneficial, and when we did our two girls begged to go, and when Mathilda heard about it her pleas were added, and Charles and Margaret consented. Now the four of them will enter the Academy in three weeks."

"Catharine, too?" Sam was incredulous.

"Yes, Catharine too. Her enthusiasm doesn't match that of

the younger ones, but she has seemed less dispirited since Joe has undertaken her guardianship and has completed all of the arrangements for the four of them."

That evening after the excitement had died down and the young people had been "ordered" to bed, Sam, his half-brother Charles and Rebecca attempted in a few short hours to bridge the months that had passed since they were together. Catharine volunteered to see that the young ladies and the children were bedded down for the night, and had brought a pang of disappointment to Sam by suggesting that she was fatigued and would pack herself off to bed with the children. He wondered if the Fates were pitted against him, and if indeed he would have an opportunity to speak with Catharine alone.

His reverie was interrupted by a question from Charles. "What brings you to these parts, my boy. Have you finished your carpentry?"

"What carpentry? I don't understand you."

"Do you never have to mend your fences—your political fences, or are you so firmly entrenched in the minds and hearts of the people you represent that you can trust them to support you come what may?" Noting the serious expression on Sam's face, Charles hurriedly changed the subject. "I'm glad you are visiting in this section that has put Western North Carolina on the map. And I do speak for myself and for the miners in the Brindletown area when I commend your efforts in our behalf. But what makes the Government so confounded slow? We need that mint now, not when we're too far gone to profit by it. I'm gettin' old Sam, my boy, and I'd give ten coins with a Philadelphia hallmark for just one with a North Carolina indentation, but I'm afraid I'll never live to see it."

Charles had been so impressed with the prospect of prospecting for the precious metal that he had removed his family temporarily to Brindletown to be nearer the operations. Small wonder that he was impatient with the slowly revolving wheels of national legislation. He did not speak patronizingly to his younger brother, for he was inordinately proud of him and of his devotion to public life, but he lost no opportunity to tease him unmercifully.

Rebecca had a stake in the mining industry through her

husband's expanding holdings, and she joined avidly in the conversation till the men switched to politics, when she suggested that they repair to their quarters where they could "talk till daylight if they were a'mind to do so," and they were. They welcomed the opportunity to air their mutual interests and concerns. Among other things, they discussed the factions that were in control of North Carolina politics and the contest between Mangum and Governor Owen for the senatorial seat. "I expect to add my weight for whatever it is worth to Mangum's prospects, for I believe he is the better man, and I shall welcome him again as a legislative colleague and friend. We were very close when he was in Washington in 1825, you remember."

But there was one concern that Carson did not discuss with his brother, and that was his utter chagrin and disappointment that Joe intended to circumvent his romantic plans by taking Catharine bodily to a place of incarceration, and in his wild imaginings—although he knew better—he was sure that the object of his affections would be as unattainable at the Academy as if she were in a walled city or in the cloistered security of a convent. He was exasperated because there would be no opportunity for him to press his suit if she continued to evade him as skillfully as she had done. The little minx! If she were playing a game, he did not know the rules unless it was that he should feign an indifference that surpassed her own. And this strategy worked well during breakfast, but after the meal the women were off to their cutting and measuring and stitching, and he had no opportunity to sweep her off her feet with the impassioned words he had been rehearsing. Besides, nine o'clock in the morning was not the most auspicious trysting time, and he could not tarry until the shades of night provided a more romantic setting. He had not spoken of his departure, and lest he upset the sewing bee he secured Charles's promise to convey his loving felicitations and explain his abrupt departure.

Dejected as he was at the outcome of his Green River visit, Carson felt a great satisfaction in arriving in Raleigh in time to assist somewhat in securing Mangum's election.

It was one of the most bitterly contested elections ever held in North Carolina, and to make it more difficult, Mangum insisted on staying away from Raleigh, and at one point he purposely circulated the intelligence that he had withdrawn from the race. His friends and some of his former enemies pleaded with him to add the prestige of his presence to the scene of action, even securing a postponement of the balloting to enable him to reach Raleigh, but to no avail.

At the height of the electioneering, Mangum and his opponent, Governor Owen had exchanged inflammatory letters which hinted at "satisfaction on the field of honor," but friends interceded, and friends secured his election—the election of one of North Carolina's ablest citizens who continued to exert his influence on the national scene for more than two decades.

Carson was in the visitor's gallery at the State House in Raleigh on November thirtieth when Colonel Polk presented a resolution for the appointment of a select committee to procure all documents relating to the Mecklenburg Declaration of Independence "for the purpose of having same printed under the direction of the Governor of North Carolina,"—a salutary move and one long overdue, Carson thought.

Although he was unable to secure accommodations at the roominghouse where his brother Joseph was settled, the two had a number of opportunities to confer between sessions of the Legislature. They made an appointment with Charles Fisher at a time when he could divest himself of his obligations as presiding officer in the House of Commons, and the three discussed at length the strategy in bringing to an early conclusion the matter of a branch mint for North Carolina. They were unanimous in the feeling that it would be wise to have the Legislature propose the establishment of such a convenience, thus giving weight and influence to the proposal introduced by Carson in Congress and still in committee in the National Assembly.

When they at last had time for personal matters, Sam expressed his sentiments to Joe on his plans for Catharine. Immediately his older brother responded with some vehemence. "It took me some time to be persuaded that you had much to do with Catharine's unusual apathy and her debilitated condition. In short, she has been in love with you all of the time you were paying court to another. Indeed she has confided to

Rebecca that when you left last year, after she had been all night at the bedside of the little victim of that venomous attack, that you professed a love for her that you evidently did not feel. Did you discuss this with my wife?"

"There was no opportunity—too many people around almost every minute. I tried to talk with Catharine, but she studiously avoided me."

"Sam, I have never been harsh with you before—except perhaps when you were growing up, but I am going to say to you emphatically, don't do anything to upset the plans already made. Do you understand? I intend to have the girls at the Academy on December tenth and that means I must leave here no later than tomorrow for Green River. It will be my fondest hope that both you and Catharine will use all of the powers at your command to improve your health and well-being. I feel I have every reason to be concerned about both of you."

In thinking over Joe's parting words, Sam began to feel a return of the emotional upheaval that he was confident had been brought under control. He slept little that night and in the troubled hours decided against a visit to Halifax. In fact, he welcomed the days of solitude that would be his while en route to the Capital City. He must and he was confident that he could discipline himself to the extent that he could look forward hopefully and enthusiastically to the future. What was that Biblical injunction that applied in his case? "He that controls his spirit is greater than he who takes a city." That was the gist of it. Strange that he should remember too at this time a toast at a Birthnight Ball celebration: "To Washington—who more than all and above all was master of himself. He guided the passions of others because he was master of his own."

In spite of his high resolves his thoughts returned again and again to the object of his affections. Before leaving Raleigh he posted a letter and a box of confections that should be waiting for her when she reached the Academy. The letter? Just the sort of thing a fond uncle might address to the other three who were his nieces. He hoped they would find their dearest hopes realized in this, their most exciting adventure.

The Congress convened for the last of the Twenty-first

Session on December 6, but Carson did not answer roll call, and was not to make his appearance until a week after the convening. It was the first time he had been late for any of the sessions. A quick look around on his first day indicated that one of his friends was missing. Usually on time for the opening roll call, Crockett took his seat on the fourteenth, two days after Carson had qualified for attendance. Thinking to playfully reprimand him, Carson exclaimed, "What kept you so long? Did your horse develop a spavin?"

Crocket grinned. "Nothin' wrong with my horse, Samuel, I jus took my time. Stopped off to visit friends now and then. I knew if you wuz here, nothin' could shake the foundations of the govermint. Made my last visit in Staunton with friend Henry McClung. Believe he's some kin of yours. He was askin' about our mutual esteemed friend, Sam Houston. That's where Sam come frum, you recollect."

"Where else did you stop, David, and what's the news from back home? How are Elizabeth and the family?"

"Busy mindin' their own bizness, I reckon. Had a weddin' in the family. This here whippersnapper frum up this away seen my girl Margrit when she was up here onct, and he wrote me fer her hand in marriage. I wrote right back and said, 'Go ahead!' And blamed if he didn't do it!"

Just at this point Thomas Chilton, member of Congress from Kentucky, joined them, and with apology he pulled David to one side for a private conversation. During the last session of Congress David and Chilton had been seen frequently together in long and close conversation. Indeed the news had been circulated in the cloak rooms that Chilton, quick to take note of the unusual life pattern of Crockett and his increasing popularity among the members, had begun to weave around him an aura of mystery, stimulating a modicum of hero-worship and endowing him with legendary attributes, the essence of which had found its way into the columns of the press and elsewhere by word of mouth. Although Crockett was prevented from telling him about other stops he had made on his way to Washington City, much later Carson heard the tale of at least one other visit.

It was a miserably rainy afternoon when a stranger was

184

observed to pass through the little village of Ninevah at a slow and easy place, apparently unconscious or inattentive to the rain that was more than a drizzle. Someone followed him to see what manner of man this was who was not in a hurry during a freshet. Overtaking the stranger, they fell into conversation which showed that this was no ordinary man—not that there was anything extraordinary in his conversational powers, but that they were unlike anything he had ever heard before. He invited the stranger to spend the night, and was gratified at his acceptance.

Even when the family had joined them, the host had not determined the identity of his guest, but when the peculiar and marvelous conversation continued, something occurred which led his host to exclaim, "Why, you are Colonel Crockett!"

"I am," was the laconic reply.

Excited whispers ran through the entire household. Colonel Crockett! A member of Congress! How could they believe it?

Before the evening was over Crockett took the children on his knee, caressing and playing with them, the while going over his entire life—his career in the Tennessee Legislature, his election to Congress, his dining with Mr. Adams, for which he was caricatured in the newspapers. He avowed freely his political opinions, saying he had forsaken Jackson because Jackson had forsaken him (a statement he was yet to make in the Halls of Congress). He spoke of the abuses of the government and held the family in close attention until past midnight.

In the morning he departed for Washington City, where on the floors of Congress he would no doubt proclaim his voluble sentiments!

Actually his sentiments became more and more opposed to Jackson and his party, and with this "disallegiance" Crockett became more vulnerable to political sniping, and to the shafts of his enemies.

As for Carson, conversation with other friends—notably Branch and Davis—revealed serious dislocations in the body politic—more serious than was apparent at the close of the last session, for summer had brought a rash of developments that did not augur well for the state of the Union. South Carolina, Davis's bailiwick, was seething with discontent because of the

185

increasing burdens of the tariff restrictions, and Branch, Secretary of the Navy, was having more and more frustrations and less and less compatibility with the President.

Calhoun had already split with the President through the medium of a letter written by Jackson to Calhoun the past May revealing to the latter that word had come to him of an act of disloyalty in asking President Monroe to punish Jackson for his conduct in the Seminole War. Calhoun answered the President's letter by avowing the truth of the accusation. He *had* said in a Cabinet meeting that he believed Jackson had overstepped his authority in Florida, and he *did* propose an investigation of Jackson's conduct. This blow to Jackson's vanity was to trigger a dissolution of his Cabinet, of which Branch was then Secretary of War. Indeed, the insult was of far more significance than the Eaton affair that stirred the Capital and furnished a prime subject for gossip in which both the ladies and the gentlemen indulged, and in which the Cabinet was involved.

A bit of gossip of another sort had reached Carson's ears. It was that Jackson was already beginning to think of his successor—someone most likely to carry on and carry out the democratic reforms he had begun. It was apparent that Jackson was playing an intricate game of chess, in which the stakes were high, and although he was content to move his pawns slowly and with sagacious deliberation, move them he must if he would win the game.

For perhaps the first time Carson began the reassessment of his boyhood hero. He remembered having read in his youth an apt description of Jackson—"the ugly redheaded Scotch-Irish boy who had been hit on the head by a British officer for not blacking his boots, whose poverty at his birth and for years afterward was painful and pitiable, who never knew his father, and could not ascertain after search, the burial place of his mother, a boy whose outlook on life in his early days was about as desolate as human destiny could possibly appear."

This was one side of the coin, and it was not the side that had aroused in him the beginning of hero-worship. Rather, if the forlorn side had been emphasized, it might have induced pity, not acclaim. Rather was it the courageous lad of fourteen who ran away from home to fight in the Revolutionary Army, and who loved horses and horse-racing, and who was ambitious enough to get an education and study law, one who dreamed that somewhere there was a ladder on which he could climb, one rung at a time, as high as he was a'mind to go.

Carson wondered if he had climbed too high—if the shafts of his enemies might topple him from his lofty height. In the reassessing process Carson remembered that Jackson was a clean fighter, that "he went in for a clean victory or a clean defeat," according to his friend Tom Benton. Furthermore he did not like to compromise, although it was known that some of his worst enemies had become his closest friends—this same Tom Benton, for instance. It was true that Jackson was a sworn enemy of the United States Bank, and that he was using his powerful influence to counteract the influence of Nicholas Biddle's institution—an institution that in Jackson's opinion might have been unconstitutionally created, one certainly that had failed miserably in establishing a uniform and sound currency.

These and other thoughts ran through Carson's mind as he reviewed his association with his friend and his President, and he concluded after painful soul-searching that so far—even with the howling about the tariff, the disaffection of Calhoun and the rumors and the gossip—even with all this, he could truthfully say, "Jackson is still my man."

SEVEN

Early in January Carson welcomed his friend, Mangum, into the ranks of the North Carolina delegation, and because they were of the same mind on issues that now, with an increasing amount of heat and vituperation, were being debated, Carson's welcome was unrestrained. Mangum, even as Carson, was a supporter of Jackson. Nevertheless, soon after his arrival he began a close association with the South Carolina congressmen. That brought Davis, Carson and Mangum together on more than one occasion, and their ties became strong indeed.

It was after a pleasant evening engagement with these two friends that Carson found, upon returning to his room, a large assortment of personal mail, as usual delayed in transit. Catharine's communication was read first, and as he read and reread it he was unable to restrain his impatience with her because of its meager contents. She limited herself to polite expressions of appreciation for the confections awaiting her when she reached the Academy and conveyed the intelligence that his nieces were well and happy in their new arrangements. "Many of the new students cry themselves to sleep at night. They miss their families, and homesickness can be more painful and debilitating than physical sickness. Because there are four of us, our family ties have not been completely broken, and we revel in the excitement of each new day." And she closed by saying, "Your three nieces wish me to convey to you their deep affection and high regard."

Carson laid the letter aside and sat for a while in bemused contemplation. "Still aloof and sparing in *her* felicitations," he said almost audibly. But the more he thought about his untenable situation, the more determined he was to enlist Catharine in a plan to bring about the happy ending of his bachelorhood. He was in love with her, he needed her, and both Joseph and Rebecca had assured him that she was in love with him. He must find a way to break down the barrier between them—an aloofness born of distrust. She had accepted his hurried avowal of love in good faith, and he had been a cad in

188

continuing to seek the begrudging companionship of another. Now he must prove the reality of his love for her.

When his mantel clock chimed the hour of midnight he was still at his desk, and by his side was a basket filled with discarded sheets on which was an assortment of prose and poetry, alternate pleading and passionate wooing—most of it effusive and lacking in convincing sentiment—none of it suitable. He was often more effectively persuasive in extemporaneous speech, at least so he had been told by his colleagues on the floor. He believed that if Catharine were in his arms or within his reach he could recapture the response she gave on that most beautiful day in November more than a year ago. But she was many hundred miles away, and he had no intention of waiting until vacation to press his suit.

He gathered up the discarded sheets and after burning them one by one he poured a glass of French brandy, and, sipping it slowly, concentrated on a different approach, planning as carefully and as logically as he did in his successful political campaigns—a straightforward presentation of facts as they are—complete honesty, absolute sincerity and a powerful emotional appeal. Once his decision had been made he lost no time putting quill to paper and in framing the most effective, if not the most eloquent speech of his career.

As he posted his missive next day, he was reminded of his brother's stern, uncompromising demeanor when he was warned not to interfere with plans for Catharine's immediate future. He could see no possibility of jeopardizing her immediate future. What with the hazards of winter weather and the unreliability of postroads, he could not possibly know his fate before the middle of February.

The next few weeks were to be among the most difficult of his life. He could not eat, he could not sleep, except fitfully. The suspense of waiting was agonizing. One day he would be light-hearted, the next day melancholy. He found solace in one of the poems of old:

> O what a plague is love.
> How shall I bear it?
> She will inconstant prove,
> I greatly fear it.

> She so torments my mind
> That my strength faileth
> And wavers with the wind
> As a ship saileth.

Happily, no major bills were under consideration, and while there was wrangling aplenty and party clashes, the serious business was discussed behind closed doors and in caucuses—official and unofficial.

When Carson addressed himself to Catharine during the early days of January, he had no idea that the business of the last session of the Twentieth Congress would be terminated at such an early date, but by the last of February a possible adjournment early in March was forseen.

By writing to and hearing from the leaders in his District, he had kept in touch with the sentiment of his constituents on the explosive matters of the tariff, the United States Bank, and other issues. He relied on his family, too, to keep the channels of communication open.

After the fifteenth of February, the date when he began anxiously to watch every mail, he received a letter from his brother, the Doctor, reporting that a committee of the Legislature had made a report recommending the establishment of a branch of the United States mint in the gold region of North Carolina: "This salutary move should bolster your efforts for a favorable disposition of this matter. Pursue it diligently." And Doctor John went on to say:

> The rumor that Governor Branch is about to tender his resignation as Secretary of the Navy, which has been making the rounds for several months, has flared into new intensity, fanned by the flames of discontent with the President. Whenever such charges emanate from Washington, they are accompanied by quick partisan denials. "Don't believe a tithe of tales you hear from that den of mischief," is the admonition.
>
> Let me back up a minute to make clear the position of President Jackson among the people of your District. There is a deal of mumbling and grumbling about the tariff, about the Bank question, and about some of the President's appointments. And I might add that whenever the women join in, the Eaton affair is "rolled as a sweet morsel under their tongues." But the Legislature have passed a resolution approving Jackson's administration and declaring that the best interests of the Union will be preserved and promoted by his

re-election. So you see, my dear brother, you are still on solid ground. I must warn you that North Carolina sentiment is not as rabid as is to be found in South Carolina, and it behooves you to exercise restraint in your private thinking and your public utterances.

By the way, Charles has just dropped in, and as usual has a bit of family news—I might say family gossip—that may interest you. I'll repeat it as he has told it to me. He and Margaret have just heard from Mathilda with news from the Academy, and she reports the strangest happening. It seems that some of the students were reading their mail after the arrival of the coach and that Catharine had not had time to read half of her letter from a certain Washington Congressman when she swooned—toppled over in a dead faint. I have an idea from what I can piece together that it was her heart. Can you shed any light on that diagnosis?

Mathilda, let me hasten to add, reports that Catharine is quite recovered, and has never looked better nor happier.

Yours in good faith,
John

On the very last day of February the long-awaited letter from Salem arrived, and Carson's joy knew no bounds. Catharine was willing—praises be!—to trust herself to his keeping "till death do us part." "I must confess," she wrote, "that often I have been embarrassed because I was older than most of the girls here, and it did not make me any happier to learn that here, as elsewhere, if a girl was not through school and ready for marriage at sixteen, she was an example of retarded development. Now that you are eager to rescue me from spinsterhood, I can face the remaining months of the school year with a head full of dreams, a heart full of love, and—dare I say it?—with a heart full of longing, too."

Carson was in a daze. He could not believe that in so short a time the whole world could be transformed into such a glorious and resplendent paradise—sunkist and dewey in the morning, star-studded and mystic at night. He went back to Catharine's letter to note, "The sisters have told me that the last of May, after public examinations, classes are suspended for two weeks. We have no vacation until then. Perhaps I shall see you during the two weeks at Green River, for Joseph has written that the four of us may go home then if we make good marks in our studies."

Little did Catharine dream that other plans would soon be in

191

the making—plans that would not wait for vacation time.

Carson was about to enter the Hall of Representatives on the morning of March third when he felt a hand on his shoulder, and he was pulled back into a corridor by his friend—his recently estranged friend, David Crockett.

"Samuel, you seem uncommon pleased about somthin'."

"I am, David, for I have spent the past two nights planning the most important and most unexpected campaign of my life."

"Wish I cud hear whut it is, but we need to git inside. Gess we'll both go home like yaller dogs with our tails between our legs admittin' we couldn't pull off our rispective bills, an 'shamed to face the gallery back home. I thought fer shore you'd git your bill for that Branch mint passed. But I done give up—not on my bills, but my loyalties."

"The winding of the wheels of progress in government takes a long time, David. Don't be discouraged!"

"I am right smart discouraged. No use to take time to explain, Samuel. You know whut my gripes are. They're all aired in this here Circular Letter I had printed. I'll give you a copy. It's mostly about the President. You'll hate me fer whuts in it, but thems my sintiments. Me an the Gineral has parted company as of now. It's as final as the Day of Judgmint. I gess I done committed the unpardonable sin, an I ain't shore that I want fergivness—except from you."

Carson started to comment, but David went right on. "Back yonder when I spoke in the heat of battle about North Carolina grabbin' them Tennessee land warrants, I ment no reflection on you. We've bin friends a long time. I'm willin' fer it to stay thataway if you are, an' here's my hand on it!"

Carson grasped the outstretched hand and the two entered the Hall together.

The members were standing around in groups and by two's and three's talking informally and in jovial mood on the last day of the session. When they were called to order by Mr. McDuffie, of South Carolina, temporary Speaker, the business of the day was dispatched in a few minutes. Then Carson rose to say, "Mr. Speaker, the House of Representatives of the Twenty-First Congress have met for the last time, and when we separate today,

192

many of us will have parted to meet no more forever. My heart admonishes me to say that this is a fit occasion for us to offer up all of our animosities on the altar of peace, kindness and good will." Carson looked straight at David and smiled. He was in an expansive mood and wanted to share his exultation with all and sundry.

Requesting Andrew Stevenson, Speaker of the House, to come forward, Carson, for himself and in behalf of the members paid a well-deserved tribute to the gentleman from Virginia who had presided over their session with fairness and equanimity. Enthusiastic applause greeted Mr. Stevenson as the members rose in a body to attest their feeling and to honor their Speaker, and the profoundest stillness prevailed during the delivery of Mr. Stevenson's valedictory.

After the gavel sounded, signifying adjournment, Warren Davis accosted Carson as he was about to quit the room. "My friend, have you been studiously avoiding me? I have not seen you in weeks. But I have been busy working out plans for an important excursion to Philadelphia this fall."

"I want to hear about it, and as I have important news for you, I suggest that we repair to Carusi's this evening, where our annual farewells are always celebrated. My news calls for champagne, does yours?"

"Not at this stage, but I am very hopeful."

Under soft candlelight Carson listened as Davis went into some detail outlining his plan to promote a meeting in Philadelphia which would bring together tariff dissidents, not only from the South, but from other sections chafing under the tyranny of increased tariff burdens. "As you know, Carson, this issue gets more heated as time goes on. If something is not done to give us relief, there will surely be a disruption of the Union we cherish. We must stop this merciless attempt to infringe on the sacred rights of those whose geographical location serves as a severe penalty. I am counting on you, my friend, not only to be present but to assist me in any number of ways."

"May I bring my bride with me, and will you do me the honor of attending my wedding in the meantime?"

"Carson, my friend, is this some kind of joke, or do you really mean it? This *does* call for champagne!"

No more was said that evening about the anti-tariff meeting, and when later they went their separate ways, Davis had assured Carson that barring an unforseen act of Providence, he would help to ring the wedding bells on whatever date would be agreed upon.

Carson tarried ih the Capital long enough to make a number of necessary adjustments, looking toward his return for the Twenty-second session in December. The National had been his home for so long he was loath to make a change, and after numerous consultations he prevailed on the manager to let him have two connecting rooms and asked that one be furnished as a sitting room or parlor. This could be accomplished by rearrangement of furniture and by adding a few pieces he would send from home that would make the suite more attractive.

He spent one morning looking at gigs and phaetons, but ruled out a purchase until he could ascertain the wishes of his bride. Her sister had made her honeymoon trip on horseback over the Great Smokies. Catharine was not an expert horsewoman, but was not averse to that kind of transportation. Nevertheless, her wishes in the matter would be consulted.

When ten days later he knocked for admittance at a building quite near a hitching block where he had secured Missy, Carson's heart was pounding like a trip-hammer. The village was Salem, a part of the Moravian settlement of Wachovia. It was twilight, and the soft glow of candles inside bespoke an invitation and a welcome that was immediately apparent when the door was opened by one of the Brothers.

"This is the Congregation House, Mr. Carson. The young ladies are at their evening meal in the basement of another building. I would suggest, since you are not expected, that you have your nieces meet you in the sitting room, which also serves as a study hall, in their dormitory."

"Very good, sir—except that for very special reasons I would like to see Miss Wilson alone."

The Brother looked curiously at the stranger. "You do not bring sad news?" he questioned.

"Far from it, sir, but since it has to do with Miss Wilson's possible withdrawal from the Academy, perhaps I should apprise you of my mission. You see, sir, we are to be married in a few weeks."

"Does Miss Catharine know of this?"

"No, sir," replied Carson, and noting the expression of amazement, "I mean, sir, she——"

"Just call me Brother Vogler."

"I mean, Brother Vogler, that she does not anticipate such an early date, but I assure you I have gained her consent to our marriage."

"In that case, I congratulate you, and while we are waiting, perhaps I can tell you something of this building and the ones nearby.

"As I told you, this is the Congregation House, or *Gemein Haus*, as the older villagers call it. It is made of stone and half-timber construction, and as you noticed has two doors that open directly on the street. On the second floor is the chapel, used each morning for worship service and for other special occasions. It accommodates the entire congregation, who, divided by sex, age and marital status, are also divided into separate choirs. The men and boys enter by the north door and the women and girls by the south entrance. Once inside, the men and boys sit to the left of the minister, the women and girls to his right. Each age group of women and girls wear white linen caps with ribbons of different colors, indicating the singing group to which they belong."

"Miss Wilson has told me about the part that music plays in the life of the community," commented Sam.

"Yes, music is as much a part of the daily lives of these Moravians as prayer. They sing hymns in their homes, at harvest time, and always at their lovefeasts. And since June 18, 1783, it is often John Frederick Peter's *Freudenpsalm*, or Psalm of Joy."

"Does that date have special significance?" inquired Sam.

"It does indeed! That was the first year of peace following the Revolutionary War. When Governor Alexander Martin announced the victorious end of the War to the members of the General Assembly, then in session, the good news brought great rejoicing, and before adjournment the Legislature recommended a statewide observance of the Fourth of July as a day of worship and thanksgiving and called upon Governor Martin to issue a proclamation to that effect. This was done on June 18, 1783."

"And so it can be said that the first celebration of the Fourth of July by legislative enactment took place here in the village of Salem," Carson responded.

"That is true, although other states began later to take similar action. But North Carolina was first in all of America to make an official proclamation setting July Fourth as a day of Thanksgiving and prayer in commemoration of our freedom as a new nation.* And so far as is known, the Moravians of the Wachovia settlement were the only North Carolinians to respond to the Governor's proclamation with a planned observance.

"But here is Sister Graff, who will show you to Miss Wilson's dormitory."

Opening the door of the newest building, Carson was shown into one of the four living rooms on the first floor. His first impression was of its size, its modest furnishings, and the cold, bare floor.

"The sleeping quarters are upstairs," Sister Graff indicated. "There are no separate rooms—just a large hall. In summer the bed tickings are filled with chaff, as are the pillows. We are having a late spring, and so the girls are still sleeping on feather beds, which we use in winter." And looking about her, she commented, "The young ladies study in these sitting rooms."

"What do they study?" Sam inquired.

"They are taught history—American history, though many of the students detest it, and only a few really enjoy English grammar. They like composition, and luckily all of them want to learn to 'sew a fine seam' and to embroider. Some of them seem much interested in the course in globes."

"What, pray tell me, is globes?"

"It is the physiographic aspect of geography, and it may interest you to know that the questions and answers concerning latitude and longtitude were based on the location of Salisbury—a place I am sure you know quite well."

Even though he consulted his watch more than once, Carson's polite interest in the recital of Sister Graff belied his

196

impatience. Finally the door opened, and in spite of the decorum usually required and practiced in the presence of the prim and proper sisters, the two met in warm embrace, oblivious to all restraints.

Although reluctant at first, Joseph, as Catharine's guardian, gave his consent to the marriage plans. Fortunately the policy of the school was so flexible that a student could enter or leave at any time of the year, though it was generally understood that once a young lady was enrolled she was expected to remain for two or three years, or until her course of study was completed.

It was not necessary for Joseph or Rebecca to be convinced of Catharine's avowed love for Sam. What they wanted to be sure of was the seriousness and steadfastness of his feeling for her. But Rebecca did not hesitate long. With a woman's intuition of the right thing to say she began enthusiastically, "Of course you will be married right here at Green River. We will begin preparations at once, and will notify all the relatives as speedily as possible. With only six weeks to spare, it will take a bit of doing, but you need not concern yourself, Sam—it can be done! How I wish Father could be here, but since you plan to go to Brentwood on your honeymoon that will console him." Rebecca was thinking quickly of everything. "Since Catharine was so well outfitted for school, her bridal dress and one or two formal gowns for Washington society will suffice."

"Just one thing, Rebecca. Catharine has become devoted to the way of life at Salem. She will probably insist on a Moravian wedding—simple and unpretentious. I know she wants to use some of their beautiful music. Indeed she would be happy if she could transport the whole choir and musicians, trumpeters and all. But I must be on my way. There are some things a bridegroom needs to be concerned about—a best man, groomsmen, conveyances, enough ready cash, and so on. I am buying a chaise and must see to that. And, though you would scarce suspect it at this point, there *are* matters of State that need attention."

"I wish you could stay long enough to discuss some of those matters, Sam. Is it true that Governor Branch is going to resign his cabinet position, and that Jackson is riding high, wide and handsome over the wishes of his Southern advisors?"

"I doubt if he is listening to his Southern advisors, if indeed he has any, Joe. But Branch has not resigned yet. The papers will be full of it when he does." And the papers were full of it. They quoted Branch's letter of resignation to Jackson, and the President's reply. Branch's letter, dated April 19, 1831 noted, "In the interview I had the honor to hold with you this morning, I understood it to be your fixed purpose to reorganize your Cabinet, and that as to myself it was your wish that I retire from the administration of the Navy Department. Under these circumstances, I take pleasure in tendering you my commission, which, unsolicited on my part, you were pleased to confer upon me."

The letter and commission were delivered to the President by a son of Governor Branch, and by him the President returned Branch's commission, stating, "It is your own private property, and by no means is it to be considered a part of the archives of the government."

In his reply Jackson wrote that he had received the resignation of the Secretary of War and the Secretary of State, and after due reflection and mature deliberation he concluded to respect them. He then could not but perceive the propriety of selecting a Cabinet composed of new material as being calculated, in this respect at least, to command public confidence. Justice to the individuals whose public spirit impelled this required this position. "In accepting your resignation, it is with great pleasure that I bear testimony to the integrity and zeal with which you have managed the concerns of your office."

Reaction following the publication of the executive correspondence was immediate. In North Carolina the *Oxford Examiner* stated that the American people had a right to know the truth behind all of this upheaval. "The President should explain what he meant by the statement that there had been lack of harmony in the Cabinet."

It was to be expected that Carson's thoughts and concerns in the weeks immediately preceding the wedding were not entirely of the bloodless revolution taking place in Washington and in the affairs of the new "Kitchen Cabinet."

When the Carsons at Pleasant Gardens came together to welcome the young legislator, the ladies vied with the men in taking the reins of conversation in their own hands. They wanted to discuss the wedding plans, and their plans for attending, and their wardrobes, while the men sought to draw him out in reviewing the national scene of battle.

"Well, at least Jackson's game of chess has proceeded to the point where we know the disposition of his pawns. It is no longer guess work," said Doctor John, with a hint of bitterness in his voice.

"Branch is certain to continue to exercise his fine talents in the national government in some capacity," suggested Colonel John, who for the first time admitted his displeasure with the President.

"In all of this 'lolligaging,' the interpretation of the Constitution is the basic question," asserted William, "and Calhoun believes he has the correct interpretation."

"Yes, he believes 'that the object of the Constitution is to restrain the government, while the object of laws is to restrain the individual,' as one of our older statesmen has said. It is difficult now to predict the shape of things to come, but we must find an honorable way to weather the storm."

May tenth was the date agreed upon for the evening wedding. The bachelor's house would become for one night a benedict's haven for the bridegroom and his beloved, while the relatives and guests would be taken care of by doubling up and putting down pallets. Fortunately Charles and Margaret could entertain almost as many relatives at their nearby home. Soon after her arrival from the Academy early in April, Catharine presented the nuptial plans she and the nieces had made, and it was evident that the wedding music would have almost as much emphasis as the ceremony itself.

"Rebecca, although it would please me to have a service exactly like the Moravian ritual, our Episcopalian service is beautiful and we will use that, except that we *must* have a choir. I wish it could be our Moravian choir, but that is out of the question. You know what wonderful voices our Negroes have! Let me train them to sing the Moravian hymn that is as appropriate for a wedding as for Thanksgiving, and I'd like for Sera to sing. Her voice is as beautiful as any I heard at the Academy."

"Catharine, dear, your happiness is a joy to see. Do as you wish about any of the plans. I only hope that you and Sam will be as happy as Joseph and I have been."

While Catharine and Rebecca were talking, young Peter appeared in the doorway holding a small boy by the hand. "Miss Catharine, dis is Martin. You know, the boy whut you nussed all night when he wuz bit by a copperhaid. He wants you to know he is well an' fine, an' whut kin he do for you?"

"It was very thoughtful for you to come, Martin, and if you really want to help, you and Peter can go with Jubel to get the evergreens to decorate the house. We need rhododendron and ivy and clematis vines, and if the mountain laurel is in bloom we can use bushels of that."

The wedding cake and confections came from Philadelphia. The cake provided the centerpiece arrangement for the dining room table, on which was cut glass and gleaming silver that reflected the light of a score of candles in the crystal chandelier above.

All day many hands were busy with preparations for the prettiest wedding in Western North Carolina—at least so the principals thought.

How could so many people who had been crowding and jostling each other all day, laughing, talking and calling out greetings to each new arrival be suddenly calmed? How could so much noise be hushed and so many voices stilled in one moment of expectation?

It was the music—piano and violins blending in the joyous strains of Hayden and Schubert, an introduction to the antiphonal singing of the Negro choir and Sera's secular solo, *There Was A Lady Passing By*.

Then all eyes were turned toward the stairway, where preceded by Rachel Rebecca, as maid of honor, and Ruth Maragret and Mathilda, as bridesmaid, the bride and groom descended arm in arm. At the foot of the stairs they walked through a festooned aisle through the parlor to an improvised altar flanked on each side by tall candlesticks with lighted tapers. The festoons, ropes of evergreens and ribbon, were held by young nieces, nephews and cousins, whose participation Sam had personally insisted upon and planned.

As they knelt and after the prayer of blessing had been spoken, the voices of the choir rose in quiet harmony in the Moravian hymn:

> Now thank we all our God
> With heart and hand and voices,
> Who wondrous things hath done
> On whom the world rejoices,
> Who from our Mother's arms
> Hath blessed us on our way
> With countless gifts of love
> And still is ours today.
>
> O may this bounteous God
> Through all our lives be near us
> With ever joyful hearts
> And blessed peace to cheer us
> And keep us in His grace
> And guide us when perplexed
> And free us from all ills
> In this world and the next.

* * * * *

"It is seldom that any bridal couple can spend months on a honeymoon, and although I hope ours will last forever, the time has come, Mrs. Carson, for your husband to begin to think about more mundane affairs. I must warn you that even though a number of months intervene before your life in Washington begins, the fall months are always busy ones in any congressional district—now more than ever when there is so much controversy and bickering over national affairs."

After spending the summer in Brentwood with Catharine's father, James Wilson, the young couple was traveling toward Pleasant Gardens over much the same route as that taken by Joseph and Rebecca on their honeymoon. "August is half gone and as soon as I deposit you at Pleasant Gardens I must be going again—this time to Virginia. My close and esteemed friend Colonel Isaac Avery and I will begin our trip next week. We must be there on the third of September."

"Is it a political convention?"

"Oh no. The meeting is called to decide the matter of a

survey of a new road that will cross the Blue Ridge at a point which will be easily available to Eastern markets. The decisions should be productive of much good for Western North Carolina. Will you mind staying with your new relatives while I am away? I must warn you, the boys may make it rough for you!"

"Since it will actually be the beginning of my new life as the wife of a distinguished congressman, I am eager to embark on my career. Of course I will love staying with your family. If the boys make it too rough, I will fly to Almyra's protecting arms."

Almyra was her first cousin who had married Sam's brother William, and whose home was "in flying distance" of Pleasant Gardens—less than a mile away. "Will we go through Raleigh when we go to Washington?"

"No, that's too far east. Besides I do not relish the thought of seeing the desolation wrought by that terrible fire last June. It will be years before our state capital will recover from its effects. You have no idea how the place had grown in the eight years since I went there in 1822. And now! I dare not picture it!"

"Will you share your friends with me when we get to Washington? I know about Governor Branch, but there are others I'd like to meet."

"Oh, my dear Cathy. I shall be so proud to show you to my friends. Beside Warren Davis, who is really my closest associate, there is Senator Mangum, a North Carolinian, and Senator Benton, whose two daughters you will like, I think. Tho I can't really count him as a friend, there is John Randolph from Virginia, who knows how to be civil but often prefers to be blatantly uncivil. You may not like him. I'm sorry you will not meet Nathaniel Macon, one of the representatives from North Carolina. He has just retired from his post. He and John Randolph were close friends; in fact, their close friendship will be perpetuated for all time following the establishment of a college for men in Ashland, Virginia last year that bears the name Randolph-Macon."

Catharine had settled back among the cushions—a far-away look in her eyes—probably trying to visualize the Washington scene, and Sam proceeded in his recital.

"Yes, John Randolph is a rather peculiar individual. He made

202

a parade of his friendship with Macon, referring to him in nearly every one of his speeches as his honorable and respected friend from North Carolina. They lived in the same hotel, spending hours together on long winter nights. I suppose that was when they began the promulgation of their dogma of absolute States' Rights."

"Who is the most outstanding and the most talked-about man in Washington beside the President?"

"Who is the most outstanding? I honestly believe that very few would contradict me were I to say that it is John C. Calhoun—our South Carolina neighbor—and I'll tell you why——"

"Oh, don't tell me why. I think I know. It's because he has the courage to stand up to the President, but I'm not sure I know enough about Nullification. Could you explain it in simple terms?"

"Well, you know what the word 'nullify' means—that's elementary. It means to destroy the effect of or to make void. Now suppose South Carolina believes that a state may nullify an act of Congress which she believes is unconstitutional, and that the tariff law is not only highly inexpedient and unjust but also violates the provisions of the Constitution and, therefore, they wish to make it of no effect. And then suppose the majority of the United States with the President at its head should be of a different opinion, and should call South Carolina's actions by a different name—say rebellion. And then suppose—which may or may not be the correct supposition—suppose that General Jackson threatened to call out the fleet to force the people of South Carolina to obey the law of the land and to suppress the rebellion——"

"But you're making it worse than it is—it hasn't gone that far yet."

"You're right. It hasn't gone that far yet. That is the reason that I am still with Jackson, though as far as I'm concerned, I think he is skating on thin ice. There is one bright spot to consider—there is a good chance that we are going to wipe out the public debt next year. That means we could expect relief from his burdensome tariff, and all would be well."

"You haven't mentioned your friend David Crockett—at least

you haven't mentioned him in a day or two. Do you think I will meet him?"

"I am sure of it, Cathy, if he is re-elected. He has been so outspoken in his criticism of the President that he may lose the election. I hear that the reaction to the Circular Letter he sent out last spring that was filled with venom and invectives against the administration has had the effect of a boomerang and that he may have to spend the next session 'shootin' bars and ridin' the rapids in Tennessee.' I saw a flyer in the *Raleigh Register* lampooning Crockett for his defection from the ranks. It was probably copied from the *National Intelligencer*. You know the *Raleigh Register* follows the *National Intelligencer* as truly as the big wheel follows the little wheel—or so say its critics. But look over to the right. I see our overnight lodging place in the distance. I'm hungry and thirsty and a bit weary, and bless you, dear little Cathy, I know you are too!"

The year 1832 was ushered in in Washington with the icy blast of winter venting her fury on the shivering populace. The thermometer registered thirteen degrees below zero and snow measuring to depths of a foot lay on the ground for weeks. It was reported that a number of persons had frozen to death. But the cold was somewhat mitigated by the heat generated at the Capitol. It was a foregone conclusion that where two or three politicians were gathered together there the tariff dispute was in the midst of them. One wondered if, indeed, other important matters of State were being bypassed or ignored in this preoccupation with the controversial fiscal concern.

At this point Carson was not preoccupied to any great extent with anything but his new marital state. For the first time in his political career he had a home away from home, and the enjoyment of it with his dearly beloved wrought a noticeable change in his disposition and personality. No longer was he tense and anxious. How could he be with Catharine around? She was full of surprises, amusing herself while he was away by writing verses to him which he would find in the most unlikely places. This one he had found only today among the papers he had taken to the House:

When I was just a little girl
You were my Lochinvar,
And all the while I was content
To worship from afar.

Then with a grown-up eagerness
I gave the love you sought,
Until I thought I'd lost you
My heart in anguish caught.

But now you're mine forever
We must cherish every minute
Of this blissful State of Matrimony
Now that we are in it.

Sam laughed at the change in meter that made the verses more appealing. Yes, he was determined to savor each new experience that he shared with Cathy as equally satisfying in wonder, in excitement, and in delightful adventure.

They had attended the Open House at the President's Mansion on the first day of January. It was a thrilling experience for Catharine when she met the President, who, as was his custom with ladies, treated her with gallant consideration, and in her case with noticeable affection. With Warren Davis and a young Washington socialite, they attended the eighth of January celebration of the Battle of New Orleans. And now the Birthnight Ball was imminent.

"Would you mind if we did not go to the Birthnight Ball tomorrow, Cathy? I am in the midst of important negotiations for a friend."

"Of course I wouldn't mind. Do you want to tell me about it?"

"Senator Mangum and I have been asked to act as seconds if a duel is the last resort in a difference between two friends— Governor Branch and Jesse Speight, of North Carolina. It seems to be a matter of misunderstanding, and Mangum and I are hopeful that oil can be poured on the troubled waters in time."

"What happened, Sam?"

"It originally had to do with Van Buren and the West Indies trade. Speight accused Branch of playing 'a bold fist in the dark' against the President. Naturally Branch resented this. Tomorrow

Mangum and I will see the injured parties and attempt a reconciliation."

"Why, this is more important than a ball, Sam. You'll prevent a duel if you can, I know."

"You *know* that I will, my precious wife."

The efforts of Mangum and Carson were fruitful. A letter was sent jointly to the two antagonists signed by the proposed seconds, noting that General Speight had disavowed in the most unqualified terms any inference of disrespect toward Governor Branch.

In reporting their successful intervention to Catharine, Sam said, "You must meet Senator Mangum. He is quite a speaker when he is full of his subject. On the seventh of this month he spoke for two and a half hours on this ever-present tariff question. In spite of its length, it was a moderate and restrained presentation of the unfairness and sectional imbalance of the tariff. His friends hailed the speech as a careful judicial approach to the ill-fated tariff bill, his enemies shouted that he had gone over to Calhoun."

Although Catharine had not made close friends among the feminine contingent in Washington, she was never bored. Something was always happening to challenge and interest her. There was the day in April when Sam came home with the latest episode from the House.

"One of our respected Congressmen fell by the wayside yesterday, Cathy."

"Was he ill? What happened?"

"It was Congressman Stansberry, and the trouble began about two weeks ago when he made a speech on the floor of the House that reflected on Houston's part in a proposed contract for Indian supplies. Governor Houston, about whom I have often spoken, came to Washington to intercede for the Cherokees, to whom he is devoted and with whom he has lived from time to time. Although as an ex-congressman he has the privilege of the floor, he was not in the House that day, but heard of the reflection on his conduct and character through the press. He wrote Stansberry, asking if his speech had been accurately reported. To this Stansberry replied that he did not

206

recognize the right of Houston to put such a question to him. Governor Houston at once declared his intention to horsewhip Stansberry on sight, and that is what happened today. Armed only with his walking stick, he met Stansberry on the street quite by accident. Stansberry, having been warned of Houston's threat, was armed. 'Is your name Stansberry?' he asked.

" 'It is,' Houston's adversary replied. Whereupon the Governor exclaimed, 'You're a d—— rascal,' and struck him down with the stick, beating him severely. Passersby said as Stansberry lay on the ground he pulled a pistol and snapped it at Houston, but it did not discharge, whereupon the latter turned and walked away. The whole tale was related to the group by an eyewitness."

"Poor man! I hope he was not seriously hurt. Do you admire Governor Houston, Sam? I really believe you do."

"Let me answer your double-barreled question this way. Yes, Stansberry was hurt—his pride sustained a lasting blow, but he was not mortally wounded, I assure you. As to Houston, let me say that he has fallen on evil and unfortunate circumstances in his life. I will not say that these events have embittered him. He is a man without a country. I pray God I may never be in a similar situation."

"You have mentioned your friendship with Governor Houston, but you have never told me about his life. Of course I know that he was Governor of Tennessee."

"Before he was governor," Sam explained, "he served two terms in Congress. He was in his second term when I came into the House as a freshman congressman. We were often together, officially and unofficially, in those days. He was a candidate for a second term as governor when the citizens of Tennessee were astounded to learn that he had resigned as governor and was going to leave the state."

"What happened so suddenly? I remember only vaguely."

"His marriage to a young, ambitious wife came to an untimely ending. It was then that Houston left the state, bitterly denounced by his enemies. He went to live with the Cherokee Indians in Arkansas, where earlier he had been an agent appointed by the adjutant general, and where he had many friends who welcomed him as their very own. He made

207

his home with them for two or three years, and recently he has been in Washington negotiating with the government in their behalf."

"I would think," interrupted Catharine, "that Governor Houston is a very valuable citizen—one who is loved and trusted by the Indians can be a great asset to our country."

"You are right, my dear, but I'll tell you a secret. Can I trust you?"

"Oh yes, Sam. I want you to trust me and to share your thoughts with me."

"Although the matter is being discussed in privy councils only, it may well come to light soon. With the blessing of the President, and with his advice, General Houston of the Tennessee militia—no longer to be called 'Governor Houston'—will go to Texas where many of the settlers are greatly outnumbered by the Mexicans. His mission will be one of investigation of this vast and rich country—now ripe for the taking by the Mexican government. Recently there have been sanctions employed that are disturbing to the citizens of the United States who haved settled in this alien country. But remember, Cathy, this is in strict confidence. There's much at stake in this secret diplomatic mission."

During the summer of 1832 the presses of North and South Carolina worked overtime to publish the vast amount of copy made available to them on the controversial subject of Nullification. The heat of the summer was intensified by the heat generated over this explosive issue.

But the rebellion in South Carolina and in her neighboring states did not receive all of the publicity, nor even a major portion of it, because in that year an enemy of dire proportions invaded the nation, and this time North, South, East and West—jointly and severally were pitted against the invader—the deadly malignant cholera. Stealthily the enemy infiltrated towns and cities, hamlets and villages, borne to our shores by the frightened fugitives from Europe, reaching our harbors only to sicken and die from the plague they brought with them. Here indeed was an enemy they were helpless to battle!

There was the case of a very elderly man who journeyed from

New York en route to his home in Rhode Island. After leaving the boat, he was taken ill on the stagecoach, whose passengers were alarmed and made an attempt to put him off at some house along the way, but none would receive him. In this critical condition he was denied a seat in the stage, was taken out and lashed to the top, being too sick to sit up, and in this way was brought to Providence, where for the sum of five dollars he was taken to the home of his brother, who refused to allow him to enter the house. He was taken to the barn, where he was looked after till his physician could be summoned, but not in time to prevent his death.

The disease, it was said, apparently depended upon some poisonous property in the air—made more receptive to persons who allowed themselves to be afflicted with passions of anger and resentment. Temperance in all things was highly advocated, and in all things regular habits of mind and body.

Perhaps a more scientific judgment was evident in the story of a woman who was chided for bringing the dread disease into a city where as a result there had been many deaths. "Do you not feel responsible for carrying death to so many people—to ninety or more in this place?"

The woman denied the accusation. "You're wrong," she replied. "Thirty may have died from cholera—the rest died from fright."

In the press, columns were devoted to suggested treatment of the dread disease, and many instances of man's inhumanity to man came from many quarters as the summer lengthened and the malady progressed. Governor Stokes of North Carolina set apart a day of fasting and prayer "that God in His infinite mercy would avert the impending judgments and ward off further inroads of the terrible plague."

There was no panic in Washington, albeit the city was visited with the scourge, and although the legislators were anxious to get on with their business and get home, the session dragged out interminably. It had been a disruptive session, climaxing a power struggle between the President and his cabinet, during which Vice President Calhoun resigned—the first time in the history of the country that a Chief Executive and his next in line had been faced with such irreconcilable differences as to force the subordinate to quit the field.

In the closing days, Catharine, concerned about her father, pleaded with Sam to allow her to accompany the family of one of the representatives whose return journey led him very near to Brentwood.

Carson was loath to give his consent. He could not bear the thought of such a long separation. While they were debating the question, a communication came to him from Halifax, North Carolina, over the signature of sixteen members of a committee appointed to issue him an invitation to attend a public dinner in his honor. "Be assured, sir, your public services have been appreciated in this section of the state. The principles for which you have contended have taken deep root in our soil, and we believe upon their maintenance depends the existence of our once fair and happy Union. It is with pride and pleasure we have ever found you fighting on the side of principle and fearlessly advocating the cause of an injured and oppressed community."

"Oh Sam, that's splendid. You'll go, won't you?"

"I would like that very much, Cathy dear, but what I like more is that here is a congressman from Western North Carolina, recognized and honored by representative leaders in an Eastern Carolina community. In a state in which East and West are split asunder and at loggerheads, a testimonial like this gives me the deepest satisfaction."

"And don't forget that your efforts are noted and appreciated by citizens of Boston, a typically Northern city, or is it typical?"

"There's nothing about Boston that is typical, my love. It is unique—a city set upon a hill in its urbane exclusiveness."

"Nevertheless, when the *Boston Daily Advertiser* admires the bold and independent stand you have taken on the floor and adds that you are second to none of your colleagues in asserting the rights and upholding the dignity of your native state, it, too, should give you deep satisfaction," Cathy declared.

"But you must remember that there are many outbursts of a different nature in my files that serve as counter-agents if I should become smug and self-satisfied. It is important that a politician's wife be better prepared for the worst than for the best."

It was not long until more expletives of the kind that he referred to were added to those already filed. It came about in this way: the officers of a large Protestant denomination, disturbed about the increasing devastation wrought by the dread epidemic of cholera, wrote to the President asking him to dictate a proclamation to the American people to set aside a day of humiliation, fasting and prayer "that God in His Infinite Mercy would halt the spread of this terrible disease and spare our land from its effects."

The President did not concur in this suggestion, and so stated in a letter addressed to the president of the Dutch Reformed Church that was published first in a New York paper and later in the *Globe*. At the same time, but before the President's action was known, the Congress was besieged to take action to insure that a Day of Fasting and Prayer was observed.

To that end, a joint resolution of both houses, calling on the President to act in the matter, had been introduced and was being debated in the House of Representatives, the extent and ramifications of which were unbelievable. Mr. Adams proposed to amend by striking out the word "Asiatic" because the malady was confined to no specific area of the world. Congressman Burgess saw no reason to change the designation already given to it. All were agreed that it was the most dreadful and frightening calamity ever visited on the human race, yet days were spent in needless proposals that skirted the issue itself.

Finally, Carson rose in his seat to say, "I believe this matter might be suddenly arrested simply by reading the letter from the President. For myself, I make no profession of love for prayer and fasting. I think the measure improper and likely to end in no good purpose. The communication from the President is not long. I think it is a very good letter and I request it to be read at the clerk's desk."

The request brought a stormy reaction. There were cries of "No, no—we have all read it!"

Carson refused to be intimidated. "I shall read it myself then," was his reply. Then standing in his place, he read the reply of the President to the Synod of the Dutch Reformed Church on the subject of the proclamation. He was neither interrupted nor reproved as he read the entire communication:

Dear Sir: I have the pleasure to acknowledge receipt of your letter of the 10th instant, submitting to me an extract from the minutes of the Synod of the Reformed Dutch Church in America, relative to a day of fasting, humiliation and prayer at this time, and which your Committee requested the President of the United States to appoint.

Whilst I concur with the Synod in the efficacy of prayer, and in the hope that our country may be preserved from the attacks of the pestilence, "and that the judgments now abroad in the earth may be sanctified to the Nations," I am constrained to decline the designation of any party or mode as proper for the public manifestation of this reliance. I could not do otherwise without transcending the limits prescribed by the Constitution for the President, and without feeling that I might in some degree disturb the security which religion now enjoys in this country in its complete separation from the political concerns of the general government.

It is the province of the pulpits and the State tribunals to recommend the time and the mode by which the people may best attest their reliance on the protecting arm of the Almighty in times of great public distress. Whether the apprehension that the cholera may visit our land furnishes a proper action for this solemn notice, I must therefore leave to their consideration.

I am, Sir, very respectfully

Your servant
Andrew Jackson

When Carson finished there was strong objection to further debate. The previous question was then moved and seconded—the yeas and the nays ordered and the resolution passed 99-62. Carson and Davis voted against the measure. But this was only the second reading, and Carson felt that there was still a chance to defeat it. He did not count on nor foresee the abuses that would be heaped upon him for his part in acquainting the House with the President's views.

Debate was resumed on Monday, July 5, with Mr. Adams of Massachusetts and Mr. Coulter, together with Congressmen Wycliff and Dearborn bearing the major burden of the heated discussion as to Mr. Carson's lack of judgment in introducing the letter of the President.

Carson was not present. On July 2, he had asked for and

obtained a leave of absence for the remainder of the session, and was already on his way home to North Carolina happily out of ear-shot of the ranting Congressmen.

Foremost among his critics was John Quincy Adams, who, after lengthy accusations slanted toward the perpetrator of this questionable procedure, said, "It was not my intention to open my lips on this subject, but I must confess that I heard the letter read with a feeling of indignation, and I am sorry that the member who introduced the letter is not here to hear me say so. It is the first time I have yet witnessed an attempt to influence the House by referring to private communications." He then turned to history for precedents, referring to the history of England, with particular reference to certain individuals of renown.

Congressman Coulter then observed that "the letter which had been read by Mr. Carson had, by being published in the papers, become a matter of history. It was now known to the nation and to the world, and the reading of it in these walls gives it no added publicity. There is no member of the House who would more decidedly and more promptly resist any improper attempt of the Chief Magistrate to interfere with the legislation of this Nation than Carson would. His votes and his conduct during the past four years show that fact." And then in sarcastic vein Mr. Coulter continued, "He ought, however, to have remembered the *Lex Parliamentaria* on the subject. In England, any direct interference of the King with members of the House of Lords was not a mere breach of order, but a high crime, a misdemeanor, and a breach of the high privilege of Parliament. If that rule were to prevail in this country, the gentleman from North Carolina who read the letter from the President ought to have been called upon in a different manner and should have been proceeded against for a breach of Congress. That was the spirit of the British Parliament. Had I known that the gentleman from Massachusetts would so methodically have referred to the laws of Parliament, I would have endeavored to keep my remarks within the range of British requirements. But Mr. Adams should remember that there is a great difference between the King of England and the President of the United States. The King was almost wholly responsible to

213

the people on whose throne he sat—not by appointment or election, but by Divine Right."

Here, the subject of the debate was shunted to one side, while some of the members heatedly clamored for the speaker to be censured for his lack of parliamentary procedure in failing to charge Carson with a breach of order in reading the letter.

The entire day was taken up with charges and counter-charges, and with appeals from decisions and rulings of the Chair. In the absence of the speaker it had fallen to the lot of Congressman James K. Polk to fill the chair. He attempted to explain his ruling, but was interrupted by Mr. Adams in charges that necessitated prolonged and lengthy elaborations, provoking the comment of Mr. Polk that either the gentleman from Massachusetts was so learned or he himself so simple that he could not comprehend the object of his remarks.

Mr. Polk then went on to say that he trusted the day would never come when the representatives of the people would be prohibited from referring to the public or private opinion of any individual, if such opinion were relevant to the question before the House. He pointed out that the gentleman from North Carolina, Mr. Carson, had, for the purpose of illustrating his views, read from a newspaper the copy of a letter written by the President of the United States. The letter was referred to by later speakers without objection. The Chair, then, had decided that he could not declare Mr. Carson out of order.

Bristling with contempt, Congressman Stansberry charged that in allowing Mr. Carson to read the letter, the Chair had sacrificed the dignity of the House. "Never," he stated, "did the monarch of the British throne exercise such power over his Parliament as the President had exercised over the deliberations of the House." Turning to Mr. Polk, the speaker exclaimed angrily, "Your predecessor in the chair never crouched before those in power. I defy any gentleman to point out such an instance—until *you* were placed in the chair. In the discharge of your duties your eyes have been too often directed toward the White House."

Seldom had so much fire and brimstone been evident in the deliberations of the House. Mr. Stansberry was called to order for his insinuations against the chair, which were unfounded and untrue, and a motion at a later session was introduced to bring formal charges against the irate member.

More than a week had been spent in destructive argument about the resolution and all of its implications. When no agreement was in sight, the House agreed to refer the resolution to a select committee with instructions to amend.

When the news reports of this long drawn-out hassle reached Carson several weeks later he felt cheated that he had had to miss the shafts and barbs of his opponents and the ready support of his friends in this another exhibition of the ineptitude of politicians looking for a scapegoat. Too bad that the Great Physician had to wait indefinitely to be implored to save the health of the nation whose affliction was daily growing more acute and terrifying, while a few puppets played a game of tweedledum and tweedledee until the session adjourned on July sixteenth.

EIGHT

As usual, following Sam's return, the house was filled with his nieces and his nephews, his cousins and his aunts—all bent on celebrating the occasion. The adults were holding forth in the parlor when Colonel John turned to Sam. "Your brother has some private matters to discuss with you, son, and the rest of us will clear out."

Doctor John, for once, looked solemn. "Sam, there is a matter of grave concern facing you right at the wrong time. I have uncovered a bit of family history that you will have to deal with. Did you know that you have a daughter who is more than ten years old?"

Sam reeled from the impact of the news. He did not need to be told who, nor why, nor when. These things he knew without prompting. But he asserted flatly, "You'll have to believe me when I say that I knew nothing of a child. How did you find out?"

"I was called to the home of a little girl who was sick. I seldom go that far back into the mountain coves, and I honestly don't see how you stumbled on such a place of rendezvous. The child was in a bad way with a high temperature, but no delirium. I asked her to tell me her name. 'Emily,' she said. 'And what is your father's name?' I asked. 'Sam Carson,' was the immediate answer. I turned to the mother, and she nodded her head in assent. 'Why have you not told my brother about this long ago?' I asked her. 'They's some things a woman keeps to herself if she thinks it's better that-away. He was young and I was young—but old enough to know better. I think now it wasn't right to keep quiet all this time. A child needs a father, and Emily will be eleven her next birthday.' "

Doctor John eyed his brother rather fiercely. "I can forgive you Sam, and so can Father, for sowing a few wild oats in your youth—maybe a double handful—but this will blast your political career, no doubt about it."

"How can you say such a thing, John? You are worldly-wise

216

enough to know that I am not the only man in public life who has had his peccadillos. Just now I am thinking about Catharine, and strange as it may seem to you, I am thinking of my responsibilities to the child and her mother. It has not been long since I read a statement written a few years ago by Doctor Elisha Mitchell, who measured the elevation of our high mountain over there, and who said, if I remember it correctly, that a woman is more likely to forgive another woman than a man is to forgive a woman in a case like this. Maybe Catharine will be understanding."

"Well, you know we have a way of meeting crises in this family by coming together in consultation."

"Not this time—not all of us. I believe you and Father and I can make a determination, and I'd like to do it now."

The three men were closeted for more than an hour. When they emerged, a course of action had been agreed on, subject to Catharine's approval and to the wishes of the child and her mother.

Chafing under the separation from Catharine at a time when he needed her so desperately, Sam became more physically depleted than he had been for a long time.

"Catharine will be outraged. If she isn't she ought to be," his father had said when the three men were discussing the unexpected turn of events.

He tried to put the nightmare out of his mind, praying that he would wake up to find that it had indeed been a bad dream. But the morning always brought the stark, relentless truth.

Cathy had prolonged her stay because of her father's condition, and would not reach Pleasant Gardens until the last of September.

Carson had been summoned to a meeting to be held in the Burke County Court House, presumably to discuss the matter of the tariff. Because of the men in charge, he did not know what to expect. He felt physically unable to go, but John had also been summoned, and he would do the driving.

The meeting was in progress when they arrived. Among the resolutions presented for consideration was this: "That we look upon the doctrine of Nullification, as lately promulgated by our

217

sister state of South Carolina, as neither a Constitutional nor peaceful remedy, but one which tends to a dissolution of the states—to anarchy and civil war, and we therefore highly disapprove of same."

During the discussion Carson rose and expressed his surprise at a meeting of this kind that was no doubt called together for the purpose of ascertaining his views upon certain points. "As your representative," he said, "I am willing to state my views, but this meeting was unexpected. I am quite unwell, and I request an adjournment until tomorrow. A statement of my views will take time to prepare, and I have no doubt that my request will be granted me."

Carson's request brought on a few heated remarks and some confusion, and an extraordinary move was made to the Presbyterian Church, where the report of a committee was read in a very emphatic manner. Then followed a speech full of sound and fury, in which the speaker dared any man present to avow himself a "Nullifier." Carson, from his seat replied, "I am a Nullifier, and I dare avow it, sir." Continuing, the speaker asked, "Is there a Nullifier in the house?" Carson replied, "There is one—I, Samuel Price Carson."

The speaker pretended not to hear, or deliberately tried to needle Carson by expressing the hope that there was not one Nullifier in the room. Carson rose, and speaking in tones loud and clear, said, "I hope to God there is not *one* Nullifier, but many." He then walked to the front and offered an impromptu resolution: "That this assembly does explicitly and preemptorily declare that it views the powers of the federal government (as resolved from the compact of the states that are partners) as limited by the plain sense and intention of the instrument constituting that pact—the Constitution; that the states who are partners thereto have the right and are in duty bound to interpose for the arresting of the present evil and for maintaining in their respective limits the authorities, the rights, and the liberties appertaining to them." There followed a brief discussion, the question was put by the chairman, and Carson's resolution was adopted as the expression of the meeting—only three voting against it.

When he left the building, Carson reached in his pocket, brought out the emblem of the Nullifiers that he had heretofore hesitated to flaunt in the faces of his constituents, and placed the Blue Cockade on his hat. Now all the world could see on what side he intended to throw the weight of his convictions.

As they started out on their long and weary journey back to Pleasant Gardens, Doctor John laid his hand on his brother's arm. "Mark up one tremendous victory for a sick man!" he said with affection. "For one who at heart is not a Nullifier, I'd say you put the enemy to rout."

"Well, you know, John, that these meetings will probably be more and more frequent as time goes on—at least until some measure of relief is evident. It amazes me that in spite of the inconveniences of travel, our people in droves will go great distances in order to hear both sides air their contentions."

"That's right. Remember that meeting in Salisbury last fourth of July when you were on your way home from Washington City, and when in spite of the plans the anti-Nullifiers had made to disrupt the meeting, our friend Charles Fisher saved the day by requesting the 'antis' to leave the room. Only a dozen or so complied, leaving an immense crowd who went on to adopt strong resolutions to proceed with every lawful means short of Nullification to obtain redress from the wrongs imposed on the South.

"I suppose you know, Sam, the identity of the man who is responsible for putting some backbone into the Nullifiers in Salisbury, and by the same token putting some of the antis to flight?"

"I have no idea."

"None other than Doctor Ashbel Smith, who has recently returned to Salisbury after having superintended the care of cholera patients in a northern hospital. He has returned to active practice and has become part owner and editor of the *Carolina Watchman*."

"I assume, then, that he is a Nullifier," observed Sam.

"An ardent one, and the *Watchman* will reflect some of his convictions. He is a Yale graduate—Phi Beta Kappa."

"I remember only that during the two years I was in the North Carolina Legislature in 1822 and 1824 that he was teaching school in Salisbury," Sam continued. "What happened to him after that?"

"He studied medicine. Has only recently returned from Paris

219

where he furthered his medical education."

"And with wide horizons like that he is a Nullifier? That's the most encouraging news I have had recently. I must pursue acquaintance with Doctor Smith. But to get back to those mushroom meetings throughout my district, do you think that from the considered judgment of a majority in those meetings I will have a mandate to guide me in my ultimate decisions?"

"In a democratic society, any responsible representative must move with the spirit and intent of the majority—or resign," John replied.

"Sometimes I am overcome with all of this dissension—even though I know it is healthy. One of these days I am going to hear a statesman who will clinch the matter for me, and then, as Crockett says, 'I will spit on my hands and plow a straight row.' "

"Well, if one man is more convincing than a majority, I hope you will find the right spokesman. Yes, poor old David, he sowed so many seeds of hatred of Jackson in his straight row that his electorate deserted him." And looking mischievously at Sam, he added, "You know there just might be a lesson for you there, son."

"You know I don't hate Jackson, and if we do come to the parting of the ways, it will be a sad day for me. If it hadn't been for my high regard for him I would have stopped this vacillating that upsets me and gone 'hook, line and sinker' for Calhoun."

Before they reached home, past midnight, they had had time to speculate on what the next move in South Carolina would be—about the ability and judgment of former Senator Hayne, soon to be installed as governor of the state, of Calhoun's maneuver to secure his own election to the United States Senate after he had resigned the Vice Presidency, and of the impending clash of wills that would inevitably follow if Jackson proposed the use of force to bring South Carolina into line.

"My allegience to President Jackson has been predicated on my sincere belief that he would show a willingness to compromise on tariff matters, and thus reduce the tensions that are all but ready to consume even the most reluctant leaders in our neighboring state. I believed with all my heart that he did not want disunion, and would prevent it at all costs. You have only to read the proposed bill for the collection of the tariff by force to see how misguided I was. I have no doubt the bill will be enacted next year, and I shudder to think of the results," Sam said.

"Why was it impossible to bring about a climate of reconciliation in the closing days and weeks of the last Congress, Sam?"

Sam sat in thought for a minute, remembering how he had joked about missing the pitched battle over the Day of Fasting and Prayer. The more he thought of the wasted hours that might have been used for purposeful achievement, the more upset he became.

"My dear brother, let me answer your question by declaring that if anyone would like to see a demonstration of the witlessness of a body of supposedly enlightened men in a time of national calamity, let him go back and read the proceedings that emanated from the mighty representatives of a great and mighty people in the closing weeks of the last Congress. Read it—read it and mourn that our system of government would tolerate such a time-wasting exhibition."

Doctor John laughed at Sam's earnestness. For his brother to be so vehement and critical of the Congress when he himself had caused much of the trouble and the delaying tactics by his insistence on reading the letter from the President struck him as ludicrous and inconsistent. "Bye the bye, Sam, William mentioned the day we started on this trip that he and Almyra were contemplating a trip to Brentwood. If they go, Catharine can return with them. I hope that happens, because as your medical advisor, I would frown on such a long journey for you, prostrated as you are at this juncture. If you are willing to obey orders and put yourself under my restrictive care, I believe you can be sufficiently restored to make the trip to Washington City in December."

Doctor John had never told a patient that his illness was more mental than physical, but he knew how great a part the psyche played in manifestations such as this, and he was convinced that much of Sam's indisposition was occasioned by worry lest Catharine would not accept the fateful news that awaited her return.

"Would you like for me to apprise Catharine of your wish to

221

have Emily accepted into the family as a member in good standing? Maybe I can ease things a bit for you if I convince her that our family wants to make a place for her among us."

"You don't really believe that I am that kind of cad, do you? She hasn't even been apprised that there is an Emily yet. I am trying to prepare myself for her violent reaction and her rejection not only of Emily, but of me. This is the most difficult assignment I have ever had, but I have no one to blame but myself. Your kind offer is not acceptable, Doctor, but I will willingly and gladly do everything you advise to build myself up physically for whatever ordeal faces me. We have already overcome one hurdle in securing the consent of Emily's mother to her adoption. Thank God she approves of our plan to take the child into the family at once."

Just before Catharine's return, Sam had Eli saddle Missy and a small pony, and later in the day he rode up to a small log house—the only home Emily had ever known. He had made a number of visits to become better acquainted, and to prepare her for a change into another environment. She was beginning to lose some of her shyness and to accept him—not as her father, but as someone she could trust. This was to be her first excursion from the home in which she felt comfortable and in which she had a sense of belonging.

Carson was surprised at the ease with which she mounted the pony. She was accustomed to riding bareback on the one animal that might be listed as part of the goods and chattels of her grandfather. And he was surprised, too, that at the end of a long ride she seemed reluctant to have him leave her.

Whether it was Catharine's nurture and admonition in things of the Spirit that led her to forgive even as she might expect to be forgiven, whether it was her unqualified and increasing devotion to her husband, or whether it was the latent stirring of quiescent motherhood—whatever the reason, Catharine was able to give her qualified approval of the plans to accept Emily on equal terms with other members of the family. They had been married almost two years, and there was still no prospect that she and Sam would have a child of their own. The qualification that Catharine had insisted upon was that Emily be legally adopted and taken into the family home at Pleasant Gardens, where she would have a tutor who would help her overcome some of the deficiencies of her early schooling and manner of life.

Sam had waited until they were on their way to the Capital City to enlighten Catharine. He did not want the news to break upon her while she was surrounded by so many family members. They had been forced to delay their departure because Sam early in November had succumbed to one of his recurring attacks of pneumonia and influenza. Even now he was debilitated with a racking cough.

On Monday, December 10, the Congress convened, having had little more than a month's vacation, most of which, in the South, at least, was interrupted by political conventions, States' Rights conclaves and Nullification meetings. Singularly, about this time, Sam Houston entered Texas, and the entry portended vast changes, not only for Texas, but for the United States. He went to this far country with the advice and consent of Jackson to prepare for an inevitable clash with Mexico, and these two had in mind, even at this early date, the eventual annexation of the Texas empire into the American Union.

Carson was in his seat in Congress on December 19, having arrived in the City the night before, and he immediately got into committee hearings on the establishment of a mint and the coinage of gold in North Carolina. One of the members noted that Mr. Carson had been assiduously careful to oppose any infraction or violation of the Constitution, and he wanted to ask if the Constitution gave him the power to propose such qualifications of the bill already introduced to establish a branch mint.

Carson answered, by questioning, "Where did Congress get the power to establish a mint? The Constitution states only that it might coin money. A mint is a place where such coinage takes place and is implied in the directive 'to coin money.'" He stated that the assay was the first step in giving coins their accepted value, and he again pointed out the dangers inherent in the transportation of gold to Philadelphia to be coined. Because of this, his constituents were clamoring for Congressional action.

A number of gentlemen in the House refused to be convinced

223

of the need for establishing a mint in the South, and Carson asked if they had read the reports and documents bearing on this subject, specifically referring to the amount of gold from North Carolina that had been coined last year. "It amounted to $204,000," he stated, "and unfortunately little of it found its way back to North Carolina."

Mr. Polk opposed the measure on principle. He believed the government did not have the power to do what the bill proposed, and if compelled to vote immediately, he would vote against the bill. Therefore he moved that the committee rise, report progress, and adjourn to sit again. Accordingly, Carson's last chance to insure provision for a branch mint in North Carolina would be buried in committee, to be resurrected when he was no longer a member of the Congress.

Neither House sat on New Year's Day but in the North Carolina Legislature the members heard the report of a select committee of the Senate in resolutions that proclaimed:

1. A declaration of warm attachment to the Union
2. A similar attachment to the Constitution of the United States
3. An emphatic declaration that the tariff is unequal, unconstitutional and unjust
4. Denouncement of Nullification as revolutionary
5. Instruction of the delegation from North Carolina in the Congress to use their best efforts to produce reconciliation.

On Friday, January 4, John C. Calhoun, having decreed it objectionable to remain as a member of Jackson's much talked about Kitchen Cabinet, took his seat as a duly elected senator from South Carolina.

In his speech on the State of the Union, the President gave a summary of events leading up to the critical situation in South Carolina, delineating each step that had been taken without success by the government of the United States to prevent the present crisis from developing. "The state of South Carolina," he said, "has forced upon the general government the unavoidable duty of deciding on a new and dangerous alternative—the use of *force*. We cannot allow any state to obstruct the execution of the laws within its limits, or see it attempt to carry out its threats to withdraw from the Union, both of which are revolutionary in character and in tendency."

The President then outlined the steps he had taken to protect the interests of the government within the state of South Carolina:

1. Removal of the Custom House from Charleston to Castle Pinckney, a necessary precaution.
2. Provision of a law that would enable the President to take other drastic measures in the interest of preserving the Union.

The President went on to say, "A recent proclamation of the governor of South Carolina has openly defied the authority of the Chief Executive, and I have expressed my determination to accept the services of volunteers who are ready, if needed by their country. They have been told to hold themselves in readiness to take the field at any moment, and at Charleston a rendezvous has been opened for the purpose of enlisting men for magazine and municipal guard."

The excited emotion of the Southern members—pent up while observing the rules of protocol inside the chamber—burst forth in unrestrained pronouncements once the members were outside the halls. "This is WAR! The President cannot get by with this drastic measure. Let him try it and see what happens!" While others shouted, "We should not submit to his revolutionary Force Bill—even if it means armed resistance!"

When, during the following weeks, Davis and Carson found opportunity to confer on the dominant opinion of the electorate in their respective states, there was no question that Davis, backed by Calhoun, and with a clear mandate from the majority of his South Carolina constituents, had a decided edge on Carson, whose mandate was not clear—certainly so far as pulling out of the Union was concerned.

"Davis, I have been doing a good deal of soul-searching, and I find I can no longer teeter-totter on the uncertain tariff platform that now supports the North Carolina electorate, and so I expect to take a stand that may result in political ruin for me, and no doubt will separate me from many of my friends in the Congress, and most particularly and regretfully from my friend, the President."

"It is my sincere hope Carson that your constituents will

225

support you in this declaration that I am sure you must make in order to live with yourself. I cannot conceive of continuing my service here without you for consultation and advice and for the good comradeship we have enjoyed these several years. I will not allow myself to think of such a deprivation. Tomorrow, which I believe is the twenty-third day of February, I intend to sound the tocsin in behalf of South Carolina. Will you be present?"

"You know that I will, my friend. Not only will I be there, but Catharine will be in the gallery. She wouldn't miss such an auspicious occasion, nor of course would I."

They and many others were there as Davis spoke on his resolution to request the President to communicate to the House whatever evidence he may have received that the Government and the people of South Carolina, or any portion of them, had at any time contemplated or intended to seize the forts or property belonging to the federal government.

"This resolution," he said, "was not introduced with a view to imputing blame to the President or the Secretary of War for the mode or manner of publication of the order of the chief executive. The government and the people of South Carolina have been charged with plans to seize the arsenals and the stores, the munitions and other property of the United States within the limits of the state of South Carolina. The last order of the series went even further and charged them with worse. It was charged that they contemplated crossing the border into Georgia to plunder the United States arsenal at Savannah of its arms and its munitions. Is it expected of the representative from South Carolina to keep silence in the face of these allegations? I deny the charges from whatever source they emanate—whether from the lowest private station or the highest public office— from whatever quarter they come, I say in reply,

> Highland or lowland
> Prince or Peer
> Lord Angus—thou hast lied!

Cries of "Bravo! Bravo!" were hushed immediately.

Davis denied that the South Carolina delegation had employed delaying tactics that resulted in the "snail's pace" at which the tariff bill had proceeded. "We have not impeded it by

226

frivolous amendments. We have acquiesced in and followed suggestions of friends on the floor, and we have remained silent on this deeply interesting subject, lest to our participation in debate might be attributed whatever dilatory or stormy character it might assume.

"You have all witnessed that we submitted in silence to the reading and discussion of public documents containing false and defamatory libels on the State of South Carolina and its people. We submitted to language of contumely and reproach upon our public functionaries that shot like fiery arrows through our veins. Yet we were dumb!

"Still more, Sir, the bitter cup was not yet filled. We felt it our duty to let the sacrifice be complete. We remained in our places. We kept our seats and bore the torture. You all knew from the beginning of the session that such would be our course, yet we were baited from the start.

"What friendly voice of truth or justice was heard in vindication during those hours, days, weeks, of burning agony—what did we hear from those who ought to have defended us? Why, that we should precipitate—fall headlong from our height. Precipitate! Away with such stuff and nonsense!

"And what, Sir, do we see now? The tariff question that has been creeping, loitering, driveling, dragging itself through six weeks of session—the very bill we were desirous to abstain from discussing lest we might shake rudely the leaves of the olive branch. This bill, entitled to all parliamentary right and usage to precedence, is to be shifted aside and the firebrand to be flung before us! Why? Forsooth because the President wills it!

"And by whom is the attempt made to substitute this sword in place of the olive branch?

"By the fast friends of the President on the floor. Can I be mistaken? . . . No, we understand it now. The President is impatient to wreak his vengeance on South Carolina. Be it so! Pass your measure, Sir—unchain your tiger—let loose your war dogs as soon as you please. I know the people you want to make war on. They await you with unflinching, unshaken, unblanching firmness. I know full well the State you strike at! She is as deeply enshrined in warm affection, brave hearts and high minds as ever formed the living ramparts for public liberty.

"They will never receive this bill, Sir—this odious *force* bill,

227

whether you pass the other or not. They will never submit to it! They will see in it the iron crown of Charlemagne placed upon your Executive. They will see in it the hideous features of pain and penalties, the declaration of war in all but its final form. They are the best informed people on the face of the earth, or that have ever been on it, on the great principles of civil and political liberty. They will see in it the prostration and demolition of States' Rights, State Constitution—ay, and the Federal Constitution, too.

"But say you it is a mere bill for collecting revenue, intended to prevent civil war and to preserve the peace?

"With an Army and Navy in your fist, you tell us that this bill of pain and penalties is a mere matter of revenue collection! A very quiet and peaceable affair! You collect taxes at the point of a bayonet and call it civil process!

"I heard a gentleman near me say that it is only a question of dollars and cents. To be sure that is the very gist and marrow of it. If it were not for such things as Southern dollars and cents we would never have heard the question raised. All governmental appropriations, exactions and tyranny throughout the world and from the beginning of time have been perpetrated for the dollars and cents of honest people, earned by the sweat of their brow for the purpose of giving them to the powerful or roguish who did not earn them.

"Why, Sir, if the President must be gratified, why not give him a tee-to-tum or some other harmless toy? Do not give him the purse and the sword of the Nation—the Army and the Navy and the whole military power of the country—as a peaceful plaything to be used at his discretion.

"Sir, South Carolina has received an insolent mandate of the President, commanding her to retrace her steps, tear from her Archives one of the brightest objects of her glory and alter the fundamental principles of her Constitution—and she sends back to him, through her humble representatives, this answer:

> Bid him disband his legions,
> Restore the commonwealth to liberty,
> Submit his actions to the public censure,
> Abide by the judgment of a Roman Senate,
> And strive to gain the pardon of a people!

"That, Sir, is her answer!"

At the very earliest moment allowed by protocol and practice, Carson went to his friend, and putting his arm about him as he clasped his hand, he spoke with highly-charged emotion, "Any further word from me or from anyone on this subject would be a fatal anticlimax. You have spoken for us all, and in terms so eloquent and moving that we will say to Webster and Hayne, to Henry Clay and to Pericles, 'Move over! Make room for one who is entitled to sit with you in the seats of the mighty orators of all time!'

"Now, let us hear from the Union Party in South Carolina—from Poinsett and his cohorts—the minority spokesmen of your great state who would compromise with right and justice and honor to the detriment of the commonwealth! Months ago I told my brother John that my hard and fast decision on this matter would be made when I heard a statesman who would convince me of the right course for me to take. I have heard him, my friend. Thank you for showing me the way."

On the following Monday, Carson made an attempt to have the odious Force Bill referred to the Committee of the whole House. He made the motion, he said, to permit the freest and fullest discussion on this important measure, which he stated was of a more despotic nature than the Alien and Sedition Law. The attempt did not bear fruit, and so between Monday and Wednesday he strengthened his determination to make his stand clear once and for all.

As always, he talked things over with Catharine, and noting his emotional involvement and his unusual pallor, she begged him not to become overwrought in the unfortunate controversy. And as usual, he reassured her. "Oh, it's just a 'tempest in a teapot,' " he said lightly. "I'll be all right." But on Wednesday, the twenty-seventh of February, when he rose to speak, he was deadly serious.

"From the obvious majority against me, it seems useless for me to persevere in my attempt to have this tragedy-laden bill referred to a committee of the whole; therefore I have withdrawn my motion. I now rise to perform a solemn duty, such a

229

one as I had hoped would never have been my lot, and one which fills me with the deepest regret. It is to part with many of you with whom it has been my pride and pleasure heretofore to act. I regret this the more because I know it will operate to banish me from the regard of a man whom I have delighted to honor—a man I have served, if not with as much ability, certainly with as much honest zeal as ever a son felt toward the person and reputation of his own father. Never has my heart known such a feeling of devotion toward any human being unconnected with me by blood, as toward Andrew Jackson. But I have arrived at the spot where we must part. I find it difficult when feelings of devotion and affection of the heart enter in to indulge in censure—even when the object of those affections are most in error. On the contrary, I feel that I would rather hide such things from the world and let them be consigned to perpetual oblivion. With the popularity he has enjoyed, this man could have done more good than any President since the days of Washington. But alas! Along with the power to do good is the corresponding power to do evil, and that is what will be inflicted by this bill."

Carson's remarks continued as he referred to a similar incident in the early days of his incumbency. "A gentleman who sits near me now, former President Adams, sent to the House a message relative to a treaty with the Creek Indians—which message strongly hinted at the use of force to 'coerce' the Indians into submission. I well remember that I and my coadjutators pounced upon the passage in question as hungry pikes would pounce upon a roach. We were all ready with our gaffs on to fly at the man who presumed to send such a message."

All eyes were turned on Mr. Adams as Carson continued. "I would say to any of you who voted with me on that occasion that before you vote for the present bill, you ought to go to former President Adams and seek his pardon. Everyone remembers what a sensation his message produced; everyone must remember the able report on it in the Senate, and certainly everyone remembers that because of the strong opposition of the House and the Senate in 1826 and 1827, the Chief Executive—that man who now sits within our midst as a congressman—refrained from using force to bring the Creeks into submission.

"I apprehend, sir, that this bill must pass because it is necessary to appease the Union Party in South Carolina. It is due them, perhaps. South Carolina has many distinguished sons. There are gentlemen here whom I highly respect who belong to the Union Party. But I regret that from them should come a demand for a bill like the present which will operate against their own state.

"I am reminded, Mr. Speaker, of some appropriate lines from the Irish poet, Moore, in relation to Ireland, now equally applicable to South Carolina:

Unprized are her sons till they've learned to betray,
Undistinguished they live, if they shame not their sires,
And the torch that would light them through dignity's sway
Must be caught from the pyre where their country expires."

That Carson's allusion to the lack of filial patriotism on the part of the Union Party was to go unchallenged was unthinkable. It did not. Mr. Blair of South Carolina, a Unionist, tore into the kindling at the sacrificial altar with vengeance and with enough brimstone to start a major conflagration.

On March 2 the last vote was taken on the Force Bill, and in spite of the eloquence and grave concerns of Carson and Davis and forty-six of those who agreed with them, the odious bill passed with 149 affirmative votes. When the vote was announced, McDuffie of South Carolina rose to perform a solemn act of duty. "The House," he said, "is about to destroy the rights of the states—to bury the Constitution. I therefore ask the poor privilege of writing its epitaph." He then offered an amendment to the title of the bill by striking out the present title and by inserting the following, "An Act to Subvert the Sovereignty of the States of this Union, to Establish a Consolidated Government Without Limitation of Power and to Make the Civil Subordinate to the Military Power."

McDuffie's amendment was defeated.

"You seem to take for granted that you are already beaten. Do you expect to campaign for re-election?" was Catharine's

231

question after Sam had related to her the events of the day.

"That I do, my dear. I have no intention of quitting under fire. I'll let the voters decide."

"What do you mean by 'under fire?' You have already vindicated yourself in every political meeting in North Carolina so far."

"Yes, but there's one prospect now that might not deal so kindly with me. I have a communication here from a committee in my district calling me to appear in Morganton in three weeks to be censured for my course in opposing the Administration and endorsing 'the extreme views' of Mr. Calhoun. That means I should start at once. I dread the winter travel. I dread, too, another separation from you, my darling Cathy, but I will go with all possible speed."

"You will not go alone, Sam. Surely you'll not be so foolhardy. You'll be too exhausted to defend yourself, and that's what you will be called on to do. You can't drive all that distance yourself."

"No, I intend to procure a driver. I'll leave next Friday. Will you pack for me? Just the barest necessities. From the summons, it appears that the meeting will last two days. I'm not sure I can stand up to two days of censure."

The meeting was held in the First Presbyterian Church in Morganton where the first day, Colonel Burgess Gaither delivered a well-considered speech that did him great credit. The celebrated lawyer, Samuel Hillman, esteemed by all who knew him to be one of the most profound thinkers and one of the best informed men in the state, was held in reserve for the second great day when the resolutions were to be offered.

Shortly after the meeting opened next day, to the surprise of all concerned and to the dismay of many, Carson's carriage was driven rapidly through the village and to the Church door, while the bells were calling the indignant clans to meet for the purpose of condemning his course.

Always ready in an emergency, he took his stand in front of the pulpit when the crowd gathered and appealed to those present to say whether, without a hearing, it was fair to convict him of misrepresenting his constituents. The crowd voted in favor of allowing him to speak first and Hillman to reply.

According to the custom, there was a large pitcher full of the finest French brandy near at hand. Looking about him as though to assess the temper of the crowd, he delivered a speech that abounded in flights of eloquence that charmed and seething invectives that made his opponents quake. It contained a clear and logical presentation of the reasons upon which the Calhoun party relied to sustain the principle that Congress had no power to levy a tariff that would raise a sum sufficient to defray the expense of government, economically administered, and of the still more startling proposition that the States had a right to declare null and void a law enacted for the purpose of protecting certain manufacturers.

As he began his speech, Carson poured out a glass of toddy for Hillman, and raising his own glass pledged health and prosperity to the brilliant lawyer. Carson spoke for two hours, and from time to time he replenished his accuser's glass. When he concluded his remarks and gave Hillman a chance to make his charges, the lawyer was unable to rise from his seat. While the newspapers proclaimed a complete triumph for Carson, it was hollow victory,—a victory through default and by questionable means, and while Carson's friends congratulated him for his expediency he was plagued with the thought that his political downfall might be imminent.

Since Carson was only twenty miles from home, it was unthinkable that he would return to Washington City without a visit to his family at Pleasant Gardens, albeit a most hurried one. It gave him an opportunity to see for himself that Emily was already one of the family, and except for occasional homesickness, had adapted herself to the change in environment in a manner becoming a well-dispositioned child. He had brought a little gift for her, and a nice warm coat that Cathy had selected.

As he unpacked he found a note from Catharine, and in it was one of her verses apropos of a recent statement he had made to her:

> A tempest in a teapot did I hear you say in fun?
> Well that is quite unlikely when all is said and done.
> That something strange was brewing is more than just a pun
> For 'twas in a Kitchen Cabinet that the mischief was begun.

When Sam joined the family circle, the Carson men indulged in a long, sometimes heated discussion of "Andrew's folly," and while they were not fully agreed that Sam's political doom had been sealed, with one accord they accepted the course he had taken as the only one compatible with the exercise of a man's conscience and convictions.

"As long as our country endures there will be conflicting views of the Constitution. Whomever is president, he will make his own interpretation, and God help us if he be incompetent, or a demagogue, or possesses the will of a tyrant, as some are now attributing to our Andrew." It was Colonel John who spoke, and he added, "The convention which framed the Constitution refused to delegate to Congress the power to coerce a state into submission. I cannot bring myself to believe that Jackson will carry out his threat to our neighbor." Then turning to Sam, he said, "I want you to make the strongest race of your life, Son. Stand up for your convictions even if you go down in defeat."

"By the bye, Abner tells us that Crockett plans to make another race for Congress this year. I doubt if Tennessee has become embroiled in the tariff question to any great degree," volunteered Logan.

And so it came about that both Carson and Crockett campaigned in their respective districts—each in his own individual style, and with opposing effects. Carson was defeated, while Crockett was again sent to Washington. Sam's opponent, James Graham, had waged a powerful campaign, and David Newland, a new competitor, made a favorable showing. Carson easily carried his own county, Burke, with Newland running second, but he was outvoted in the other counties.

There was little time to brood over his first political defeat. While his campaign was in progress he had been solicited by a personal friend who was a political enemy to act as his second in an affair of honor. The principals were his trusted friend, Charles Fisher, and his political foe, D. F. Caldwell, both of Salisbury.

Caldwell had asked Carson to act as his second, a fact that caused contention among Carson's friends in the area, particularly to Burton Craige, who had been solicited by Fisher to act as his second. Craige scathingly rebuked Carson for aligning himself with one who had worked to defeat him in the last election, and who in the ensuing duel might take the life of his adversary, Carson's friend of long standing, who had again and again proved the integrity of his friendship. Fortunately the affair ended happily for all concerned when Carson, after repeated consultations and missions of good will, was able to bring about a reconciliation of the injured parties.

The newly-unseated Congressman was now faced with a decision about establishing his residence in North Carolina. His home had always been at Pleasant Gardens, and he was at a loss to know what decisions to make. His brother Charles approached him at the most opportune time. "I am moving my family back home at the end of the year. Why don't you move in at Brindletown? You'll be near the mines and can look after my interests and yours too, and you'll be just a few miles from Joseph and Rebecca, which should be pleasing to all concerned."

It was a happy solution for everyone. Charles had gone to Brindletown when the gold rush started, and Margaret much preferred her own home. Carson had not determined his future course, and was grateful for an opportunity to reestablish his health in an environment so familiar. Accordingly, during the last week in December the move was made, and with a refreshing sense of humor he immediately christened it "Nullifier's Retreat."

They had spent a happy Christmas with his nieces and his nephews, his cousins and his aunts at the old home on Buck Creek, where he had received the most wonderful Christmas gift of all—Catharine's announcement that another little Carson was on the way. "It is time you determined to begin to put down roots in North Carolina," Catharine teased, "so that our heir can claim the rightful heritage of a true Tar Heel."

With Emily, his was already a happy family, but he was certain the new arrival would compound that happiness many times. So contented was he with these dreams of the immediate future that he resented deeply a summons to attend a meeting in Morganton—one of a number to be held throughout the state to protest Jackson's removal of bank deposits.

His erstwhile antagonist, Hillman, having apparently undergone a change of heart, introduced resolutions condemning the President's action as unconstitutional and unwise.

Both Carson and Hillman spoke effectively on the dereliction of the Chief Executive and the resolutions of condemnation were passed without opposition. The resolutions represented the sentiment of a large part of North Carolina where the bank had many supporters.

After the meeting, Carson and Hillman tarried to discuss and compare the previous meeting at Morganton when they were on opposing sides in a similar battle of wits, with the productive session just held. No reference was made to Hillman's final, unfortunate incapacity on the former occasion, however. "Whether or not the resolutions we have just passed tonight will be productive of any measure of relief, will be dependent upon the actions of the United States Senate. It is apparent that we can expect more from Senator Mangum than from Brown, who undoubtedly is a wholehog Jackson man," Hillman commented.

The gentlemen then discussed the relative merits of the two senators from North Carolina—Mangum, who had been walking a tight-wire in his advocacy of States' Rights, but his unwillingness to come out for Nullification, and Bedford Brown, whose expediency in political matters had reflected more of self-interest and less of the qualities of statesmanship. One of Senator Brown's harshest critics had said that on the matter of the banking measure, he did not know his political arithmetic. Carson was sure that Mangum could be trusted to follow through in the most effective way, even though he had not broken with Jackson.

"Mangum is a prudent man, Carson, but I am not sure he knows the extent of the unpopularity of the President in North Carolina. There is no one better qualified than you to recognize and proclaim the complete change in public sentiment here. One year ago, when you were about to be censured for being ahead of your time in expressing your convictions, the man in this county who would in public dare to say anything against General Jackson, would be insulted, as you were about to be. Now you can hardly go into any crowd without hearing him denounced in the most unqualified terms, and those who are

236

most bitter against him are those who have heretofore been his most devoted friends."

"I suppose the almost universal state of collapse of our banking system, brought on by the President's unrealistic tampering with the Bank of the United States, will swell the ranks of his enemies," suggested Carson. "There is nothing that so affects the fighting instinct in a man than a measure that reaches into his pocket as does the Bank bill. It will be interesting to see what happens when this measure of condemnation of the President reaches the floor of the Senate."

Although they did not see it, they heard later what happened when Mangum presented the resolution in the Senate. In his powerful speech he emphasized the point that the question was no longer "bank or no bank" but "Constitution or no Constitution." In this speech he definitely broke with Jackson, for which he was severely criticised in Congress, and warmly praised in North Carolina.

After Senator Mangum presented his resolution, his colleague, Senator Brown, denied that the resolution represented the sentiment of the people of Burke County, stating that the miserable petitions came from a group of "pot-house politicians." He was joined by other friends of Jackson who denounced the resolutions; one of whom was Senator Forsyth of Georgia.

The political implications of these sporadic outbursts were not lost on the associates of the President—Van Buren, Clay and Webster, the last two having thrown the weight of their conviction and eloquence in opposition to the President's bank bill when political rallies were held, reflecting the sentiment in large metropolitan centers.

A citizen of North Carolina, writing to David Crockett, now a member of the House, observed, "I think the reports of the meetings in New York, Philadelphia and Baltimore will have a mighty influence in opening the eyes of the American people to the true character of the President. His treatment of the members of those committees—the rough and insulting manner in which he spoke to them—is enough to disgust all high-minded, independent and honorable men with the man."

To Crockett, who long before had "unharnessed himself"

from Jackson with the statement, "I did not leave Jackson— Jackson left me," these pronouncements must have produced a warm glow of satisfaction.

It was Doctor Carson, who in April wrote to Senator Mangum a letter of commendation. "We had a meeting in Morganton the week of Superior Court," he wrote. "It was convened in consequence of the debate on the resolutions from Burke County recently heard in the Senate, and further stimulated from the indignant feelings at the course our Senator Brown took on that occasion. The meeting was called to disabuse the participants at the January meeting of the aspersions cast upon it by Mr. Forsyth, followed up by Senator Brown. The vote on the resolutions was unanimous, save two."

Doctor Carson went on to refer to the Webster bill to extend the charter of the Bank of the United States for six years, a move he sanctioned, and to Calhoun's speech in regard to it. He spoke of the presence at the meeting in Morganton of Colonel Isaac T. Avery, and of his own brother, Samuel P. Carson, and closed by saying, "I cannot but express to you the pride I feel in having one from our state who has the fearless independence to march forward in the vindication of principle, and the ability to sustain himself in the high and honorable course which you have adopted." He added a postscript commenting on the decline in the price of gold in the area in the wake of the Bank controversy.

Sam was grateful that there was a bright side to his political misfortunes. The turn of affairs had given him opportunities he might otherwise have missed of being often with his favorite brother, Doctor John. Jogging along toward Brindletown after one of the numerous political conclaves, they fell into their old pattern of conversation, Sam commenting that so far he had been almost as busy, though without compensation, as he was when he was a congressman. "I'm beginning to chafe under the pressures that take me away from home to attend these political meetings. I need to be with Catharine, now that she needs me in a rather special, protective way."

"I would think she would have plenty to do managing the increasing number of your Negro population."

"There's an overseer for that, John, and I am fortunate that many of them are able to dig enough profit out of the mines to pay bed and board for all the rest."

"While your mother was alive, Sam, she looked after the needs of the women and children at Pleasant Gardens as if she were a paid female overseer, and she did it with a kindness and gentleness that endeared her to them—especially to the children."

"I remember well her ministrations, often getting up in the night hours to visit a sick child, that is, if she couldn't or wouldn't waken you to attend him."

"Speaking of mines, I'm glad to hear that your successor in Congress intends to keep alive the matter of establishing a mint in the area. Did you notice what Colonel Avery said in his speech the other night about the calibre of men who have been drawn into the state because of their mining interests?"

"Yes, he stated that the mines have attracted here a body of men who will be found to possess as much enterprise and intelligence as can be found among an equal population anywhere—that among them are men who have filled the highest offices in our State."

"And to think that with such a showing we cannot wean away from Philadelphia a small portion of her coinage profits, nor light a fire under our Southern obstructionists like Polk, who are responsible for the slow death of your bill."

"It is so irritating, John, that sometimes I am tempted to hitch my wagon to another star."

"Do you have any particular star in mind?"

"Yes, I may as well admit it, I have given an occasional serious thought to joining my friend Houston in Texas. He needs help from red-blooded Americans who have some of the know-how of governmental procedure and practice."

"I think you're crazy, my boy. I really think you are touched in the head with an ailment I know how to diagnose but not to treat. My God! I can't think of anything more revolutionary than that! You'd be jumping out of the frying pan into a fire that all the devils in Hell would delight to see. Look at me, boy! I do believe you're a sick man! A sick, sick man!"

Sam laughed good-naturedly at John's vehement objections, and since they were in sight of "Nullifier's Retreat" he thought

239

the subject should be temporarily put to rest.

Later, after the evening meal, and while Catharine was putting Emily to bed, the two, unable to escape the jungle of politics, began to speculate on the possibility that North Carolina would repudiate Senator Brown because of his recent unmitigated insolence. "It depends upon whether the Jackson forces can get control of the North Carolina electorate," Sam suggested. "It is difficult to tell how strong the President really is after all the onslaughts he has suffered. One would think that after Henry Clay's resolution to censure him for the removal of the deposits, Jackson's influence, both in Washington and in the hinterlands would be abated."

"It would indeed. I am glad that Mangum voted for the resolution to censure, even if his vote was cancelled out by Brown's negative one. In any event, the resolution stood up, and Jackson's censure has become a matter of Congressional record."

Thinking to interest his brother in North Carolina politics, and if possible distract him from the idea of going to Texas, Doctor John asked, "Have you considered going back to the North Carolina Legislature, Sam? Much has happened since you were a member of the General Assembly in 1822 and 1824. The elections are months away. Why don't you run for the Senate and plan to stay in North Carolina? I know that Catharine would applaud such an idea."

For quite awhile Carson sat staring in the distance, apparently in deep concentration—perhaps weighing the two alternatives—exploring Texas territory or casting his lot with friends and relatives in his native state.

"You know, John, your idea may not be as sound as a dollar, but it intrigues me nonetheless. I have nothing to lose, and it may enable me to chart my future course more realistically."

NINE

During the summer of 1834, all of the controversy about Jackson's policies brought about a significant change in North Carolina politics, as elsewhere in the nation. For the first time in the history of the state there were now two definite national parties, Mangum emerging as the leader of the Whig Party in North Carolina, and gaining recognition in the national party to such an extent that he was beginning to be mentioned as a candidate for the Vice Presidency.

Carson was now sharing most of his time with Catharine, who, nearing the time of her delivery, became more and more dependent upon him for the little attentions that psychologically, at least, prepare a woman for the often traumatic experience of childbirth. Everything was in readiness for the event, even to the midwife who would attend her if there was not enough time to summon the Rutherfordton doctor, who shared with John the responsibility of medical supervision of the family.

They wanted a boy, but would not go so far as to settle on a boy's name. It was just as well, for in the early hours of the morning on July 24, a daughter was born to Catharine and Sam. They christened her Rachel Rebecca—a name so widely used in the Carson and Wilson families that it was a matter of speculation as to whom should go the honor of godmother for a little namesake.

In the fall of 1834 when the votes were counted, the Carson men began to realize that the thing they feared had come upon them. The Jackson forces won control of both Houses in the Legislature and re-elected Bedford Brown as Senator. Mangum, whose term had not expired, became the target for the jubilant majority.

In the face of the Jackson landslide, Carson did not expect to win a seat in the North Carolina Legislature. He was astounded when his popularity once again proved the exception to the rule. On November 17th he would be sworn in as Senator from Burke County.

Governor David Swain was at the helm when preliminaries began on the opening day. Sam and his brother, Joseph McDowell Carson and Alney Burgin representing their respective districts, pooled their thoughts and convictions in a brief reunion, later mingling with the larger group to renew friendships of long standing.

Three major proposals emerged during the short session. One of the first was for a convention to amend the Constitution of North Carolina. The bill called for the necessary directives and procedures to be followed in qualifying the delegates-elect to participate in the deliberations, even to the wording of the oath to be administered.

Delegates from Western North Carolina were jubilant when the measure passed, setting among its provisions the directive for the people to vote on the question "Constitution" or "No Constitution."

Sam Carson was made chairman of "a select committee" to consider amendments to the original bill and provide some mode of ratification by the people.

But by far the most inflammatory issue was brought up on December 19th when a resolution was proposed "that the Legislature of the State, acting as the representative of the people, have a right to instruct their senators in Congress . . . when it appears that a given Senator misrepresents the will of the State." This barb was aimed at Mangum and was a prelude to the arbitrary instruction that followed demanding that Mangum and Brown vote for Thomas Benton's resolution to expunge from the records of the Senate the bill to censure President Jackson for his unlawful and unconstitutional act in the matter of the removal of deposits.

A heated debate followed over the authority of the Legislature to instruct a senator, and Carson found himself in the middle of controversy about which he had spoken at some length in the House. His exertions on this occasion were not equal to his strength, for as had happened so many times before, exposure to the severe winter weather had threatened him again with complete disability.

On December 27, a third and final reading of the resolution to instruct the senators on the way they should vote in soothing the President's vanity was ordered. Mangum, impressed with Carson's speech against instruction, sought to have him submit it for publication, for now that news of the act of Legislature had spread, he was being besieged on the one hand with demands to resign, and on the other to stand fast and hold his ground.

To Mangum's letter Carson replied by courier from his sick-bed on January 4, "Your favor of the 29th ultimo was received a few days since. I fear I shall be unable to comply with your request to send my speech for publication. I would willingly do so if bad health and more business than I can possibly attend to did not constantly plague me. My spirits are broken, and it is with considerable difficulty I can keep up, resulting from the villainous dyspepsia, which is the most miserable of all curses the human flesh is heir to. When I get home, and at ease, if I can collect my wandering thoughts, I may try to write out what I said, but I shall want the excitement which the occasion provided to make my speech interesting.

"Now, sir, with regard to yourself. Your friends from every corner of the state say stay where you are, regardless of the efforts of the miserable panders of power.

"I received a letter this morning from my brother, Charles Carson, dated Salisbury. He requested me to write you and say that the resolutions have been the subject of conversation from the time they were introduced, and every intelligent man that he had seen (including Jackson men) deprecated them and also the idea of your being influenced at all by their passage. He says, 'Stand to your post and do the talking,' and if necessary send for him *and he will go and do the fighting*, for he is confident that he can whip 'the d——d dogs.' You know Charlie, and I give you his own words."

Because he was far from well, and before he left home, Catharine had tried to prevail on Carson not to attend the hearings, and to forego the idea of taking any part in the proceedings. When she saw that he was determined to go and use his influence and persuasion in behalf of his friend Mangum, and against the conspiracies of the Jacksonians, she announced that she would accompany him to Raleigh to see that he was well cared-for in the event of a collapse. It was well that she did, for before he was able to leave the city he required and was thankful for her ministrations and those of his friends.

Finding himself too ill to argue, at her earnest request, he promised to forego all political involvement and rest at home during the remainder of the month. The enforced rest gave him leisure to plan the details of a revolutionary scheme that had occupied his spare moments. Despite the warnings of Doctor John, he was bent on a migration to Texas to join forces with Houston in the evolution of an independent government. He intended to weigh the matter with as much prudence as his adventurous spirit would allow, but before he got into too much detail of planning it was necessary to persuade Catharine that the rewards of such a venture far outweighed the diffi-culties and dangers of an expedition of such major proportions. This was difficult to do, now that there were two children—one less than a year old—who would be required to face the perils of travel through raw and uncivilized areas, in some instances inhabited by Indians who were as likely to be unfriendly and savage as they were to be friendly and co-operative.

"But we will have with us our own family of Negroes, Cathy. I will take only those who want to brave the perils and who will swear to defend us and each other if need be."

"How many do you think that will be, Sam?" And thinking to discourage him or bring him to his senses, she said, "What will you do when you are too sick to sit up in your carriage?"

"I'll have a bed laid for me in one of the covered wagons we will have in our caravan."

Carson's eyes lighted up as he went on, "I've done more planning, Cathy, than you know, and much of it is for your safety and comfort and mine, and for the well-being of the little girls, as well as for all who will accompany us.

"Some of the experts I know in Washington are working out details for me—matters of itinerary, major equipment and minor necessities. They have made intensive studies from some of our recent travelers to the West, and I will have the benefit of it."

Carson looked appealingly at his wife, as he took both her hands in his. "I'll promise you all of the necessities and some of the luxuries too, my dearest Cathy, for I want you to be Queen of the Caravan—without a care or worry in the world save to love and cherish me and those we love so much."

Cathy was almost persuaded to give her assent, but she had one more high card to play. "Sam, you were too sick in Raleigh to rejoice over the fulfillment of one of your cherished desires. This Jackson-controlled Legislature provided the first steps for reforming our state constitution. Do you realize that after all of these long years of waiting, the Western half of North Carolina has been recognized and given a chance to bring about the reforms that all of our leaders are clamoring for, including a strong voice in shaping our future course?"

"Why Cathy, I do believe you have come of age politically these few weeks since you've had to listen and sit in on so many committee sessions of necessity brought to me in my illness. I do indeed remember that the Legislature provided the machinery for the people to cast their vote for or against holding a convention to amend the constitution under which our state has been operating since 1776."

"And now that the election has been set for the first and second of April, you plan to be on your way to Texas, relinquishing your responsibilities and denying yourself the satisfactions of debate and decisions in framing a new constitution or an amended one that may last another century."

"I have weighed all of these matters, Cathy, and I have balanced them with the prospect of helping to frame the *first* constitution of an independent Texas! Is such a prospect preposterous?"

"Preposterous! It's absolutely ridiculous! Do you think you'll live long enough to see that wasteland transformed into any semblance of civilization and its people freed from the tyranny of Mexican rule?"

"I do think that is possible, else I would never have taken the first step, dear little Cathy. Please trust me to take care of you and to provide you with safeguards——"

"And sanity, Sam? Can you guarantee that, too? Do you realize what you are asking me to do—to cut myself off from those I love, many of whom I may never see again, to pull up roots so firmly planted and tended and to put them down again in a Godforsaken, savage-infested region where I may never see a white woman the rest of my days?"

Catharine burst into tears and fled, locking herself in her room, where she soon dried her eyes and took under consideration a number of schemes to save herself from "a fate worse than death."

Sam had not expected Cathy to accept his plans eagerly, but he was not prepared for the intensity of her resistance. While he was thinking about his next step, he saw a rapidly-approaching rider whom he soon recognized as Doctor John.

"Sam, I have bad news for you, and news of an astounding nature, too. I'll give you the second first. An attempt has been made to assassinate the President!" John breathlessly exclaimed. "Now calm yourself, boy, the President is all right—the pistol was discharged twice, but misfired both times—a miraculous escape! Sit down here while I tell you the news that has stunned the nation. I've just come from Salisbury, where the whole populace is upset."

"Get to the point, John, without descriptive details!"

"It happened on January 29—about two weeks ago. Jackson was attending a funeral in the Legislative halls and the procession was proceeding through the rotunda of the Capitol when a man named Lawrence fired at the President. The culprit was immediately taken into custody. It was a shocking experience, made doubly so because of the circumstances."

"You're sure the President is safe? Thank God for that! You see, John, in spite of my tirades, the President still owns part of me—this part right here," he said, placing his hand over his heart. "Whose funeral was he attending, John? It must have been someone of importance to command the respectful attendance of the President."

John drew closer and put his hand affectionately on the arm of his brother. "It *was* someone of importance, Sam. It was Warren Davis!"

Sam's face blanched as he leaned back in his chair, too stunned to speak. Doctor John stayed over that night to be of any help and comfort possible to Sam and Catharine, who, on hearing the sad news, had pulled herself together to share her grief with Sam. She was sure that only the death of one of his immediate family would cause sorrow like this. Early in the friendship, a friendship that had grown more meaningful and interdependent through the years, Carson had spoken of the Damon and Pythias relationship between them.

The next morning John could tell that his brother had had very little sleep. He had seen the manifestation of grief in men, but Sam's was more acute than any he had ever witnessed. "Will they bring him back to Pendleton?" Sam inquired of his brother.

"No, he is already interred in the National Cemetery in the Capital." Thinking to distract his brother, Doctor John, who had had second thoughts on the sanity of Sam's proposal to go to Texas, inquired, "How much further have you gone in your planning to join your friend, Houston?"

"On my long range plans, the details are in the 'blueprint' stage, but if Catharine gives me her consent to do some exploring on my own, I will leave immediately."

John was sure that he had unwittingly precipitated a decision just made—on the spur of the moment, for Sam had added, "Now, more than ever I want to go."

Catharine crossed the room and sat on a hassock at his feet. "You do want to go, very much, don't you, my dear?"

"I do, Cathy, my heart has been set on it even before I took a plunge from my lofty Nullifier's seat in Congress. Let me go first," Sam implored. "Let me view the land, brave the dangers, assuring and reassuring you that I will never force you to take the final step. If you go, it will be because you, too, have an adventurous spirit and really want to go."

"See, John. You are a witness to these safeguards my husband has thrown around me. It won't be necessary to put quill to paper on it. I'll call on you to attest this promise if it ever becomes necessary."

When he left home, the snows of winter were still to be seen in glistening white patches on northern exposures. When he reached the Texas border, however, there was a noticeable change in temperature. He found the atmosphere dry and conducive to clearing the throat and cleansing the lungs in a most therapeutic manner. He breathed deeply as he surveyed the promised land.

The further he advanced into the Texas territory, the more convinced he was that he had found the pot of gold at the foot of a many-colored rainbow. Not that there was any actual evidence of the precious metal, but the fertile soil, the lush,

247

green grass, sending out its invitation to hungry cattle, the burgeoning harvests, and the acres and acres of virgin timber beckoning the saw and the builder—these practical tokens of a good life cheered him and invited further speculation as to future possibilities.

On April 18, he could resist the prospect no longer, and he bought a thousand acres on the west side of the Red River near Cedar Bend. Twelve days later he bought a tract believed to contain two to three hundred acres at a cost of $3,750—not actually in Texas, but near the Texas-Arkansas border.

By the last of April he had traversed a good portion of his newly-acquired holdings, and he was pleased with what he saw. He had talked with every settler he met—white man or Mexican—and from them he learned much about the history, the geography, and the topography of this wild and inviting country.

He visited San Antonio de Bexar, one of the oldest towns in North America, founded in 1692. There he found accommodations that enabled him to soak up much of the ancient lore that set it apart from the vast, uninhabited expanses surrounding it. Sam described the town in a letter to Cathy:

San Antonio is built in an oblong square, and the streets extend at right angles. The houses, covered with flat roofs, are one story high in most cases, with a parapet raised some two or three feet, giving the appearance of an extensive fortress. There are some large houses and a very ancient church. These and a mission they call "The Alamo," which is situated in the northeast part of the old town, are relics of an ancient civilization begun nearly 200 years ago. The Alamo is a large, oblong, walled enclosure containing about an acre of ground. The walls are about eight to ten feet high and three feet thick—a formidable and I would think an impregnable fortress, from all appearances.

Along the San Antonia River below Bexar are many imposing structures built of massive stone in the frequently seen mission style of architecture. For the most part these are fortresses and churches, some of the latter sufficiently large to accommodate six or seven hundred people, and usually covered with lofty arched roofs of stone. I am told that they were formerly surmounted with enormous bells and ornamented with numerous carved statues and paintings. The entrance to the Mission Espada is by a magnificent arched gallery, through which six horsemen may ride abreast.

During the last century and a half, these missions, and indeed the two oldest towns, Bexar and Goliad, have been repeatedly plundered and attempts made to destroy them, but in vain. I am told that in them the pious fathers of others days, with a sword in one hand and a Bible in the other, gathered the wild bands of the prairies to bend the knee to the shrine of the Virgin.

I am told, too, that the climate of the region is delightful—the summers not oppressively warm, and the winters exceedingly mild. Snow hardly ever falls here, it seems—even to the depth of an inch. It would seem my dear, to be a region admirably suited to my health—and to yours and the children's—if—the one big obstacle—if you have decided to become an adventuress for the sake of your rightfully wedded husband. What think you, Cathy?

Sam did not reveal the fact that he had already purchased extensive holdings in this faraway western world. He reasoned that Texas or Arkansas land would increase in value as American colonists continued the migration already begun, and that he could always sell it at a fair profit if Cathy was unwilling to make a new life here.

It was at Bexar that he had given instruction for his mail to be forwarded, and when he went to post the letter to Cathy, he found a number of communications that offered interesting reading. He eagerly opened the letter postmarked "Brindle-town"—a letter filled mainly with news of the family, who, from the report from homes and hearthstones, were well and prospering in a manner that would be encouraging and heart-warming to the absent member. They were beginning to chafe under his prolonged absence, Cathy wrote, and they hoped to receive word very soon that he and Missy were homeward bound.

He opened next a letter that was in Doctor John's familiar handwriting. It was postmarked "Raleigh." John really gets about, was Sam's immediate thought. Then he read:

Since you would not stay around until after the election, perhaps you have not been informed that North Carolina went to the polls on the first and second days of April to vote "yea" or "nay" on the matter of changing our outmoded constitution. While it is true that the vote was in the affirmative, there are some interesting points that developed in connection with the election that will reveal some of the weaknesses in our body politic.

You may or may not have the figures at hand, so I will remind you that by the census of 1830 there are 97,633 eligible male voters in North Carolina. Give heed to this! So lacking is the interest of our people in the grave constitutional question that one-half of the qualified voters took no part in the election. In spite of that, it was the largest vote ever cast in our glorious state—except for the Presidential election of 1828. With a total vote of 49,244—27,550 were for the convention, and 21,694 were for the *status quo*—they were "agin' " it. At any rate, the "ayes' had it, and at last—read this, my boy, and shout!—at last Western North Carolina, the miserable stepchild of our g-r-r-eat commonwealth, has come into her own. Glory be! Praises be! Hallelujah!

But that is not all. You must begin at once to pack your saddle-bags. If you start in the next hour after reading this, you have barely time to reach home, get a change of clothing, pick up your credentials and start out again for Raleigh. The assembly of delegates will convene there on the first Thursday in June. Hurry! You'll just barely make it.

Your friends in Burke County have signally honored you with their trust and confidence by electing you as a delegate to this auspicious and gratifying convention.

Now maybe you'll give up your ideas for increasing the population and expanding the territorial possessions of the United States in the foreign fields of Texas. And once you're back, maybe you'll decide to stay to serve these people, who may actually be trying to say they're sorry for messing you up and throwin' you in the Nullifiers' encampment at the last election. You can tell 'em back home that you found the grass not one whit greener across the border.

You'll rejoice in being again with old friends and compatriots—Nathaniel Macon, your venerable and respected associate of other days; John Branch, your mentor from Halifax County. (I forgot to say that each county was instructed to elect two and only two delegates.) Then there will be William Gaston and Richard Speight, from Craven; Charles Fisher and John Giles, from Rowan; from Rutherford County there will be your distinguished brother and mine, Joseph McDowell Carson, with Theodore Birchett, and last, but by no means least, Samuel Price Carson and Burgess Gaither, from Burke. These are your friends! Of course before the great undertaking is over, many more may claim you as an enemy—only time will tell.

Now therefore, I adjure you—waste not a minute more in your orgy of speculation. Return to the place of your nativity, where duty does not beckon, but calls in stentorian and commanding voice! Adieu, and God speed you on your way.

Your sometimes exasperated, but usually proud (of you)
Counsellor, Physician and Brother

The delegates to the Constitutional convention on June 4 overflowed the room in the Governor's mansion where they assembled, and before the day was over, it was determined to accept the offer of the Presbyterian Church to hold subsequent sessions in their edifice. Joseph McDowell Carson was in attendance on the first day, but Sam had not reached Raleigh.

The dissension began immediately. The clerk, having finished the registration of delegates, called on the representative from Anson County to come forward and take the prescribed oath.

The gentleman from Anson rose and threw the first stumbling block in the way of orderly dispatch of the business at hand. He doubted if the Legislature had a right to impose the oath, and he thought it best to postpone the oath-taking until certain matters of interpretation were taken up and clarified by a committee appointed for that purpose, whereupon he proposed the appointment of a chairman *pro tem*. Accordingly, David Lowry Swain of Buncombe was placed in the chair.

The second speaker found himself in a state of confusion as to the implications of oath-taking, just as the first speaker had pointed out, and he proposed to adjourn until the following day in order to enable the delegates to know what limitations, if any, the oath would place on the free exercise of opinion and judgment of each respective delegate. And then the debate got into full swing. Mr. Speight referred to what had been done in the early years of the nation to revise the old confederation of the federal government. "Though they were appointed only to revise the articles of the old confederation, they transcended their limits and actually formed an entire new constitution, and that instrument was approved by the people of the United States," and he added, "I think that if this constitution were to take a similar course (and remake the constitution of North Carolina) the people would approve it."

It was pointed out that at this stage they were not a convention, but merely an assemblage of private citizens, with a chairman temporarily appointed to keep order.

William Gaston rose to oppose the motion to adjourn. "Under the plain language of the act under which this meeting was called, there can be no convention until the prescribed oath is taken," he announced, and he quoted from the tenth section

251

of the act: "No delegate-elect can be permitted to take his seat until he shall have taken the oath prescribed." He further stated that "if we transcend the limits of the Act of Assembly that called us together, or refuse obedience to the conditions therein proposed, we are not a convention called by the people, but a self-constituted body."

Because of his brilliance and perspicacity, William Gaston's pronouncements weighed heavily in all assemblies and convocations of the state, and in committees. He was one of North Carolina's foremost jurists, and his opinions were respected. "In matters of such grave concern, it is safe to adhere both to the letter and the spirit of the act that created this convention, the ninth section of which states that the convention shall convene on the first Thursday in June. It makes provisions for an omission to convene on this day in one case, and in one case only—'provided that if a quorum does not attend on any specific day.' It is ascertained that a majority of delegates is present," continued Mr. Gaston. "Do we then have a right to adjourn *as delegates* of an unformed body? Can we be said to have convened until we are formed into a convention?"

Going back to the objection to taking the oath until there was time to inquire into the effect that the oath-taking would have, he asked, "Is it not enough that the people who have delegated us to act on these grave matters have demanded of us an oath for the faithful performance of our duties? When it is taken, then each person must act according to the best dictates of his conscience, and with a solemn sense of his responsibilities to that Great Being to whom he shall have made his religious appeal."

After a few informal remarks, the question, "Shall the meeting proceed to organize the Convention?" was voted on in the affirmative, and the members then without exception took the oath prescribed.

John Branch then moved that Nathaniel Macon be appointed president of the convention, which motion was unanimously agreed on, and Branch and former Governor John Owen then led the venerable Macon to the chair.

In low and feeble tones he addressed the delegates: "My powers are weak and I fear that I cannot fulfill the arduous duties of presiding over this important deliberative body, either satisfactorily to myself or acceptably to you. It has been some time since I retired from public life and I am sensible that I shall be found rusty in the rules of proceedings, and will therefore, in advance, invite correction from my friends in the convention. I urge on you mutual forbearance and good temper in the prosecution of business, and I pray that each of us, with an eye single to the welfare of our commonwealth—may agreeably unite in such measures as will redound to the glory and happiness of North Carolina."

Five additional days were required in which to perfect the organization of the convention, the delegates often becoming involved in histrionics and often harking back to what was done or not done by the convention of 1789 that finally ratified the federal constitution.

Sam Carson, making the return trip from Texas to Brindletown with as much haste as Missy's aging pace would allow, tarried at his home only long enough to enjoy his family for a few days, and reached the convention hall on Monday, June 15. He found his co-delegate from Burke, Burgess Gaither, involved on the wrong side in debate on the relative responsibilities of whites and Negroes in sharing the tax burden.

The work of the convention was essentially a compromise between the diverse interests and views of the East and the West. Important changes were proposed in the constitution as the days passed, and some of the proposals were truly democratic. It was evident from the first that many delegates were guided in their voting by consideration of what the electorate back home would approve, even while thinking themselves in terms consistent with equity and justice. More than were expected expressed satisfaction in the constitution of North Carolina as presently worded. Some of them were argumentative about matters like the two-year term proposed for the governor and members of the Assembly, as well as on the distribution and allocation of senators and the appointment of members of the House of Commons.

Wisely, these amendments were agreed upon and ratified in the early days of the convention, after full but not always harmonious debate. But the greatest debate in the history of North

Carolina was launched when a motion was made to amend the thirty-second section of the constitution. The section, stated in negative form, declared, "That no person who shall deny the being of God, or the truth of the *Protestant* religion, or the Divine authority of the Old and New Testament, or shall hold religious principles incompatible with the Freedom and Safety of the State, shall be capable of holding any office of public trust or profit in the Civil department within this State."

For fifty-nine years, since the adoption of the constitution at Halifax, this section excluding Catholics and Jews from holding public office was allowed to stand—a blot on the fair name of North Carolina. True, the thirty-first section restrained ministers of the Gospel from holding office, and very little had been said about the discrimination.

The debate started on June 26, after halting and delaying preliminaries. Leave of absence was granted the delegate from Cabarrus, whose health demanded a visit to the north for medical aid. Governor Branch said on arrival that morning that he had left a sick room to vote on the question, and he hoped it could be prosecuted with all justifiable speed. Mr. Edwards reminded the delegates "that we have had proclaimed to us the truth of the Bill of Rights in language so clear that 'he who runs may read'—that all men have a natural and inalienable right to worship Almighty God according to the dictates of their conscience." He was at a loss to conceive why this section was ever introduced in the constitution—"but it is there, and it is our duty to examine the influences it exercises on the great fundamental principles of civil and religious liberty." He said that in coming into the convention he had understood that the public mind was greatly agitated on this subject; that in some counties the excitement border on phrenzy. He had had other opinions on the reaction of the public mind and affirmed that such discrimination did not reflect the true intent of enlightened men. Moreover he hoped that there was but one opinion as to the propriety of expunging from the constitution this foul stain on our character.

One by one, the members rose in support of this sentiment or against it. There was brilliant and effective argument at times, and at times long, drawn-out, effusive and discursive displays of

254

oratory and rhetoric. Many speakers pointed out the obvious truth that in actual practice the citizens of North Carolina had bypassed this section of the constitution, and had elevated to places of public trust both Catholic and Jew. William Gaston was a notable exception among the Catholics, and no one had objected to his wise pronouncements as he presided over the courts of the state, and no one questioned his right to fill the office of superior court judge in his district.

Carson, like Branch, was in favor of removing the entire section, thus precluding discrimination of individuals of any sect. "I had not anticipated on my arrival here that there could be any difference of opinion on this subject. I thought the age in which we live forbade it. The principal argument I have heard presented as the reason why the clause should not be stricken out, was that in its practical operation it did no harm. But suppose we allow it to remain where it is and thus virtually re-enact it, will it continue long innoxious?

"I shall not go into history, Mr. Chairman, to draw thence any conclusions, but shall base myself on this great fundamental right—I am a creature of God, and to that God I am accountable. Who can interpose between my conscience and its Almighty Maker? If any man can convince me that he is made responsible for my conduct on earth, and I am consequently released from personal responsiblity—then I may acquiesce in your religious tests. But until I am so convinced I go for striking out the whole article. No man should presume to dictate to me as to what church I should attach myself. Whence could any man derive that right? Has anyone been instructed by his God to instruct any delegate here? No earthly authority, certainly, could confer such a right.

"I have not attached myself to any church. I have my preferences, arising however, more from the influence of education than any religious feeling. It might be that at some day I would wish to attach myself to the Catholic Church; if so, and there should be anything in the constitution of the state which gave me birth, and in some degree has honored me, that would prevent me from aspiring to office, I would indeed think it hard. But I protest again and again against the right of any man to interpose between me and my Maker."

Concluding, Carson said, "If this article is retained in the constitution in its present shape, I shall vote against ratification of the amendment, I do not care how beneficial the remaining portions are. And more, if my voice should ever again be heard by my constituents, it will be raised for the purpose of denouncing an article so unbecoming the spirit of the age in which we live."

Mr. Branch said he had voted for every liberal proposition to amend the objectionable article, but he did not think the amendment in question would remove the stain from our constitution, and therefore he would not vote for it. "We met to amend our constitution, and we ought to do it effectually and not accommodate the ill-founded prejudices of our people. Why," he asked, "are the Jews to be excluded from office? Our Savior and his disciples were Jews, and are there not many among the Jews as talented, as virtuous and as well-qualified to fill any position in our government as any other citizen in our community? The Jew can be appointed to any office in our national government—he may even be raised to the Presidency of the United States. Why shall we refuse to admit him to any office in our state government? I am opposed to all religious tests for office and shall therefore vote against this amendment." Another wording of the amendment was proposed and summarily voted down.

Charles Fisher, delegate from Rowan rose and announced that he would vote for an amendment in which the word "Protestant" would be replaced with the word "Christian," so as to allow all who believe in the Christian religion to hold office in the state. Mr. Fisher said, "I have listened with very strict attention to all that has been said on this subject, and of all of the debates I have ever witnessed, this has taken the widest range. As regards time, it has swept over eighteen centuries, and as regards space, it has traveled around the globe; its range has been circumscribed only by the limits set to human imagination. If a stranger, uninformed to the true state of the question, had dropped in here and had listened attentively to all that has been said, he must have come to the conclusion that we are about to establish the Holy Inquisition in North Carolina; that we are now preparing the wheel and the rack, the thumb screws and the hot iron for the punishment for recusant Papists. The only question now before us, 'Shall we amend it, or shall we leave it as it is?' "

The debate continued interminably, in truth, until the delegates were worn down and worn out, and with the passing days it seemed highly unlikely that the section in question would be materially changed. On one of these days Carson rose to say, "I believe that no man is more honest in his course than the gentleman from Halifax, Mr. Branch. I, with him, have gone for the most liberal amendments. We are in favor of a complete religious tolerance but we have been defeated. But because we cannot obtain all of the liberal amendments, shall we refuse that which is in our power to get? If we cannot make room for the Jew, if he be thought worthy of office, let us not refuse the privilege for Christians of every denomination."

And thus, the delegates decided the issue, falling short of their opportunity to sweep clear the prejudices against one increasingly large segment of their population. The only change that was made in the section was that the word "Christian" was substituted for the word "Protestant."

Saturday, July 11, was the last session of the convention, and this day was given over largely to the amenities with resolutions expressive of thanks to civil authorities and to the Presbyterian and Methodist churches for use of their sanctuaries, and to the Reverends McPheeters and Jamieson for their ecclesiastical services.

Carson asked leave to offer an amendment to the resolution returning thanks to the chaplains "and that Doctor McPheeters and the Rev. Mr. Jamieson be requested to accept $50 for their services." The affirmative vote having been taken, Mr. Gaston rose to say, "I am about to offer to the convention a resolution on which I know I shall meet with perfect unanimity. However we may have been divided on other subjects, in returning thanks to our venerable president for the able manner in which he has presided over this body, there will be no difference of opinion."

A resolution of affection and appreciation was read, but before a vote was taken, Carson instantly rose and expressed the hope that this mark of respect and well-deserved appreciation to Mr. Macon for probably the last public act of his life would be testified by the members standing. The words were no sooner spoken than every man in the Convention was on his feet!

Macon stood, acknowledging the accolades of his friends. "I have for a long time been engaged in public business, and though no one will charge me with being a flatterer, I must say that I have never witnessed such good order and decorum of conduct in any public body with which I have been associated. This, I expect, will be the last scene of my public life. We are about to separate and it is my fervent prayer that each of you may reach home in safety and that your days may be long, honorable and happy. While I live, if any of you should pass through the county in which I live, I shall be glad to see you."

On the President's resuming his seat, and after the applause of the convention had ceased, Carson rose and said, "The concluding remarks of our president has called me up to say that I am about to leave North Carolina to reside in the far West, where I shall be happy at all times to see any friend from the old state. To be a North Carolinian would be sufficient recommendation. My house and my corncrib shall be at the service of my friends."

The body then rose as Doctor McPheeters petitioned, "Give to the people of this state, before whom its amended constitution shall soon pass in review, wisdom, that they may be directed in their final action thereon. Deliver them from passion, prejudice, and all unreasonable prepossessions. May they approach the question before them with honest, liberal and enlightened views, and decide thereon calmly, conscientiously, and in the fear of God." Thus, on Saturday, July 11, 1835, the historic constitutional convention of the state of North Carolina came to an end.

Carson accepted the suggestion of his brother, Joseph, to ride with him and let Missy follow along. There were so many things to discuss, and there had been no opportunity throughout the session, each having been in separate living quarters. "From your invitation in the last minutes of the convention, I take it that Catharine has finally given her consent to accompany you on your wild goose chase, Sam."

"Yes, I hope I did not paint too rosy a picture of the West in the short time we had together. She has agreed, bless her! and I am as excited as a schoolboy."

"I understand some of our mining population hereabout, having satisfied their itchy hands in digging gold, are now afflicted with itching feet and want to go to Texas, where the sun shines perpetually and the grass is green all year. How soon will you be going, Sam?"

"If all goes well, I shall start toward the last of August—six weeks should give me enough time to get things in readiness. Of course you know, Joseph, that the thought of leaving my family brings an onrush of emotion that is hard for me to control, especially when I think of Father. A man past eighty may be called without much warning."

"Don't worry about Father, Sam. He's hale and hearty. Now that he has got over the initial shock, I believe he is more tolerant of your wild ideas than any of us. Father has always been an adventurer, as you well know. Can't you just see him at the tender age of seventeen leaving the sanctuary of a well-ordered Irish home and setting sail for America—the promised land?"

"Do you think he has ever regretted it, Joe? I've often thought of it."

"Nonsense! With all of his barns filled to overflowing and with a rich harvest of children and grandchildren who are making the Carson name known and respected in the councils of state—how could he have any regrets?"

"I'll tell you what, Joe, we are going to Pleasant Gardens in two weeks. If we can do without the shedding of tears, let's have a family get-together with as many as possible the first week in August in the old home."

"Capital idea! Rebecca will help me round them up. Leave everything to me, and we'll speed the parting guests in fine style. And by the bye, before I forget it, I was proud of your able speech for the thirty-second amendment, my boy. I believe you made history that day."

Sam looked at his brother to see if the compliment was in jest or in earnest, but before he could comment Joe continued, "You have a lot of fight in you for a sick man. Did you not leave your bed to make this fight singlehanded for religious tolerance?"

259

"When you say 'singlehanded,' I presume you mean that my co-delegate from Burke, Mr. Gaither, deserted me in the thick of battle. He was safe in saying his constituents would not vote for any liberalizing of the thirty-second amendment, because he knew I had not been here to feel the pulse of the electorate, but the fact that my words had sufficient weight to help carry the amendment is an indication of the false premise on which he took his stand. Even Gaither was finally convinced and voted for the measure, you remember. I think he was talking through his hat when he said there is a strong prejudice against the Catholics in our area. If there is, I have never been aware of it."

The Green River Carsons laid well their plans for a family houseparty to speed the parting Texans. William and Almyra, Charles and Margaret opened their homes for those who could not be accommodated at Pleasant Gardens. They had not had a summer like this in many years, and it was a happy occasion. All of the children, save the very youngest, were billeted at William's, and for years they remembered and talked about "the sending-off party" and the pranks they played on each other and on their several black mammys.

Rebecca had suggested that the womenfolk bring scraps for a quilt or two, which might be finished and presented to the travelers. They secreted themselves in an upstairs room where frames were readied, and for three days their tongues and fingers vied with each other in noisy competition. They held up for inspection several sample patterns, and finally decided on the "Double Irish Chain" and "The Rose in the Wilderness." Naturally, they discussed the forthcoming trek to "a foreign country," and debated the relative merits of Mexican and Indian neighbors.

"You'll have to learn to speak Spanish, Catharine," was Almyra's suggestion.

"I may not see a Mexican for years, girls, and by that time I'll know more than just *si, si*. As for the Indians, we are not inexperienced in dealing with them—up to this point more or less satisfactorily." And she added, "I've forgotten, if I ever knew, the names of the tribes we will likely encounter. The only Mexican I have ever heard of is Santa Anna. He is President of Mexico and a general in their army, you know. Sam says that he is already in Texas with his Mexican hordes seeking whom he may devour, but he is not in the section where we are going."

"See how nonchalantly she speaks of the dangers ahead of her! I, for one, believe she is pretending—putting on an act to make us think she is not frightened out of her wits at what they may encounter," said Margaret, as she began adjusting the frames in readiness for the final quilting.

Meanwhile the men were covering acres of ground in their discussions—digging up past events for reappraisal and closer scrutiny, and tiptoeing over painful mistakes long buried. Uppermost in their thoughts, however, was the forthcoming journey, and after they had satisfied themselves that Sam and his Washington advisors had made adequate plans for the removal of Sam's family and his retinue of slaves, Doctor John asked, "Why are you taking so many of your retainers, Sam? Don't you know you will have a drove of 'mourning doves' on your hands, if not before you get there, then certainly when they get to their destination and never see a black face?"

"I have been told that more than half of the settlers have brought their Negro families with them; otherwise they would make poor progress in developing the country that someday may be part of the good old U.S.A. And to answer your other question, I am taking so many because I do not want to separate families."

"Then you must have in mind planting a number of staple crops after you have cleared the land," Colonel John suggested.

"Yes, Texas cotton is said to be superior in quality to that generally produced in the United States. A cotton planter from Alabama says that he believes Sea Island cotton will produce well there, due to the salubrious climate. I am told, too, that ten bales of cotton may be made to the hand, and that a hand can make two and a half bales to the acre. That is probably too optimistic, so I am counting on my hands to make a bale and a half to the acre. My men and women are experienced in the field, and my sacks of cotton seed are already stored away in our seed and harvest wagon. I intend to introduce good old North Carolina cotton to compete with the Sea Island variety."

"What about other commodities, Son? Do they grow wheat in abundance?"

261

"There has been some experimenting in the neighborhood of Bexar, Father, and it has been found that Mexican wheat is superior to that raised in the United States, but my understanding is that it is not grown in other sections. Corn, rye, oats and potatoes produce as well in Texas as in our Southern states. My most sanguine hopes are derived from a plan for cattle-raising in their lush prairie country. This holds bright prospects for us for the future.

"You're surely not going to drive herds of cattle on this precarious expedition, are you?" inquired Logan.

"Only enough to feed my entourage and provide milk for the babies while on our way. Twenty to thirty head of cattle and twice as many sheep. We'll take no hogs. They do not drive well. They're too temperamental and unmanageable. They are not quiet and amenable as sheep are; besides, pork is the first thing I'll deny myself in my present state of health," Sam ventured, and Doctor John pronounced a loud, "Amen."

Here Sam laughed in anticipation of his next remark. "We are already saving eggs for the trip—hen eggs, guinea eggs, duck and goose eggs. Catharine has deputized certain trusty women to have in readiness enough setting hens to hatch a sizeable brood when we reach our destination, and to tend them carefully on the way. It is just an experiment and may not work out."

"I think what you'll have is a lot of scrambled eggs when you get to your destination," Logan commented.

"Well, so much for the anticipated harvest. Now I want to know about the political climate, and how you'll accommodate yourself to the general state of unrest that prevails and about which you have remained eloquently silent," Charles teased. "I remember back in 1833 while you were still in Congress, Sam, General Houston wrote to President Jackson that a majority of the population of the province was anxious for the United States to take possession of Texas; that the people are determined to form a state government, separate from Mexico, and that she had already beaten and repelled all of the troops of Mexico from her soil."

"That was in 1833, Charlie. The story has radically changed. Santa Anna, with 6,000 Mexican troops, is solidly entrenched on Texas soil, ready to do battle with any and sundry who

262

attempt to wrest the territory for the United States," Sam explained. "I am putting my faith in Sam Houston. He is a master strategist. I am sure that he has laid plans as carefully as has Santa Anna."

"Do you think that General Houston will welcome you as a ready accomplice in his plans for emancipation?" Doctor John inquired. "Seems to me I remember in that very letter to Jackson in 1833, he expressed pride and satisfaction in the President's handling of the Nullifiers of the South, bidding him Godspeed in preserving the Union, and he further observed that all voices—even in Texas—approved the course he had taken with the Nullifiers. That does not augur well for you, Sam, now does it?"

"I'll reserve my judgment on that at this point, my dear counsellor, advisor and brother."

About this time, the ladies, tiring of their quilting, joined the men in preparation of the feast spread for them under a large beech tree near the creek, and it was not until next day that they resumed their mutual tasks at the quilting frames. "Do you expect to find fruit in abundance in your future abode?" It was Rebecca, remembering Catharine's fondness for jellies and jams, pickles and preserves.

"One would think that I'm going to the North Pole instead of to a climate very like our own. Of course we'll find an abundance of fruit. Sam heard that nowhere are peaches to be found that are better, and grapes are in abundance—apricots and figs, too. And would you believe that oranges are to be found in the southern part of Texas?"

"Sounds very enticing, my dear," Almyra interjected. "It almost makes the thought of wild Indians and Mexicans bearable."

The men had weightier problems to discuss—the recent Constitution Convention, the stubborn tenacity of Jackson in holding out against the threat of violence in the matter of removal of deposits, and his banking policies in general.

"Is it not a fact, Sam, that you and Webster, among others, were cited by the President for having borrowed sums from the United States Bank—something the President frowned upon for members of Congress?" Charles asked.

263

"That's so much water over the dam now, Charlie. The moneys were repaid. Certainly the President had no quarrel with me personally about it, and as for Webster, there may have been political implications in his case, things being as they were at that particular time."

"It's good to know that your record is clear, Sam. As for Jackson's stubbornness, no amount of vituperative assassination from the Southern press and the opposition could shake him from his determined course. And yet, in his suicidal obstinacy, one gem of purest ray is seen," Charlie commented.

"What gem is that, pray tell us?"

"Guts," rejoined Charlie, "and if you think that analogy ill-chosen, forget it or choose your own words."

Sam evaded any complication in the discussion of Jackson. Any thought of him just now brought on a depression he could hardly cope with. For with Jackson he associated Warren Davis, and the recent death of his friend.

Thinking to change the subject from reminiscences that he was sure were painful to Sam, Colonel John observed, "Well, at least we have one cause for rejoicing since we were all together last, and this is something that Sam has a stake in. Although you were not in Congress to hear Tom Benton take up where you left off, he did introduce a bill in February to provide for branching the United States Mint to the south—one branch to go to New Orleans for coining gold and silver, and one branch to Charlotte for coining gold."

"No, Father, being an itinerant ex-Congressman sojourning temporarily outside the United States, I missed that great moment of history and the satisfaction of following the fate of the Senator's bill."

"You mean I did not write you about this important development?" Doctor John inquired.

"If you did, John, the letter miscarried."

"Well, that's not all, the Congress acted on March third to accede to your initial pleas and to Benton's second attempt to get action by voting to establish a Branch mint in Charlotte, in the heart of the goldmining section of the United States, and I predict that this long-overdue action will change the economy of this region and perhaps enrich us in ways we've never

264

dreamed of. In that respect, Congress has done well by us this year, and speaking of our National Assembly, has anyone heard the results of the Tennessee elections and whether or not our friend Crockett was elected?" Doctor John inquired.

"I saw Abner a few weeks since," ventured Colonel John, and by this time he must be as nervous as a June bride waiting at the church."

"What's he waiting for, Father? I thought Abner had had his bride these many years," Logan commented.

"He has, Son, but the last time I saw him he was all steamed up about going to Texas with David—if this election puts David's opponent in Congress. The election ought to be right about now. In ten days or so we ought to hear something."

Sam sat bolt upright at this piece of news. "I should have known that David would hear the call of the Texas wild," he said. "In my own adventuring I had lost sight of David except to know that since the publication of his autobiography—with Chilton's assistance—he has become famous at home and abroad, abroad meaning anywhere outside of Weakly County, Tennessee. But Father, Abner is the last man I'd associate with pioneering. Are you sure you have your facts straight?"

"Abner seemed serious enough when we talked. He said that as far back as the early part of July, David had declared his intention of headin' for Texas if he were defeated for Congress."

"I wonder which route he will take. My reason for close inquiry is that from all I hear the Jacksonites will defeat him. I would even be safe in saying that Texas will soon need to roll out the red carpet for her distinguished visitor."

By this time Sam was pacing the floor. "Did Abner say anyone else is going?"

"Yes, he's taking William Patton, his wife's nephew, and a neighbor, Lindsay Tinkle, talks like he wants to go."

"Two from North Carolina and two from Tennessee. Now *I'm* all steamed up. I want to hear how that Tennessee election came out." Sam considered for a moment and then added, "Good old David. It's strange how our paths seem destined to cross, isn't it?"

Well into the night hours they talked, for all of the visitors

265

were returning to their homes the next day—all save Sam and his family.

So exuberant was Sam over the prospect of having David in Texas that it did not occur to him that this might be the last time the family would all be together, and it was just as well. Had he not staked his all on the great adventure ahead—one that might bring him fame and fortune? Sentimentality must give place to practicality in times like these.

Seated at his desk in his home in Enfield, John Branch, former governor of North Carolina, U.S. senator and Secretary of the Navy, was on the point of opening his mail, when a communication from Raleigh turned his thoughts to the recent monumental achievement in amending the state constitution. He rejoiced in the opportunity the convention afforded him to strengthen and renew friendships of long standing. Especially was he happy to see again a young man of talent and promise in whose behalf he had in 1825 associated himself as mentor and friend.

In Raleigh at the convention he had been moved by the serious and eloquent defense of religious tolerance that Samuel Price Carson had made, as he had been equally dismayed by his apparent ill health. Remembering the handsome, exuberant neophyte in the halls of Congress in those early days, it pained him to see the change that time had wrought in the decade just passed. It pained him even more that his young friend planned to encounter the rigors and hardships of a wild and alien country when the East needed men of his integrity, eloquent persuasion and charm to fill many positions of honor that well might open up to him if he should elect to stay in North Carolina.

Recalling the past, he reached in his desk and brought out a letter in Carson's familiar handwriting. The letter was dated February 28, 1832, and signed by Carson and Willie P. Mangum reporting that they had poured oil on the troubled affair of himself and General Speight that had seemed headed for 'the field of honor.' How grateful he was to be spared that duel! And from another file he drew a letter in the same familiar hand of the young Burke legislator, containing the plea, "Let nothing goad you to resign," and he was reminded again of the fateful days in Washington when Jackson inaugurated his spoils system, and without regard to seniority, efficient administration or sensitivity, he began maneuvering the resignation of Cabinet officers and forming his own Kitchen Cabinet.

Carson's letter had warmed his heart.

He remembered, too, happier occasions when his daughters, Margaret and Rebecca, and their beaux, with lovely Mary Eastin and the gallant young blades who were always in attendance brought gaiety and the sparkling vivacity of youth to the White House parlors. His protégé Sam Carson, was often there paying court to the President's niece who was the 'unofficial hostess' at the Executive Mansion until the Eaton scandal made untenable the position of both Mary Eastin and her cousin Emily Donelson, who was the official White House hostess.

He was not sure what had happened to Sam's White House romance, only that Mary Eastin did not marry for a full year after his protégé from Burke had married his cousin from Tennessee, and that Carson's successor in Congress, James Graham, who had been a political rival, ungallantly referred to Sam's former White House romance and later marriage to his cousin in this wise, "Sam Patch must have decided that if he couldn't get honey, he would take molasses."

Through some mystic quirk of fate, less than a week after Branch's morning reverie, he received a letter in Sam's flourishing style. It was postmarked, "Brindletown, September 9," but on the inside, the inscription was "Nullifier's Retreat." He read:

> My dear Governor, I am bearly able to walk and have written but little since the sixteenth ultimo, on which day I was suddenly and most violently attacked with cholera (I think the *real* cholera, but the physicians add "morbus").
>
> I was at my father's when taken, and lay two weeks before I could venture to be brought home on a bed in my carriage. I am improving fast and my system appears in better condition than it has for years past. I have abandoned "spirits" in toto and Mrs. Carson has also "snuff." This I am confident you will be pleased to learn.
>
> We start lock, stock and barrel for Texas on the twenty-second instant—should have started this day but for my sickness. Inclosed is your bill of sale for Benny—poor fellow, I should have liked to have had him to wait on me in Red River.

267

Shall expect to see you during the winter or spring and should you come I will probably return with you and spend the summer in old North Carolina.

Mrs. Carson joins me in our love to self, Mrs. Branch and Family.

Your Friend Truly,
Sam P. Carson

Honbl John Branch

Branch folded the letter, returning it to its outside covering that served as an envelope. He looked troubled as he sat in thought for a few minutes. Was it a strange foreboding that prompted him to say to himself, "What stamina and determination this man has! Now, more than ever, I wish he wouldn't go." And he went to make plans for Benny's arrival.

TEN

By the time Governor Branch received the letter from his Texas-bound friend, Carson's caravan had traveled only a short distance. Even though the cattle drivers, the wagoners and their cargo had three days' start ahead of those riding on horseback and in the several carriages, the late starters overtook them at a point in Georgia where they planned to make camp.

Carson had selected his faithful overseer, George Cathey, to have general supervision of the wagoners, and had spent hours with him rehearsing the plan of travel and the several alternatives that might be resorted to should contingencies of weather or a surprise attack by Indians necessitate a change in plans.

The responsibility of Catharine and the children rested heavily on his shoulders. In the foreguard were covered wagons bearing precious cargo—the household and personal effects of the Carsons. One wagon was loaded with provisions to last the journey through, another held utensils for preparing meals and setting up camp for a hundred-odd people, plus varied labeled roots, herbs, linaments, ointments and an assortment of home remedies in case of sickness or injury.

Eli and Moses, with one or two assistants were in charge of the livestock—cattle and sheep that would furnish them food and milk along the way. Their number was augmented by couriers on horses who were designated to ride to and fro to keep lines of communication open between the fore and aft sections. A young Negro, a second generation African named Siphargon (called "Si"), was chief courier. He was charged with the responsibility of finding suitable campsites where water for man and beast was easily attainable. In the event of extreme emergency, these couriers would ride swiftly to spread the word.

Old Cumbo, dearly beloved of all the curious admixture of old and young, black and white, insisted that she would see to the health and well-being of the younger travelers, "an' deze ole eyes won't never close till deys all done asleep an' counted

269

for—ever las' single one of dem, Miss Catharine. Ize got my remedies where I kin get my hans on 'em quick."

Peter Carroll and his wife, Harriet, with their son, Empsey, Billy Dagen and his wife, Nelliemae, together with Abe Green and his wife, Nelly, were in charge of the cooking, and that included the preparation of fish, fowl, and livestock.

Sam's brother, Doctor John, was a member of the caravan. His presence was easily accounted for. After Sam's severe illness at Pleasant Gardens, and after he had gone to Brindletown to make haste their leave-taking, the Carson men, as was their wont, came together for a consultation about Sam's physical condition. There was little doubt that this last bout had been caused by a choleroid type of illness, but they were all agreed that he had had too many debilitating attacks of "the cold plague."

It was Sam's father who raised the question uppermost in the minds of the others. "John, I can't see why you encouraged your brother to embark on this senseless mission, when you know better than anyone that his constitution is not equal to such hazards."

"I did encourage him to move to Texas, Father. Let me tell you why. Last spring I encouraged him to go because his grief over the death of Warren Davis was so acute I thought a change would be beneficial, but you remember I saw to it that Jason accompanied him. Sam's health seemed better while he was in Texas, and Jason told me that he rarely coughed while he was there; in fact, he was like a new man healthwise."

"I think, John," observed Jason, "that this is the opportune time to tell all of us what your fears are."

Doctor John watched his father closely as he replied. "It seems to me that Sam has many symptoms of consumption, for which we know there is no cure, but which can be greatly alleviated by living in a beneficial climate. Jason is of the opinion that Texas affords such a climate. Until we learn more about this dread disease, for which there is no medication, a healthful climate is the only answer. If I seem to have encouraged Sam in a senseless endeavor, I did so in the hope that it would prolong his life."

A sudden silence fell over the group. Each in his own way

exhibited the great concern he had for a member of the family to whom they were all devoted. It was reminiscent of that fateful day in August, 1827 when they came together on the eve of the duel that cost the life of Carson's friend, Doctor Vance. "I think that Sam has been a sick, sick man since that day," Logan ventured.

"Yes, I heard Silas McDowell say once that Sam would never be the same again, and in some respects he hasn't," William added.

Charles and George had joined the group, and, as they often did, they turned to Joseph McDowell Carson, who had always been Sam's mentor. "What do you think, Joe?" they asked almost simultaneously.

"I am of the opinion that Sam's physical illness, his recurring attacks of influenza and pneumonia, have little connection with that unfortunate duel—no matter what Silas McDowell says. But this I will say with a great deal of certainty and a great deal more of pride—for a sick man, he has accomplished wonders! His record of daily attendance at the national Congress was surpassed by very few, and he had a far heavier load of committee work than many older and more seasoned members. I would say his entire Congressional record compares favorably with that of any of his contemporaries, and often his duties were performed when he was too sick to carry out his responisbilities.

"But now I am concerned about him. I am deeply grieved because of John's pronouncement." Joseph's voice broke and he was visibly shaken, "Sam is like my own son, Father. It is a great mistake for him to attempt such a journey. I cannot think of his being away from home and loved ones, facing the adjustments and hazards of a wild and foreign country, if indeed he does have the dread disease. I think John should make arrangements to accompany him."

Doctor John looked up in surprise, but before he could reply Colonel John faced the issue. "Your brother is right. You have no wife nor children to detain you. It will relieve me very much if you would go." John sat for a while without responding, but he could not hide his troubled expression.

"Will you accept a compromise, Father? Let me go with the

caravan halfway—well, perhaps as far as the Mississippi. Once they get all their paraphernalia across, there would be no turning back for Sam. By that time I will decide if he should go on."

And so it was agreed. John took his own horse, and rarely was he out of sight of the carriage in which Sam and Catharine were riding, and he was greatly encouraged as the caravan proceeded to see no evidence of a physical relapse. Perhaps the cholera had indeed cleansed his system and given him a new lease on life.

Their route lay south from Brindletown through Rutherford-ton, whence they continued in a South-Westerly direction through the upper part of South Carolina, then due west through Georgia and Alabama. In every case they traveled over rough but well-defined roads calculated to be the least difficult and treacherous for a group numbering one hundred or more individuals. Sometimes, in order to avoid mountainous sections and rivers that were not easily navigable, they were obliged to travel in zig-zag fashion. And as far as possible they tried to avoid known Indian settlements.

The first campsite where they stayed more than one night, the children were wild with excitement. They wanted to wander off in search of nuts and muskedines, to wade in the clear streams, and generally to expend some of their pent-up energy.

Later, basking in October's bright, blue weather, they suffered their elders to bathe and dress them in a change of clothes "from skin out" in order that the garments they had worn since they started could be washed, dried, and smoothed out with the aid of flat-irons heated near a bed of coals. "Dis shore is a pore make-out," Cumbo complained good-naturedly. "Effen Mr. Sam had started us in de summertime, we wouldn't had dis pile of clothes an dese dirty chilluns."

Some of the more enterprising elders had spent the morning fashioning bows and arrows to amuse the young boys, and had taught them how to clear out a small space, leaving a fringe of young saplings. They removed the small branches, now bereft of leaves, bending them toward the center, tying them securely at the top to simulate a skeleton wigwam. Over this they spread the skins of animals that had been slaughtered to provide food for the travelers. The children watched each step in wide-eyed curiosity.

Although the older ones had encountered Indians many times, the younger ones—most of them, had never seen a red man.

It was Doctor John's idea to gather the travelers around a blazing campfire to sing some of their corn-husking songs or the spirituals they loved. Lustily they sang, and then as their mood changed, nostalgically. But the younger ones saved the day. "We wants to see some sure-enough Indians," one of them called out. This seemed a propitious time to prepare them for the varied experiences that faced them—in particular, the more warlike tribes they would encounter once they reached the border. Later they could be told of the Mexican boys and girls, who might, if all went well, become their playmates once they were ready to begin their new life. But before his narrative could be started, one of the older women answered the child's question.

"You wants to see some shore 'nuff Indians? You'll see 'em soon enuff. I tells you I is clean scared outen my wits jes thinkin' 'bout it, Mr. Sam." Emily sidled up near her father and he drew her down beside him. He did not want the children terrified, and he was provoked with Nellie for her outburst.

Putting his arm around Emily in a protective sort of way, he reassured them. "Not all Indians are fierce and warlike," he began. "Many tribes live in peace with their paleface neighbors for long periods, but sometimes without warning they go on the warpath, seeking revenge for some real or fancied wrong that has been done them. The fact is, Indians make war on each other more often than they do on the white settlers. You will be hearing of many tribes, and some of them you will come to know by name, but right now I am going to tell you about the three tribes you will be hearing a lot about when we get to the Texas country. The Caddo Indians will be our neighbors. They are one of the oldest nations in Texas. When we get settled, we must try to make friends with these Indians who live along the border of the Red River where our plantation is."

Carson knew that making friends with the Caddos was a dubious business, if for no other reason than their awesome

273

appearance. He had seen them and he thought it was only humane to prepare the children for this new experience.

"They look like nothing you have ever seen before. Unlike most Indians, the warriors do not have long hair. Their heads are bald, except for a single bunch of hair on top. Around this they paint wavy red lines running down to and around their necks. They know how to make chains of silver and sometimes of tin, and they make small silver horses and buffalo to hang on these chains, which they suspend from their noses and from their ears. I am told that our Cherokee Indians used to dress like this." Sam went on, graphically describing their pecularities of dress and adornment. "Their ears are pierced to enable them to wear silver rings, bright glass tubes, feathers and sometimes dried bird skulls as permanent ornaments."

The women and children listened in consternation. Carson intended to tell them more about the customs of the Caddos as they progressed on their journey, but he decided judiciously that their preparation should be given in small doses when Nellie called out, "Mr. Sam I'ze bleeged to turn back. I an' Abe would thank you to let us go home. I done tol him I'd die afore I'd live next to dem savages."

"Aw Nellie, you is allus stirrin' up trouble. Go ahead, Mr. Sam, we'se lisenin'," contradicted Abe.

"Let me tell you about the Comanches. They live west of the Caddos along the river Brazos, and they have the finest hunting grounds in all of Texas. They own many horses and live in tents or wigwams."

"Will we live in wigwams where we are goin', Mr. Sam?"

"No, we will live in cabins like we did at Brindletown, and soon you won't know whether you are in North Carolina or in Texas."

With this note, the children, shepherded by Cumbo and their mothers, were hustled off to their make-do beds, but the men and boys were full of questions, particularly about the Caddos.

"Talkin' about huntin', Mr. Sam, what does dey hunt?" Si asked.

"Any wild beast, but mainly the buffalo and the black bear. The buffalo go from north to south, according to the season. Just about this time of the year they will be going south. When my brother and I were on our way to Bexar last spring, we met a large herd going north. We gave them wide range, for woe is the traveler who gets caught in their midst—especially if they should decide to stampede.

"As for the black bear, the Indians, especially the Comanches, depend upon him not only for skins, which they value, but they are hunted mainly for the oil they produce—oil to use for seasoning, oil to burn, oil to make ointments and salves. There are many uses for this valuable commodity. You've seen bears a'plenty. They are all more or less alike except for size."

Eli reminded Carson that they had not heard about the third tribe they would likely encounter, "but if they's Cherokees, we know about them."

"You're right, Eli. When my brother and I were in Texas last spring we found out many things that we had never known before about the Cherokees. Those now in Texas have come west with the encouragement of the U.S. government, hoping eventually to own their own land. They have migrated from Tennessee, Georgia, Alabama and some from North and South Carolina. In appearance they are like the ones we see back home. They are tall and light-skinned, not coppertoned like the Caddos and the Comanches, and they are friendly with their neighbors. They have established their own government, with a constitution printed in their own language. Their homes are built like their white neighbors'. They have a few grist mills and saw mills, and the women have their looms and spinning wheels to make cloth for their wearing apparel and household needs. They even have their own slaves to do the menial work in the compound. I have told you about my friend, General Sam Houston, who has encouraged me to make this move. He gets along well with the Cherokees since he lived with one of their tribes in Tennessee. He knows their language, and has always been a friend to them."

The campfire was burning low. They had a long journey ahead of them, and at the suggestion of Doctor John, they rolled themselves in their blankets and sought the sleep they sorely needed—an uneasy sleep it was for those who could not escape the frightening spectre of the Caddos who were soon to be their neighbors.

Twenty moons and twenty suns later they came to the Father of Waters, the mighty Mississippi. If Carson had been a deeply religious person like his mother, he probably would have turned the campsite into an old-fashioned camp meeting to offer up thanks for a safe journey, with relatively few minor casualties and for a relatively happy band of campers. The Negroes did sing songs of praise and rejoicing, and as he listened, Sam's heart was full to overflowing. For his own sake and for Cathy's, he dreaded Doctor John's departure. It had been a solace to both of them to have him along. The only good thing about his leave-taking was his assurance that Sam was physically fit for adventure, and for whatever uncertainties were ahead.

For the first time on the trip, Cathy could not control her pent-up emotions. She felt an uneasy premonition in parting with what she thought was the last vestige of her former life. She employed every pretext known to womankind to detain him, even after he was mounted and ready to go. With little Rachel in her arms, and holding Emily by the hand, she and Sam exacted promises that he would write often, giving news of the family, and they promised to do likewise.

Outwardly displaying his usual bright and sunny optimism, but inwardly suffering pangs of grief, Doctor John rode away, looking back as long as he was in sight of them, remembering every detail of their appearance to share with their uncles and their cousins and their aunts, to say nothing of their brothers and their sisters, and more importantly of all, with Colonel John.

As soon as John was out of sight, Sam placed his hands gently on Cathy's shoulders, turning her around to face the West.

"Look ahead, dear little Cathy; dry your eyes and look ahead. Somewhere out there across the Mississippi and later on across the Red River is our future paradise. Once you get there and we are settled, you will be caught up in the routine of plantation life just as you knew it at Green River and Pleasant Gardens and at Brindletown. You have been Queen of the Caravan, just as I promised, and you have been wonderful. Soon you'll be Queen of our Texas Prairie. I will tell you every day what a brave and gracious lady you are, and how very much I love you."

But Cathy was not easily consoled. Deep down there was a longing for familiar faces of loved ones left behind and an insistent foreboding that could not be ignored.

At intervals along the way she had felt a compulsion to cry out, as Nellie had done, "I want to go back—I want to go back—please take me back home!"

That night her dreams were tortured. She sat up in bed sobbing uncontrollably and calling out, "I'm afraid—I'm afraid!" In an instant Cumbo opened the partition that separated them. She took Cathy in her ample arms, comforting her. "Miss Cathy, honey, jes' yo' cry yo' fill. Cumbo knows how yo' feels. She knows how ha'd dese days is bin. Jes' don' wake de chillun an' don' let Mister Sam hear yo' cry. It'll kill his soul to hear yo' cry, honey. Come mawnin' an you'll feel better. Git yo' res' now, honey. We gota git on dat steamboat in de mawnin'. Lie back down an' let me pull up dese kivvers, honey. Cumbo'll be rat here. Everthin's gonna be all right—come mawnin'."

As Catharine closed her eyes, old Cumbo shook her head mournfully. Her words of comfort that "everthin's gonna be all right" belied her inner convictions. But now she'd pray harder than ever. She'd pray for every last one of them. She'd ask the good Lord to clear up the path in front of them and trust in Him to lead the way.

Old Cumbo was not the only member of the caravan who was filled with doubt. Had Sam Carson been realistic when he turned Cathy's gaze toward the West, he could never, by any stretch of the imagination, have painted so rosy a picture of optimism and hope. For Sam Carson was well-informed, and he knew that before there could be any semblance of peaceful habitation for Americans in Texas, there must be a revolution. He knew because of what had already happened that it would not be a bloodless revolution, and that in all probability they were riding full force into the path of a storm that might break at any moment, the relentless impact of which could very well sweep them into eternity unless they could soon be established and organized with others in a common purpose. He must hurry and begin to put down roots in the Texas soil. They must not be content to make haste slowly. They must push forward with all possible speed.

Sam spent much of his time with quill and drawing board while others attended to the long process of loading, and he came to what he considered was the best possible solution to their dilemma. It was the most feasible plan if all would agree to co-operate in it. Once they set foot on Arkansas territory, the members of the caravan who could make the best speed would be the *avante garde*, leaving the cumbersome equipment with the others, who of necessity were slow of movement, to follow at their own speed. They were equipped with maps and all needed provisions.

"Hallelujah!" exclaimed Si, who had been chosen to advance. "Now them whuts a'mine to can spen' they time diggin' an' swimmin' an' wallerin' in the mud all the way to Pecan Point—ain't that where we goin', Mr. Sam? Yas Sir, they kin take they time 'thout havin' to be pushed an' shoved an' prodded to move."

Talking to the ferry hands on shore was almost like getting an express from the scene of agitation and conflict. Sam made the most of this opportunity. And once on board, he continued his quest for knowledge. The captain was a weather-beaten adventurer with an English accent, but a Mexican vocabulary that enabled him to get both sides of the current picture from his passengers, and he was not loath to share his gleanings. He did so with emphasis that his news was unclassified—free for the asking, but totally unreliable. You could take your pick of whatever suited your fancy. What difference did it make? What was true today would be a lie tomorrow, anyway. Besides, with all of this traffic coming and going he was lining his coffers without the usual prospector's tools.

Asked if more were coming out than going into Texas, he replied jovially, "More women and children coming out, and that I like, even if most of them are scared stiff and weeping because they are leaving their husbands and sweethearts behind. For the most part, those going in are of a different breed—hard, disciplined in other wars, adventurers, raring to go. If they guzzle as much liquid refreshment once they join up with

Houston as they did on board I can't see them being much help to Texas. But then," he added, "I'm told that Houston can guzzle more and walk straighter than any man west of the Mississippi."

"Do you know the exact whereabouts of Houston now?" Sam inquired.

"Most likely at Refugio. I couldn't say for sure. He has no family here, so he is free to roam at will. I do know that since word has gone abroad that the Americans have given up trying to pacify the Mexicans, the leader of the pacifying group, Stephen Austin, now says 'orgainze for rebellion,' and groups in several locations are getting together to try to form an independent government. Of course you know that already there have been clashes between the Texans and the Mexicans, and it is amazing how well the Texans, who are vastly outnumbered, have been able to stand their ground—not only to stand their ground but to put the enemy to rout."

During the ferry trip Sam walked among the passengers, gleaning additional information. He refused an invitation to join a hilarious drinking party, only half intent on the cards spread out in front of them. "No thank you boys, I'm on the wagon," Sam replied pleasantly. He noted they were all in uniform of one kind or another. But he accepted the proffered chair at another table where coffee mugs and beer steins were about equally divided.

"My name is Carson. I'm from North Carolina, and I have a party on board going to Texas." The others proceeded with introductions, and as luck would have it, one of the party had ferried back and forth innumerable times of late, and he appeared so knowledgeable about what was going on that Sam wondered if he was a spy for the Texans. Asked about Houston, the gentleman replied, "I left Natchez yesterday, and an express had come in from San Augustine with what must be the latest intelligence. Seems that less than two weeks ago a provisional government was formed at San Felipe. They did not declare for independence, but they did declare to reinstate the constitution of 1824 which Santa Anna had set aside, and they elected Stephen Austin, William Wharton and a name named Archer as commissioners to go to the United States Capital to ask for aid. They are now on their way."

279

One of the gentlemen present, apologizing for his lack of information, remarked, "I thought that the Mexican government had become more conciliatory toward the colonists."

"They are conciliatory when there is something to be gained by it. But this on again-off again policy works no longer. You remember early this year, Santa Anna sent a company of soldiers to Anahuac to assist in the collection of duties. Up to that time duties had been collected without the threat of armed intervention, and the colonists resented the insult. Headed by William B. Travis, they marched on the town, forced the Mexicans to surrender, and sent them off to San Antonio."

"Yes," Sam replied, "and as a result, the brother-in-law of Santa Anna, General Martin Cos, ordered the arrest of Travis and others. Travis, you know, is from my sister state of South Carolina, and the event was broadcast pretty thoroughly in our state papers. There was speculation that that engagement might be considered the first battle of the revolution."

"No—that was just a skirmish. The first real battle was fought at Gonzales, the second day of last month, and it is my understanding that it was a notable battle in many respects *and* was favorable to the Texans."

"But what has happened now that Austin, the commander-in-chief, has started on his mission?"

"General Burleson took over the army around San Antonio."

"Well, what of Houston?" Sam asked.

"He was named by the convention at San Felipe as commander-in-chief of the whole Texas army to succeed Austin."

"Was it an election or an appointment?"

"It was an election, but not a unanimous one. The report is that he was rejected both by his neighbors at Nachogdoches and his own soldiers at Refugio, but was sustained by votes from other municipalities."

"You seem to be especially interested in General Houston, Mr. Carson. Do you know him?"

"Our paths have crossed on several occasions, sir, but I am interested also in another 'soldier of fortune' who I suspect is now in Texas."

The group indicated their curiosity, and Sam proceeded.

280

"Before I left home word had come to our little community at Pleasant Gardens that if one David Crockett of Tennessee lost his election to Congress he had in mind bringing a few friends to explore the Texes country, as he called it. He lost the election. I wonder if by any chance he has been heard from hereabout?"

There was instant attention. Crockett's name and fame had apparently preceded him. They had heard of him; they were impressed with what they had heard and were anxious to hear more, but none had any knowledge of his presence in Texas.

Had Sam been endowed with occult powers, he would have known that even now Crockett and his party were entering the Red River area, having been hilariously wined and dined in Memphis on November first. They had traveled by boat down the Mississippi to the mouth of the Arkansas River, and ascended the Arkansas to Little Rock, then overland to Lost Prairie along the Texas border—only a few miles from the northernmost border of Sam's newly acquired property.

The river boat after a slow crossing pulled up to the landing point about dusk, and because there was such a load of passengers and their belongings to unload the Captain recommended that they stay on board overnight and enjoy a carefree evening with the other passengers.

That night Sam shared with Cathy some of the highlights of his afternoon briefing, and later, more appropriately dressed for the usual riverboat festivities and surrounded by his family and other celebrants, he shed some of the concerns that had been increasing with every passing hour. He listened to the music of stringed instruments and the voices of happy Negroes temporarily released from their burdens. When the strains of music became livelier, he persuaded Catharine to join other dancers and take a few turns with him in the cramped space available for dancing. And Cumbo, eyes shining, feet tapping, and her face wreathed in smiles was heard to say, "Thank you, blessed Jesus. Miss Catharine's happy agin'. Now old Cumbo can res' in peace."

Colonel Hall and his laborers, who had been occupying the cabins Carson had bought when in Texas in April, gave every possible assistance in settling the newcomers, and he was able to

281

make a good report of his stewardship. The crops had been better than average and the cattle and other livestock looked sleek and well-conditioned.

"How was your trip, Mr. Carson? From outward appearances I would say you fared better than most of the settlers who are coming in sizeable numbers."

"We had no major difficulties that I had not anticipated, but the expenses of the trip were double what I had expected, and I find myself temporarily in a cramped financial condition. The fact is, Colonel, it may be necessary for me to sell this property and some of my Negroes to relieve a temporary embarrassment."

"In that case, Mr. Carson, I know of two who will be glad to accommodate you, both as to real estate and retainers. The two own property in the area and are desirous of increasing their holdings. I will, with your permission, speak to them of your possible intentions. But you own enough acreage that you do not need to dispose of all of it. I suppose you will keep this tract that has been so greatly improved."

"That is the very reason I thought to dispose of it. It will bring in more revenue than all the other property combined, and I intend tomorrow to purchase a tract from William Miller, a Tennessean, who bought it three years ago."

"Yes, that is the tract known as Little Prairie. It is a very desirable property, but why buy more when you intend to sell all adjacent land?"

"I believe I will realize from the sale of it, as part of the larger tract more than double the $2,000 it will cost me."

"I see, Mr. Carson, that you are an astute trader—an asset not usually ascribed to a politician, but one that will serve you well in the vast expanses of this undeveloped area." At Catharine's insistence Colonel Hall accepted Carson's invitation to the evening meal, and he noted that his hostess had apparently adjusted to her new environment and that she showed considerable pride in their new cabin home. "What a pity it will be," he thought, "if she has to be uprooted so soon and forced again to make adjustments calculated to upset womenfolk."

During the next two weeks Carson was busy with his several transactions. James Bass and William B. Hemphill came at

Colonel Hall's behest and on December 8 signed an agreement to purchase for the sum of $107,000 the several properties and tenements involved in the transaction.

Carson again demonstrated his business acumen in accepting annual payments from the two purchasers that would give him a guaranteed income for the next six years. He reported the prospects to Cathy at the same time that he promised he would build on a site of her own choosing the most complete and most beautiful pioneer home on the Red River.

"What will we do while you are building? I am just beginning to feel comfortable here, and now we will have to get out," Cathy complained.

"Not on your life, we won't Cathy. It's all in the deed." He handed her a copy of the instrument so that she could be satisfied of the stipulations. "You can see right here. The first payment of $25,000 is to be made in a matter of three weeks on the first day of January. The buyers will have possession then of all except our cabins here. These are reserved until such a time as we can conveniently leave—and that will be when our new home is completed. And that's not all, Cathy. On the first of every January, beginning with 1837, we will collect $16,400 'til the full amount of $107,000 is paid."

Catharine could not avoid showing her relief that they would have a guaranteed income—no matter how the winds of adversity might blow. The fact dissipated her fears of what might become of them if her husband reverted to his former pattern of debilitating illnesses. Nor could she avoid showing a special tenderness toward her good provider. "When can we go looking for a new homesite, Sam?" she asked enthusiastically.

"Before we do that I want to visit a man who came to Red River about two years ago. He is a man of wealth and integrity— a Scotsman who emigrated to North Carolina and settled for a while in Granville County. He has been here long enough to know 'the lay of the land.' When we were here last April, Jason and I spent some time with him and he gave me excellent advice about the properties I acquired then. Perhaps he will have suggestions about our permanent home."

"Who is he, Sam, and where does he live?"

"He is Robert Hamilton, a bachelor about ten or fifteen years older than I, and he lives in Red River County on a valuable estate—considerably to the west of us."

"I'm sorry he is a bachelor," Cathy interposed. "I had hoped I would soon get to know some wives."

"You will, you will, of course, little Cathy. Colonel Hall tells me that one of our neighbors—only twenty miles or so away—has a very personable wife. They came two years ago, and brought with them a large number of Negroes. Before coming to Texas he was a supreme court judge in Alabama."

"You haven't told me his name," Cathy broke in.

"He is Judge Richard Ellis, a jurist of some distinction, and a most desirable asset to our colony here."

"Then if he has a wife, let us go to see them first."

Before they could make their first call, Judge and Mrs. Ellis came calling on the Carsons. Through the kind offices of Colonel Hall they had learned about their new neighbors. For weeks they had been planning a Christmas celebration. On the three days before Christmas they would extend the hospitality of their home to those in the Red River country who could attend, and they had come especially to invite the Carsons. While the ladies continued their conversation, Sam and Judge Ellis in another part of the room appeared to be in serious discussion. "This affair, Mr. Carson, is to be more than a 'fandango.' You have been apprised of the apprehension that is daily building up to the south of us. The general council now sitting at San Felipe has notified the residents of Pecan Point, through an emissary to me, that we should send two delegates to the constitution convention that will meet early in March, I presume at San Felipe. I have discussed the new directive with one or two of the older residents hereabout, and we feel strongly that this area is entitled to more than two delegates in a matter so portentous as this. It is for the purpose of discussing this issue that you, along with other responsible citizens are invited to share our hospitality."

"And you are inviting the women, too?"

"Let me explain. When I made a trip to Texas in 1826, roads were horrible and both travel and mail were unpredictable, as indeed they are today. My wife did not hear from me for five months, and in her anxiety appealed to Austin to find out what had become of me. When I reached home a few months later she let me understand that she would be most uncooperative if I ever left on a scouting trip without her. She feels so strongly about this that she arranged the Christmas festivities to tempt the wives to accompany their husbands on this ostensibly social mission."

"My wife will find in Mrs. Ellis a strong ally, for she has some extreme reservations about this whole idea of pioneering," Carson replied laughingly.

Meanwhile the second portion of Sam's caravan had arrived and were directed to the site Cathy had chosen—a tract with improvements, situated west of Big Bayou and a little northwest from Fisher's Prairie. All of it was in Lafayette County, Arkansas, but part of it near the Texas-Arkansas border. Carson had agreed with Alexander Bole, the owner, to consummate the transaction after January first when he would receive the $25,000 payment from Bass and Hemphill, and secured his permission for part of his goods and chattels to be taken to the place immediately on their arrival.

Among the Negroes were enough skilled artisans to insure that their new home would be sound and enduring, and enough unskilled labor for completion by the middle of February. No time was lost in planning. Together Carson and Cathy worked out details agreeable to both. Although the majority of settlers built log cabins, occasionally on the larger plantations more pretentious houses would be found, sometimes with siding and cedar shake roofs that made a more elegant appearance.

They finally settled on a weatherboarded house with a shake roof and twenty-by-twenty rooms separated by a wide hall, partially enclosed at either end. Two huge chimneys of sandstone daubed with lime afforded open hearths and fireplaces— two in the hall and one in each of the adjoining rooms.

An ample stairway, patterned after the one at Green River, led to the half-story above. Here there were two large rooms with gabled ends and another room, long and narrower at the front, designated for Cumbo where she would be close to the little girls. The third bedroom would be reserved for guests. Catharine objected to the puncheon floors seen in many of the houses, arguing that the skilled labors they had could hand-plane pine boards, and using wooden pegs they could produce an attractive, compact and durable floor on which to place the prized pieces they had brought from Bindletown and Pleasant Gardens.

Remembering the details of these homes, Catharine included a number of innovations seldom seen in the west. There would be ample mantle boards, and shutters that opened inside offset windows, on each side of which shelves would be built for books and bric-a-brac.

If Catharine's enthusiasm in planning could be matched with equal enthusiasm in living in the home of their creation, Sam was convinced that half his problems would be solved.

As they approached the Ellis home it became evident to the Carsons that they were not the first arrivals. Hobbled horses and a number of conveyances were in a front enclosure. Once inside the house they were cheered by the sound of many animated voices and by the appetizing aroma emanating from the kitchen quarters.

Judge and Mrs. Ellis greeted them warmly and introduced them to Albert H. Lattimer and his new wife, Elizabeth; the venerable Scotsman, Collin McKinney and his wife and handsome twin daughters, Anne and Peggy, and a number of unattached gentlemen—James H. Robinson, Robert Hamilton, and James Clark. They needed no introduction to Colonel Hall and his lady, who joined the party later.

Late in the afternoon, after all the guests had arrived, the gentlemen were assigned a cabin outside the main house, where their discussions next morning were to take place, and the ladies occupied one large bedroom adjoining the living room and dining area. Cathy said it was just like being at the Academy again, for in spite of the threatening clouds, they were determined to be gay.

The first evening was given over to social enjoyment and an opportunity to get acquainted. Thinking to enliven the conversation, one of the gentlemen observed, "I understand that the famous David Crockett is on his way with companions to lend support to the cause of Texas independence."

Carson sat bolt upright. "Has anyone in the area seen or talked with him, or is this just a wild rumor?"

"My information, Mr. Carson, came from *The Arkansas Gazette*. It seems that he has lingered in and around Little Rock to recoup his fortunes, and being much in demand as a speaker, he entertains a gullible public with the tall tales for which he is famous. Indeed, *The Arkansas Gazette* has published one of his tongue-in-cheek tales describing how he broke one of the Arkansas banks."

The ladies asked for a recital of the tale, and the gentleman was obliging. "Crockett said it was the custom of one of the banks thereabouts to bolster its revenue by taking skins and pelts in exchange for a loan—the rate of exchange being a raccoon skin at par for a dollar, while a bear skin was good for ten dollars and a beaver for twenty-five. Now this particular bank had a capital of $100,000, of which about $3,000 had been paid in, and with which the building was mortgaged to secure the rent and the cashier's salary.

"Crockett allowed he saw himself a chance to capitalize on his prowess as a hunter and trapper. He had great luck, and trudged off to the bank with his plunder, insisting on payment in specie rather than taking their notes. The skins were safely deposited in the bank safe—a long shed in the rear—and Crockett marched away.

"A few days later he called with another haul, which he said were finer than the first skins. The next day he called with a third lot, still finer. It was the next lot that broke the bank, he said, and he explained his remarkable feat in this wise: After selling his haul during bank hours, the Colonel made tracks, but he returned to the bank safe during the night, and thrusting his screw ramrod through the logs, he fished out the skins and sold them over again the next morning till the bank was broke."

Carson kept his own counsel, while the ladies talked excitedly of the possibility of seeing the famous Crockett as he made his way south. It would be useless to explain how much it would mean to him to see his former associate, who never hesitated to tell "tall tales" that reflected on his own conduct, but rarely, if ever, made a friend the scapegoat of his many anecdotes.

By unanimous consent, Judge Ellis took charge of the discussion next morning. "There are a number of important decisions to be made, gentlemen. As you know, the Red River area has not been clearly defined as to the borders between Texas and Arkansas. In addition, the counties and municipalities are loosely defined. The residents in the Pecan Point vicinity, separated as we are from the settlements in Texas proper, have shown only slight interest in the revolution now taking place. Likewise, until very recently, Texas has paid little attention to us!"

Here Judge Ellis took a memorandum from his pocket. "It was the consultation meeting in San Felipe that on last November 11—a month ago, in fact—resolved, 'That as the settlements on the Red River are remote from other settlements in Texas, they be formed into a separate municipality, and that they send two delegates to the convention which is to meet the first day of March next.' This was followed by a communication I have just received that the council has voted to permit the citizens of Pecan Point to send two delegates to the convention.

"Now gentlemen, the reason I have called you together is to ascertain if we can secure more adequate and just representation at the convention. How we are to consummate these ends is a matter for discussion and decision. Please express yourselves freely."

Mr. Hamilton rose. "Judge Ellis and gentlemen, we are probably of one mind as to the gravity of our situation, and the fact that we are far removed from the scene of action does not release us from interest in nor responsibility to the causes of our delicate position. If anything, the fact that we are not in the direct path of danger, that our homes are not likely to be plundered and our women and children ravaged by Santa Anna's hordes, places on us a more peculiar and more humane involvement in discussions and decisions pertinent to the March convention."

From his seat, Collin McKinney spoke out. "But the voices of two representatives will not sway the assembly one way or another. This is a large area, and should be broken up into a number of municipalities, each jurisdiction being entitled to two representatives."

"Right you are, sir," Albert Lattimer agreed. "We will have to move with all possible speed, and I suggest that we send a representative immediately to the council at San Felipe to discuss and remedy our unfavorable situation."

"I am in full agreement, gentlemen," Carson explained. "The Red River area has greatly increased its population in recent months. I am of the opinion that three municipalities should be formed, each having two representatives, and I move that we proceed to the selection of one of our number who will present our petition to the general council. Perhaps someone who can go immediately will volunteer for the assignment."

James Clark got to his feet at once and indicated his willingness, indeed his eagerness to perform the mission.

"Most of us are not citizens of Texas, but of Arkansas," interjected James Robinson. "And all of you know that there is no municipality designated as Pecan Point—or Red River either, for that matter."

"Then we'll form these respective municipalities when we get a directive from the council," Colonel Hall observed. "In the meantime we should decide on methods of selection of the six representatives while we are all together."

Judge Ellis consulted his memorandum again. "The council has designated February first as the date for election of the delegates to the convention. Let us act on this directive as if we would be given as many as three municipalities and six delegates and set up the machinery for such an election. We can issue handbills to acquaint the people with our plans, designating the several polling places agreed upon."

Question piled on top of question, and once the restraints of formality had been broken, it was with difficulty that order was restored. In the midst of the confusion, the aged Collin McKinney rose and pounded on a table for order.

"Remember, Gentlemen, that this is but the beginning of our responsibilities, and that we have taken only the first step. I would remind you that General Houston has said that until Texas has a responsible, well-organized and functioning government no step can be taken to free us from Mexican oppression and subservience. Since he is known to have the ear of President Jackson of the United States government, it would appear that all of our future hopes and aspirations lie in the speedy declaration of our independence from Mexico. To that end I offer the hospitality of my home for counting the ballots and determining the election of those men who will guide our destinies in the March convention. And may the God of our Fathers direct us in these momentous days!"

There is no record to show that the council received or passed upon the letter delivered by James Clark seeking larger representation from the Red River area at the convention, and in spite of there being no municipality of Red River and at this time no Republic of Texas, and that the general council had stipulated February 1 as the election date, Pecan Point sent the following statement on January 27:

> We, the undersigned judges appointed in Resolutions passed at Collin McKinney's to compare polls of the different elections, after examining the same do certify that Collin McKinney, Robert Hamilton, Samuel P. Carson, Richard Ellis and James H. Robinson are duly elected to the Convention to be held in Washington, in the Republic of Texas, on the first day of March next, for the purpose of framing a Constitution.

When the news of his election reached him, Carson was faced with multitudinous problems. In the first place it was necessary for him to supervise closely and urge to completion their new home if they were to get settled by the middle of February. This required a number of trips to the new site, and exposure to the inclement weather was beginning to take its toll. Besides, Cathy was none too happy about the prospect of his long absence from the home he had represented to her in such glowing terms. She lost interest in the details of packing and moving that otherwise would have challenged and excited her.

Finally he was faced with two alternatives: either leave Cathy with the full responsibility of moving and getting settled—too much to ask of a woman who had been protected all of her life—or refuse to accompany his associates and fellow-delegates who were leaving for the convention shortly after the fifteenth of February.

Could he refuse to accept the responsibilities of citizenship in his adopted country, and forever rue the day when he failed to measure up to his ideals of service to his fellow man? Seldom had he been racked with such painful decisions and such a bleak prospect for the future. He dared not conjure up the prospects of Cathy's well-being and that of the children. Suppose the Caddos should take the opportunity provided by this internal upheaval to go on the warpath.

The more he wrestled with the prospects, the more depleted he became, and with sheer physical exhaustion came the final awareness that he would be wholly unfit for any useful contribution at the convention unless he left his family as well provided for as was humanly possible. Then only could he invoke the protective care of a Benevolent Father.

"The other elected delegates from Pecan Point must go on without me," wrote Carson in an express to Judge Ellis. "I shall join you as soon as my health permits and my family is settled in our new home."

Christmas had passed without a single word from relatives in North Carolina, even though their new address had been sent out immediately. Cathy's disappointment and heartache left her inconsolable. "We're cut off from the world, Sam—our world and everything we hold dear. What good can come of an expedition like this—what possible good?" she agonized.

"Cut off from everything we hold dear? Why Cathy, we have each other, and we must learn the lessons of self-reliance. That is part and parcel of this often lonely and unrewarding experience of pioneering."

"If there were only a way to communicate without having to wait for the mails to come through! Our letters from North Carolina are probably at the bottom of some swollen river. You know yourself that the mails are totally unreliable."

"I know that, Cathy, and things are likely to get worse before they get better. Let's give ourselves another year before we give way to despair. Next Christmas things will be better, little Cathy. I won't promise, but we can live expectantly—we *must* live expectantly. There's no other choice."

Had the truth been known, Carson's ardor for the new life he had forced on Cathy was at its lowest ebb. Discouraged because of his health, uncertain of the immediate future of his adopted country, sometimes at the point of desperation when he thought of leaving his family to the mercy of uncertain but potentially merciless savages, he was beginning to lose faith in

291

himself, and in his ambitious undertaking. Seeking solace in the past for want of satisfaction in the present and optimism for the future, he relived some of the less agonizing days of his service in the United States Congress.

Many times since his unexpected and precipitate involvement in Mexican affairs, he was reminded of a former antagonist whose political philosophy he had once opposed with all of the vigor at his command, but whose ideals for preservation of the Union in the Nullification controversy he could now, with the passing of the years, look upon with tolerance, if not admiration. Joel Roberts Poinsett, well-born, wealthy Charlestonian of Huguenot descent, and Carson's senior by a score of years, had represented the United States as its first ambassador to Mexico. He was eminently fitted for the assignment. His education in the states and on the continent had been thorough and protracted—as thorough as his frail constitution would permit, and protracted because he, like Carson, was plagued with an illness that sent him from one recuperative climate to another in search of health.

His health eventually repaired, he served a number of years in the Legislature of South Carolina, where he distinguished himself by his independence of thought and action. He was elected to the national House of Representatives in 1821, where he emerged as an ardent admirer of Jackson, whom he idolized as the hero of New Orleans, as a champion of agrarian civilization, and as an advocate of the recognition of the Spanish American republics.

Carson's term of service had begun just as Poinsett's was interrupted to accept the new post he had been tendered by President Adams, and while his association with the South Carolinian was brief, he had read the published report of Poinsett's earlier visit to Mexico, and had come to know the man through his pen and his associates.

Carson recalled all this and much more about his contemporary, whose appointment as Minister of Mexico and subsequent stormy diplomatic mission had brought about his recall by Jackson, then President. He had become an increasingly unpopular symbol of United States foreign policy—hated by the

British, whose plans for the conquest of Mexico had been thwarted, and despised by many disaffected Mexicans who demanded his recall by President Jackson.

It had been almost six years to the day since Poinsett had returned to Washington. Carson remembered the circumstances of his arrival in Washington. It was neither the "return of the prodigal" nor the triumphant entry of "the conquering hero." News of the events of his last fear-ridden days in the Mexican capital had preceded him—his personal friendship with leaders of power and influence in the capital—Guerrero, Santa Anna, Zavala—had proved ineffectual in stemming the tide of revolution now heightened by threat of a counter-revolution that might spell disaster. But whatever the ultimate effect of his recall on the public, Poinsett's Washington friends welcomed him with open arms, and Carson was among them.

How vividly he relived those and other event-filled days while he was gaining strength to make his next move! He dared not continue the unfolding of his relationship with Poinsett, for suddenly he was weary, too weary to live again the dramatic days of Nullification when he and the fiery South Carolinian were again arrayed as political enemies, each against the other, each ready to do battle for the cause he believed was right.

"If I were not so tired and ill, I would try to put on paper my thoughts on this strange unraveling of fate. Santa Anna, no longer a disciple of republicanism, is now the arch enemy of Texas. Zavala, I am confident, will continue to espouse the republican principles set forth by the redoubtable Poinsett, who now has become active in promoting internal improvements in the United States, concentrating particularly on development of railroads. And here am I at the crossroads! Impotent! Ineffectual! No longer able to carry my share of the colonists' load!

"Catharine," he called, "bring me a large potion of spirits! Oh yes, I know I foreswore that vile habit before leaving North Carolina, but I'll be damned if I will be beaten by an enemy that encamps within me and robs me of my strength and capabilities when I need them most. Don't look at me like that, Cathy, my precious Cathy. I am a sick man, and I need the strength that this potion will give. Let me have it, Cathy, and tomorrow I will be better and we can set out for our new home."

Before the day was out the mails came, an accumulation of personal Christmas messages, family letters, and a bundle of newspapers.

Cathy was as excited as a child, and alternate tears of joy and nostalgia splashed the pages of the Green River letters and the letter from her father.

Doctor John's communication was the first that Sam opened. Posted January tenth, it was received February nineteenth.

Dear Pioneers, let me convey to you the love and belated Christmas greetings of young and old at Pleasant Gardens. Your nieces and your nephews, your cousins and your aunts, to say nothing of your brothers and your sisters and our venerated father, with one accord join me in the hope that your first Christmas in Texas was filled with a host of things to be thankful for—good health, comfortable and happy surroundings, a plenteous table, and congenial friends to share your festive board.

We missed you! Individually and collectively, we missed you! Shortly before Christmas old Eben came to the kitchen door with two wild turkeys he had caught and Becky had dressed. "Dese is fo' Mr. Sam. Please see dat he gits 'em in time for Christmas."

Poor Eben! Distance and the limitations of Uncle Sam's delivery system mean little to him in his fast-fading awareness. He knows only who are his friends, and you have always been "the top rail" with him.

If I live to be a hundred I'll never forget the picture of you and Emily and Catharine and the baby standing amidst the smoldering campfires that cold November morning on the banks of the Mississippi.

My homeward journey was made without too much inconvenience, but with ever-increasing loneliness. I never liked solitude, Sam, and so I decided to go a little out of my way to visit an old friend. I remembered that James Pinckney Henderson, of Lincoln County, had moved to Canton, Mississippi to practice law, and just in time I thought to renew my friendship with him, sleep in a 'shore 'nuff bed, and put my feet under a real dining table once more.

Although he is yet unattached, he is set up comfortably for the niceties of life, and he welcomed an old North Carolinian with unfeigned pleasure. When I told him of your trek to the wilds, he was quite delighted. "Texas needs more men who are experienced in government like Sam Carson," was his comment, and he went on to say, "I'm afraid that our country is not aware of the importance of

294

wresting this outpost of Mexican domination, nor of the still more important fact that we have no time to lose. The enemy is already advancing! They're saddled and bridled, and equipped for slaughter!"

So much in earnest is he that he is making plans to raise a company of volunteers which he will command, and which he will equip at his own expense. They will set out when the cry from Texas becomes unmistakable and insistent.

Henderson is young, dynamic and personable, and I suppose you would say that he is ambitious. Texas can use men of his caliber, and I know that he will leave his imprint there.

In my next communication, I will reveal the excitements of the balance of my journey, for I have time and space only to say that we are all well and eager to hear from the Carsons of Texas, particularly of your health, Sam.

Your no-longer-protective
Doctor John

P.S. Speculation is rife in these parts as to whether Texas will emerge from the expected clashing of swords as a state or an Empire. It is surprising how much interest is shown in the scattered news reports of the turmoil out there, and I almost forgot to report that Abner Burgin is back home, entertaining neighborhood groups and individuals in hair-raising accounts of his journey to Texas with "Crocket & Company." Seems that Abner and Lindsey Tinkle lost their taste for adventure the further they got away from civilization, and according to Abner, they came home twice as fast as it took them to go to Texas.

Doctor John's letter, although a poor substitute for Doctor John in person, served as a restorative, or was it the Texas punch Cathy had provided? In any event, the news of James Pinckney Henderson's active interest in Texas afforded Sam great satisfaction, and the report that Abner Burgin had returned in one piece from his perilous adventures with "Crockett & Company" again made him wonder what had become of David and his young nephew, William Patton.

When Sam at last set out for Washington on the Brazos, after settling his family in their new home, thoughts of the historic events ahead of him served to buoy his spirit and enliven his journey. That it would be his good fortune to encounter James Clark, returning from San Felipe after presenting the petition from the Red River council, was one of the imponderables of Fate. At once Sam asked for news from the Council.

"I did not wait for action on the petition," Clark indicated. "Things were getting too hot for comfort, and so I left the petition and started home."

"Did you see or hear anything of David Crockett and his companions on your journey?" Sam inquired.

"I not only heard of him. I saw him. You remember, I set out immediately on my journey to San Felipe without returning to my home. I had not gone far when I met Crockett's party. Never having seen 'the Colonel,' introductions were in order, whereupon Crockett asked if I were a-kin to a Mrs. Clark who had shown him a special favor. He proceeded to explain that he and his party were riding through the Red River country, traveling westward, when two women overtook him and warned him of danger in that direction. They urged him to procure a guide and change his course. I told him that one of the women was very likely my wife, and so it proved to be.

"There were several in Crockett's party, and I advised them to turn back, as the Indians were on the warpath. Seems like they had been exploring all the Red River country from Fulton to Lost Prairie. Strange how you have managed to miss your friend, Mr. Carson. I'm sure that a number of times you have been near enough to throw a rock into his camp, if you'd been a-mind to."

Sam thanked Clark for his report, asked and received advice on the safest and surest way to reach Washington, and started for the nearest boat-landing on the Red River where he could get transportation for himself and his horse to a point below Shreveport, the course suggested by Clark.

From Nacogdoches, Texas, Carson wrote to Catharine reporting on his journey.

Although I will be late arriving at the convention, my trip so far has been satisfactory, my health improved, and my spirits elevated accordingly.

We left the boat at a point near Nachitoches, Louisiana, and I spent last night in San Augustine. I believe that on this route our mail can come and go with the surest dispatch.

In spite of the laws prohibiting immigration and the imminent dangers, the migration into Texas continues. I passed an impressive number of ox-drawn wagons piled high with household effects, the families following on horseback or in wheeled vehicles of one sort or another. The weather was balmy and pleasant until yesterday, when a "norther" blew in, the gale causing temperatures to drop precipitously.

"You'll be hard put to guess who recently occupied the room I now have at Nacogdoches! None other than Jesse Benton, brother of the eminent Senator, my godfather emeritus. Jesse was on his way to "the scene of action" with a sizeable group of volunteers when he was stricken with an illness that kept him immobilized for near a month. Having been reduced to skin and bones, I don't see how he can carry out his plans to enlist in the infantry as a private, but such is his intent, reports mine host, and he is now on his way. Seems he became much discouraged because the volunteers who accompanied him consumed all of his provisions, and a great many of them had cleared out.

As can be imagined, rumors and tall tales circulate freely in the saloons and in the streets—wherever people congregate, for there's nothing on their tongues now except the war with Mexico. One rumor has it that the Indians are joining forces with the Mexicans, and that our friend, Houston, has visited them attempting to transfer their loyalties and help turn the tide in our favor. Another is that the Mexicans outnumber our soldiers ten to one, and that Santa Anna's army has laid seige to the Alamo at San Antonio de Bexar, and that Colonel Travis, in command of our defenders, has sent out a desperate call for reinforcements. The bearer of this tale said he had heard that Crockett is among the defenders. How true this is in fact or in substance may soon be revealed. It is logical, for if he is still harboring malice against Andrew Jackson, he would never "join up" with Houston's army, and apparently he wanted to be a part of the liberation forces.

Still another rumor is that Texas now has two governors, Henry Smith and James Robinson—one vetoing and revoking the orders of the other. Such is the state of confusion in and around the temporary seat of government. I fear I have missed some of the dramatic incidents and vital transactions that have already taken place.

Don't worry about me, dear little Cathy. The Alamo is a long way—more than 150 miles from the new seat of government at Washington-on-the-Brazos, which I expect to reach on the day after tomorrow.

Your highly-exercised but extremely devoted
Delegate-to-the-Convention, S. P. C.

P.S. It is a foregone conclusion that this Convention will declare the Independence of Texas. I hope they have not already done so, for I want to have a hand in this historic event.

297

ELEVEN

Carson had no illusions as to what he would find in the way of physical comforts and conveniences at Washington. There were none. At the only tavern in the town all the guests and the keeper and his family slept in one large apartment—some in beds, some on cots, but the greater number on the floor. Main Street was just a wide clearing in the woods, and clustered around were new but primitive log cabins, and a few hurriedly patched-up shanties.

The large unfinished building used for the Convention Hall was left with openings for doors and windows, but with little protection from the elements until someone stretched cotton cloth across the windows to stop the force of the biting wind. The Hall was rented by a number of Washington merchants, and made available to the Convention rent free.

"I wonder why they chose such a God-forsaken location for such a note-worth occasion," Carson speculated as he approached his destination. Surely San Felipe, the seat of Texas government until now, couldn't have been worse. The town had been laid out for less than a year, he remembered. "I think when they changed the seat of government, they jumped out of the frying pan into the fire," he concluded.

It was shortly after noon on March 10 that Carson slipped unnoticed into the Convention Hall. Taking a back seat, he was thus afforded an opportunity to become oriented without attracting attention. He did not count, but there appeared to be about half a hundred men of different ages and in contrasting mode of attire. Some were outfitted in rough buckskin, while others wore more sartorially correct broadcloth frockcoats with elaborate colored vests. Some were bearded, others mustached, while many were smooth-shaven.

Wall pegs were hung with a curious admixture of headgear— the Texas wide-brim and two of its Mexican counterparts, at least one coonskin cap, and a stovepipe or two, with a score or more of beavers in conventional style.

Carson recognized a few acquaintances. Judge Ellis was in the chair, and seated in front were Collin McKinney and Robert Hamilton. Looking further, he noted Albert Lattimer, but James Robinson was missing. Strange, he did not remember Lattimer's election as a delegate from Red River. He had expected to see Sam Houston, but apparently the General had not arrived.

Carson listened intently. The Chair recognized Mr. Maverick, a delegate from San Antonio de Bexar. "As you know, gentlemen, I reached the Convention Hall on March fifth after the day's session had adjourned, and just as the engrossing clerk was about to close the list of Signers of our historic Declaration of Independence." (So the Declaration had already been framed and signed, Carson noted with surprise.)

Maverick continued, "In view of the excitements that have prevailed since the Convention was called into extraordinary session to hear the urgent communication from Colonel Travis at the Alamo, I feel that I am in duty bound to explain that Mr. Badgett and I do not represent San Antonio. These citizens— largely Mexican—are represented by Ruiz and Navarro. The Anglo-American soldiers stationed at the Alamo were not permitted to vote for delegates to this Convention. The Mexican judges would not allow them to vote, primarily because most of them have so recently arrived in Texas that they are not considered citizens. So they ordered an election of their own. Jesse Badgett and I were elected. We have the honor to represent the stalwart invincibles at the Alamo, and you will recall that with my credentials I presented a petition signed by the officers of the Alamo requesting that Badgett and I be seated along with the Mexican delegates. I want this body to know that we feel it is an honor to represent our beleaguered soldiers in this memorable convention."

"Well spoken, Mr. Maverick! Are you a native of Texas, sir? I do not have your credentials before me," the president inquired.

"I am a native of Pendleton, South Carolina, sir, but I came to Texas from Louisiana."

Carson raised himself in his seat to get a better view of the man with whom he undoubtedly would have much in common.

299

The Reading of the Texas Declaration of Independence
From the Painting by Fanny V. and Charles B. Normann in the San Jacinto Museum of History

He was sure of it when Maverick noted, "I left South Carolina when Calhoun's doctrine of Nullification changed the political future of that state."

Judge Ellis, who was presiding, noticed Carson as he rose to get a look at Maverick, and immediately announced, "The chair recognizes the honorable Samuel P. Carson, late of Burke County, North Carolina, formerly a three-term member of the United States Congress—a new-comer to Texas. He is a member of our delegation from Red River, but was prevented from accompanying our other representatives to the convention because of the urgency of family matters. Mr. Carson, will you come forward and present your credentials?"

As he walked toward the clerk's desk, Carson remarked, "I hope I am not too late to sign the document that for Texans will be second only to the United States Declaration of Independence in point of historic significance."

Permission was given by acclamation for Carson to sign. He lifted the document, noting the heading, "The Unanimous Declaration of Independence Made by the People of Texas in the General Convention at the Town of Washington on the 2nd day of March, 1836."

There was no time to read the nine or so pages, handwritten in legible style, but he paused long enough to read the last paragraph: "We, therefore, the delegates with plenary powers, of the people of Texas, in solemn Convention assembled, appealing to a candid world for the necessities of our condition, do hereby resolve and declare that our political connection with the Mexican Nation has forever ended, and that the people of Texas do now constitute a free, sovereign and independent republic, and are fully invested with all the rights and attributes which properly belong to independent nations; and, conscious of the rectitude of our intentions, we fearlessly and confidently commit the issue to the decision of the Supreme Arbiter of the destinies of all Nations."

Carson's eyes were misty, as he reached for the pen to affix his signature. He was conscious of the drama of the occasion, and his emotions were deeply stirred at the thought that he and those who surrounded him were fortunate participants in a stirring epoch of American history—the Birth of a Nation! He followed the pattern already set for decorative signatures, the flourishes possibly denoting each man's determination to arrest the attention of all who would in time wonder what manner of men these were who were bold enough to take this decisive step, and he wrote his name in large flowing style under that of James A. Maverick, a former South Carolinian.

As he turned to resume his seat, Carson's eyes met those of a short, stocky man, smooth-shaven except for a curly beard that extended from one ear to the other and under his chin, in much the same fashion as the Mennonites and Amish. His dark hair was thick and curly, and was brushed back from his forehead and from his ears. Carson was arrested by the intensity of the look in his eyes, and by his benign expression. He was later to learn that this was David Burnet, with whom his own immediate destiny would be enmeshed, and that the beatific countenance camouflaged a disposition as hard as nails and a less-than-conciliatory stubbornness.

At the close of the session, and much to his surprise, Carson was accosted by Maverick. Extending his hand, the ex-South Carolinian ventured, "You are well known to me by reputation, Mr. Carson, and as you may surmise, I came to know you through our fellow townsman, the late-lamented Warren Davis."

"You were friends?" Carson asked eagerly.

"Pendleton is a very small village, sir. But contrary to what you may be thinking, the Nullification issue did not separate us. Only men of small concepts will allow friendships to suffer because of issues. I am not sure I can be so charitable where John Calhoun is concerned, however."

"Well, at least we can be charitable toward each other, and who knows but that your political philosophy and that of President Jackson was right. Certainly, if it were not for the Nullification issue which I espoused, I would not be here among the Texas midwives, and would have been deprived of the opportunity to cultivate your friendship."

"I can see that our mutual considerations and interests bid fair to strengthen us in the tasks that lie ahead, and I dare say we will need all of the strength and cooperation that we can muster to tide us through this painful experience."

"Then you think that the worst is yet to come?"

"I have no doubt of it. You see, I know firsthand of the strength and ruthlessness of Santa Anna and his cohorts. I know, too, of the pitiable condition of our defenders at the Alamo. I was one of them, as was also Jesse Badgett." Maverick's voice faltered. "I know of their stamina and guts. We were under bombardment for twenty-four hours without the loss of a man. Before I left, the enemy demanded a surrender, which, if not complied with, would result in the annihilation of all within the fort in the event that it was taken. Colonel Travis answered the demand with the burst of a cannon shot, and our flag was proudly waving from the garrison walls when I left.

"You were not here when Colonel Travis's letter was read to our delegation on the sixth, Mr. Carson. Much of what I have just said was incorporated in his plea for reinforcements. I am familiar with its contents because I accompanied John Smith, who bore the letter I referred to—a letter that produced a profound effect on all assembled."

Carson himself was profoundly affected by this firsthand accounting of events. Insistent questions flashed and pounded in his mind, and realizing that the other members had been dispersing as they talked, he motioned Maverick to a chair where they could continue their conversation uninterrupted. "Mr. Maverick, is David Crockett among the stalwarts you referred to?" Carson inquired.

"Indeed he is, sir!"

"What about William Patton, his nephew, and my friend, Jesse Benton?"

"Neither was there, as I recall."

"Then tell me, what was the response to Travis's letter, and where in the name of God is General Houston? I heard rumors when I stopped at Nacogdoches, but I want facts—if they are available."

Maverick was impressed with Carson's impatient concern. It was in noticeable contrast to the casual reaction of some of the delegates.

"Let me answer your last question first. General Houston, I am told, arrived at the Convention on the last day of February riding a small Mexican pony. He was attired in a buckskin suit and Indian moccasins, and had a brightly-colored Indian blanket

303

wrapped around him. The delegates who had assembled gathered around him and plied him with questions. 'What of the rumors that Santa Anna was gaining ground at Bexar?' 'Would it not be the better part of valor for them to arm themselves and go to join their fellow Texans in the conflict?'

"Houston quieted them with the admonition, 'Attend first to the business for which we have come together. We must declare ourselves free of Mexican oppression, establish an independent government and frame a constitution that will be noted and respected by other sovereign nations. We must elect officers to govern us, and to give direction to our purposes.' This, in substance, was General Houston's advice, and he repeated his admonitions when, on March third the first message from Travis was read to the convention. And again the delegates, impatient to get to the scene of action, were placated by Houston, who insisted that they had more important work to do and should proceed with the organization of a provisional government."

Carson was impatient to hear more, but he waited for Maverick to resume his briefing.

"You may not be apprised of this, Mr. Carson, but General Houston, as long ago as January seventeenth last sent James Bowie to the Alamo with orders to blow up the fort. Colonel Travis refused to acknowledge General Houston's authority, refused to obey orders, refused to retreat. You see, I know, for I was there."

"Perhaps this insubordination had much to do with Houston's calm acceptance of Travis's tragic plea," suggested Carson.

"Indeed it could very well have influenced the general's action, but if it did, more's the pity."

"I did not see him in the hall this afternoon. Is the general here?"

"No. He was here on the opening day when the committee was appointed to draft a declaration of independence. He was not a member of that committee, though it was on his motion that the instrument was adopted. Something of the calibre of the men who drew up the paper is evidenced by its ready acceptance. Mr. Childress read the declaration from his seat, it was received by the convention, delegated to a committee of the whole, reported without amendment and adopted unanimously in one hour from the time of its first and only reading. General Houston was the only member who spoke to the subject, and his speech was in the nature of a declamation."

Maverick paused to note two gentlemen in close conversation near the exit. "Do you see the gentleman on the left, Mr. Carson? He is William F. Gray, and he has given me much of the information about what preceded my arrival. He is not a delegate, but is writing a sort of diary of events that he hopes to have published. The gentleman next to him is George Childress, of whom I have just spoken. He is a native of Tennessee, and next to General Houston, I would say that he is the man of the hour. I understand he wrote the Declaration. At any rate, it was largely his workmanship.

"But going back to General Houston, Mr. Gray reports that on the second day of the Convention when one of the delegates rose to move that the members of the body arm themselves and wear their arms during the sessions, Houston, determined to keep tempers cool and get on with the business of organizational procedure, again reminded the delegates of their responsibilities. The motion to arm was withdrawn. Later Houston was confirmed as Commander-in-chief of all military forces.

"It was during the extraordinary meeting called on Sunday, the day after my arrival, that the appeal from Colonel Travis was read. Houston immediately addressed the Convention, and then with two of his staff, took his leave."

Carson received the news of Houston's departure with great disappointment. Remembering that it was while he was in Congress in 1832 that Houston's direct appeal and persuasive arguments had kindled his first spark of interest in the opportunities and challenges of Texas, Carson pondered the strange fate that had brought the two together in defense of Texas liberation. And he had missed him by only four days!

At the 7:30 session that evening Carson announced he had been officially notified that the steamers *Brutus* and *Invincible* were berthed at the mouth of the Brazos, ready for any mission that the Republic of Texas might have for them. He thought it was important to commission these vessels. He would therefore move that a select committee on naval affairs be delegated to

305

inquire into and report in relation thereto, a motion that was immediately approved by the Convention.

Thus Carson was launched in the most active, grave, exciting and tension-filled period of his life. He was soon recognized by his fellow members as one of the superior delegates in terms of experience in legislative and constitutional bodies, and his counsel was sought in all major decisions.

Following the close of business that evening, Robert Potter, colorful and brilliant former North Carolinian, who had followed Carson as a member of the national Congress, and later as a member of the North Carolina Legislature, came forward, and the two were seen in animated conversation. Potter was an outrageous but attractive renegade, whose checkered career in North Carolina politics had been climaxed by expulsion from the Legislature at the insistence of indignant citizens, enraged at his highhanded escapades. Shortly after, he left North Carolina for Texas, where he was ready to carve for himself a more enduring and respectable career.

"Well, Carson, since that portentous year when we were together in the late-lamented North Carolina legislature of 1834, here we are in the middle of this treacherous and dubious business of collaborating in the painful birth struggle of an infant Nation." Carson smiled, and was about to speak, but Potter continued, "I heard rumors that you were in Texas, and I had my suspicions about the reason for your coming. I doubt not that General Houston had a hand in it. By the way, did he ever repay the $200 he borrowed from you in the spring of '32?"

"If you are implying that I came all the way to Texas to collect that paltry sum you have treed the wrong possum, and besides, that is a purely personal affair between the General and me. I prefer not to discuss it. But I am not averse to being enlightened on the subject of your presence here in Washington. I know full well why *you* came to Texas."

"Suppose we skip over that, if you will. I am now representing the people of Nacogdoches in this grand experiment, and I intend that they shall be well represented, my dear Carson. But if you should pin me down as to how I was elected a delegate, I might be evasive. Suffice it to say that my North

Carolina experience did not stunt my ambition, nor have I forgotten the strategy of handling men, even though my wiles were not equal to the determination of the clergy and the sixty-two members of the House of Commons in North Carolina, who voted me out of that august body."

Carson had been told that a large percent of the emigrants to Texas had come to live down their past. Apparently Potter had made strides in doing just that, for he had been accepted on equal terms with the most reliable and knowledgable of the delegates and Carson intended to give his associate every encouragement in his good intentions.

Nevertheless, he looked at Potter searchingly. "You are one year my junior, you know, and always your life has been full, exciting and fruitful. Remember, I did not say fruitful of what. But seriously, your many years in the United States Navy should be of inestimable value, even if you were just a boy when you served on the high seas. You grew to manhood under that discipline, and let us hope you have found here the right niche for your talents and abilities."

"I am grateful for your confidence, Carson, but I may have got off to the wrong start. You see, as soon as Colonel Travis's letter was read last Sunday, I presented resolutions urging the convention to keep steadily in mind the organization of the government, but to adjourn and hasten to the field of battle, there to show our colors in time of emergency. I urged immediate action to organize the militia, provide arms, ammunition and supplies, and in addition to draft an appeal to Texas and the United States, at the same time explaining our reason for adjournment."

"Were the resolutions passed? You see, I have just got here and I am ill-advised."

"No," Potter replied impatiently, "they were turned down. Childress, Collinsworth and Rusk led the opposition."

"They may have opposed this particular strategy, Potter, but they will make use of your widely-acknowledged experience in our new government, or I miss my calculation.

"And since we intend to stay right here and not 'scatter our shots,' I suppose the first thing to do is to complete the drafting of the Constitution, already in the initial stages, I understand,

307

and to pursue the matter of floating a loan for an improverished but aspiring new Nation."

"Yes. I'll bow to superior judgment, if I must, and go along with the majority, though I'm not sure but that my plan was a wise one. We won't have a government to use a Constitution if these damned, infamous Mexicans are not stopped in their tracks."

On the following day, two latecomers, Andrew Briscoe and James Wood, appeared and asked permission to sign the momentous document that lay on the table. Permission was given, and the engrossing clerk, Mr. Kimble, then closed the roster with his testament. Now the Texas Declaration of Independence was complete—ready to be shouted to the world as soon as copies could be made and sent on their way.

By the afternoon of the eleventh, the drafting of the constitution was well under way. When the question of requirements for exercising the franchise was introduced, it was proposed to change the voting age from twenty-one to eighteen. Carson was opposed in principle to lowering the voting age, but the army needed men *and* boys in the present emergency. The motion was defeated and Carson offered a substitute motion with the qualifying provision "that all young men of the age of eighteen years and upward who shall have served faithfully in the present War of Independence be entitled to vote upon presentation of certification of such faithful service."

The motion, deemed unnecessary by most of the delegates, was defeated. This was a blow to Carson, who felt that any young man old enough to bear arms for his country was old enough to vote. It proved to be the only defeat on any important motion or suggestion that he experienced during the convention.

There had been no news from the Alamo since Colonel Travis's letter was read to the assembly on the sixth, but wild rumors persisted that thousands of brutal Mexican soldiers were marching eastward, bent on exterminating the government, and the tension of the delegates was manifested at any unusual sound or movement. Each was conscious of the grave concern of the other, and all recognized their plight and the need for drastic measures. Committee work, important in the extreme, was accomplished by sheer force of will.

The Convention had been considering the draft of a Constitution, article by article, section by section. This had been a time-consuming process, and on Monday, March 14, Carson moved that the House resolve itself into a committee of the whole. This was done, and he was called to the Chair. Within a reasonable time, he was able to report the completion of the Constitution as amended—perhaps not the wisest but the most expedient solution to their urgent race against time.

The document as reported and amended was referred to a committee of five for correction of phraseology and of errors. Other matters under consideration—the disposition of public lands and the matter of reconstituting the militia—were disposed of negatively.

On Sunday morning, Carson, with the delegate from Matagorda, was appointed a committee to forward commissions to naval officers. Carson was well aware of the importance of the Navy in the present emergency. He believed that the sea routes were vital to the success of the revolution, and that therefore the Navy should be a subject of major concern. He saw to it that sufficient time was taken to insure that a standing committee of five would provide a liason between the officers of the Navy and the Texas government to insure proper communication between these two vital agencies. These specifications and provisions proved to be the nucleus from which the Navy Department grew.

With increasing rumors that Mexican forces were approaching, Carson on the morning of the sixteenth had requested a suspension of rules with leave to introduce a resolution "that spies be immediately dispatched under the direction of this House for the protection of this convention, and also for the procuration of arms."

Other business occupied the uneasy delegates, and they adjourned in the late afternoon to reconvene at 9:00 P.M. to make final approval of the Constitution. But during the recess, word was brought by express of the fall of the Alamo, and the delegates hurried spontaneously to the Convention Hall, where great confusion and excitement tended to disrupt an orderly transaction of business.

Some of the delegates had gone home, and those who were left were in constant alarm because of news that kept coming in of the flight of families and livestock in the path of the invaders. The news was borne by stragglers and deserters from the Texas army, who, as they traveled eastward, spread over the country such exaggerated reports of the large force of the enemy, of their unheard-of cruelties, and the small number of Texans to stop the hordes that the panic became universal.

When sufficient order was restored, the Convention proceeded to business. The Constitution was not quite ready, and the delegation adjourned to 10:00 P.M.

The brief respite gave the members time to talk among themselves. The Constitution, they agreed, could not be implemented in time to make decisions affecting the immediate urgent needs of a responsible Texas government, and some measure should be adopted to provide for an interim government, the officers selected to form a cabinet, through which the functions of government could operate in the emergency.

When they came back into the Hall at 10:00, they seemed to be invigorated, and they immediately got down to the work at hand. At midnight the constitution was finally adopted, and before they adjourned, an ordinance organizing a provisional government was adopted, consisting of a president, vice-president, four secretaries and an attorney general.

The ordinance creating the provisional government enumerated other provisions. The officers were to be chosen *viva voce* by the convention. They would have full powers to negotiate treaties, and they were specifically authorized to negotiate a loan, not to exceed one million dollars, for which they would pledge the faith of the newly-constituted Republic of Texas.

When details of the executive ordinance were agreed on, the Convention proceeded to the election of officers. A delegate from the municipality of Jasper presented Carson's name in nomination for President of the *ad interim* government. David G. Burnet, who had been in constant attendance at the convention, but who was not a delegate, was also put in nomination for the same office. He received twenty-nine votes, six more than Carson, who was then elected Secretary of State. Robert

310

Potter, as Carson anticipated, was made Secretary of the Navy, Thomas Rusk, Secretary of War and Bailey Hardiman, Secretary of the Treasury. The new officers were sworn in at four o'clock on the morning of March 17, and the group adjourned to get whatever rest they could until the session convened again at 9:00 A.M.

Carson, recognizing that some of the most urgent concerns of the new government had not been resolved, got no rest in the intervening hours. He wrote a number of dispatches and orders, and a few letters, and made a rough draft of matters to be brought before the Convention when it reconvened. At that time he sought authority "to issue notes in an amount adequate to the present exigencies" and permission to raise funds to administer the government. He recommended the appointment of fellow delegates George Childress and Robert Hamilton to go to the United States and seek recognition of Texas independence, and their aid in carrying the war to a successful conclusion.

Agents of the prior government, Wharton, Austin and Archer, had succeeded in raising funds, but in terms that many considered unacceptable—so unacceptable as to bring on heated discussion from time to time since the first days of the Convention. That they were morally obligated to recognize the efforts of these agents and meet their terms or effect a compromise was such a strong conviction of Carson that he later spoke at length on the subject, pointing out that one of the fundamental rules by which the Cabinet should be guided was that the faith of the government should be preserved. In the end, the Convention voted to leave the adjustment of the loan in the hands of the Chief Executive.

With further reports of the encroachment of the enemy, the administration decided to go to Harrisburg, and they thought not on the order of their going. They went in haste and confusion, dispersing in all directions, their panic increasing when they were confronted with a constant stream of women and children and a sprinkling of men, with wagons, carts and pack mules rushing to cross the Brazos.

President Burnet issued a proclamation urging the people to stop their flight and listen to reason, but even with the assurance that the enemy was still some distance away and that General Houston had been encouraged by large reinforcements, the panic persisted, and the exodus continued unabated. To add to their misery and discontent, it was raining, and wagons, heavily loaded with household goods, were often mired in the mud, the pedestrians sloshing along in the wake of the pack mules and wagons.

Although President Burnet got a late start, he rejoined members of his cabinet at Groce's Landing, between Washington and Harrisburg. They remained there through Sunday, the twentieth, with Zavala, the vice president, and Carson, ill from exposure to the elements.

During the day the Cabinet was called into extraordinary session to hear unexpected tidings. Joe, the Negro servant of the ill-fated Travis and the only male of all in the Alamo to escape with his life, had arrived during the night, and was to be questioned by members of the Cabinet.

He made an excellent witness, giving, with great dignity and becoming modesty, a full account of that awful day. The recital was painful in the extreme, both to the boy and to his listeners. There were among the delegates those who had lost brothers and other kinsmen in the tragic battle, and Carson had lost a friend of many years. He buried his head in his hands when the boy described Crockett's last hours. "The biggest pile of dead Mexicans wuz found near the stockade fence where Colonel Crockett took his stand. He would fire and without taking shelter, he reloaded the gun right in front of the enemy. Maybe it wuz reckless, for he got his arm shot to pieces by a musket ball. But he kept on firin' at close range with just one arm, and then when the Mexicans crowded in on him, he used Ole Betsy like a club, swingin' her an' knockin' dem Mexicans ever whichaway. When his rifle broke, he went after dem greasers with a knife till they put a sword through his body."

"When General Houston left the Convention on March 6, he assured the delegates that he would go to the Alamo and do all in his power to help the men there. Did he reach San Antonio?" inquired one of the delegates.

"No suh, but I wuz in his camp on my way here, an' the men told me they rode as fas' as they cud thru the mud, tryin' to get

312

dere. They said ever little bit the General would git off his horse an' put his ear to the groun' to tell if they wuz still shootin'. He learned that trick from the Indians. Then at las' he got up off the groun' after lisenin' an' said 'De guns at de Alamo is done quit shootin'.''

Asked for the latest news from General Houston, he reported that the commander seemed to be retreating before the enemy. The Cabinet members were of the opinion that that could very well be the case, for now that he had been victorious at the Alamo, Santa Anna, no doubt, would consolidate the Mexican forces and try to complete the rout of the Texas army.

Now that the Cabinet was together again, President Burnet was anxious to keep it that way as they traveled toward Harrisburg, where once again they would try to take up the reins of government.

It was dark when they crossed Buffalo Bayou and entered the village. They found accommodations at the home of Mrs. Harris, widow of the gentleman who founded the town. The house was overrun with transients. Most of the Cabinet slept on the floor under blankets, but Mrs. Harris provided beds for Burnet, Zavala and Carson. The three chosen ones agreed that they were fortunate, but Carson and Zavala were sure the lady had detected their indisposition and had had pity on them.

Taking advantage of a lull in activity, and with the intelligence that a mail would soon be dispatched up the Red River to northern Texas, Carson wrote hurriedly to Cathy.

Harrisburg, Texas
March 30, 1836

My dear and long-suffering wife,

I have time only for a hurried note, written by dim candlelight.

This is an inauspicious time for great optimism—perhaps I should not write at this juncture, when the affairs of Texas are at their lowest ebb.

My position with the newly-formed Republic of Texas is responsible, time-consuming and, in the very nature of things, hazardous. Nevertheless we are all grateful that so far we have not encountered the enemy face-to-face.

We hear that Houston's army, now recruited with a considerable number of volunteers, is on the east side of the Colorado, and the enemy is on the other side, in sight. No fight yet. We are provided with the news of Houston (and the enemy) by Mexicans friendly to our cause, but Houston, himself, sends no communications.

William Fairfax Gray is our chronicler. He keeps a diary, which I hope is accurate. If his written opinions are as unpleasant and derogatory as he expresses in conversation, we will present a miserable picture to the world, should his diary ever reach the public.

Now for some news of the immediate future, which I hope you will keep safe from prying eyes. The President (in private) is sympathetic to my desire to go to the United States on a mission of importance. He realizes the extent of my physical needs and he knows that I have discharged my official duties when I was unable to burn the long-past-midnight oil in order to write all of the dispatches, orders, letters, etc. that the business of the Republic demands.

The steamboat *Cayuga* came up yesterday afternoon. How long she will stay in the docks I do not know, but I have high hopes that orders will come through in time for me to board her.

Two of my compatriots, like myself, are ill. Zavala is going home (he lives not too far away) to recruit his health, and Rusk has had to postpone his plans to join the army until he recuperates. So much of the time lately we have had to live in damp clothing—a day and night experience. The weather has been atrocious.

Talk to the children about me, Cathy. I need not ask you to do this, nor to keep your hopes high for my safe return. I know that you will.

With deepest affection and respect,
Carson

Sam did not write of Crockett nor the Alamo. He still could not bring himself to think unemotionally of that terrible tragedy.

On April 1 Carson received by special dispatch the order of President Burnet for his official leave. "The infirm state of your health rendering it necessary for you to repose from the fatigues of office, and the recognition of your physician that a change would probably conduce to your restoration, I have submitted to the gentlemen associated with us in Government the propriety of your proceeding forthwith to the United States, and there employing your valuable time in the service of Texas. . . . You will proceed to Washington City as fast as your circumstances will permit, there to unite your exertions with our commissioners in procuring a *recognition* from the government of our Mother County, and take charge in a general supervision of all of the interests of Texas in the United States."

The president went on to say that an acting Secretary of State would be appointed, "but the Department will await the return of its most esteemed incumbent. Your absence will be too sensibly felt not to be deeply regretted. You will make it as little irksome as possible, not only by frequent communications, but by shortening the period of your absence as much as a prudent regard for your health and the ulterior objects of your visits will permit."

Carson received the reprieve both with exultation and disappointment—joyous relief that his ordeals would be temporarily abated, but genuine disappointment that he would no longer continue his association with those who were undergoing a period of such stress. Before he started packing he wrote a number of important communications—two to the agents of the Republic, Childress and Hamilton, one to John Forsythe, Secretary of State of the United States, and one to Colonel James Morgan, confirming the intent of the government to purchase for the sum of $8,500 the freighter *Flash* for use by the Republic.

Later, while engaged in last-minute preparations for going on board, Carson was given a briefing by Captain Andrew Briscoe, who, because of Carson's intercession, had been permitted to sign the Declaration of Independence on the eleventh of March, and who was the next to last man who signed. He had rejoined the Army when the Convention dissolved on the seventeenth. He reported the dire straits of Colonel Fannin. "Day before yesterday, Santa Anna and a large force of Mexicans were three miles from San Felipe and have no doubt engaged our men by this time. There is probably nothing left of the place by now."

Before the ink was dry on notes that Carson had finished just before retiring, intelligence arrived that Fannin's small company at Goliad fought valiantly until there were no more than thirty left, when he raised the white flag. They had expected to be made prisoners of war. Instead they were taken out a distance from the village and shot—the last man of them.

"We are dealing with barbarians, who either do not know the rules of civilized warfare or have so little conscience they do not care," Carson declared emphatically.

Carson's informer agreed, and cited the recently-acquired intelligence that the bodies of the victims at the Alamo had been piled high and a torch put to them. The Secretary of State shuddered. His sympathies for all of the brave ones that had been so victimized overwhelmed and sickened him.

There was one last personal obligation that Carson must attend to before going on board. Thomas Rusk, Secretary of War in the new Republic, had been ill for several days—too ill to rejoin the Army as he had planned. He, like Maverick, was a native of Pendleton, South Carolina, and for understandable reasons Sam felt drawn toward anyone who had had any association with his friend, Warren Davis. He had been attracted to Rusk even before he knew his place of nativity—perhaps because he spoke with a trace of the Irish brogue that often showed up in Colonel Carson's conversation. Rusk, a lawyer and protégé of John Calhoun, had organized a company of volunteers at Nacogdoches, and had been elected captain. When delegates to the Convention were chosen, Rusk had received a majority of the votes cast. It was in that election that Robert Potter, by his dubious maneuvering, garnered barely enough votes to put him across the finish line. And now Rusk was secretary of war and Potter, secretary of the Navy.

Carson found Rusk improving and impatient to get on his way to his command. The butchery at the Alamo had fired his zeal for retribution. "We have not heard all that transpired on that fateful morning of March sixth, Carson, and in our lifetime we will not hear the last of it. It will someday dawn on the imagination and conviction of a later generation that no purer example of self-sacrifice has ever been witnessed than that demonstrated a few weeks ago at the Alamo. Those men could have saved their lives by fleeing from an enemy ten times their strength. They had ample time to save themselves. But each one of those heroes surely made up his mind that the enemy must be held at bay until the colonists could move their families to safety. They lost their lives, but they gained two precious weeks for us. Now our troops can consolidate and take an invincible stand. Pray God that we may.

"Yes, Carson, for sheer courage, cold nerve and deliberate

self-immolation, there is nothing that will compare with the Alamo and Travis's resounding shout, 'We shall never surrender nor retreat!' The Texas army now has a rallying cry, 'Remember the Alamo!' We must go on to victory with that cry on our lips."

"But what of Houston? Is it true, as some of these fleeing civilians say, that he has retreated, and if so can you fathom his reasoning for such a tactical move? Or, are we already whipped, doomed to serfdom by these aliens?

"I know it to be a fact that Burnet has written to him in tones of scathing criticism. 'The enemy are laughing you to scorn,' he wrote. 'You must no longer retreat. The country expects you to fight. The salvation of our country depends on your doing so.'"

"Hand me my saddle bags, Carson," Rusk requested, and he brought out a letter still damp from exposure to the elements. "This came today—just before your arrival." It was from General Houston, dated March 29. It answered some of the criticism that had been directed toward him. "I consulted none—I held no councils of war. If I err, the blame is mine."

"If his strategy works, Carson, he will become a hero for all time; if not——But tell me, Mr. Secretary, you say you are about to board the *Cayuga*. What is your mission?"

"I am on my way to Louisiana at the direction of President Burnet, there to confer with General Edmund Gaines at Fort Jesup with a view to having the United States move troops into the Sabine to compel the Indians to respect their treaty. It appears that they have been stirred up by the Mexicans to harass—perhaps emasculate the settlers in that area. After that, according to my recent orders, I am to repair to the Capital of the United States, there 'to take charge in a general supervision of all of the interests of Texas.' Perhaps along the way I can attend to my health. I find myself very much depleted and in need of rest and recuperation.

"And you, Rusk? I don't need to ask. You are a true soldier. On you and Houston and those like you depend our salvation. Believe me when I say that I envy you."

Carson had never worn the uniform of his country. Fate had decreed that his would be a less-hazardous service. But his admiration for Rusk and Houston—yes, and even for Potter, was genuine and sincere. There were no heroes who could be compared with those of any rank who were willing to fight for their country in a just and honorable cause. These things were very much a part of his thinking when he grasped the hand of Rusk in bidding him good-bye and Godspeed.

On board the *Cayuga*, Carson made every effort to unwind and rid himself of the deleterious effects of the preceding hectic days, but it was impossible to get away from the nightmare of the war. There were those on board who could talk of nothing else but the terrible plight of the families who had been uprooted from their homes and had been compelled to flee before the entire Mexican army—innocent, suffering victims of man's inhumanity to man. Each time a frightened baby's scream or the anguished cry of a mourner accompanied the staccato of gunfire, the pathos of this merciless exodus was seared into the hearts and minds of the sensitive.

There were moments when the secretary of state had time for reflection. In retrospect he could not believe that so many official duties had been crowded into so few hectic days. It would have been a physical impossibility for him to have written by hand all of the official communications that were sent out under his signature from different locations where his "runaway" government kept pace with the fleeing civilians. Without the services of his chief clerk, Thomas Hill, it would have been utterly impossible.

Carson was plagued by the thought that the answers to most of the pleas sent for men, munitions and supplies might never be received in view of the ever-changing location of the seat of government.

On the twenty-third of March he had written from Harrisburg, "We stand in need of supplies of all kinds—sugar, tea, corn—at least one hundred bushels must be sent up. Flour must be had if possible, and liquor suitable for genteel men to drink. In short," he wrote, "I leave to your imagination to supply what we shall need. Every article of comfort is wanted. The Cabinet wish to see you with regard to fortification necessary to the protection of the bay."

318

He wondered if the proclamation of President Burnet "urging every man of Texas able to poise a rifle or wield a sabre to fly to the army" had reached the populace—already flying in the opposite direction. The government printing had been done under great difficulty by the Bordens at San Felipe, the same agency that had been publishing *The Telegraph and Texas Register.* They did get an issue of the *Register* on March 24, but Carson remembered seeing a memorandum from Gail Borden, Jr. reporting that it had been necessary to remove their press. They would try to put it over the river, and if the government could send a team, they would set it up at Harrisburg.

The *Cayuga* had halted at Liberty to take on cargo and passengers, and Carson took advantage of the opportunity to get a letter off to his superior officer, David Burnet.

State Department, Liberty
April 4th, 1836

My dear President,
 I lay on the opposite bank of the River last night. I have issued orders to two different persons (one for Trinity and one for the Neches) to press boats to aid the people in crossing. The panic has reached this place, and the people are all leaving Trinity from the opposite side. The river is rising rapidly, and I fear by night it will be impassable for any kind of carriage. The slue on this side is belly deep. Destruction pervades the whole country. Never till I reached Trinity did I despond, I *will* not say despair. If Houston has retreated or been whipt, nothing can save the people from themselves—their own conduct has brought this upon them. If Houston retreats, the flying people must be covered in their escape. He must be advised of the state of the water and the impossibility of the people crossing. If under the Providence of Almighty God he has whipt them, the panic can be allayed. I state facts as they now exist here, nothing can stop the people unless Houston is successful.
May God protect you,
Sam P. Carson

Apparently after he had affixed his signature he had had an encouraging word, for at 12 midnight he penned a postscript.

News—good news
 I have just heard through a reliable source that a company or battalion of U.S. troops left Fort Jesup eight or ten days since,

crossed the Sabine and are marching toward the Neches. This news has infused new life in all of the people here. I will send this news to the distressed movers, which will turn many a one back.

Carson

Before morning Carson's elation had turned to great personal anxiety. He had been coughing for days, just as Rusk had been doing. He was awakened just before dawn with the most severe paroxysm he had ever had. He lay back on his pillow, the sweat pouring off his body, blood staining the towel he held to his face in what was his first hemorrhage from the lungs.

He was too weak to rise the next morning, and he was frightened. "Thank God," he thought, "when I perform one more official mission, I will be on my way to Catharine where I can gather my strength and my determination to take up my mission again."

Unseasonably warm days followed the spring rains, and for the next few days Carson baked in the sun on the *Cayuga*, recovering his strength to such an extent that he was able to confer with General Gaines, and on the fourteenth of April to send this communication to the Cabinet of the Republic of Texas:

Nachitoches, Louisiana
14th of April, 1836

Gentlemen

On my arrival here last night, I met with General Gaines, and have had with him a full and satisfactory conversation. The object of the concentration of forces at Fort Jesup is to protect the frontier and the Neutral Ground, also to keep the Indians in check and repress savage aggressions. This he is bound to do in fulfillment of treaty stipulations between the Govt of the U States and Mexico

An Express arrived here at 2 o'clock A.M. last night directed to Genl Gaines advising him of the concentration of from 1500 to 2000 Indians, and a conjunction of their forces with about 1000 *Mounted* Mexicans. This is the detachment no doubt which Jo, (Col. Travis's servant) spoke of as having left San Antonio and which took the Bastrop Road. There is no doubt of this information being correct. On Sunday night last (10th inst) they camped about 60 Miles from Nacogdoches. The gentleman who brought the express says there is at least 300 families west of Nacogdoches which have I feare been slaughtered before this

Genl Gaines *immediately* on receipt of this Express issued an order to prepare 13 companies to march this evening to the Sabine with two field pieces with 75 rounds for each and 35 rounds for the infantry—also 12 days provisions, etc.

In the last paragraph of his letter, Carson noted that he was enclosing a copy of General Gaines's requisition to the governors of Louisiana, Tennessee, Mississippi and Alabama to furnish a "brigade of Mounted Volunteers," which would augment their troops by seven to eight thousand men.

His mission completed, the ailing secretary of state turned his face northward—to Cathy, his beloved family and the haven of home. He was sure that if any individual could nurse him back to health, it was Cathy. Could it be possible that he had been gone from her only forty-two days? It seemed an eternity. Looking back on his brief tenure of activity as an officer of the Republic, it seemed humanly impossible that so much could have been accomplished in so short a time. He was too sick and tired to speculate on the effectiveness of the measures taken. In his present state he sometimes wondered if the events had actually happened or if it had been one long nightmare. He slept a great deal, often having to be aroused at mealtime.

Thankful that there was a boatlanding within thirty miles of his new home, he had dispatched an express while he was at Liberty announcing the approximate time of his arrival. He knew that someone from the plantation had met every northbound steamer since the arrival of his letter. And now, almost at journey's end, he would summon all of the will power and determination he could muster to present the appearance of a man hale and hearty when they saw him for the first time. But will power and determination were not enough to enable him to carry out his well-planned ruse. When he reached the haven of home, he was put to bed immediately and the nearest doctor summoned. The diagnosis was typhoid-pneumonia.

It was during the ten days he was confined to his home that Cathy announced her determination to accompany him on his trip to Washington City. Together they made plans to leave the plantation in charge of George Cathey, his faithful overseer. Other plans Cathy outlined in a letter to Doctor John.

Will you come to our rescue? There is barely time for me to make

321

this communication. You are no doubt better informed of recent events in Texas than I, so I will not elaborate.

Sam insists on carrying out President Burnet's request that he go to Washington City, there to intercede with the United States government for recognition of the Texas Republic and to join efforts with agents of the Republic in securing a loan. He has with him Burnet's orders to the agents, who are already on their way to the Capital.

In his present weakened condition, I cannot allow him to make this journey alone. The little girls and their beloved Cumbo will accompany us as far as Nashville. There we will put them on a stage to Asheville—a long, long journey, but our only alternative. We will then proceed by steamer to the Capital. Please see that someone meets them. We should reach Nashville by the first of June.

Sam implores you to send news to Nashville in care of Joseph Bryan, who, as you know, is a transplanted North Carolinian—one who may use his influence for the cause of Texas with Van Buren, whose prospects as a successor to President Jackson seem highly propitious.

He hopes that North Carolina will take a stand for Texas—and soon!

Devotedly and in haste,
Catharine

Perhaps it was just as well at this juncture that Carson was unaware of the vacillating tendencies of the acting head of the Texas government, for even at the moment that the secretary of state was making plans to disrupt his household and rally his strength for the arduous journey ahead, Burnet, having had a change of heart, was seeking to replace Carson as secretary of state. In a letter from Burnet to Carson dated May 23, the President diplomatically suggested the propriety, indeed the necessity of Carson's immediate return, or that he resign his office to enable the cabinet to procure the best talents of the country in his stead.

And thus began the unfolding of a drama that in less portentious and ominous times might have been designated a comedy of errors. That the overtones were tragic in the extreme was easily discernible by those who, uninvolved, watched the players from the wings or on the sidelines. In the drama, personalities were involved to a certain extent; human frailties, too, played a part. But the tragedy of errors was in a total breakdown of communication between the seat of government in Texas and the several emissaries sent to the United States Capital bearing positive and documented instruction to achieve desired ends—the recognition by the United States of the Republic of Texas, and the securement of a loan to enable the Republic to survive. The tragedy involved men of good faith who were, perhaps unintentionally, placed in delicate and embarrassing positions, their dealings suspect, and their integrity questioned before the nation.

Proceeding to Nashville, blissfully unaware that he had already been replaced by an acting secretary of state, Carson was urged by Catharine to tell her of events and personalities that had meant the most to him in the preceding weeks. This he did, singling out Rusk and Potter and the colorful Zavala—all members of the cabinet and his closest associates. "But the two I wanted most of all to see, I never did," Carson confided, "Houston and Crockett." Knowing that sooner or later he must face up to the loss of his friend, Carson told her of the visit of Colonel Travis's servant Joe and of the impact of his words on the members of the convention—turning many from the conference table to the field of battle, so incensed were they at his disclosures.

"But Cathy, the only way I can survive is to look ahead, and I want to start now with you as my wonderful helpmate. You may have to shoulder some significant responsibilities these next weeks, acting as my chief clerk until one can be provided."

"In that case, you should tell me about these agents you have spoken of. How many are there imploring President Jackson for assistance?"

"Austin, Wharton and Archer have been in the Capital for some time, you remember, and to some extent have been successful in their procurement of funds. You remember Robert Hamilton who was at the houseparty at the home of Judge Ellis last December? He is one of the agents, and George Childress is the other. It was necessary for me to write them just before I left Harrisburg, urging them to attend at once to a matter of grave concern to the Republic. We had received rumors that the Mexican minister to the United States had been sent by their government with one objective—to sell Texas to the United States. Hamilton and Childress were instructed in my letter to

323

enter a solemn protest in the name of the Republic of Texas against the right of Mexico to sell, or the United States to purchase, setting forth in full our declaration of independence."

"That is so ridiculous, I'm surprised you gave the rumor serious consideration. I do remember Mr. Hamilton, the handsome bachelor who is one of our neighbors when he is privileged to be at home, but what of Mr. Childress?"

"He is an admirable fellow, though I am told that he is often subject to fits of melancholia. It was he who was almost wholly responsible for the wording of the Declaration of Independence, and who proposed an emblem for the new Republic—a single star of five points, either of gold or silver that would be worn by every officer and soldier and every member of the convention.

"We have long known that Childress has felt a compelling interest in Texas, and that before coming here he was the instigator of several mass meetings in Nashville, where he was born. As editor of *The Nashville Banner & Advertiser*, he used his talents persuasively in the editorial columns of the paper to excellent advantage. He is also a lawyer. In short he is one of our most talented leaders."

"Then you will have very little missionary work to do in Nashville, I would say," Cathy suggested. This surmise proved to be correct, because it took only a short while to importune Joseph Bryan to intercede with the powers that be in Washington City.

They found that Childress had done his work well, for General Dunlap was actively engaged in raising troops for Texas, and to further encourage the general, Carson authorized borrowing up to $25,000 on the credit of his government to defray expenses of the expedition.

"Has the Congress authorized the sending of troops into Texas?" Catharine inquired of Sam.

"I wrote Burnet today that seventy men under Captain Grundy are now ready to leave Nashville. He states that he has formal orders to prosecute every man who in any way may violate the act of neutrality or who may take up arms for that purpose. He says he will accompany them to the border line as peaceful emigrants, and if, when they arrive, the boys think it proper to step over the line his authority in the government will cease, and he thinks it highly probable that he will take a peep at Texas himself."

On his second day in Nashville, Carson was caught up in a wildly enthusiastic crowd in front of the press building that housed *The Nashville Banner*. A courier had brought the news of Houston's victory at the battle of San Jacinto. The word was being relayed to the uproarious crowd even before the type was set for printing the message. Shouts of "Give us more details!" served to swell the ranks of the eager participants.

The spokesman held up his hand to restore order. "If you will remain quiet, I will give you all the news I have." And he proceeded, "It was on the morning of the twenty-first of last month that a division of the Mexican army, under the boastful and confident Santa Anna himself, was surprised in a series of maneuvers by Houston. The Texas general had decided that it was time for the conflict for the soil of Texas to be decided. He held a council of his officers. Orders were given to burn the bridge over which they had passed—the bridge that afforded their only means of escape. Within 200 yards of the enemy they formed the battle line, and were met with a shower of musket and grapeshot. When within seventy yards of the enemy, the word was given to fire, instantly a blaze of missiles mowed down the enemy into the arms of death. When the command 'Charge!' was given, accompanied by the soul-stirring strains of 'Yankee Doodle,' the effect was electric. New ardor seized the souls of the Texans! Santa Anna was captured and 700 Mexicans lay still and lifeless on the battlefield."

"What of Houston?" someone shouted.

"He received an ankle wound that will no doubt incapacitate him for a time, but we can pour out our hearts in thanksgiving that his life was spared and that the Mexican hordes are no longer 'the invincibles.' "

When later Carson joined Cathy he did not have to put his elation into words. Never had she seen such a transformed human being! He seemed to have found a wellspring of hope and enthusiasm—yes, and a renewal of physical strength that was evident when he clasped her to his heart in joyful embrace. "Do you know what this means, Cathy? Do you really know

325

what this means? I can now face President Jackson without apology, and with pride in the accomplishments of our mutual friend, General Houston, and the army he commands. It is glorious beyond words!"

"I share your elation, my dear, but here are letters from home sent by a messenger from Colonel Bryan. Would you have me read John's letter? I am anxious to see if he has received our request to meet Cumbo and the children in Asheville."

John had received the request, and he assured them that he would be on hand when the proper stage arrived, even if it meant camping at the stagecoach stop several days. He gave news of the family, and commented at length on recent developments in Texas.

We are mindful of the sacrifices that are being made, of the bloodshed and suffering among the people of Texas, and to that end we had recently right here in your home in Pleasant Gardens what was probably the first meeting of citizens in the United States to go on record recognizing the sovereignty of the new Republic of Texas. That should afford you abundant satisfaction. Also at a meeting on the twenty-seventh of last month at the courthouse in Morganton, forceful and rousing sentiments in behalf of Texas were expressed in resolutions that proclaimed their recognition of her independence. They petitioned Congress to take note of the heroic contest of kindred people for the dearest rights of man and to bring an end to the cold-blooded indifference of a nation that was the first to recognize the independence of the Mexican Republic.

Your humble servant and brother was a member of the resolutions committee, along with Dr. William A. Graham, Samuel Fleming, Captain Charles McDowell and other eminent gentlemen.

Now to less nerve-shattering incidents. I have recently acquired another horse—a spirited animal, not yet broken in for family use, but sleek and beautiful, the pride of Eben, who insists on keeping her trim.

What shall I name her? Perhaps we can give her Missy's former appelation—Little Whirlwind, now that Missy, poor old girl, has been put to pasture permanently.

"This has been a wonderful day, Cathy. John's letter has been a fitting climax to it, but I must write my President the good news. And so saying he addressed a memorandum to Burnet:

The enthusiastic bursts of feeling everywhere in this country exceeds anything I have ever witnessed. From all accounts the spirit in the national Congress is fine. I send all the papers I can to let you see what is passing there. Public meetings are getting up in all directions petitioning Congress to recognize our independence. A bold move has been made in my native county (Burke, North Carolina) in our favor. I am induced to believe that we should send from this country every volunteer we can. I am acting on that principle, and shall not relax my efforts unless advised to do so by the government."

Contrary to his expectations, the trip up the Potomac was enjoyable and invigorating and he and Catharine made the most of it, calling it their second honeymoon.

Congress was still in session when they arrived in the City, and Carson made plans to renew old friendships and "to strike a blow for Texas," but first he must see Hamilton and Childress, and deliver to Hamilton the commission of President Burnet which had been entrusted to him for personal delivery.

These agents had preceded him by several weeks, and had waited expectantly for some communication from the government that had sent them on their official mission. They had written Burnet, begging him to forward official reports and instructions, but these communications were never answered. They were especially anxious to have official confirmation of the victorious Battle of San Jacinto and of the capture of Santa Anna before presenting the cause of Texas before the Congress and the state department, but no confirmation came.

Carson, exasperated and indignant at the lack of support of these qualified agents, on July 3 wrote to Burnet, "In the total want of communication from the government as to their whole policy and action except as I gather it from the newspapers and letters received by friends in this country, I am at fault how to act, and indeed frequently subject to mortification because of inability to answer questions put me by our best friends here."

Carson, on the evening before, had been invited to have dinner with his former friend and mentor in the White House. President Jackson greeted him warmly, giving no hint of the break in their relations in 1833. They picked up the thread of their friendship as if nothing had happened to dim its lustre.

When, over coffee, Carson broached the subject of Texas, Jackson immediately assumed the restrained manner of Chief

327

Executive. He was still friendly, but cautious. He expressed grave doubts about the reported plan to send Texas commissioners with Santa Anna to Mexico to negotiate a treaty of peace—a development Carson knew nothing about, which put him at a decided disadvantage. He voiced other objections as well. Jackson was noncommital about the recognition of the Texas Republic, preferring to wait for decisions reached by Congress. "There has been a dearth of newspaper reports from Texas, Carson, and only recently we have found out the reason. Gail Borden's paper, *The Texas Telegraph and Register*, was widely read here in Washington until——"

"Until the presses were stilled at San Felipe and the Borden Brothers sent out an appeal for help in moving the equipment to Harrisburg! The building housing the *Telegraph* was the first to be put to the torch, I understand. All of that happened before I left, Mr. President. I know nothing since that time—nor whether the presses ever reached Harrisburg."

Beset with a desire to know what happened to the printing press, and incidentally to pick up news of further developments he knew nothing about, Carson went to the Library of Congress and pored over the final pages of *The Texas Telegraph and Register*. That night he reported his findings to Cathy. He had made notes of the important disclosures. "Apparently the Bordens determined to spend their last dollar to keep the people informed during the critical days of the 'runaway scrape,' as it is now designated. And despite inadequate facilities and despite the disorder of refugees scared out of their wits, the Bordens had issue No. 22 of the *Telegraph* ready for printing on April 14, the day after the *ad interim* government had designated the Borden paper as its official mouthpiece."

Carson took a note from his wallet. "This is the provocative statement that was buried on the last page of the edition: 'We promise the public of our beloved country that our press will never cease its operations till our silence shall announce to them that there is no more in Texas a resting place for a free press, nor for the government of their choice.' "

"They are indeed provocative words, and the statement is one that every newspaper in the Nation would do well to emulate. Were they able to live up to their high ideals?" Cathy asked.

328

Carson shook his head. "Shortly after, a cry of alarm was sounded. The Mexicans were entering the village. Thus, after only two weeks' residence, the Borden brothers, laden with records and priceless archives, took refuge on a small boat bound for Galveston. Before leaving they had instructed their newspaper force to remain at their posts—and the three printers did remain—the only persons left in deserted Harrisburg. Before the seventh paper could roll off the press, Santa Anna arrived, and he dictated the next paragraph: 'I entered Harrisburg on the night of the fifteenth lighted by the glare of several houses that were burning, and found only a Frenchman and two North Americans working in a print shop. They declared that the "so-called" president, vice president and other important personages of the cabinet had left at noon for Galveston, that the families had abandoned their homes by order of Houston, who is billeted nearby with upward of 700 men and two four-pounders.'

"What happened to the three intrepid printers is not known," Carson continued, "but the six copies of the *Telegraph* they ran off in the face of certain capture contained the only evidence extant of the authority of the *ad interim* government."

"What happened to the printing press?" Catharine inquired.

"Santa Anna was lacking in imagination and vision, else he would have used it to threaten an already distracted populace by printing and circulating handbills claiming victories he never won, thus turning the press against its sponsors. Instead he ordered the heavy machinery lowered into the somber waters of Buffalo Bayou, while he stood by watching the brown current eddy and splash about it. After it settled in the murky deep, he turned to stroll into the deserted village. The free press of Texas had been stilled."

Carson replaced his notes in his wallet. "Thanks to Santa Anna, his paragraph has supplied me with information as to the whereabouts of the cabinet. I suppose they are still in Galveston."

"But all that happened before the great victory at San Jacinto and before Santa Anna was captured," Cathy suggested.

"Of course it did! But it is noteworthy reporting, and I am glad the President set my curiosity agog, else I would have missed these important revelations."

329

Satisfying himself that the Congress would be receptive to affirmative action in the matter of the recognition of Texas, once certain requirements were met, Carson mingled with his friends and former associates. He was particularly pleased with the support of Senator Benton and Mr. Clay and with the decision to send a secret agent to Texas to report confidentially to President Jackson. His friends and new members of Congress were likewise pleased with the agents sent from Texas. Childress and Hamilton had made a good impression in both public and private circles.

There was still the matter of the loan to be pursued, and it was decided that Carson and Hamilton should go to Philadelphia to interview some of the capitalists there. Catharine would stay in Washington with friends and Childress would attempt to arouse the sentiment of the people in outlying areas in behalf of Texas. In the meantime Congress had adjourned, after conveying to President Jackson their favorable attitude toward recognition of the new Republic.

Once domiciled in the City of Brotherly Love, Carson and Hamilton conferred with two of the city's financiers, who were unwilling to make a loan without ample security. The cabinet had failed to authorize the agents to pledge Texas lands for that purpose, and so the suggestion was made that they proceed to New York, there to float a loan by selling government bonds. This they did, and having been well received, were proceeding in good faith with details of the negotiation when an item in the *New York Gazette* was brought to their attention. It was a proclamation issued by President Burnet announcing that due to frauds perpetrated by persons professing to be agents of Texas, *the only recognized agents* from that date (June 10) would be Toby and Brother and R. F. Triplett, of New Orleans.

Carson's first reaction was of disbelief. "Do you think someone is trying to play a prank on us, Hamilton? If so, it is a dastardly trick. Why, do you know that there was a rumor afloat in Washington that Burnet had replaced you and Childress with our friends Collinsworth and Grayson. Since they had not shown up when we left I decided to overlook the rumor."

"This can't be true, Carson. If it is, then you and I have been placed in an odious position from which it will be difficult to extricate ourselves. Why, I have right here on my person the order written in Burnet's own handwriting and personally delivered by you, authorizing me as an agent of Texas to secure a loan."

"And here," Carson said, extricating a paper from his pocket, "is Burnet's order to me of April first: 'You will please repair as fast as circumstances will permit to Washington City, and there unite your exertions with those of our *Mother* country, and you will take in charge a general supervision of all the interests and concerns of Texas in that country. You are fully apprised of our wants—they are numerous—as the means at present in our power of gratifying them are limited. Your exertions may be valuably employed in procuring aid of all sorts—fiscal aid is all important in this crisis!' "

The two men talked long into the night. There were ample means and ample provocation at their command to expose President Burnet to embarrassment by placing him in a similar humiliating posture. They could repudiate his highhanded and unjust methods by giving publicity through the same channels to the inept management of his high office. But they concluded in the end that it was better for the cause of Texas to bear the humiliation and submit to the injury in silence rather than bring the authorities of the Republic into disrepute.

As soon as they made their positions clear to those with whom they had entered into negotiation, they left the city for Washington, where they found that Collinsworth and Grayson had indeed arrived on the eighth—two days after Carson's departure. And on the tenth, along with all other agents of the Republic save the New Orleans team, had been summarily divested of their responsibilities.

"Where is Collinsworth?" Carson inquired of Grayson.

"When we arrived, Congress had adjourned, and the President was on his way to the Hermitage, so Collinsworth followed him, there to use his persuasive powers."

"Gentlemen, we are involved, each one of us, in Burnet's complicated game of chess, and *we* are the hapless pawns, moving willy-nilly at his direction, and I for one am disgusted."

Carson's comment was followed with a question. "Have you

seen any official of the government, Grayson?"

"Yes, before Collinsworth left we presented our credentials to the secretary of state—to no purpose, I must admit. John Forsyth made formal objections to credentials from which the seal of Texas was omitted."

"And I dare say that Collinsworth will meet with a similar rebuff at the hands of President Jackson," remarked Hamilton.

"You know, Carson, that for a time Collinsworth followed you as secretary of state. He resigned that office on May 13. The seat of government was then Valasco."

"What were his reasons for resigning?" Carson inquired.

"One of the reasons was the government's conferring the highest offices in their gift, such as a foreign minister, brigadier general, foreign agents and many other appointments upon persons who have never been in the country except temporarily for speculative purposes, to the exclusion of many better-qualified who had taken permanent residence in Texas."

"You say Collinsworth was secretary of state at one time. I thought he was in the army," Hamilton suggested.

"He was, and he made a glorious record at San Jacinto. General Houston said he bore himself as a chief, and General Rusk expressed his highest approbation of his chivalrous conduct in almost every part of that engagement. Burnet offered him the post of district judge, and hinted at the possibility of appointment as chief justice of the supreme court, now duly constituted in the new government, but he declined."

"And what of yourself, sir?"

"When I was commissioned for this undertaking, I was attorney general."

"Why, I thought David Thomas was attorney general," Carson remarked.

"He was when you left, but he was mortally wounded in April by the accidental discharge of a gun while a passenger on the *Cayuga*."

"And so the government was not impressed with the representation of Texas claims by her district judge and attorney general? Pray what kind of credentials did you bear?" Hamilton inquired.

332

"Here is the copy rejected by the secretary of state. It is dated May 26 and signed by Burnet and the present secretary of state, William Jack. 'By these presents you are appointed commissioners on the part of the government to proceed to the City of Washington in the United States and present yourselves as duly empowered and instructed by the government *ad interim* of Texas to mediate and produce a cessation of the war between Texas and Mexico and you will use your best exertions to procure the recognition of the Independence of Texas.'

"The commission goes on to suggest that the annexation of Texas by the United States would be highly acceptable to the people of the Republic."

"Well, that's a new tack. Heretofore we have asked only for recognition of our independence and the consequent status as a Republic. Now we want to get into the Union," Hamilton observed, smiling broadly.

"There's nothing wrong with that, but I'd like to add that at the same time we were given our commission, the secretary of state wrote to the commissioners already in Washington—Austin, Archer and Wharton, confirming our appointment as agents of Texas, and soliciting their aid in consummating the objects of our mission."

"And now all of us are ambassadors without portfolio, according to the *New York Gazette*'s proclamation," Hamilton concluded.

"Perhaps the injury we feel is somewhat mitigated by the fact that there are so many of us, and the onus rests no more heavily on one than on the other. If we had a decanter and glasses, perhaps we could in all sincerity drink to the success of Toby and Brother and Mr. Triplett, who, rightfully or not, have superceded us. And if that be objectionable to anyone, we can surely drink to Texas, whose potential is staggering and whose future is glorious! And now, gentlemen," Carson continued, "I intend to make a positive and constructive move. I am proceeding immediately with my dutiful wife to the White Sulphur Springs of Virginia, there to cleanse myself of all bitterness, disappointment and false pride. Who will join me in this therapeutic objective?"

333

T W E L V E

The stagecoach unloaded its passengers in front of the Old White, and the two sojourners, so recently burdened with diplomatic responsibilities, seemed gay and lighthearted as they entered the lobby. Later, by candlelight, where there was music and dining and dancing, Sam reminisced. "One of the most satisfying vacations I have ever had was spent right here, Cathy, and with your help I am going to see that this one is equally satisfying and beneficial."

"That was a full decade ago, Sam—in 1826, wasn't it? Not before you knew me, but before you knew that you loved me."

"That's the year, my dear. There have been many changes since that time. The Old White, a famous Inn then, has added to its prestige, its elegance and its renown. You know, I feel that we have just passed a milestone, and that while the road ahead will have many turnings, there will be joy at every turn. From this day forward I pledge you my undivided attention, and my heart's best devotion. Certain it is that I have been unable to give you much of either since that most beautiful of all evenings when we knelt at the altar at Green River to pledge our marriage vows. What was it that they sang for our wedding prayer? I am sure that you remember every word."

"I do, Sam, and the closing words are as appropriate for us now as then:

> *O may this bounteous God*
> *Through all our lives be near us,*
> *With ever joyful hearts*
> *And blessed peace to cheer us.*
> *And keep us in His Grace*
> *And guide us when perplexed.*
> *And free us from all ills*
> *In this world and the next."*

They sat awhile in silence, as if reliving the beauty and the sacredness of that hour, and then Sam took Catharine's hand in his. "Something strange has happened to me, Cathy. By all rights

I should be bowed down with anguish and humiliation. Instead, I feel as if the weight of the world has been lifted from my shoulders, and that I can breathe again, and love again as never before.

"Look at me, Cathy. Don't turn your head away. What are those tears for? This is no time for weeping. You and I are going to have many wonderful years together." With both hands he turned her face toward him and smiling, looked deep into her eyes. "You remember how we laughed at ourselves and my political downfall when we named our North Carolina home Nullifier's Retreat? We'll think of a name as appropriate for our new home. But whatever its name, this one we'll live in. We've only existed before. Now we can really live!"

Cathy fought back the tears. Oh God! How could she ever measure up? With all of his heartaches and disappointments and disillusions, and with his years numbered as she was sure they were—how could he put up such convincing pretense!

She was afraid she would break down and have to fly to her room, making a scene that would be embarrassing to her beloved companion. Instead, she got up from the table, and moving to his side with both trembling hands outstretched, asked softly, "Will my husband do me the honor of dancing this round with me?"

There were two weeks of pure joy at their retreat. There was no doubt about it. Sam's health was better than it had been for years, and even if he did not look as young as on his first visit to the resort, there was a spring in his step and a light in his eyes that was more eloquent than any doctor's pronouncement.

When at breakfast one morning Cathy confided, "I dreamed about the children last night," Sam knew that it was time for them to be moving on.

"If you are willing to take a little more time on our return to North Carolina, I would like to go through Halifax. I did not have an opportunity to talk sufficiently with my friend Branch, and I'd like to see old Benny again. Then on our way to Pleasant Gardens we will stop in Salisbury for a few days."

"What about Green River? We can stop there, can't we?"

"Of course, but that will be on our way to Texas. We will cover the same route that we took with our caravan when we went West."

Before they could conclude their planning, a porter came to

the table with mail that had just come in. "This came by express, Mr. Carson, and it is marked 'urgent.' Our desk clerk wanted you to have it now."

"Why, its in Joe's handwriting. I'm sure he wants us to hurry to Green River."

Carson broke the seal and read only a small portion. His face was ashen as he pulled Catharine to her feet. "I must lie down, Cathy. I'm afraid I'm going to—die."

Cathy sat beside him on his bed until he could regain his composure.

"Joe always told me that my emotions were like a woman. I'm ashamed, Cathy, that I have no more stamina than this. All of the strength I boasted has gone from me—I need yours now to sustain me."

"What is it, Sam?"

"It's John, Cathy—my brother, counsellor and physician, as he often signed himself. He's gone."

Joe had written in haste, giving only a few details. It was an accident. He was still trying to break in his new horse—was thrown violently, his head striking a boulder. He lived several days, but died at home on July 6. "None of the family knew where to send word of the mishap until Cathy's letter written from Washington while Sam was in New York indicated that you would spend a few weeks at the White Springs. There's little that you can do now, although I am sure you will want to come this way soon. The children are well and Father, stoically carrying on in a way that amazes all of us, has set an example of fortitude that you must try to adopt. Let's close ranks and meet his expectations. John would be the first to approve that course."

No sooner were they settled at the Mansion House in Halifax than an invitation was delivered to Sam to be the guest at a public dinner in his honor. The invitation lauded his participation in the struggle for independence of Texas, pledged the support of the citizens in this laudatory undertaking and conveyed the continued interest of the populace in his personal and political life.

"This is an occasion which I would like very much to share,

Cathy, but I have no heart for public functions. I shall have to decline. I will do well to bear up physically under the rigors of our continued travel, and I must conserve my strength for the ordeal of my visit at the old home with John away."

He addressed a reply to be delivered by the waiting messenger, closing with an expression of sincere appreciation:

> ... and while, gentlemen, I thank you most sincerely for your kindness toward me personally, be assured that I am proud and grateful for the anxiety you feel for the success of the great cause of liberty for which the infant Republic is now struggling, and allow me to add, Texas *will* succeed.
>
> The importance of her great move on the political chessboard cannot be overlooked by the votaries of liberty throughout the world.
>
> With the expiration of the American Congress and her resolutions of July 4 in our favor, and with the institutions of this mighty Republic as our model Texas has nothing to fear, but all hope in the great conflict.
>
> Be assured, gentlemen, of my sincere acknowledgments for your generous feelings, and believe me to be
>
> Your obd't servant

At Pleasant Gardens Cathy stayed with the William Carsons, at their cool and comfortable home on Buck Creek. She had had a joyful reunion with their two girls—Emily, now an attractive and lovable girl of fifteen, and little Rachel Rebecca, who had almost forgotten her mother in the months they had been separated. They had been taken to their uncle's home at the time of John's serious accident. Cumbo had looked after their every need, consoling them when at first they missed their parents, endeavoring in every way to offset and assuage every hurt and to fill their days with the stuff of which happy memories are made.

"Cumbo's too old to go back to Texas, Miss Cathy. She wants to stay here where she can recollect things that make her happy. She thankful she got away fum de wild Indians and dem Mexicans."

Sam did not report to Cathy how he was hard-put to spend the days under his father's roof without the presence of Doctor John, nor did he report many touching incidents of his reunion with all who meant so much to him, including old Eben and

Missy. But he did tell her that his father had insisted that his brother, Jason, accompany them on the return trip to Texas. "Father wants me to take John's carriage and a team, and Jason can help with the driving. The roads west have been much improved, and we will find comfortable overnight accommodations. There will be no 'camping out' as before, I promise, Cathy."

Charles and Margaret joined them at Green River, and the three Wilson sisters who had married the three Carson brothers made every effort to insure that there would be happy memories of this, as of other reunions.

As at other times, there was animated discussion of events of moment. They were particularly concerned about Houston, and his personal encounter with Santa Anna, and they asked for Sam's version.

"Of course you know that I was not in Texas at the time of Santa Anna's capture. Indeed I knew nothing of the victory at San Jacinto until I reached Nashville. My knowledge of the events I will relate is on the authority of an officer who was present, and knew personally of the events that immediately followed.

"It was the day after the battle that turned the tide for Texas that Santa Anna and a few of his comrades in arms were surprised and surrounded by a small contingent of the Texas army ten miles from Houston's camp. Orders had been given not to kill any prisoners, but to bring them to camp where General Houston lay wounded. The search party had not proceeded far when they spied four or five deer on the west side of a branch. As they rode toward them, the deer started, and on looking to the right they saw a Mexican bending his course toward a bridge. He stopped a moment to gaze around him, and the Texan soldiers rode up to where he was. Whereupon he flung himself to the ground and covered himself with a blanket. When they called to him to rise he only took the blanket from his face. After a second and third command, he rose and, finding himself surrounded, he advanced and desired to shake hands. One officer offered his hand and the Mexican pressed and kissed it. He offered them bribes—valuable jewelry, his splendid

338

watch and a large amount of money. To the credit of the American as well as the Texan character, they refused.

"He asked them where Houston was, and through an interpreter, an officer asked who he was. Bursting into tears, he said he was an aide to General Santa Anna. He was told in a mild tone not to grieve, that he would not be hurt. He was dressed in common clothes, bore no arms, and appeared dejected, complaining of pains in his heart and legs. They started with him to camp, allowing him to ride until in sight of it, when he dismounted. General Houston was lying on a blanket at the root of a tree with his saddle for a pillow. He was half asleep with his face turned away from the party as they approached. The first he knew of their presence, the Mexican squeezed his hand, calling his name. When Houston looked at him he drew himself up in salute and explained with extreme agitation '*Soy Antonio Lopez de Santa Anna, Presidente de la Republica, Mexicana, y General en Gefe del Egerito de Operaciones.*'

"Houston suggested that he be seated upon a medicine chest nearby. When seated, he asked for opium, which was given him. He swallowed a considerable quantity, and soon became calm enough to ask what was to become of him. General Houston ignored the question and spoke of his cruelty to the Texans—especially at the Alamo and at the massacre at Goliad.

"They entered into an animated, though not heated discussion of the ethics of civilized warfare, Santa Anna attempting to justify his acts as commanding general because, he said, the Texans had no right to be in the territory over which he had authority. The Americans were bandits—land pirates, he insisted.

"When night overtook them, Houston had a bed for the prisoner put inside of his own tent and a guard set over him for the night. Houston's men clamored for the assassination of the prisoner, but Houston was adamant. Santa Anna was far more valuable to them alive than dead."

No sound had been uttered throughout the dramatic narrative, and when Sam finished Joseph Carson was the first to speak. "Although I am sure your interesting report is valid, it occurs to me that there will be as many versions of this history in the making as there are persons who record their thoughts and observations."

"It appears from our North Carolina press that Burnet has called a convention to elect a permanent government," Charles commented.

"That was provided for in the constitution, and I suppose that Burnet has been happy to serve until Houston's return to Texas. You know the General went to New Orleans shortly after Santa Anna's capture to have his ankle wound treated."

"Have you seen our former Lincoln County citizen, James Pinckney Henderson? The state papers say he raised a detachment of volunteers from Mississippi and set out for Texas sometime last spring," Jason commented.

"No, he had not reached the battlefields when I left. At least I saw no report of it." And Sam went on to comment, "When the present *ad interim* government gives place to the permanent one, Houston will undoubtedly be a candidate for president of the Republic."

Carson's surmise became actuality. Following the tradition of the Mother Country to elevate successful generals to positions of honor in public life, Houston was elected president of the Republic on September 5.

That heartening intelligence reached Carson's ears shortly after they crossed the border into Arkansas, where they were detained almost a week to allow Sam to recover from a severe setback. He had been cheered by Houston's election, even as he was dispirited by a rumor that had come to him that Burnet had written disparagingly of his efforts while he was in the United States. "If you will be my chief clerk, Jason, I would like for Houston to have a full accounting of my efforts."

"I shall be proud to serve as your amenuensis, my boy. You owe it to yourself to set this record straight, for if ever a man in public life endangered his personal life by determination to carry out a mission that could have been eminently successful but for circumstances over which he had no control, it was the first secretary of state."

Jason sat by Carson's side as he dictated:

Douglass Place,
Pulaski County, Arkansas
November 28, 1836

General Sam Houston,

I take leave to lay before your excellency (not knowing who may compose your Cabinet) a brief statement of the manner in which I fulfilled the mission upon which I was dispatched by the government *ad interim* of Texas under a commission bearing date of first of April, 1836.

Carson traced his every step from the time he left the temporary capital. Explaining how he carried out first Burnet's direction to confer with General Gaines at Nachitoches, he discussed in detail how he was forced to interrupt his travels at various locations to recruit his health. This caused an unexpected and frustrating delay in reaching Washington City, but on arrival he delivered personally President Burnet's commission to Robert Hamilton, and the two arranged to meet in Philadelphia with certain capitalists there. He explained further that when the meeting took place, the capitalists assured Carson and Hamilton, that they "would take liberally at whatever we could start our stocks or bonds in New York."

Upon this Mr. Hamilton and myself proceeded to New York, sounded the money market and were arranging our plans of operation when to our surprise and astonishment, there appeared in the Gazettes of New York the following proclamation: "Due to frauds perpetrated by persons professing to represent Texas, after this date (June 10th) only Toby and Brother and R. F. Triplett of New Orleans will be recognized as agents."

To judge our feelings and decide upon our deep mortification could only be done by persons placed in similar situations. But great as our chagrin we deemed it better for the cause of Texas to bear it in silence—had we taken any other course we could have been compelled to give flat contradiction to the president and publish in the public prints the authority under which we acted and had presumed to borrow money upon—but we preferred submitting to the injury rather than bring the authorities of the Republic into disrepute in the only country from which we could expect aid, and in which our dissensions at home had been sufficiently magnified and done sufficient injury.

Springtime in the valley of the Red River was almost as beautiful as springtime in the foothills of the Blue Ridge mountains, and certainly as soul-reviving and invigorating. The delicate green leaves of the live oak, and the burgeoning of the peach, plum and apricot, wafting the sweet scent of their flowering fruit, brought renewed life to the plantation and its occupants.

Sam was spending much time out in the open, visiting the fields, inspecting the cattle, and conferring with George Cathey, his overseer.

"Mr. Sam, looks lak we goin'ta have a good crop of cotton dis year. Shore wuz a bust last year, but den it were de same wid everbody's crop. Twern't jes ourn—no suh, twern't. Lessen a killin' fros' comes, we goin have plenty of fruit. I'ze sorry 'bout de cotton. Hits yore money crop, I know. Takes all de corn we kin raise to feed de livestock."

"Well, George, I want you to cultivate more and more of this land till we get it all productive. Put more in cotton and wheat. You saved plenty of seed, didn't you?"

"Yassuh we got plenty."

"We're going to have no trouble getting our grain to the market on the river now. Next year we'll have a bumper crop, and though things are going to be pretty tight for me this year, we'll make do. By the way, George, bring me all your records so I can see just how we did make out."

Next morning he went over the slips with Jason. "Looks like there is a pecuniary shortage," Jason observed. Sam had known of the cotton failure, but he had not reckoned on the large deficit that the records showed. His absence from home at a crucial planting time and tremendous expenses he had had from March 1 of last year until his return in early December had depleted his resources far beyond any expectations. Extreme financial embarrassment was something new to him, and he was at a loss to know how to handle it.

"I can help you out, Sam, or Father or Joseph—any one of us will be glad to advance what you need."

"Not by a long shot, Jason. I've been standing on my own feet since I was twenty-two. I don't intend to start leaning now. I'll think about it and come up with something. In the meantime we won't let Catharine know what the situation is."

The next morning he revealed his plan to Jason. "I'll get the consent of enough of my Negroes to act as surety for me and I'll go to New Orleans and borrow $10,000 to tide me over until my next harvest.

"Can you spare twenty hands, Sam? I figure that's about the number it will take for that amount of money."

"I don't have to spare them. They'll stay right here. I will get full description of them and assign them as collateral till the note is paid. All I will have to do is to swear I won't dispose of them in the meantime, and to register the mortgage in this county, their present habitation. I have no idea of defaulting on this note, if that's what you had in mind."

Sam and Jason went around to Eli's cabin and gave him a list of each Negro who would be involved in the transaction, instructing him to see them personally and get their consent. "And if any on that list can't understand that they will never have to leave this place, nor change the way they now live, send them to me and I'll talk with them."

As he stopped to speak with and reassure George Cathey, who had managed the plantation as well as anyone could have done, Jason reflected on Sam's way with the Negroes. When he was growing up the "hands" on his Father's plantation idolized him, and there certainly seemed to be mutual respect and good will between Sam and his Negro families now.

As they walked toward the house Sam spoke to his brother about a plan he had in mind. "How would you like to take a voyage with Cathy and me, Jason?"

"To New Orleans?"

"Exactly. Do you know, Cathy and I have not celebrated our wedding anniversary since we came to Texas? It's coming up in April, if you remember. What do you say the three of us go down to New Orleans. I have in mind to see John Preston there about accepting my note and mortgage. Then when all of the legal affairs are attended to, we can celebrate. I want very much to do this for Cathy. I don't have to tell you that without her care and her devotion I wouldn't be here today."

"I'm sure of that, and I like your plan. Once I get to New Orleans and we have our celebration, I will turn my face toward

North Carolina. Think I'll go up the Mississippi to Memphis, then home by easy stages."

One evening before they started, Robert Hamilton dropped by on one of his frequent visits. When Houston became president of the Republic, he had nominated Hamilton as chief justice of the Red River district of the several supreme courts that had been established.

Hamilton had not suffered severe financial reverses because of his efforts in behalf of the new Republic. In the first place, he was a bachelor and his expenses were not comparable to Sam's. In the second place, he was said to have been the wealthiest man to sign the Texas Declaration of Independence, and as such could afford losses that the others on this abortive mission for Burnet could ill afford.

"Hamilton, I am conscious of one very large dividend that I have garnered in the otherwise disappointing trafficking with President Burnet's foibles. It is that I have won a friend in the Honorable Robert Hamilton, of Pecan Point and vicinity."

"Then you will perhaps better understand my mission today, Carson, and not let your pride get in the way of accepting the offer I want to make."

Sam looked at Hamilton quizzically.

"I know the tremendous expense you had on our fruitless mission, more than the rest of us because of your illness. Besides, our plantations are too close and our overseers too compatible for it to escape my knowledge that you have had serious reverses. Will you let me come to your assistance?"

"Hamilton, you are indeed the friend I thought you to be, and I am everlastingly indebted to you for your offer of help in my present embarrassment, but we have just made plans that will be two-fold in purpose," and Carson related the things that he and Jason had discussed.

"And as to our 'fruitless' mission, the more I think of it in retrospect, the more I am convinced it was not fruitless except insofar as the six of us involved tended to feel a sense of personal failure and frustration. Our generation may not properly evaluate our remarkable victory over Mexican tyranny, and the emergence of Texas as a promising nation, but in years to come when the tragedies of war and our personal tragedies

344

are forgotten, this magnificent achievement will be recognized for the monumental epic it is."

"Then you believe that the unsavory reputation we now seem to have that villified the new Texas as the resort of criminals, of insolvent and fraudulent debtors and bad characters of every description is not the picture that will go down to posterity?"

"I believe that our history will be what we determine to make it. Having now laws for the punishment of immorality and crime, and aware of the character that we have generally, though unjustly sustained in the United States, the people of Texas should resolve that their laws will be rigidly enforced. And that is where you come in, Hamilton. Do you, as our new chief justice, have any comment?"

"Only that I agree with you that our laws must be executed without fear or favor, and that a respect for law and order and justice should be nurtured. It must be the watchword in every home and family and in every court of law; it must be the foundation on which this new nation is built. That proposition goes for all of America as well as for Texas, who already has the eyes of the world upon her. All of the states of the Union have their quota of undesirables. Isn't it true that the Carolinas, Maryland and other states were first settled by criminals and outlaws, Carson?"

"It seems to take a certain breed of reckless adventurer to blaze the trails of civilization, Hamilton. Yes, the Carolinas and Maryland had their fair share of renegades. The iniquity is not in having such shameless conditions, but in allowing such conditions to prosper and procreate for want of eternal vigilance in this matter of respect for and obedience to the law. America will follow the path of dissolute nations of all time unless we give heed to strengthening the foundations of our beloved land in matters of justice and equity. And I, for one, believe that Texas will measure up to her great potential as a leader of nations."

"The pace at which the picture changes makes one dizzy. It is almost incomprehensible," Hamilton noted. "Zavala's death last November was a blow. Seems that for two months he had not been well enough to participate in the affairs of state, and that at Burnet's suggestion he resigned the vice presidency in late

October. Stephen Austin was made secretary of state and James Pinckney Henderson, attorney general when the permanent government was formed."

"Yes, and with Austin's death following almost immediately, Henderson succeeded him as secretary of state," Carson commented. "I hope that he does not meet the dire fate that has overtaken his many predecessors in office. Bailey Hardeman, you remember, died in that office while he was filling the vacancy caused by my absence and later resignation," Carson explained to Jason.

"When you think that in the short space of seven months, for one reason or another—most of them valid—there were five secretaries of state, poor Burnet must have been as confused as anyone. He changed secretaries as often as the government changed capitals. And only once was he in danger of losing his official head."

"And that was——" began Jason.

Hamilton provided the answer. "That was after Collinsworth, Grayson and Hardeman, with Burnet, signed one secret and one open agreement with the notorious but now captive Mexican general. Each signed in his respective official capacity as an officer of the Republic. That is ancient history now, for it happened nearly a year ago."

"But it is dramatic and exciting history, my friend, and I would be glad for you to proceed in the telling of it," Jason urged.

"The agreement was that the prisoner be allowed to return to Vera Cruz, where he would use his influence in effecting a treaty with Mexico. The stipulations were that he would not again take up arms nor use his influence to cause them to be taken up against the Republic, that the Mexican troops were to march immediately beyond the Rio Grande, that all captured property be released, and that all Texas prisoners be released or exchanged with Mexican prisoners. Indeed, the cabinet went so far as to provide transportation for Santa Anna and his associates on the *Invincible*, bound for the Mexican capital.

"But in their official strategy they reckoned not the temper of these fighting men of Texas—the soldiers in the regular army and the volunteers newly arrived from the United States, who

346

were violently incensed at the thought that the man most responsible for death and carnage and pillage, and who was the symbol of their collective anger could so easily escape the assassin's sword or the hangman's noose.

"They must fix on one on whom they could vent their anger and reprisal. Burnet was the scapegoat, and at a mass meeting of the angry mob, a resolution was passed denouncing him and ordering his arrest—the directive written out meticulously: 'You are hereby ordered to proceed to Velasco and there arrest the person of David G. Burnet. You will take into possession the books, papers and records of his cabinet. Keep them safely and report forthwith.' "

Hamilton paused, then took up the thread of his narrative. "The newly arrived volunteers were represented by an officer who went to Velasco and attempted to seize the person of Burnet. He mistakenly thought that he had a mandate from the citizens and the army, so great was the clamor for Burnet's punishment. But to the credit of the citizens and the army, they would allow no mob rule. Their ultimatum was that, right or wrong, the government should be sustained."

"That is an important link in the chain of Texas history," Carson commented, "and now Zavala and Hardeman are dead and Santa Anna lives on. Strange, strange are the twistings of fate."

"Carrying the analogy further," Hamilton reflected, "Burnet's head is 'bloody but unbowed.' There is much to be said for his perseverence under fire. When the clamor for his resignation reached proportions that he could not ignore, he made a declaration that indicated his cool courage and determination. He avowed that he had been called to the duties of his office without any solicitation on his part; he had sworn to execute those duties faithfully, and no amount of harrassment or danger or suffering could induce him to resign, when in so doing he might jeopardize the cause of independence.

"He then directed the commander of the *Invincible* to bring the prisoner on shore, but Santa Anna vowed he would not leave the vessel alive. A second order met the same response. Two of your fellow North Carolinians, General Pinckney Henderson and General Hunt, had a hand in persuading the

347

defiant Mexican to leave the ship. There were five in the party who boarded the *Invincible*, only to find Santa Anna in a state of extreme agitation, alternately raving like a madman and crying like a child.

"The prisoner continued to act this strange part for about two hours, stating meanwhile that he had taken a large overdose of opium and would soon die. Assurances that he would receive no bodily harm while under the protection of those who had come for him fell on deaf ears, his aide declaring that no amount of reassurance would affect him while his mind was so completely under control of the self-administered drug. Meanwhile, Santa Anna lay on his back, breathing with apparent difficulty. The surgeon of the *Invincible* was called, who, on examination, pronounced the prisoner perfectly healthy and only temporarily incapacitated.

"Later a new ruse was tried. Restraining irons were brought, and as they were about to fasten them in place, Santa Anna jumped up, adjusted his collar, put on his hat, and gave evidence of his full compliance with the wishes of his captors."

"I believe there is more of interest to be told, Hamilton, and I know Jason is anxious to hear it all," Carson suggested.

"As the five Texans were rowed toward the shore with their prisoner, Santa Anna took alarm at the presence of a body of Texas soldiers on the beach and threatened to drown himself if the boat were not pulled to the opposite shore.

"General Greene, one of his captors, assured him that the soldiers were there out of sheer curiosity and that if he was ambitious to portray the character of Napoleon, whom he had sometimes imagined himself to be, he could do so by taking the Texan flag and calmly waving it in view of the military in token of respect for the cause they were pledged to maintain. The boat proceeded, and at a given signal to the soldiers, the whole company cheered the prisoner as he tremulously waved the Texan flag."

The inexorable passage of time continued to take its toll of Carson's strength and vitality. With Christmas of 1837 came the full realization and, for the first time, the acknowledgement that he was losing the battle for his life. But still he did not give up all hope.

348

Nothing was said to mar the pleasure of the holidays, but while the others were celebrating, he was laying well his plans, which he confided to Cathy at an opportune time after Christmas Day.

"I have been told that the healing waters of the Warm Springs in Little Rock have been known to revitalize and restore those in my condition. With your full agreement, Cathy, I would like to make one more stand before the enemy depletes me entirely. I have already lost the battle on the economic front, and if I go to Little Rock, I shall have to sell the better part of my holdings here. What think you of moving temporarily to the Springs? We will take only enough to maintain us on a less ambitious scale, and leave George Cathey in charge here."

Tears welled up in Cathy's eyes, as she nodded in acquiescence, and Carson misconstrued their meaning. "It's asking too much of you, little Cathy. You have been uprooted so often these past years, and each time I am less able to cope with any part of it. Forgive me for a selfish act that will be harder on you than on anyone. It is not in me to give up without a struggle, and I want to make one more supreme effort."

"When shall we begin to pack?" was Cathy's reply, as she put her arms around him reassuringly.

"There are a number of matters to attend to. As you know, many years ago I made a will which I entrusted to the care of General Waddy Thompson of South Carolina when I came West. I shall have to revoke its provisions and make a new will in keeping with my depleted resources. My good friend, my very good friend, Robert Hamilton has consented to become my executor."

In Shreveport, Louisiana, on January 1, 1938, Carson executed his last will and testament—a short and simple document that arranged for his just debts to be paid, and after that all of his property, real, personal and mixed, would go to his beloved wife, Catharine, for and during her life or widowhood. In the event of her remarriage, according to the stipulations of the will, she would receive only one-fourth of the estate "over which her husband would have no control," and the remaining portion would be divided between his two daughters.

There was a final stipulation: "my old and trusty servant,

349

George Cathey, I leave to the protection of my family, with as much freedom as the law will permit."

Once again a caravan—a greatly diminished caravan—left the Carson homestead bound for the Hot Springs in Arkansas. On that beautiful morning in May of 1838, as Eli assisted his master to the wagon on which a bed had been made, Sam turned to his overseer, now in sole charge of his small plantation. "You keep everything well in hand, George. I'll be home before the snow falls."

George managed an expansive smile as he grasped Carson's outstretched hand. Who was he to displace the rock of hope on which the tired, wan traveler had taken his stand? He knew that miracles sometimes happen to those who have a special kind of belief, but he also knew that only a miracle would restore his beloved "Mr. Sam" to health.

The summer was long and hot and exhausting, but as best he could, the old manservant kept hope in his heart until summer's end and long after the frosts came. And then one day Robert Hamilton read to him from *The Arkansas Gazette* an inconspicious notice: "DIED on November 2, 1838 at the Warm Springs, the Honorable Samuel Price Carson, former resident of North Carolina and first Secretary of State of the Republic of Texas."

The old Negro was silent for a while, and when he did speak the words came slowly and in a quavering voice. "He wuz countin' on comin' back, Mr. Hamilton. The folks hyah wuz all countin' on it, too."

"I know, George. None of us want to lose our friends, but we must think of Miss Catharine and the little girls now. They will want to go back to North Carolina, and you will be the one in charge. They will have to depend on you to hold things together and see them safely home."

Hamilton watched as the old man walked away, leaning heavily on his cane. He had not gone far when he turned and said, "Dis is goin' to be a long day, Mr. Hamilton."

Hamilton recalled immediately Carson's recollection of the day of his tragic duel. "Yes, George," he called to the old man, "it *is* going to be a long, long day for November."

BIBLIOGRAPHY

General

Green, Thomas Marshall. *Historic Families of Kentucky.* Baltimore: Regional Publishing Company, 1964.

Heiskell, S. G. *Andrew Jackson and Early Tennessee History.* Nashville: Ambrose Printing Company, 1918.

Stone, Irving. *The Immortal Wife.* New York: Doubleday, Doran & Company, Inc., 1944.

Jones, Katharine M. *The Plantation South.* Indianapolis: The Bobbs-Merrill Co., Inc., 1957.

Thomas, Jean. *Ballad Makin' in the Mountains of Kentucky.* New York: Oak Publishing Company, 1964.

Kane, Harnet T. *Gone Are the Days: An Illustrated History of the Old South.* New York: Bramhall House, 1960.

Schlesinger, Arthur M. Jr. *The Age of Jackson.* Boston: Little, Brown & Co., 1945.

Kauffman, Henry J. *Early American Gunsmiths.* New York: Bramhall House.

Work, John W. *American Negro Songs & Spirituals.* New York: Bonanza Books, 1940.

Dolan, J. R. *The Yankee Peddlers.* New York: Clarkson N. Potter, Inc., 1964.

Shackford, John B., ed. *David Crockett: The Man and the Legend.* Chapel Hill: University of North Carolina Press, 1956.

Lathrop, Elsie. *Historic Homes of Early America.* New York: Tudor Park Co., 1927.

Clark, Glenn. *The World's Greatest Debates.* Saint Paul, Minn.: Macalester Park Publishing Company, 1940.

Shaeffer, E. T. H. *Carolina Gardens.* Chapel Hill: University of North Carolina Press, 1939.

Parrish, John. *My Mountains, My People.* Asheville: Citizen-Times Publishing Company, 1957.

Howard, Robert West, ed. *This Is the South.* New York: Rand McNally & Company, 1959.

Rights, Douglas L. *The American Indian in North Carolina.* Winston-Salem: John F. Blair Publishing Company, Inc., 1957.

Hosmer, Charles B. Jr. *The Presence of the Past.* New York: G. P. Putnam's Sons, 1965.

Smith, Page. *John Adams*, vol. 1. Garden City, New York: Doubleday & Co., Inc., 1962.

Bassett, John Spencer. *The Constitutional Beginnings of North Carolina, 1663-1729.* Baltimore: The Johns Hopkins Press, 1824.

Bassett, John Spencer. *The Life of Andrew Jackson.* Garden City, New York: Doubleday, Page & Company, 1911.

Dowdy, Clifford. *The Great Plantation.* New York: Simon & Schuster, Inc., 1955.

Editors of American Heritage. *The Revolution.* New York: Bonanza Books, 1957.

Schlesinger, Arthur M. Jr. *The Age of Jackson.* Boston: Little, Brown & Co., 1945.

Kane, Harnett. *Gentlemen, Swords & Pistols.* New York: William Morrow and Company, Inc., 1957.

MacManus, Seumas. *The Story of the Irish Race.* New York: The Devin-Adair Company, 1966.

Phillips, Ulrich. *Life and Labor in the Old South.* New York: Grossett and Dunlap, Inc., 1929.

Furnas, J. C. *The Americans: A Social History of the United States.* New York: G. P. Putnam's Sons, 1969.

Dodd, William E. *Life of Nathaniel Macon.* Raleigh, N.C.: Edwards & Broughton, 1903.

Henderson, Archibald. *Conquest of the Old Southwest.* New York: Appleton, 1920.

Coit, Margaret. *Andrew Jackson.* Boston: Houghton Mifflin Co., 1965.

James, Marquis. *The Raven.* Indianapolis: The Bobbs-Merrill Co., Inc., 1929. *Andrew Jackson: Portrait of a President.* New York: The Bobbs-Merrill Co., Inc., 1937.

Parton, James. *Life of Andrew Jackson.* New York: Mason Brothers, 1860.

Appleton's Encyclopedia of American Biography. New York: D. Appleton & Company.

Benton, Thomas Hart, *Abridgment of Debates of Congress,* vol. 17.

North Carolina

Arthur, John Preston. *Western North Carolina: A History from 1730-1913.* Raleigh: Edwards & Broughton, 1914.

Wheeler, John H. *Historical Sketches of North Carolina,* vol. 1., Lippincott, Grambo & Company, 1851.

Wheeler, John H. *Reminiscences & Memoirs of North Carolina.* Greensboro: Van Noppen Publishing Company.

Smith, A. Davis. *History of Western North Carolina.*

Henderson, Archibald. *The Old North State and the New.*

Ashe, Samuel. *Biographical History of North Carolina,* vol. 2. New York: Harcourt, 1908.

Connor, R. D. W. *North Carolina: Rebuilding an Ancient Commonwealth.* Chicago and New York: American Historical Society, Inc., 1829.

Draper, Lyman C. *Kings Mountain and Its Heroes.* Cincinnati: Peter G. Thompson, Publisher, 1881.

Griffin, Clarence W. *Western North Carolina Sketches.* Asheville: Miller Printing Company, 1937.

Lefler, Hugh Talmadge. *History of North Carolina,* vols. 3 & 4. New York: Lewis Historical Publishing Company, 1956.

Debates of Convention of 1835 to Amend the Constitution of North Carolina. Raleigh: Joseph Gales & Son, 1836.

Griffin, Clarence W. *History of Old Tryon and Rutherfordton.* Asheville, N.C.: Miller Printing Company, 1937.

Murphy, Archibald D. *North Carolina History,* vol. 1.

Ramsay, Robert Wayne. *Carolina Cradle.* Chapel Hill: The University of North Carolina Press, 1964.

Zeigler & Crosscup. *Western North Carolina.*

Foote, William Henry. *Sketches of North Carolina.* New York: Carter Publishing Company, 1846.

Rumple, Rev. Jethro. *History of Rowan County.* Salisbury, N.C.: J. Bruner, 1881.

Boyd, William K. *History of North Carolina,* vol. 2.

Connor, H. G. *The Constitution of the State of North Carolina,* Annotated. Raleigh: Edwards & Broughton Printing Company, 1911.

Couch, W. T. *Culture in the South.* Chapel Hill: The University of North Carolina Press, 1935.

Frank C. Brown Collection. North Carolina Folklore Series. Durham: Duke University Press, vol. 1.

Texas

Dixon, Sam Houston. *The Men Who Made Texas Free.* Houston: Texas Historical Publishing Company, 1924.

Fulmore, Z. T. *The History and Geography of Texas as Told in County Names.* Austin: E. L. Steck, 1915.

Gammel, H. P. N., ed. *The Laws of Texas, 1822-1897,* vol. 1. Austin: The Gammel Book Company, 1898.

Garrison, George P., ed. *Diplomatic Correspondence of the Republic of Texas,* vol. 1. Washington, D.C.: Government Printing Office, 1908-1911.

Gray, A. C., ed. *From Virginia To Texas, 1835: Diary of Col. William F. Gray.* Houston: Gray, Dillage & Co., 1909.

Binkley, Wm. C., ed. *Correspondence of the Texas Revolution, 1835-1836.* New York and London: D. Appleton - Century Company, c1936.

Winkler, Ernest W., ed. *Secret Journals of the Senate: Republic of Texas 1836-1845.* Austin: Texas Library and Historical Commission, 1911.

Kemp, Louis Wiltz. *The Signers of the Texas Declaration of Independence.* Houston: The Anson Jones Press, 1944.

Roosevelt, Theodore. *The Winning of the West.* Current Literature Publishing Company, 1905.

Morgan, Edmund S. *Birth of the Republic, 1763-1789.* Chicago: University of Chicago Press.

James, Marquis. *The Raven.* Indianapolis: The Bobbs-Merrill Co., Inc., 1929.

Webb, Walter Prescott, ed. *The Handbook of Texas*, vol. 1. Texas State Historical Association, 1952.

Tinkle, Lon. *13 Days to Glory.* New York: McGraw-Hill Book Co., 1958.

Johnson, William Weber. *The Birth of Texas.* Boston: Houghton-Mifflin Co., 1960.

Barker, Eugene C. *The Life of Stephen Austin: Founder of Texas, 1793-1836.* Austin: Texas Historical Association.

Davis, Robert E., ed. *The Diary of William Barrett Travis*, Waco, Tex.: Texan Press, 1966.

Foote, Henry Stuart. *Texas and the Texans*, vol. 1. Philadelphia: Thomas Cowperthwaite & Company, 1841.

Hogan, William R. *The Texas Republic.* Norman, Okla.: University of Oklahoma Press, 1954.

Texas Almanac, anniv. ed. 1966-1967. Dallas: Dallas Morning News, 1967.

Yoakum, Henderson. *The History of Texas: First Settlement in 1685 to Annexation in 1846*, vol. 2. New York: J. S. Redfield, 1853.

Turner, Martha Anne. *The Life and Times of Jane Long, "Sweetheart of the Republic."* Waco: The Texan Press, 1969.

Rippy, J. Fred. *Joel Poinsett: Versatile American.* Edited by John C. Evers. Durham: Duke University Press, 1935.

Rossi, Paul. *The Indians in Texas in 1830.* Washington, C.C.: Smithsonian Institution.

Smithwick, Noah. *The Evolution of a State; or, Recollections of Old Texas Days.* Austin.

_____ *Journal of Convention of 1836*—Unindexed book of about 363 pages.

_____*Union List of Texas Newspapers*, H. W. Wilson Co., 1930.

Baker, D. W. C., ed. *A Texas Scrapbook.* New York: A. S. Barnes & Co., 1875.

Bancroft, H. H. *History of North Mexican States and Texas*, vol. 2. San Francisco: The History Company, 1889.

Newell, Rev. Chester. *History of the Revolution in Texas*. Austin: The Steck Co., 1935.

Jones, Anson. *Official Correspondence of the Republic of Texas*.

Frantz,_____ *Gail Borden, Dairyman to a Nation*. Norman, Okla.: University of Oklahoma Press.

Hogan, William R. *The Republic of Texas*. Norman, Oklahoma: University of Oklahoma Press, 1946.

_____*Secret Journals° of the Senate: Republic of Texas, 1836-1845*. Austin: Austin Printing Company, 1911.

Richardson, Rupert Norval. *Texas, The Lone Star State*. New York: Prentice-Hall, Inc., 1943.

ARTICLES IN *NORTH CAROLINA HISTORICAL REVIEW* (RALEIGH) USED FOR DOCUMENTATION AND INFORMATION

Boyd. "Constitution of 1788." 16:36-53.

Hoffman. "Electioneering in North Carolina in 1830." 32:31-55.

Vinson. "Electioneering in North Carolina, 1800-1835." 29:171-188.

Chambers. "As the Twig Is Bent: The Family of Thomas Hart Benton." 26:385-416.

Des Champs. "John Chavis, a Preacher to the Whites." 32:165-172.

Phifer, Edward W. "Champagne at Brindletown." 40:489-500.

Calhoun, John C. "Correspondence Relating to Presidential Campaign of 1824." Edited by Thomas Robson Hay. 12:20-24.

Newsome, A. R., ed., "Correspondence of John C. Calhoun, George McDuffie and Charles Fisher, Relating to Presidential Campaign of 1824." 7:477-504.

Knight, Edgar W. "Notes on John Chavis." 7:326-345.

Wenhold, Lucy Weinbach. "Salem Boarding School between 1802 and 1882." 27:—

Blair, Marian H. "Contemporary Evidence—Salem Boarding School, 1834-1844." 27:142-161.

McCorkle, Donald M. "The Collegium Musicum Salem: Its Music, Musicians and Importance." 33:483-498.

Johnson, Guion Griffis. "Camp Meeting in Antebellum North Carolina.' 10:95-110.

Mahon, John K. "The Carolina Brigade Against the Creek Indians in 1814." 28:421-425.

Avery, Isaac T. "Isaac T. Avery to Samuel Price Carson: Report on Gold-mining." 40:494.

Phifer, Edward W. "The Averys: Saga of a Burke County Family." 39: Winter, pp. 1-17; Spring, pp. 140-147; Summer, pp. 305-339.

Hoyt, Elizabeth Stone. "Reactions in North Carolina to Jackson's Banking Policies, 1829-1832." 25:167-178.

Harrell, Isaac S. "North Carolina Loyalists." 3:575-590.

McFarland, Daniel M. "North Carolina Newspapers, Editors and Journalistic Politics, 1815-1835." 30:376-414.

McLean, William. "William McLean's Travel Journal from Lincolntown, North Carolina to Nashville, Tennessee, May-June, 1811." 15:377-388.

Corbitt. "Congressional Districts of North Carolina, 1789-1934." 12:173-188.

Crittenden, Christopher. "Means of Communication in North Carolina, 1763-1789." 8:373-383.

Shackford, James Atkins. "David Crockett and North Carolina." 28:298-315.

McPherson, Elizabeth G., ed., "Unpublished Letters from North Carolinians to Andrew Jackson." 14:361-392.

Rippy, J. Fred. "A View of the Carolines in 1783." 6:362-370.

Miller, Zane L. "Senator Nathaniel Macon and the Public Domain." 38:—

PUBLISHED AND UNPUBLISHED COLLECTIONS, PAPERS, HOLOGRAPHS CONSULTED FOR PERTINENT INFORMATION AND DOCUMENTATION

John Branch Family Papers
Carrington-McDowell Papers
Elisha Mitchell Collection
Dr. John Calhoun McDowell Collection
James Sprunt Historical Monograph #8, pp. 15, 16 and 17.
John Gray Blount Papers
Charles Fisher Papers
Mirabeau B. Lamar Papers
Clarence Griffin Collection (Scrapbook)
John Heritage Bryan Collection
Willie P. Mangum Papers
William A. Graham Papers
Silas McDowell Manuscript

Allen T. And Theodore Davidson Papers (1813-1931)
Dodd's *Life of Nathaniel Macon* (S. P. Carson Letters)
Sketch of Founders—Washington & Lee University (The Academy)
Randolph-Macon Historical Papers (Nathaniel Macon to Samuel Price Carson, February 9, 1933)
L. W. Kemp Collection. University of Texas Library, Austin
Niles Register, vol. 44, p. 418
Earl Vandale Collection. Barker History Center, University of Texas
Thrall, Rev. Homer. *Pictorial History of Texas*. p. 522
"Bulletin," North Carolina Historical Commission, Raleigh, N.C.

ARTICLES AND DOCUMENTARIES OF THE McDOWELLS AND CARSONS APPEARED IN THE FOLLOWING NORTH CAROLINA NEWSPAPERS AND PERIODICALS FROM 1830 to 1967

Roanoke, Va. Advocate, May 20, 1830; Aug. 25, 1831; Dec. 6, 1832; Jan. 3, 1833.
Raleigh Register, Apr. 30, 1831. "Crockett Splits with Jackson."
North Carolina Review, Mar. 2, 1913. (Judge Alphonso C. Avery).
Greensboro Daily News, Nov. 4, 1928. (Ruth Moore).
Asheville Citizen-Times, Aug. 31, 1930. (Mary Johnston Avery).
Forest City Courier, Oct. 9, 1930.
Greensboro Daily News, Jan. 5, 1939, "Jackson, Crockett and Houston Frequent Visitors at Carson House."
Star and North Carolina Gazette, Oct. 10, 1835.
Asheville Citizen-Times, Feb. 4, 1951. "Congress Race Resulted in Vance-Carson Duel." (George W. McCoy).
Asheville Citizen-Times, Aug. 12, 1951. "David Crockett at Vance-Carson Duel." (George W. McCoy).
Hickory Daily Record, 1946. "Congress Seat to Burke 119 Years Ago." (Mabel Miller Rowe).
Asheville Citizen-Times, Mar. 12, 1956. "Green River Plantation Stirs Memories of a Mellow Past." (Clarence Griffin).
State Magazine, May 23, 1964. "Historic Home Becomes a Museum." (Rosamond Braly).
Salisbury Post, Apr. 11, 1965. "Historic McDowell Mansion Has Colorful Background." (Helen Chaney).
Charlotte Observer, Mar. 26, 1967. "Carson Home Visit Turns Time Back to 1810." (Stover Dunagan, Jr.).
Asheville Citizen, "Portrait Recalls Noted Figure and Duel." (Rachel Dyes).

Asheville Citizen-Times, May 21, 1967. "Carson Never Forgot Fateful Duel." (John Parris).

North Carolina State Ports, Winter 1965. "Down Historyland Trail.".

Greensboro Daily News, Nov. 4, 1928. "Buck Creek Mansion." (Mary Johnston Avery).

Carolina Watchman, July 15, 1837; June 30, 1829.

Asheville Citizen, Dec. 24, 1933.

State Magazine, Sept. 25, 1943; May 23, 1964.

NEWSPAPERS

Texas Telegraph and Register
Arkansas Gazette
Niles Register
National Intelligencer
The Asheville Spectator
The Greensboro Patriot
State and North Carolina Gazette
The Halifax Minerva

The Charleston Mercury
The Memphis Enquirer
The Roanoke Advocate
The Salisbury Watchman
Western Carolinian (Salisbury)
The Raleigh (N.C.) Register
The Houston Telegraph
The Houston National Banner

NOTES

Chapter One

Page 1 " ... a last long look ... " The scene that met his eye is described in Wilbur Z. Zeigler's *Heart of the Alleghenies*, p 247.

"Only rarely did a hint of the Irish brogue ... " Samuel Carson's father, Colonel John Carson, was born in Fermanagh County, Ireland. He came to America with his sister's family and other Protestant immigrants.

5 Bealnath Buiedehe—pronounced Bailnau bwee (town of Buidehe)

6 "One who has written of the Highlanders ... " *Ballad-making in Old Kentucky*, p 137.

7 "Pressing at the same time the pistols and LaFayette's hand ... " *The Halifax Minerva*, and doubtless all news media in the states, reported this moving account of the visit of the French General to the Hermitage.

11 James Graham—older brother of the future governor of North Carolina and United States Senator, William Alexander Graham.

Felix Walker—Revolutionary soldier and Republican member of Congress (1817-1825).

Dr. Robert Branck Vance—Native of Buncombe County, uncle of a future governor of North Carolina, Zebulon Baird Vance. Doctor Vance was a member of Congress 1823-1825.

13 " .... the Academy ... " Colonel George Moffett (Moffitt), whose father settled in Burden's grant, and whose name appears among the Scotch-Irish immigrants, fought with honorable distinction from the beginning to the end of the Revolutionary War. As a friend and promotor of education, as one of the founders of the Academy at Lexington, Virginia, which grew into Washington and Lee University, he was no less prominent as a soldier." Green's *Historic Families of Kentucky*, pp 15-18.

21 " ... should have named you 'Falada' ... "—the talking horse of *Grimm's Fairy Tales, The Harvard Classics* p 184.

22 " ... that a rich vein was found ... " Shaeffer's *Carolina Gardens* p 239; *Western North Carolina Sketches*, Clarence Griffin, p 73.

" . . . an imponderable mystery" Shaeffer's *Carolina Gardens*, p 241.

26 " . . . would be delighted to meet so handsome, a kinsman." Elizabeth Benton, born in the beautiful Cherry Grove Plantation, near Fairfield, Virginia, was the daughter of Colonel James McDowell and brother of Governor James McDowell. According to genealogical tradition of the day, Thomas Hart Benton's wife and Samuel Carson were first cousins, once removed.

"Cherry Grove" had been paid in grant to Sam's great uncle, Elizabeth Benton's grandfather, by the King of England in return for his military services in the colonies—Irving Stone, *The Immortal Wife* p 46.

28 Carson's speech in Congress on April 3, 1826, relative to the proposed "Mission to Panama," as do all subsequent speeches, appears in *Benton's Abridgement to the Debates of Congress*, Volume 17 p 102.

31- *The New York Evening Post* and other news media reported at
33 length on John Randolph's departure and subsequent arrival at the English port of Liverpool, where he went as an Ambassador of Good Will for the United States government. The sending-off party is not documented.

Chapter Two

Page 34 Warren Ransom Davis (1793-1835) of South Carolina, a cousin of John C. Calhoun, a graduate of South Carolina College, member of Congress 1827-1835 and an active Nullificationist— *William A. Graham Papers*, 169[n].

The author is indebted to Dr. W. Edwin Hemphill, who is presently editing the *Papers of John C. Calhoun*, for clarification of the above documented relationship between Warren R. Davis and Calhoun, which he states is not close enough to warrant any simple statement to that effect. He states that Davis and Calhoun each had homes in Pendleton, South Carolina; that they were obviously friends and agreed with each other in politics; that they were quite distantly related, if at all. From further detailed explanation furnished by Doctor Hemphill, it would appear that Davis was more closely related to the wife of Calhoun (born Floride Colhoun) than he was to her husband.

40 "My father has in his possession a copy of letter written to an Andrew Reid, of Lexington . . . " Green's *Historic Families of Kentucky*, p 92.

41 " . . . pioneered in abdominal surgery . . . "—now designated as an ovariotomy. "This operation, performed without an anaesthetic, was without precedent in the whole history of surgery since the world began. Had Doctor McDowell lived in France, he would have been elected a member of the Royal Academy of Surgeons, received from the King the Cross of the Legion of Honor, and obtained from the government a magnificent reward." Ibid. p 96.

". . . . John Adams had written to his wife . . . " Monograph, *A Day to Remember*, written by Frances Griffin, is an account of the first Fourth of July celebration by legislative enactment in all America. The celebration was held at Old Salem, the Moravian settlement of Wachovia, July 4, 1783.

John Frederick Peter's *Freudenpsalm* (Psalm of Joy) a cantata form performed by soloists, choir, congregation, organ and orchestra, was put together in barely two weeks, following Governor Martin's proclamation of June 18, 1783. Ibid. p 6.

55 ". . . . daughter of my step-grandfather." This "Hunting John" McDowell and his brother Joseph McDowell, Jr. of Quaker Meadows emigrated from Ireland at the same time. Green's *Historic Families of Kentucky*, p 18.

61 ". . . . gold-mining as a favorable industry." The first gold found in America was a huge chunk, the size of a flatiron, discovered on a Sunday morning in 1799 by a twelve-year-old resident of Cabarrus County, North Carolina, Conrad Reed. *Greensboro Daily Record*, May 15, 1949.

62 "A pot of gold at the end of a . . . rainbow." Gold-mining, introduced in this chapter, was to be a factor in the economy that enabled the Carson men to prosper. It was to be the indirect cause of frustrations that plagued Sam Carson's legislative career in Washington, for try as he did to get action on his bill to establish a mint in the gold-mining section of the South, the delaying tactics sponsored by John Knox Polk prevented the fulfillment of his dream.

On December 23, 1829 Carson moved the following resolution: That a select committee be appointed to look into the expediency of establishing a branch of the United States Mint in the gold-mining region of the South." *National Intelligencer*, December 24, 1829.

The resolution was finally tabled, never to be reinstated during Carson's incumbency, and so it was left to Thomas Hart Benton to win acclaim for introducing later a similar bill that passed both Houses and became law. "The mint was built by Act of

Congress, March 3, 1835 at Charlotte, North Carolina. The building, now standing, has simplicity and dignity, and a great golden eagle spreads its wings beneath the sloping pediment of the front door. It now houses treasures of art rather than gold." Helen Fetter Cook in *State Magazine*, October 23, 1954.

66 "Contrary to all expectations. . . . " *The National Intelligencer* reported in great detail the circumstances surrounding the election of John Quincy Adams, the first President of the United States to be chosen by Act of Congress when the electorate failed to establish a majority vote.

67 ". . . . no less than four large eagles were seen. . . . " *National Intelligencer*, March, 1824.

Chapter Three

Page 71 The Council Oak and Quaker Meadows" *Colonial Records of North Carolina*, Vol V. *Historical Handbook of the National Park Service* and Theodore Roosevelt's *Winning of the West* p 13.

73 This method of completing the formation of the company was unique—Draper's *Kings Mountain and Its Heroes* p 13.

Theodore Roosevelt, in *Winning of the West*, sums up the Battle of Kings Mountain in these words: "The mountain men had done a most notable deed. They had shown in perfection the best qualities of horse-riflemen . . . then, leaving their horses, they had shown in the actual battle such courage, marksmanship, skill in woodland fighting that they had not only defeated but captured an equal number of well-armed, resolute men in a strong position. The victory ranks among the decisive battles of the Revolution—the turning point in the southern campaign.

" . . . a song in the Gaelic" *Gur Muladach A Tha Mi* (Translation by Ian Grimble). The author is indebted to Reverend James MacKenzie, Gaelic student and an authority on the poet John MacRae, Tory soldier at the battle of Kings Mountain. MacKenzie holograph in files of author.

75 " . . . but that precious Binah . . . " In his will, Joseph McDowell, Jr. left Binah to his young wife, Mary Moffitt, as long as she remained a widow. (Burke County, North Carolina *Records*)

76 " . . . the arduous journey on horseback . . . " E.T.H. Shaeffer's *Carolina Gardens*, p 238.

78 "They found grandfather's grave . . . " Arthur's *History of Western North Carolina*, p 250 and *Davidson Papers* in Sondley Library, Asheville, N.C.

80 "Colonel Carson was a patriot in the guise of a Tory"—Draper's *Kings Mountain and Its Heroes*, pp 24-25; 197-198.
(This guise was indirectly responsible for the tragic duel fought between Samuel P. Carson and Doctor Robert B. Vance in 1827.)

" . . . about an encounter . . . " This and other stories in connection with Colonel Patrick Ferguson's experiences in Western North Carolina, are documented in Draper's *Kings Mountain and Its Heroes*.

In the sketch of Patrick Ferguson (Ibid., pp 48-67) his rank is indicated first as Captain, then Major and then Colonel. On October 1, 1780, one week before the fateful battle, he signs himself "Patrick Ferguson, Major 71st Regiment."

88 ". . . . his able speech at Hillsborough against adoption of the Federal Constitution without qualifying amendments." McDowell's speech weighed heavily in decisions made by the Convention of 296 delegates. They did not reject the Constitution, but adopted the report of the Committee of the Whole, which was in the form of a resolution "that a declaration of rights, together with amendments . . . should again be presented by Congress before North Carolina should take a stand for ratification." Hugh Talmadge Lefler. *History of North Carolina*, Vol 1., p 275.

Schenck, in his history of the invasion of the Carolinas, includes a photograph of Joseph McDowell of Quaker Meadows, under which is the caption "Hero of Ramseur's Mill, Kings Mountains and the Cowpens."

Chapter Four

Page 94 ". . . . sorry to see Mr. Clay and Mr. Randolph pretending to shoot at each other" *Willie P. Mangum Papers*, pp 275-276.

95 "Crockett . . . would like to extend his political boundaries . . . " Shakford, *David Crockett: The Man and the Legend*, p 73.

Crockett's campaign for Congress in 1825 was premature and unsuccessful, but he was elected to represent the Ninth Congressional District in Tennessee in 1827. Ibid., p 74.

97 "... and started down the Obian River." Ibid., p 77.

104 "... much of Alexandria, the beautiful sister city of Washington, is in ashes." *National Intelligencer*, December 7, 1826.

106 "Mr. Carson rose in an effort to bolster ... " *Benton's Abridgment of the Debates of Congress*, Vol 17, p. 386.—Photocopy in files of author.

113- Complete and factual transcript of inflammatory dialogue
119 between Carson and Vance is preserved in *Silas McDowell Manuscript*, made public at his request thirty-five years after his death (when supposedly members of the two families involved would have no interest in the affair). McDowell, born in the York District of South Carolina, became a resident of Burke and later of Macon county. He married a niece of Governor David L. Swain, and was a close personal friend of both Carson and Vance. Copy of Silas McDowell Manuscript in files of author.

There was an addendum to Mr. McDowell's lengthy account: "I did propose to give Sam Carson's subsequent history after the duel, but when I remembered that his name is linked with Texas while it was 'The Lone Star State' and he one of its executive officers, and that in consequence his name belongs to the general history of our country, I therefore deem it proper that history alone deal with his name."

Attached to the Manuscript is a clarifying statement signed by the late Judge Alphonso Calhoun Avery, prominent and widely-known jurist of Morganton, North Carolina, as follows: "The foregoing is a correct copy of manuscript left by Silas McDowell in the hands of Theodore Davidson as a matter of history to be written by a future generation ... " Judge Avery gave publication to the statement in the *North Carolina Review* of March 2, 1913. (Copy of the *Review* of this date is in the files of the author.)

Chapter Five — The Duel

Page 125 "... there is no fight in him." Carson's gentleness of nature and slowness to anger resulted in the charge. Shackford's *David Crockett, the Man and the Legend*, p 85.

127- Crockett's election and campaign. Ibid., Chapter Six.
128

128 "Davis had come to Pleasant Gardens in Calhoun's carriage ... " Holograph—Rebecca Carson Whitson (Samuel Price Carson's daughter) to W. C. Erwin. Copy in files of author.

130 "... give them to my friend, David Swain." David L. Swain, born in Bumcombe County, North Carolina, one of the truly great of North Carolina's public servants. He served three successive terms as governor of the state, and became president of the University of North Carolina in 1835, continuing in this capacity until his death in 1868. Arthur's *History of Western North Carolina*, p 383.

The bequest to Swain was recognized by law and allowed to stand. Stephen B. Weeks in *Magazine of American History*, December 1891.

131 "The doctor spoke haltingly...." Last words of Doctor Vance reported in *Silas McDowell Manuscript*. Copy in files of author.

A letter from James Graham to his brother William Alexander Graham states that Carson's belt was cut by a ball from Vance's pistol. *William Alexander Graham Papers*, p 169.

Historian Hugh Talmadge Lefler states that there were at least twenty-seven political duels in North Carolina between 1800 and 1860.

Facts concerning the duel between Carson and Vance have been recorded by numerous historians and columnists of every period for the past century; the last publicity known to the author was in a sketch of the life of Carson written by Robert L. and Pauline H. Jones, published in *Texana*, magazine of the Texian Press, Waco, in 1968. (Copy in files of author.)

132 David Crockett was first to bring the news of the outcome of the duel to Pleasant Gardens, home of the Carson family. Shackford, *David Crockett: The Man and the Legend*, p 86.

132 "... and all agreed it would be a fine thing to have Crockett accompany him to Washington." Ibid., 86.

137- Text of Carson's speech on Indian Affairs. *Benton's Abridgment*
139 *of Debates of Congress*, Vol 17, pp 136-137. (Photocopy in files of author)

139- Circular Letter—Holograph among records of Samuel P. Carson,
140 of which this is a condensation.

141 "... just see what they have done in Raleigh to Archibald Murphy's dream." Lefler, *History of North Carolina*, p 315.

"Archibald Murphy"—public spirited lawyer of Hillsborough, North Carolina,—the genius, leader and mouthpiece of the Progressive Reform movement in his state after 1815. He lamented the poverty, ignorance and general backwardness of the state, particularly his own western section." Ibid., p 315.

142 John Chavis—freeborn Negro, graduate of the Academy at Lexington, Virginia, Presbyterian minister, mentor of Willie P. Mangum and close friend of Mangum's mother and other members of the family. *Willie P. Mangum Papers*, pp 412-583.

Notes on John Chavis—Edgar W. Knight, *North Carolina Historical Review*, Vol 7, pp 326-345.

146 " ... as far as my friend Carson's amendment ... " Shackford, *David Crockett: The Man and the Legend*, pp 98-99.

"My measure met with no serious opposition with the exception of one." The exception must have been that of his friend, Carson. Ibid., p 99.

149 " .... paying so much attention to the President's pretty niece." North Carolina historians and chroniclers of the period identify the niece as Emily Donelson, but that is incorrect. That there was an "affair of the heart" with one of the White House hostesses who was a niece of President Jackson has never been disputed. The best authoritative consensus is that the niece could have been Mary Eastin, who was known to have many beaux. It is known that the young Congressman from North Carolina, the daughters of Secretary of the Navy and Mrs. John Branch, and Mary Eastin were often together at White House functions.

152 " ... my old friend, Sam Patch." *William Alexander Graham Papers*, p 202.

154 "Our President was a beautiful white charger named Sam Patch." S. G. Heiskell, *Early Tennessee History*, p 288.

155 "The crucible bore evidence ... " Halifax Minerva, May 28, 1829.

155- "But I can tell you a tale ... " Jackson's letter to the Creek
156 Indians was published in the *Carolina Watchman*, June 30, 1829. (Contrary to the persuasive tone of the paternal letter of President Jackson, the pathetic story of the removal of the Indians, particularly the Creeks and the Cherokees, "excels in weight of grief and pathos any event in American history. Many harrowing tales were told by the old people of the Cherokee tribes who were left behind depicting the cruel scenes which accompanied the hunting down and removal of these brave people, who clung desperately to their homes and who mourned as they were driven through 'the valley of tears.' ") Arthur's *History of North Carolina*, p 576.

158 "He sometimes asks me to speak for him on the floor of the Congress." Article in *Texana*, Vol VI, p 158 entitled "Samuel Price Carson"; also *North Carolina Review*, March 2, 1913.

"Carson was considered at the time the best impromptu speaker in the House of Representatives. He was, until his last term, the trusted friend of Andrew Jackson, and often his selected leader to defend the policy of the Administration in the House." A. Davis Smith in *History of Western North Carolina,* p 103.

158 "He is having wood cut from the land at the Hermitage ... " This walking cane, silver-tipped and engraved "Growth of the Hermitage. Presented by Gen'l Andrew Jackson to Col. John Carson—1830" is displayed in the museum of the home of Colonel Carson, now an area historic site. Also in the museum is another cane presented by President Jackson to Colonel Carson, recently donated by Admiral John Carson, ret., of Charleston, S. C., now Chieftain of the Carson-McDowell Clan.

Chapter Six

Page 161 ".... the payment of a pepper corn ... " Glenn Clark, author, teacher, philosopher, Macalaster College, St. Paul, Minnesota, compiled in one volume *The World's Greatest Debates.* Debate between Hayne and Webster, pp 31-54; 104-131.

165 " ... free or slave states ... "—free, in the sense that they were capable of working out their own destinies unhampered by broad legislative restraints; slave states, in that they would be subservient to the controls of the Federal government.

166 "Liberty and Union, Now and Forever, one and inseparable." Ibid., p 131.

Commenting on the debates, Clark states that Daniel Webster, at the very climax of what was probably the most inspired utterance of his entire life, took the word *Liberty* out of the position which the South had given it ... and placed it side by side in partnership with *Union.* "Had he gone one step further and substituted for these two words the more humane word *Brotherhood,* the cycle would have been complete and North and South might have stood shoulder to shoulder on common ground." Ibid., p 152.

166- "With whom he had disagreed violently ... " "For several years
167 a coolness had developed between Carson and the great Daniel Webster ... " Wheeler's *History of North Carolina,* p 92.

172- ".... a letter from ... Carson to Thomas Gilman." Following
173 Carson's conversations with Van Buren, he included in his Circular letter to his constituents Gilman's inquiry and his reply. Carson, at first refused to allow these letters to be published. He felt that his conversations with Van Buren could be judged confidential.

367

173 "He no longer called socially at the White House." *Raleigh Register*, March 2, 1913. *William Alexander Graham Papers*, p 202.

175 "Here were two gladiators in the forum . . . " Clark's *World's Greatest Debates*, pp 136-140.

"What Calhoun calls 'veto,' Webster would call 'nullification.' " Ibid., p 139.

"Senator Calhoun's argument, a marvel of analysis, will stand as a perfect model of deductive reasoning and a monument to the masterful intellect of this leader of a lost cause." Ibid., 139[n].

181 " . . . in securing Mangum's election . . . " Willie P. Mangum Papers, p 386.

182 "When Colonel Polk . . . " (Uncle of James Knox Polk)

183 " . . . I intend to have the girls at the Academy . . . " Record of the registration of the four cousins at Salem Academy on December 10, 1830, is in the Alumnae office at Salem College, Winston-Salem, N. C.

185 ". . . . where Crockett would no doubt . . . " *Roanoke Advocate*, July 7, 1831.

186 ". . . . trigger a dissolution of the Cabinet." John Branch, of Enfield, North Carolina (Halifax County), was the first native of North Carolina to hold a cabinet position. When President Jackson requested his resignation as Secretary of the Navy, Branch offered to serve until his successor was named.

So intense was the interest in the Jackson-Calhoun split that the *Western Carolinian*, published in Salisbury, N. C., ran a series of biographical sketches of Calhoun in May, 1831.

Chapter Seven

Page 188 "Many of the new students cry themselves to sleep. . . . " *North Carolina Historical Review*, Vol 27, p 37.

191 ". . . . ready for marriage at sixteen . . . " Ibid., p 37.

192 "Carson rose to say . . . the House of Representatives of the Twenty-first Congress have met for the last time. . . . " *Register of Debates*, March 3, 1831.

195 "This is the Congregation House or *Gemein Haus.*" Monograph, *A Day To Remember*, Moravian Archives at Old Salem, Forsyth County, N. C.

196 Description of buildings, furnishings, courses of study, etc., at Salem Academy, *North Carolina Historical Review*. Vol 27, pp 37-42.

198 Letters to and from President Jackson to his cabinet members, and related correspondence appeared in Secretary Branch's home paper, *The Halifax Advocate*, as in other news media throughout the country.

200 " . . . the prettiest wedding in North Carolina." Page 202 of the *William Alexander Graham Papers* quotes James A. Graham as stating, "There was lately a grand Washington City wedding in this vicinity, Samuel P. Carson to a Miss Wilson, a cousin of his own. . . . I believe they have been courting one or two years, and meantime, *Sam Patch* was trying his fortune in Washington City; but learning that the Fates had decreed against him, he resolved if he could not get Honey he would take Molasses." James Graham, of Rutherfordton, N. C., had been a political rival of Carson.

Carson's one regret in connection with his wedding was that his friend, Warren Davis, was unable to attend.

202 ". . . . do not relish the thought of going to Raleigh . . . " The beautiful State Capitol, with its special decorations, together with the statue of George Washington by Canova, one of the great treasures of the world, crumbled in the heat of the terrible conflagration.

203 ". . . . to obey the law of the land and suppress rebellion." Editorial in *The Halifax Advocate*, June 7, 1833.

206 "Efforts of Mangum and Carson were fruitful . . . " *Willie P. Mangum Papers*, Vol I, pp 27-28 and holograph in *Branch Family Papers*, Southern Collection, University of North Carolina Library, Chapel Hill.

207 "Pulled a pistol and aimed at Houston." Heiskell's *Early Tennessee History*, pp 482-483.

210 ". . . . a communication from Halifax." Holograph in *Branch Family Papers*. (Copy in files of author)

Chapter Eight

Page 217 ". . . . a course of action was agreed on . . . " Emily was legally adopted by Carson when she was eleven years old. (testimony of adoption in files of author)

369

217 "A woman is more likely to forgive another woman . . . " *James Sprunt Historical Monograph,* Carolina Room, University of North Carolina Library, Chapel Hill.
Doctor Mitchell's second attempt to establish the height of the mountain that now bears his name resulted in a fall to his death.

217 "Carson, summoned to the meeting . . . " Full report of this meeting was carried in *The Halifax Advocate,* October 18, 1832, as in other news media.

218- ". . . . brought out the emblem of the Nullifiers . . . placed the
219 Blue Cockade on his hat." Margaret Coit in *John C. Calhoun,* p 237, viz. "Once Old Hickory got into action, he predicted the Union leaders would make the Blue Cockade as scarce as a blue rooster."

223 ". . . . that these two (Houston and Jackson) had in mind the eventual annexation of Texas to the United States." Samuel G. Heiskell, *Early Tennessee History,* p 485.

223- Carson, still persisting in his attempt to push for legislation to
224 establish a mint in the gold-mining region of North Carolina, is needled by a fellow member of Congress, and on motion of John Knox Polk, his bill was temporarily "put to rest." *Register of Debates of Congress,* January 1833.

226- Warren R. Davis's resolution requesting President Jackson to
229 produce the evidence on which he based his statement that the people of South Carolina . . . intended to seize the forts or other property belonging to the Federal Government, was followed by his provocative dialogue with other members on the floor of the House. Congressman Davis's remarks appear in this chapter as one uninterrupted speech—one that should bring a glow of pride to every native son of South Carolina. *Register of Debates of Congress, Twenty-second Session.*
Early in November of 1832 Jackson had sent George Breathit to South Carolina, ostensibly to act as an agent of the state, observing tempers, purposes and military strength of the Nullifiers. Basset, *Life of Andrew Jackson,* p 564.
"The duty of the Executive is a plain one," Jackson wrote. "The laws will be executed, and the union preserved by all legal and constitutional means, and I rely with great confidence on the support of every honest patriot in South Carolina." Ibid.

209 "I now rise to perform . . . " Carson breaks with Jackson—Boyd, *History of North Carolina,* p 181 as also recorded in *Register of Debates of the Twenty-second Congress.* Full text of Carson's speech on Nullification in files of author.

232 ". . . . fair to convict him without a hearing." The meeting to censure Carson is documented in A. Davis Smith's *History of*

Western North Carolina, and in an article by Mary Johnson Avery, *Greensboro Daily Record*, November 1928. It was reported in many newspapers of the period.

"Three of North Carolina's Congressmen mustered up courage to defy Jackson. One of them was Samuel Price Carson, Jackson's old friend and admirer, not only denounced the Force Bill, but made it the occasion to withdraw from the Democratic party." Connor—*History of North Carolina*, Vol II, p 516.

234- Carson and Burton Craige mediate differences between D. F.
235 Caldwell and Charles Fisher of Salisbury, warm personal friend of both men, and in the process almost wrecked their own friendship. Photostat of full correspondence in files of author.

238 ". . . . Doctor John Carson wrote to Senator Mangum a letter of commendation." *Willie P. Mangum Papers*, Vol II, pp 135-136.

Chapter Nine

Page 242 The first session of the North Carolina Legislature to which Carson was elected senator convened on November 7, 1834. He was appointed on a number of important committees, one of which was to plan for a state-wide convention to amend the Constitution of North Carolina.

242 ". . . . that the Legislature of a state have a right to instruct their senators in Congress . . . " *Raleigh Register and North Carolina Gazette*, December 23, 1834.

The same issue noted ". . . . the only regret that we (the editors) felt at the close of the speech of Mr. Carson was that it could not be heard and understood by every free citizen of the State."

243 "So impressed was Mangum with Carson's speech against instruction that he sought to have it published . . . " *Willie P. Mangum Papers*, Vol II, pp 268-269.

243 " . . . my brother Charles says . . . 'stand to your post and do the talking . . . and I will do the fighting . . . " Ibid., p 272.

" . . . an attempt to assassinate the President . . . attending a funeral in the Capitol . . . " "It *was* someone of importance, Sam . . . it was Warren Davis." This tragedy occurred on January 29, 1835, was documented in news media throughout the Nation, and is often reprinted in current journals.

248 "On April 18 he could resist the prospect no longer, and he bought a thousand acres . . . " Deed Book B, pp 130-131, Lafayette County Court House, Arkansas.

253- "But the greatest debate in the history of North Carolina ... "
257 *Proceedings and Debates of the Constitution Convention of North Carolina—1835.*(One of the original copies of this rare book is owned by the author.)

All subject matter from page 18 through the closing prayer of Doctor McPheeters is quoted verbatim, with language and spelling in its original form. Note in particular the word "phrenzy," p 254.

Contemporary comment on the great debate is found in an article written for the *Morganton News Herald*, July 10, 1950 by Senator Sam J. Ervin, Jr. of the United States Congress, who stated: "Fighting single-handed, Samuel Price Carson denied the right of the government to proscribe any religious test whatever, and advocated expunging the entire section from the new North Carolina Constitution. He made a magnificent speech in support of his position."

263 " ... grapes are in abundance ... " Reverend Chester Newell in *History of the Revolution of Texas.*

263 "Were not you and Daniel Webster cited ... ?" Basset, *Correspondence of Andrew Jackson.*

268 "Branch folded the letter, returning it to its outside cover ... " Holograph in *Branch Family Papers*, Carolina Room, Library of the University of North Carolina, Chapel Hill. (Copy in files of author.)

Chapter Ten

Page 269 "Siphargon ... " "Si," having returned from Texas with all of Carson's retainers who wanted to return, was an old man at the Carson House during the War Between the States.

270 "Sam has many symptoms of consumption ... " Holograph relating to Carson at Barker Center, University of Texas, Austin.

273 "The Caddo Indians will be our neighbors." Description of appearance, dress and characteristics of this war-like tribe of Indians is taken from *Indians in Texas in 1830*, John C. Ewers, Ed., pp 106-107-108.

274 " ... about the Comanches ... " Ibid., p 50.

275 " ... an' if they's Cherokees ... " Ibid., p 113, 149[n], 112.

284 The general council of the Provisional Government, on December 12, 1835, directed that elections be held throughout Texas on February 1 to select delegates to the Constitution Convention. Red River municipality elected Collin McKinney,

372

Robert Hamilton, Samuel P. Carson, Richard Ellis and James H. Johnson. Kemp, *Signers of the Texas Declaration of Independence*, p 49.

"The Provisional Government elected Stephen Austin and William Wharton as commissioners to go to the United States capital to ask for aid." *Texas Almanac* (Anniversary Edition), p 58.

" . . . the Crockett party . . . " Shackford—*David Crockett: The Man and the Legend*, pp 212-213.

283 " . . . not on your life! It's all in the deed . . . " Record in Deed Book B, Lafayette County Courthouse, Arkansas. Photostats of deeds, mortgages, etc. in files of author.

283- Robert Hamilton's background and other statistics, Kemp,
284 *Signers of the Texas Declaration of Independence*, p 152.

287 Crockett's tale of how he broke the bank is from the *Arkansas Gazette*, May 1836.

289 " . . . no Pecan Point, or Red River Municipality either . . . " Kemp, *Signers of the Texas Declaration of Independence*, pp 104-211.

292 " . . . he was reminded of a former antagonist . . . " J. Fred Rippy, *Joel Roberts Poinsett—Versatile American*. Although in 1824, Poinsett had declared that the protective tariff should be resisted by every constitutional means, he strongly disagreed with those who advanced the doctrine of Nullification, p 134.

294 "James Pinckney Henderson . . . " Native of Lincolnton, North Carolina, successively Secretary of State and Attorney-General under Sam Houston (Republic of Texas), the first governor of Texas, United States Senator, statesman and diplomat. "There is no Texan, with the possible exception of Sam Houston . . . who was of more value to the Republic and to the State of Texas." Robert Glenn Winchester in *James Pinckney Henderson*, the Naylor Company, San Antonio, Texas.

Documentary records of this versatile North Carolinian are in files of John L. Henderson, husband of the author.

296 "Crockett asked if I was a-kin to a Mrs. Clark . . . " Shackford, *David Crockett: The Man and the Legend*, p 215.

Chapter Eleven

Page 299 " . . . and so they ordered an election of their own . . . " Kemp's *Signers of the Texas Declaration of Independence*, p 203.

301 "I left South Carolina when Calhoun's doctrine of Nullification changed the political future of that State." Ibid., p 201.

Photocopy of the original Texas Declaration of Independence is in files of author.

303 ". . . . riding a small Mexican pony . . . " Johnson, *The Birth of Texas*, p 144.

305 " . . . and his speech was in the nature of a declamation . . . " *Gray's Diary*, p 123.

306 ". . . . his (Carson's) counsel was sought in all major decisions" Southern Historical Quarterly, Vol. XXXI, p 195.

306 Robert Potter—"an outrageous renegade" Kemp's *Signers of the Texas Declaration of Independence*, pp 258-277.

306 "Did Houston ever repay the $200. he borrowed from you in the spring of '32?" Texana, Vol. VI, p 259.

307 " . . . the sixty-two members of the House of Commons who voted me out of that august body . . . " Journal of the House of Commons (N. C.) 1834, p 258.

308 Carson's efforts to give the franchise to 18-year-olds, "particularly those who have faithfully served in present war" was defeated—the only major defeat of his official career in Texas. Texana, Vol. VI pp 263-264.

309 "Carson—in a reasonable time was able to report the completion of the Constitution, as amended." Texana, Vol VI, p 266.

309 " . . . introduced motion 'that spies be immediately dispatched under direction of the House for protection of the Convention and for the procuration of arms.' " Gammel, p 901.

310 Constitution finally adopted at twelve midnight, and motion for establishment of provisional government was adopted. *Diary of William Fairfax Grey*, p 132.

310 Carson nominated for President of the newly created Republic of Texas, but lost to David Burnet. Carson then elected Secretary of State. Ibid.

311 Encroachment of the enemy results in panic and confusion, and a quick exodus of government personnel and citizens to Harrisburg, the third capital of the Republic. Thus began the famous "Runaway Scrape," designating the unorthodox removal of the seat of government from San Felipe to Washington on the Brazos and now to Harrisburg. *Diplomatic Correspondence of the Republic of Texas*, Vol I, pp 136-137.

312 Zavala and Carson ill from exposure. Ibid.

314 "Rusk has had to postpone his plans to join the army—*Gray's*

Diary, p 149. Thomas Jefferson Rusk was born in Pendleton, South Carolina December 5, 1803. His father lived on land belonging to John C. Calhoun, who was attracted to young Rusk because of his "capacity of mind," and arranged for him to study law. Joining the migration to Texas in December, 1835, seated at Convention on March 2, he was elected Secretary of War. From May 1 to October 31, 1836, he was Brigadier-General of the Texas Army. (Adapted from Kemp's *Signers of the Texas Declaration of Independence*, pp 304-312)

318 Carson's letter from Harrisburg: "We stand in need of supplies of all kinds . . . " *Official Correspondence of the Republic of Texas*, pp 585-586.

321 " . . . . the diagnosis . . . typhoid-pneumonia." *Texana*, Vol VI, p 274.

322 " . . . to send news to Nashville in care of Hon. Joseph Bryan." Bryan was a transplanted North Carolinian. Holograph "Bryan to Van Buren" in files of author.

322 "Burnet to Carson" May 23, 1836. Kemp—*Signers of the Texas Declaration of Independence*, p 51.

323 " . . . . to sell Texas to the United States." Records of Department of State, Texas Book 34, p 19.

324 Having had no information to the contrary and under the impression that he was still Secretary of State, Carson authorized borrowing $25,000. to equip Tennessee troops to go to Texas under command of General Dunlap, *Texana*, Vol VI, p 274.

325 " . . . Santa Anna was captured and 700 Mexicans lay still and lifeless." Rev. Chester Newell, *History of the Revolution in Texas*, p 107.

327 "They [Hamilton and Childress] had written begging Burnet to forward official reports and instructions. The communications were never answered." "Childress and Hamilton to Burnet," June 10, 1836. Garrison's *Diplomatic Correspondence of the Republic of Texas*, Vol I, pp 99-100.

Further evidence of frustrations of Burnet's Commissioners and/or agents sent to United States to obtain recognition of Texas and to obtain funds is seen in letter of Stephen Austin from New York, dated April 15, 1836 to Andrew Jackson, Martin Van Buren, Richard M. Johnson, John Forsyte, Lewis Cass, T. Hart Benton, "and any member of the Cabinet or Congress of all parties and all factions of the United States." It was a desperate call for help. The letter follows:

Sirs: The Commissioners appointed by the Provincial Government of Texas in November and December (1835) have discharged the duties assigned them as fully as their powers and the peculiar circumstances in which they have been placed would permit.

It is with regret that we say that the state of things at home embarrasses the labors of the government agents in this country.

The undersigned have not received one word from the Government since the meeting of the Convention in March and the public have been informed in the newspapers that we have been superceded and that we have no powers as agents.

You will at once perceive the bad effect which the news have on the public mind, for taken in common with many exagerated accounts of internal dissension, etc., they have a tendency to weaken the public confidence and to paralyze our efforts.

In our communications from New Orleans and Nashville, from Louisville and Washington City, we informed the Government of our proceedings, and that it was all important for someone to be furnished with the *Declaration of Independence* and with full instructions. For want of this document we could do no more in Washington than to prepare opinions to sustain the Declaration of Independence made by Texas.

We feel every confidence that as soon as a diplomatic agent, properly authorized, appears at Washington it will be done. . . . The loan is in progress in this City.

327 Carson—dinner guest of President Jackson—*Texana*, Vol VI, p 275.

329 Santa Anna's hordes invade San Felipe—put torch to building housing *The Texas Telegraph and Register*. Frantz—*Gail Borden, Dairyman to a Nation*, p 107.

329 ". . . . the free press of Texas has been stilled." Ibid., p 109.

330 "Carson and Hamilton proceeded to New York, there to float a loan—stunned at Burnet's duplicity—rereads letter from Burnet authorizing the mission." Kemp—*Signers of Texas Declaration of Independence*, p 50.

Full documentation of events following the abortive mission of all Texas agents—Ibid., pp 81 through 84; also Texana, Vol VI. "Carson to Houston" letter giving full description and documentation of events that took place from the time the Secretary of State received his commission from Burnet, April 1st, 1836 until he and Mrs. Carson proceeded to the White Sulphur Springs at Virginia for the restoration of his health is found in Kemp's *Signers of Texas Declaration of Independence*, pp 52-53. Holograph, marked Exhibit B in files of author.

In spite of all the hardships, physical, financial and emotional, of the several commissioners who discharged their duties acceptably to all save Burnet, the end result was a victorious conclusion that inspired one of the several historians of the period to say: "Sam Houston made Texas possible as an American state, and added to the Republic as grand an area as was ever populated by a race." S. G. Heiskell in *Early Tennessee History*, p 6.

Chapter Twelve

Page 335 "Sam's health was better than it had been for years." *Texana*, Vol VI, p 278.

335 "... to see old Benny again." Carson's old manservant, now a member of the Branch family retinue.

336 "It's John, Cathy ... he's gone." Holograph in Carson papers. John died on July 6, 1836, after being thrown from his horse.

336 "To be a guest at a public dinner at the Mansion House in Halifax in his honor. August 1, 1836. Holograph in *Asbury Papers*, Barker History Center, University of Texas. Photocopy in files of author.

338 "My knowledge of the events (surrounding the capture of General Santa Anna) I will relate on the authority of an officer who was present ... " Rev. Chester Newell, *History of the Republic of Texas* p 195-196.

339 "But Houston was adamant ... Santa Anna was far more valuable alive than dead." (As related by General Houston to Texas Historian Newell.)

340 "Carson was cheered by Houston's election as President of the new Republic, even as he was dispirited by rumor that Burnet had written disparagingly of his efforts while in the United States. *Correspondence of the Texas Revolution—the Ad Interim Government*, p 1087.

Dr. Ashbel Smith, in *Reminiscences of the Texas Republic*, commenting on the character of the outgoing President David Burnet, said "Old John Knox would have hugged such a character with grim delight. It doesn't detract from the virtues of his character that he did not possess eminent administrative capacity, nor in a high degree that knowledge of human nature and tact in managing men which inferior men often acquire. . . . "

343 Carson, greatly depleted financially, mortgages a number of his retainers to tide him over until another crop could be harvested. *Texana*, Vol VI, p 287. Note and mortgage in LaFayetter County, Arkansas, April 1837.

345 "Unsavory reputation that villifies the new Texas"—*Newell, History of the Republic of Texas*, p 190.

347- Description of Santa Anna's return in captivity—Henry Stuart
348 Foote, *Texas and the Texans*, pp 315, 342, 344.

349 Samuel Price Carson's Last Will and Textament. Probate Record Book B., LaFayette County, Arkansas, pp 111-113. Photostat in files of author. (Manuscript in County Clerk's office, Lewisville)